Tell
No
Tales

by Christine Morgan

Published by:

Sabledrake Enterprises
PO Box 30751
Seattle, WA 98113
http://www.sabledrake.com
sabledrake@sabledrake.com

*For Kathy Morgan, sister-in-law and good friend,
with fond recollections of Howie and Diana.*

* * *

This book could not have been written without the help and inspiration of the following works and people:

Mark Burnett, reality television pioneer.

Christopher Terrill, photographer/producer/director of "The Ship."

Hosts Jeff Probst, Joe Rogan, Phil Keoghan and Peter Woodward.

The NBC, CBS, and History Channel production teams, sponsors, and executives.

David Cordingly, author of *Under the Black Flag.*

Captain Charles Johnson, author of
A Complete History of Pirates.

Steffan O'Sullivan, author of ***GURPS Swashbucklers.***

And all of the competitors, adventure racers, eco-challengers, survivors, and those for whom fear was not a factor.

Chapter 1

"So, I hear this island is cursed," Larry Burlingame said from the edge of the hole.

Kelly Dagget paused and straightened up, blowing a lock of cinnamon-gingerbread hair out of her eyes with one exasperated puff. She wiped her forehead, then pulled her sunglasses down and peered up at him.

"Are you trying to make a point, Lare, or just conversation?"

Larry chuckled and spread his hands. "Who, me? Just passing the time, boss-lady."

"Boss-lady?" She turned and raised her eyebrows at Mike and Steve. "If I'm the boss-lady, why am I in this pit busting my butt with you two?"

Mike Glass snorted.

Steve Quinlan grinned and held his shovel out toward Larry. "You can always have a turn with mine, old boy."

"There's not room down there for all of us," Larry said. "We'd get in each other's way. The big man wants a hole, not a damn trench."

"Well, I'll tell you what," said Kelly. "You can fill it back in once we plant the treasure chest."

"Now, that," said Steve, "sounds like a plan made in heaven." He directed the grin at Kelly this time, and she gave it right back to him, with interest.

"Yeah, fine," Larry grumbled, plopping his ass onto the lid of the chest, a big iron-bound thing with a padlock the size of a grown man's fist. It settled deeper into the sand as his weight came down on it.

"We're not going to need to dig if you piledrive it into the ground," Kelly said.

Larry gave her a dirty look and hitched his collar away from his thick neck. He was a patchwork of burned spots and peeled spots, and the top of his head where the hair thinned was an angry red. Not a guy who was made for this sun and heat.

Neither was Kelly, who only freckled and then freckled some more but never truly tanned . . . though sometimes the freckles ran together in what could almost look like a tan. From a distance.

"Cursed, is it?" Steve pitched a shovelful of dirt out of the deepening hole. "No one told me that bit."

"Pff," Kelly said. "Folk tales."

"Do tell." Steve had an athlete's build, lean and limber. He tanned well, complementing his jet-black hair and electric-blue eyes. But it was the accent that really did it for Kelly. She could listen to him talk all day. "Pray share the local lore, dear girl."

"You're telling me you've never heard the story of Captain Smythe?" she asked.

"Can't say as I have. Except that he left a buried treasure, of course."

Mike – for whom tanning was not an issue, as he was naturally the color of polished mahogany – scooped out another shovelful and then surveyed the hole. He raised his eyebrows at Kelly as if to ask her if it was deep enough yet.

"Should be," Kelly said. "After all, the poor sap who gets to dig it up will be alone, and lucky to have a shovel instead of coconut shells and bare hands."

The three of them clambered out of the pit and sat on its edge, legs dangling. Well, Mike's legs didn't exactly dangle. Mike could damn near rest his feet on the bottom.

"Captain Smythe," Steve prompted, nudging Kelly.

"Captain Elliot Smythe," she said. "An English privateer. He sacked a Spanish galleon and made off with plunder worth over thirty thousand pounds. Smythe and his men put ashore here to bury it, somewhere in the heart of the island."

"Where," Steve said, nodding wisely, "one of them would have been left behind to guard the swag . . . with a musket ball in his heart."

"Oh, absolutely. But while they were away in the jungles, a Spanish warship came along, sank Smythe's ship, and laid a trap for the pirates. Smythe's crew walked right into it, and they were wiped out almost to a man. Smythe

was wounded, but he escaped with his wife, a cabin boy, and the ship's cook. The Spaniards searched for the treasure, but no luck. A few years later, another ship came looking for it. All they found was the cabin boy, who'd grown up half savage. He claimed that the last time he'd seen Smythe, the captain was dying . . . but swore that he would never leave his loot unprotected."

"And so I take it that his vengeful spirit haunts the island to this day." Steve glanced around. "We've been here, what, six weeks now getting ready for your father's gala affair? And no one's seen hide nor hair of a ghost."

"Don't have to *see* them," Larry said. He had gone even redder than drink and sunburn allowed, but pressed on regardless. "Haven't any of you noticed the bad-luck stuff that's been going on? Robby Willets breaking his arm? Or what about the tarps blowing away and the rain getting into the food stores? Four crates spoiled. You want to tell me that's coincidence?"

"Robby Willets was trying to scale Widowmaker Peak while in his cups," Steve said, gesturing over his shoulder at the looming craggy face of the black mountain. "If you ask me, he's lucky his arm is all he broke. It could have been his fool neck."

"With the winds whipping up the way they do around here at this time of year," Kelly said, "we don't need a ghost or a curse or any other superstition to blow things around."

"People have been getting sick," Larry continued doggedly. "And what about the cameras?"

Kelly rolled her eyes. "Everybody was told not to drink the water without boiling it. As for the cameras, equipment glitches happen too. Salt crystals from the sea air can interfere with them, make them touchy."

Mike grunted.

"See?" Kelly said. "Even Mike agrees with me."

"We'll have all our electronics in tip-top shape by the time we're ready to begin filming," Steve said. "We'd better, or Dagget Senior is going to have our heads on a plate."

"Don't mind Dad. His bark is worse than his bite."

"Oh, yes, absolutely," Steve said. "Like he's ever so much as barked at his precious little punkin-girl." He ruffled her hair.

"Hey!" Kelly twisted away. "Come on, jeez, quit with the big brother routine."

She got up, resisting the urge to kick a spray of sand into his face. This wasn't grade school, when boys and girls showed they liked each other by teasing, pinching and so on.

Unless that was how Steve showed it . . . ?

No, sad to say, no. Plenty of the guys on Veradoga with the Dagget Productions team were that immature, but Steve Quinlan wasn't one of them.

"Let's get this bastard in the ground," she said, kicking sand at the treasure chest instead and not caring that she got some on Larry. "I'm dying for a swim and a cold drink."

The others got moving. Larry, at Kelly's pointed look, heaved himself up and grabbed an end of the chest, while Mike got the other. A token gesture, really. Mike could have picked it up one-handed and balanced it on his finger. Spinning it, maybe, like a basketball player showing off.

"Thirty thousand pounds was the value of Smythe's treasure, was it?" Steve said. "And we're giving away, what, half a million? Even allowing for inflation, that's a bit of a bump."

Larry and Mike crab-walked to the edge of the pit with the chest swinging between them. Larry was huffing and panting. Mike's broad face was as impassive as an Easter Island stone idol.

"Okay, let her down on three," Kelly said. She counted it off as they rocked the chest back and forth, back and forth, and let go.

The heavy box thumped down hard enough that she felt the vibration of its landing in her feet. The padlock thunked against the purposefully-distressed wood like an old-time door knocker. Sand spit up and rained down.

"Pieces of eight, pieces of eight, awwk!" cried Steve in a high, scratchy parrot's voice. In his normal one, he added, "Which reminds me, when do our feathered friends arrive?"

"Day after tomorrow, I think."

He handed out the shovels. "Parrots. I love it. It's the little touches that make the show."

"Nah, it's the backstabbing and emotional meltdowns that make the show."

"*This* show, granted," he said. "Just the latest jump onto the reality television bandwagon."

Kelly bristled. Even though it was Steve, she bristled. "You saying that my dad's bottom-feeding?"

"One of the kings of 'celebreality'? Good Lord, no. Would I be working for him if I thought that?"

"Hey," Mike said.

Anything more vocal than a grunt or a snort from the big man was enough to cut right through Kelly and Steve's budding argument. They both turned to see Mike staring at Larry.

"You okay?" Mike added, forehead furrowed into a worried scowl.

Larry's right hand still held the shovel that he'd been using to heap sand over the chest – it was buried almost up to the lock now – but even as Kelly looked, Larry's fingers loosened and he dropped it. His left hand was clenching and unclenching, and his breath had taken on a thin, wheezing teakettle whistle.

"Larry? Larry, old boy!" Steve sounded as alarmed as Kelly suddenly felt.

Larry had gone waxy beneath his blotches of sun and peeling skin, and more sweat than was warranted stood out in greasy beads. He clawed at the left breast pocket of his khaki shirt.

"Oh, my God, is he having a heart attack?" Kelly said. "Larry?"

His answer was to keel over.

Mike moved to catch him but was a fraction of a second too late as Larry toppled head first into the pit. His skull met the top of the chest with a hollow thud. The lock knocked again. The rest of Larry crumpled and sprawled, splayed out facedown on the lid.

Without waiting for advice or instructions, Mike picked Larry up and heaved him out. Larry rolled onto his back. His eyes goggled up at Kelly in pain and surprise.

Kelly snatched the cell phone off her belt and pushed the button. Instead of the warbling signal that would tell her she was connected with the main console at Central, she got nothing. No reception bars. The phone was stubbornly silent.

"Not now, damn it!" Kelly beat the useless gadget against her palm and tried again. Still nothing. She cursed and cast it aside, then fell to her knees beside Larry and groped his neck for a pulse. "Steve, use the walkie-talkies."

He did, but only got a hissing bray of static. "No good, love."

Her mind was revving but only spinning its wheels. No way to call for help. Of all the times for the phones and radios not to work! Top-of-the-line, yeah, right! She'd have a few words for the sponsors when she got the chance, that was for sure.

She knew CPR, had gotten her re-certification every two years since she'd started taking babysitting jobs at age fourteen. Now that she actually needed to do it, she was at a loss and couldn't remember a single thing.

"A, B, C," she muttered, combing her fingers frantically through her hair. "A . . . Airway!"

While Steve and Mike hovered anxiously behind her, she tipped Larry's head back. The stale smell of his lunch wafted up from a gaping mouth. He wasn't breathing.

Steeling herself, she pinched his nose shut and sealed her lips around his.

Exhaled. Watched the row of buttons down the front of his shirt rise and then fall as her recycled air gusted back out.

"B . . . Bleeding . . . oh, damn, no, that's first aid, the Three Killers." Kelly drove her thumbs into her temples as if she could squeeze the information out of her brain.

It came back to her with a sweeping feeling of relief. She shook Larry hard by the shoulders and shouted at him, following the rote even though she already knew he wasn't okay, was light years from okay. Next, she jerked her head up and found Steve's stunned gaze.

"Go for help," she told him. "Drive back to camp, get the doc and the zappy-thing."

"Wouldn't it be faster to load him into the back?"

"I can't do CPR in the back of a moving vehicle, not on roads like these. Have Leslie bring a chopper. She can land in the field."

He went at a run and Kelly turned back to Larry. Still no signs of breathing, still no pulse. She blew two more quick breaths and then prodded at his meaty torso until she found what she hoped was the whatchamacallit, the xyphlophone . . . typhoid . . . goddammit . . . the cartilage thingie at the bottom of his sternum. Three fingers up, brace the heel of her hand, set the other hand on top with fingers laced, and she rocked up and down over Larry's prone form.

"One and two and three and four and five," she counted.

It was five and then a breath, right? Or hadn't they changed it, recommending fifteen compressions and then two breaths?

Ahh . . . screw it. They also said that *anything* was better than nothing, as long as she was pumping the blood through him and oxygenating his lungs.

Leaning down again, she forced her breath into Larry's airway. Resumed her position. Began a fresh set of compressions.

Knowing all the while that it was going to be too late.

*   *   *

Chapter 2

The buff blond guy puked first.

It didn't do the rest of their stomachs any good. The hold was already cramped, dark, dank, and smelly enough without adding someone's last meal to the overall miasma. And the motion . . . up and down, side to side, up and down some more . . . sure wasn't helping.

But at least the big blond guy had puked first. As tough as he looked, with that square heroic jaw and beach-boy tan, it was good to know that he had some kind of weakness, anyway.

Letitia Jackson glanced around at the others. What little, that was, she could see of them in the light of the one whale-oil lantern. The light, swinging with each swell and trough, only added to the disorientation, only emphasized the motion of the ship.

Conversation would have been impossible even if they had been so inclined. The boom of waves on the hull, the rolling thunder, and the shouts and hollered orders from the crew on deck drowned out everything else.

She could see them, though, glimpses at least in the nauseating sway of the light. An even dozen counting herself, and each and every one looking like he or she was having second thoughts. Thoughts along the line of, "and I signed up for this? On *purpose?*" The prospect of half a million dollars wasn't as enticing once some guy yarked all over the tarred wooden planks of the floor.

Eight were white, four men and four women. If Letitia was remember-

ing the names right, the puker was Karl, the tough old drill sergeant type was B.J., and the professor was Charles. Dale was the cute red-headed guy. Letitia hadn't caught the name of the mousy little gal in glasses, but the stocky woman with the pasty Seattle complexion was Angie, and the tall thin blonde was Calliope – now there was a hard name to forget. The hard-eyed honey with the gravity-defying breasts was either Bonnie or Connie.

Of the remaining four, two were black: Letitia herself and Ambrose, a young fellow who looked to be about her son's age. There, though, all resemblance ended. Her boy Rickie was on the varsity football team, broad as a beam. This kid was reed-slim, small. The Native-American woman was Tala, long-legged and gorgeous, and the Hispanic kid, Jimmy, sported a vivid red and green tattoo of a coiled snake on one wiry arm.

Twelve ordinary Americans from all walks of life, Letitia thought.

Except that they were all in costume, and crammed into the dark hold of the ship like so many sardines.

Karl groaned and burped. Those nearest him cringed away but another episode was not immediately forthcoming. Letitia figured that he'd already off-loaded all he had in him. He looked around, shamefaced and blushing beneath his golden-brown tan.

Tala gave him an encouraging smile and seemed on the verge of saying something when the mousy gal in glasses bent double and threw up as well. She promptly began to cry.

The ship hit a tremendous swell. Letitia wasn't the only one to squeal as her insides went weightless. They came down with a watery crash and the lantern swung so violently that it banged into a beam. Letitia suffered a brief vision of it shattering and dousing them with burning oil, but it didn't.

Her head ached from lack of sleep, jet lag, caffeine deprivation, and general disorientation. The past four days had been a whirlwind. She had been standing by, waiting to hear the final cut, and when the call came she could hardly believe it. Neither could Devon, who told her she was nuts but if she really wanted to do this, he'd be behind her all the way.

Far behind her, safe and sound and comfortable in their New York apartment. He teased her by saying this was her mid-life crisis. His had been the motorcycle, though Rickie wound up riding it more than his dad ever did. It took Letitia to do something crazy-extreme like this. She also knew that Devon had never really believed she would apply for a Burt Dagget reality show, or that she'd have a chance in hell of being chosen. Or that she'd actually go if she was.

But here she was, halfway around the world from home. On a wooden

sailing ship, loaded into the hold like so much cargo. Like the way her ancestors might have come to America, except on those voyages, it was a sure bet that two-thirds of the cargo hadn't been white.

From the moment she'd gotten the word, everything was a blur. Packing, airports, grueling flights, more airports, customs offices, Jamaica, an intense day of training camp, and finally a hotel. She had been too plain worn out by then to do anything but go right to her room.

That had been yesterday. This morning, in the wee small hours when no civilized person was awake, she'd been jolted from a sleep so deep it was almost a coma by thunderous hammering on her door. Staggering to it, bleary-eyed and confused, she could only think that there was a fire, they had to evacuate, something like that.

She'd opened the door and four people in costumes had charged in, yelling. "Press gang! Press gang!" One of them was a woman and she hustled Letitia into the bathroom, threw clothes at her, and jabbed her impatiently into the hall while she was still shrugging into her knapsack.

The others people had been similarly rousted. Letitia remembered that Ambrose had looked terrified, his dark doe eyes enormous. The mousy girl had been crying then, too, pushing her glasses up her nose and hitching for breath.

Down the stairs they went, escorted by the shanghaiers in their folded-over knee boots or silver-buckled shoes, their striped pants, their blousy shirts and bandannas and earrings. One was wearing a tri-corner hat with a plume. Another had a curved cutlass thrust through a bright red sash. The men were unshaven and fierce, one of the women wore an eyepatch, and they carried on shouting all the way down the stairs.

A pair of men in jeans and work shirts trotted backward ahead of them, one with a camera and the other with a long microphone, both trained on the action.

In the basement parking garage, they'd been loaded not into a car or a van but a wagon, a rickety old wagon drawn by a rickety old horse. Jouncing and clattering, they'd gone to the pier, where the ship had been waiting. The dark and the confusion only gave them the barest of looks at it before they were whisked aboard and stowed in the hold.

Letitia had known it was all part of the act, but she still felt indignant and frightened. This wasn't what she'd been expecting. Not after the chauffeured limousines and catered meals that she'd received when they'd flown her to L.A. for the final round of interviews. That had all been handled with the utmost politeness, even the psychological profiling. This . . . this was insane.

Ambrose was struggling not to be the third to spew. In the uncertain movement of the light, he was practically olive-green. He tried, but he didn't make it, and his retching triggered a like outburst from Professor Charles.

It was, Letitia thought, one hell of a bonding experience for them all. The others looked as bewildered and out-of-sorts as she felt. They were embarking on a great adventure together, possibly the greatest of their lives, and they started off like this. Puking their collective guts onto their collective shoes.

The sea finally smoothed out, and the pitching and heaving of the ship settled into a gentle rocking that was only mildly upsetting. Letitia had picked up her knapsack before it could get splattered and hugged it to her ample frame.

A glint gave away the presence of the camera, hidden in the beams of the ceiling and capturing everything. Dagget had told them they'd get used to that, being taped 24/7, that in time they would even look right through the camera teams as if they weren't there.

Letitia judged herself the second-oldest in the hold. Charles, who managed to look dapper even after throwing up, probably had a few years on her. B.J. was younger, but only by a little. Angie was maybe in her mid-thirties, and the rest were just kids.

The miserable voyage ended with a bone-rattling shudder – shiver me timbers, as the old salts said – as the ship docked none too gently. Topside grew loud again with commotion, feet running back and forth, voices raised, lines being thrown. Then the hatchway banged open and let in a flood of hazy tropical sunlight around the silhouette of a woman.

"Avast, ye swabs," she said. "I be Captain Kelly. All ashore that's going ashore."

Kelly Dagget. Letitia remembered her from last year's show, in which she'd played the Old West fort commander. She was a little bitty redhead and should have looked harmless with her freckles and her upturned nose, but she had Burt Dagget's commanding presence and a way of standing that made her seem taller than she was.

The dozen of them got up from the benches that lined the walls of the hold, stepping carefully around the puddles and lumps. Carrying their knapsacks and glancing dubiously at one another, they ascended the wooden stairs to the deck. Bells were clanging, people were calling and chattering, animals were neighing and bleating and clucking. Letitia was third out, and her eyes widened as she took it all in.

"Welcome to Veradoga Island," Kelly Dagget said, swaggering up to them with her hands on her hips. A black-powder pistol rode on one, a

cutlass on the other. The only thing to spoil the illusion was the squat black antenna of what looked like a cellular phone or a walkie-talkie sticking up from her belt. "This be Rum Town."

It could have come straight from a swashbuckler movie . . . or a Disney theme park. A couple of ships, smaller and less fancy versions of the one they were on, bobbed at the dock. The marketplace was busy with people moving among stalls, where everything from live chickens to bolts of cloth were for sale. A caged green parrot hectored passers-by to step into a seedy-looking tavern.

It seemed like a lot of work for them to have gone to for a television show, but Letitia knew that the ultimate plan would be for this site to end up as a theme resort. Like the Old West fortress, fans of the show would happily pay big bucks to stay at the place where it had been filmed.

Almost everyone in sight was dressed in pseudo-17th century garb. The only exceptions were the camera teams, pairs of two, who were mostly in shorts or jeans and plain t-shirts. They did an expert job of staying out of each other's way as they zoomed in to get the reactions of the players.

Letitia was suddenly conscious of how she must look, with her too-plump body stuffed into britches that ended in raggedy knee-length cuffs over striped stockings, a loose top cinched tight by a vest, and gold hoop earrings glinting in the sun.

A handsome black-haired man in tight breeches and an open-throated shirt approached Kelly with a shallow woven basket in his hands. It was filled with a dozen small leather pouches. Kelly cleared her throat for their attention and got it.

"Here's yer wages," she said, tossing each of them a pouch.

They clinked when caught, and Letitia felt the shift of coins inside.

"Ye have until sundown to spend them on whatever ye like here in town," Kelly went on. "Then ye'll report back to the docks, where ye'll sign aboard yer new ships. Godspeed."

With that, she left them and strode down the gangplank to the dock. The handsome man followed her, and the dozen players were alone on deck, exchanging looks of consternation.

"I would need an abacus to calculate all the anachronisms," Charles said, stroking his beard and shaking his head. "If this is meant to be their version of Port Royal, it's criminal."

"So it's inaccurate," the shirtless Hispanic kid said, thumbs hooked in the sash around his waist. "It's still neat."

"What are we supposed to do?" asked the mousy girl. Heather, Letitia

remembered suddenly. Her name was Heather.

"You heard the captain," said the redhead, Dale. His grin was huge, like a kid's on Christmas, exposing teeth that must have financed his orthodontist's yacht. "We've got money to spend!"

Letitia opened her pouch and poured coins into her palm. They were fakes, plated tin or copper, but they looked good. Imitation doubloons and pieces of eight, though she had no idea what they might be worth. "What do we buy?"

"Whatever we want," said Bonnie-or-Connie. Her outfit was more wench than pirate, and the cameras had to be loving the deep cleavage showcased by her tight, low-cut vest.

"Whatever we think we'll need," Angie said, glaring stonily at Bonnie-or-Connie as if daring her to talk back. "This is for supplies, necessary and vital supplies, not a shopping trip."

"We've only got 'til sundown," B.J. said, just as it seemed that the two women were about to go off on each other. "Let's get a move on."

"I'm for that," said Letitia. "Should we organize this, make sure we buy smart?"

"We don't know what crews we're going to be on," Tala said. She had startling, striking eyes that were the silvery grey of an overcast winter morning, contrasting beautifully with the rich copper of her skin.

"I think we should each get what we think we'll need, and we can pool our resources once we're divided up," Dale said.

"Works for me," B.J. said. "Time's wasting."

He was first down the gangplank, but the others followed with excitement and anticipation washing away the memory of the pre-dawn rousting and the hellish, seasick sail to their destination. As they reached the boardwalk, they were surrounded by eager merchants displaying various wares. Fresh fish, pottery, dried herbs, cheap jewelry, goats, rum, sugarcane, spices, live chickens, utensils and cloth were waved in their faces, each would-be seller trying to out-shout his neighbors.

Thanks to their training at pirate camp, they were supposedly able to recognize most of what they were seeing. A crash course in the life of the average 17th century sailor had done that much, at least. With luck, they'd remember how to cook and load cannons and rig sails and all the other things that had been drummed into them. Letitia certainly hoped so. At the moment, it was all a blur.

Dale plunged happily into the thick of it, singing *A Pirate's Life For Me* as he went. The rest of them tried to stick together at first, but their anxious little

cluster got swept apart by the townspeople.

It was a pretty good setup, Letitia had to admit. The people all around her were actors and members of Dagget's production team, but their costumes and talk contributed to the illusion. And if it wasn't authentic, as their professor groused, it was at least familiar enough from dozens of movies.

The town was tiny and made up like any Caribbean port-o-call, with a few businesses in addition to the tavern. A "Bloodletter and Chiurgeon," for instance, next to the "Apothecary," caught her eye. A dirty-faced little girl wheedled her into buying a bunch of flowers tied with twine.

She fingered her remaining coins and wondered where to begin.

*   *   *

Chapter 3

They brought more people. To the island.

To *his* island.

He had seen the first ones come. Men and women, even a few children. Building houses and ships. Hacking through the dense growth. Rearranging the landscape as it suited them.

Never knowing that he was there. Never suspecting.

It was going to cost them dearly. It already had, if perhaps not quite as dearly as he'd anticipated. The poisonous extracts hadn't killed any of them, only sickened a few. They were a tough breed. The man he'd knocked from the cliff with a well-aimed rock hadn't died either, only broken a bone or two. They thought it was an accident. He hadn't been seen.

His throat tightened at the thought of them bringing still more people to his island. Settling there. Living there. Taking his home away from him. Disturbing that which ought not be disturbed. Finding what which was not meant to be found.

He would use the skulls if he had to. If it came to that.

In the meantime, he had his pistols. And his trusty blades.

Those would do for now.

He knew every inch of the island. Knew where to hide, where the intruders would never see him. They had come with their machines and thought they had explored everything.

Not so. Not the cave. It was too well-concealed. Once, they'd passed

within a few yards of it and never had so much as an inkling.

Spyglasses. Spyglasses on posts with no eye to look through them, but they saw. He never doubted that. They saw. With their blank, glassy stares. He avoided them, slipping through the jungle as only he could. Creeping closer to their hated town.

He heard the boy before he saw him. Talking to himself, making play-noises of cannons and the clashing of swords.

Closer. His skeletal fingers came up, parted a screen of wide leaves.

The boy was on the bank of a creek that flowed from a spring into the sea. The water formed a wide pool there, partially dammed by a pile of stones. The boy had his toys on the shore. Ships and horses and men carved from wood. A play-battle.

He waited and watched. The child was alone. Small. His yellow hair was cut in a ragged bob and he wore only knee-britches, rolled up and wet from wading.

It had to be done.

The leaves whispered as he stepped through them. His bony hands reached out.

The child heard and turned. Eyes as blue as the sea went wide. His rose-bud mouth dropped open and he hitched in breath for a scream.

Smythe got to him first.

He seized the boy, plunged him into the pool. Saw the wavering lines of his stick-thin arms distorted by the water, distorted by the bubbles that rose and burst around him.

The boy kicked and thrashed. Smythe held him down, held him under, pressing hard with the heels of his hands. The pool wasn't that deep and the boy's back struck the soft muck at the bottom, stirred it up in smoky brown swirls that were torn apart by the frantic flailing of his limbs.

A final bubble exploded from the boy's lips. Water rushed in to replace it, filling him, drowning him. The little body trembled, and went limp. It lolled beneath the surface, hair streaming up around the slack face like strands of kelp.

The waters calmed. Smythe watched his own reflection return. Gaunt and horrible. The eyes dark sunken hollows. The teeth bared in a horrible deathmask leer.

He held the boy down a while longer, then let go. The waterlogged body bobbed along the bottom, through the clouds of silt, drawn slowly by the current. It turned, a drowsy movement almost as if the child moved in his sleep. It fetched up against the dam of stones and wedged there.

Smythe took up a frond and smoothed away his tracks. Then, with a backward, satisfied glance, he returned to the jungle. And the cave, where his priceless treasure waited.

*   *   *

Chapter 4

A squat stone fortress was placed to guard the town from marauding ships. Its crenellated top showed the blunt dark snouts of cannons, and a *Pirate Adventure* flag fluttered from the pole. Just as the *Old West Adventure* flag had adorned the log outpost, and just as a *Sherwood Forest Adventure* flag would fly from the medieval-style keep next year. If, that was, the world didn't end in the meantime.

All pretense at historical accuracy was abandoned at the door, in favor of comfort and technology. This was Dagget Central, with its own massive basement generator to run the electrical system. It had its own air conditioners, fridges, computers, film and sound editing equipment, even a couple of vending machines. The furnishings were sturdy and none-too-fancy, but serviceable enough.

The rec room was on the fort's ground floor, paneled in dark wood with shelves of books, board games, videotapes and DVDs, and art supplies. Half of the room was full of low couches and chairs, centered around an entertainment center. The other half contained a pool table, a Ping-Pong table, a pinball machine, and a dartboard. The gym was also on the first floor, with its two rows of stationary bikes and treadmills, a stair-climber, a rack of free weights, mats for exercising, and a *Bowflex* machine.

The second floor was taken up by the infirmary and offices. The third-floor living areas were divided into dorms full of padded cots, one for the men and one for the women, with some smaller private rooms set aside for

Burt Dagget, Kelly, Dr. Brookstone, and the few married couples and families. The accommodations were far better than what the players would be enduring. If the cafeteria's food was uninspired, it was at least plentiful, and afforded some variety.

Burt Dagget would be spending the majority of his time in the fourth floor control room, a dark and gloomy place lit primarily by the monitors that picked up the live feed from the cameras positioned all around the island. He preferred it this way. Behind the scenes. Seeing all, knowing all. Godlike.

Several years ago, a teenaged Kelly had dragged him to see *The Truman Show*, over Burt's strident protests. He hated Jim Carrey, he avowed. The man was a bona fide goofball. But the movie had captivated him. The idea, the premise . . . and most of all, the guy who ran the show from his control room in the fake moon.

Godlike. Omniscient.

That was the way it was *supposed* to be.

"One delay after another," he said with a disgruntled sigh. "What's going to go wrong next?"

"Delay?" Tyler Brookstone, who was half a foot shorter than Burt and carried himself in the aggressive rooster-strut characteristic of many such small men, looked up at Burt with narrowed, angry eyes. "This isn't just another delay, Dagget, another inconvenience interfering with your almighty Plan. A man is dead!"

They stared at each other. Burt wanted to explain how this wasn't the way it was meant to be. Everything was meticulously planned out. In control.

Godlike.

"Look, Tyler," Burt said, striving to sound reasonable when he really yearned to put his fist through a wall. "*Pirate Adventure* is the most ambitious show we've ever attempted. This is taking reality television to a new level. This isn't just pitting Man against Nature, or making people face up to their worst fears, or breaking up relationships with loads of steamy, sleazy sex. We've created an entire town here on this island, one that will live on as an educational tourist attraction long after we've finished filming. It's historical re-creation, competition, and –"

"Spare me the sales pitch, Dagget, and tell me what you're going to do."

Godlike? By the way Tyler Brookstone was acting, it was like he was expecting Burt to raise the dead, turn water into wine and then walk across Veradoga Harbor for an encore.

"I can't change what happened to Larry any more than I can change what happened to Robby Willets' arm. Accidents happen. We have to get over

them and keep going. It's the talk that I want stopped."

"People are going to talk. It's their nature."

"Talk is fine," he said. "Let me rephrase. It's the superstitious crap I want stopped. Everything that's happened has a reasonable explanation. It's a pain in the ass, granted, and you know how I hate delays, but it's really no big deal."

"A man is *dead*," Tyler Brookstone said again, his chin outthrust and belligerent.

Burt Dagget let out a breath that was almost a growl. "I mean the rest of it. You know what they've been saying. People getting sick, people getting hurt, stuff not turning up on time, things going wrong . . ."

"Yeah. Bad luck."

"Balls. They're saying it's a curse. And that's talk I can do without. Larry dying when he did is only making things worse."

"Worst of all for Larry, I'd say."

His fists curled and before they could get away from him — this flashfire temper was something he'd handed down to Kelly along with his dark-red hair, but thankfully she'd gotten a good measure of self-control from Margaret to go with it — he planted them knuckles-down on a large map of the island. The map was tacked to the table and protected by a plastic sheet that could be written on with markers.

"Tyler, I've said I'm sorry about Larry and I am, but you knew as well as I did that the man was not in good shape. How many times had you been on him about his weight, and his drinking?"

"I also told him he should avoid too much physical exertion," the doctor said. "Yet you sent him halfway across the island to dig a hole."

"He drove, for one. It's not as if I made them hike and haul. Larry didn't do any of the digging, either. According to Kelly and Steve, all he did was pick up the chest. If that's too much physical exertion, he could have done it just lugging his own suitcase. It could have happened anywhere."

"It could have, but it didn't. Burt, he fell on top of the chest and died. Doesn't that suggest anything to you?"

"Oh, for the love of God!" Burt said. "Are you telling me that you're believing it, too? Dead men tell no tales, right?"

"I didn't say *I* believed it."

"Spooky old Captain Smythe's curse. That's what's been behind everything that's gone wrong, isn't that what they're saying? We've offended his spirit, trespassed on his island, and he wants to kill us all or drive us away before we find his treasure. And you buy it. A Stanford man like you."

"I do not."

"Larry Burlingame had a heart attack. You examined him yourself. And for the record, he didn't die *in* the damn pit. Mike Glass hauled him out, Kelly gave him CPR, and you zapped him twice at the scene with your portable defibrillator before loading him into the helicopter. He almost made it."

"Almost," Tyler admitted. "We lost him for good just before we landed."

"So he didn't die in the pit," Burt said.

"No . . ."

"So there's no sense reading into it. We've come too far to quit now, you know that."

Tyler might have been about to say something more but the door opened. Kelly burst in, flinging her hair out of her face and re-settling her plumed hat securely on her head. Burt was glad for the interruption.

"They're ashore, Dad. Shopping."

"Looked like a few of them were sick on the way over."

She grimaced. "We made it a rough crossing like you said, too rough for some of the poor bastards. The *Adventure* is going to need a good hosing-out before the first Captain's Court."

"Let's see how our sailors are doing." Burt went to the bank of monitors that showed Rum Town, the cameras hidden inside palm trees and parts of walls. "Want a peek, Tyler?"

The doctor shook his head and left without a word. Kelly watched him go, then turned to Burt with one gingery brow raised in a question.

"What crawled up his nose?"

"Nothing to worry about. Ah, there they are."

The players were easy to pick from the crowd, despite being dressed in period garb. They were the ones gawking around, trying to take it all in. Only one of them was fully immersed, arms loaded with parcels.

"Sheffield," Kelly said, riffling through a stack of papers. "Dale. Works at one of the major Orlando theme parks. This must be just another day at the office for him."

"Is he a walkaround?" Burt asked. "You know, like Mickey Mouse or the Cat in the Hat?"

"It doesn't say. I don't think they're allowed to tell. Might freak out the kiddies and all, if they saw someone they knew to be one of their heroes out boozing it up in a bar someplace."

"They're going to be an interesting bunch. Who's your money on?"

"Too soon to tell." She joined him at the monitors. "I'll say right now, though, that Connie's going to be a problem child."

"Good," Burt said. "Love that drama. She's the quote-unquote dancer,

right?"

"Apparently, it's true . . . you *can* write off a boob job as a business expense."

"Don't even think it, girl."

"I wasn't!" she protested, but looked down at the front of her blouse all the same.

"I see what you mean, though."

"Dad!"

"Not that, punkin. Look there. She just passed Ms. Greywolf and I'd swear the temperature dropped a few degrees."

"No wonder. Connie was probably banking on being the island babe, and Tala makes her look like day-old meatloaf."

"Jealous?"

"What, just because Tala's got that silky black hair down to her butt, legs to the stratosphere, and a face that would make Helen of Troy turn into the Wicked Queen from *Snow White?* No, why in the world should I be?"

"Let's put them on the same crew."

"Dad, that's cheating. It's supposed to be a random drawing."

"But conflict is *good,* Kelly."

"There'll be plenty of conflict no matter how the crews shake out."

"Oh, fine. We'll leave it to chance."

Kelly eyed him. She knew that she was the one who would, at sunset, draw names and assign the players to their ships. There was no way that he could fix the results. Yet she was looking at him like she wouldn't put it past him to find a way.

"It's going to be a good show," she said. "Better even than *Old West Adventure.* I've got a feeling."

He gave her a sour look. "Now, if I'm telling Doc Brookstone that we've got to ignore everyone else's feelings, hunches, intuitions, and premonitions about bad luck and the damn island being cursed, it would only be fair to discount that, too."

"Okay, okay, forget I said it." She frowned. "Dad?"

"Yeah?"

"I did hear someone say that Arnold Warwitz was planning to sue."

Burt drummed his thick fingers on the table. "For one, Warwitz signed the same waivers as everyone else on this team. For another, nobody told him to go boar-hunting. If he'd asked, I would have said no. He's got no one to blame but himself for his goring. We should be saving that for the contestants, anyway."

"In other words, I shouldn't let it bug me."

"That's right. You've got bigger fish to fry."

"Speaking of which, I should get down to the ships and see how Steve and Leslie are doing."

"And speaking of *that,*" he said, "how's things with you and Steve?"

"There's nothing with me and Steve," she said, blushing beneath her freckles. "What gave you that idea?"

"I'm a student of human interaction," he said. "That's what this is all about. Human interaction. Ordinary people in extraordinary situations. Society at its most basic, primal level. Besides, I've seen how you look at each other."

Kelly curled her fingers into her hair and pulled. "Jeez, Dad."

"What? I'm closing on the big 5-0, and you're closing on the big 3-0. Be a shame to have this be the end of the Dagget line."

"You promised you wouldn't do this."

"I did? When?"

"When I broke up with Jack. You swore you'd leave off the grandkid thing."

"Guess I forgot."

"And look at us. Look at our life. I couldn't take a baby hiking up Korgaald Glacier, or boating down the Amazon."

"That's what nannies are for."

"Huh-uh," Kelly said, slicing her hands decisively. "I know what that's like. You'd be leading some expedition in Kenya and Mom would be on location in New Zealand, and I wouldn't see either of you except at Christmas. The rest of the time, I was stuck with Mrs. York. That's not how I want my kids to grow up."

"I made it up to you, didn't I? Started taking you along."

"Sure, when I got out of college and you said I was finally old enough to be interesting."

"Well," Burt said, looking down at the map with its coves and waterfalls and jungle thickets and rocky cliffs. "I never knew you felt that way."

"I don't anymore. I like my job, my life." She laughed, a merry sound entirely unlike her mother's shrill titter that had grated on his nerves like nails on a chalkboard. "You made me a star. I'm probably more famous already than Mom ever was. I'm Commander Kelly, Captain Kelly . . . what'll it be next time? Sheriff Kelly of Nottingham?"

"Got a nice ring to it."

"I really better run. It's almost showtime."

*　　*　　*

Chapter 5

The clanging of the ship's bell was loud enough to cut through the din of the marketplace, even over the squabbling of the chickens. As if it were a cue – which of course it was – the 'townspeople' actors melted away and the twelve contestants were left standing on the straw-strewn street, looking toward the dock.

Three figures were waiting for them, posed dramatically in front of the tall masts and furled sails of two pirate ships.

Shouldering their knapsacks and carrying their various purchases, they made their way to the dock where two gangplanks had been lowered. An open chest sat at the foot of each plank, beside the man and the woman who stood with Captain Kelly.

Karl Werner, mortified by losing the battle with seasickness on the crossing, was eager to move on and make a better showing of himself. The guys at the station, as well as his ex-wife, would never let him hear the end of it. Maybe that disgraceful incident wouldn't end up in the final edited, televised version, but Karl wasn't optimistic. These television people loved to show as much as the censors would let them get away with. He just hoped the end result was something he'd feel all right about letting Karl Jr. and Katrina watch.

He had bought a cutlass that would serve if needed as a machete, and tied it to his belt. The blade slapped against his leg as he walked toward the ships.

The contestants formed a loose group. They hadn't had time to exchange many words and Karl was leery about striking up conversations yet anyway. No telling how they were going to be divided up. No sense making a friend only to end up on opposite sides.

Camera people slid unobtrusively around. Karl ignored them. He'd been featured in a documentary about Southern California fire departments and was used to it. Some of the others still looked pretty self-conscious. The short, skinny girl – she couldn't have been that much bigger than Katrina – kept trying to ease behind someone else and out of view, pushing her glasses up on her nose.

The man to Captain Kelly's right was the one they'd seen on board, dark-haired and rugged. The woman to Kelly's left was an athletic brunette who held herself in a way that teetered on the border between arrogant and haughty. Both were dressed to the nines in frock coats, plumed hats, and the works.

"Time's come for ye to sign on for yer next voyage," Kelly Dagget said, affecting a cheesy pirate-movie accent. "The first six of ye I call will join Mr. Quinlan aboard the *Tortuga,* and the rest will be with Mr. Beaumains on the *Maracaibo.*"

The brunette smiled ironically at being called "Mr."

Kelly produced a snuffbox, wooden and carved with scenes of sailing ships on the high seas. The lid was off and it contained a dozen chits. She stirred them with her finger.

All of a sudden, as she plucked out the first one, Karl decided to go with it. Forget about how hokey it was and just go with it. They were here for two months, and nothing else mattered. Winning mattered. Competing. Playing this game as well as he possibly could. He might not make it to the end, being well aware that his size and strength would work well for him initially but be a liability later on as the others came to see him as a physical threat. No, he might not make it to the end but he was not going to be the first one sent home, either.

"When yer name's called," Kelly said, "take yer crewman's kerchief from either Mr. Quinlan or Mr. Beaumains and board yer new ship."

Around Karl, the others shifted and grinned.

"This is it," Dale said, and rubbed his hands together. "Sail, ho!"

"Angie Ellis," Kelly called.

The stocky woman, so pale that Karl wondered if she'd ever seen the sun before this, pushed to the front. Quinlan reached into the chest and gave her a scarlet bandanna with a scrolled "T" in the middle. She tied it around her neck before going up the gangplank and onto the *Tortuga.*

"Karl Werner."

Starting a little at being called so soon, Karl hitched the strap of his knapsack higher and followed Angie. He heard Kelly behind him announcing the next names.

"Jimmy Hernandez. Letitia Jackson. Dale Sheffield —"

"Tor-tu-ga! Tor-tu-ga!" Dale cried, pumping his fist in the air.

"And Calliope Glenning," Kelly finished.

The tallest of the women, the one with the kinked Stevie Nicks blond hair, stood barely shorter than Karl's proud 6' 3". She drifted up the plank as if her feet didn't touch it, and there was a distant, second-thoughts look in her luminous blue eyes.

"Ye six will be on the *Maracaibo*," Kelly said. "Benjamin Nathans, Ambrose Matthews, Tala Greywolf, Connie Berkwelter, Charles Lowell, and Heather Moss."

Mr. Beaumains handed each of them a vivid yellow bandanna with an "M" on it as they passed her. The two crews looked at each other across the gap of water that separated the rails of their ships.

"Cast the lines!" Kelly said. "Release the sails! Godspeed, and good sailing."

With that, the ships left the dock. The effect was good but not perfect, the thrum of the deck beneath their feet testifying to engine power as well as the billowing sails. Men and women in costume ran around adjusting ropes while Mr. Quinlan locked his hands behind his back and gave them all a once-over.

"Welcome aboard the *Tortuga*," he said. He didn't bother with the silly accent, but his voice was clipped and gave the impression of a British sailor fallen on harder times. "It's my duty to tell you the rules of the game. From now on, the crew of the *Maracaibo* are your rivals. You'll go up against them in contests, everything from climbing a mast to deciphering a treasure map. The winning crew of each contest will be rewarded with booty —"

Jimmy Hernandez snickered and Angie Ellis scowled at him.

Quinlan continued as if he hadn't heard. "Which you'll be able to trade in Rum Town for supplies. But both crews will join Captain Kelly for the Captain's Court, at which point you'll *both* have to discipline one of your own. The winners get rewarded, but none escape the Captain's Court."

"Discipline?" Letitia Jackson asked. "I thought we just voted them out, sent them home."

Quinlan's grin was wolfish and he went from impoverished noble to outlaw in the wink of an eye. He *had* been an outlaw, Karl suddenly remembered. Without the four-days' stubble, the cowboy hat, the bandanna and the

sneer, he hardly looked like the same man who'd led the raiding outlaw gangs on *Old West Adventure*. But it was him, all right.

"Not necessarily so," he said. "That's where these come in."

He gave each of them a little wooden box, similar to the snuffbox that Captain Kelly had drawn from to assign them their ships. Inside were six clay disks, two yellow with *keelhauled* written on both sides in piratey-looking script, two red with *marooned,* and two black with *walk the plank.*

Again, the wolfish smile. "When you vote, you won't just be naming a person, but you'll be deciding what you want to happen to them. The majority of chits will determine the fate of that crewman. Those who are to be keelhauled will undergo some test of physical endurance. If they get through it, they'll be allowed to rejoin the crew. But they're not apt to be exactly happy, now, are they?"

A few of the others swapped uneasy glances.

"Those who don't succeed in the keelhauling will go home," Quinlan said. "Those who get marooned will be sequestered elsewhere until the last Captain's Court, when they'll be brought back in judgment of the finalists. Only those who end up walking the plank, or those who fail a keelhauling, will be sent home. So hold onto your chits, and use them wisely and well."

They tucked the boxes away in pockets and corners of knapsacks. In the west, the sky had gone the color of flame and roses, and the first bright stars were starting to come out. The breeze picked up and the ship leaped. With the salt spray and fresh air in his face, Karl's stomach didn't so much as quiver this time.

"You'll have a few hours until we get to Buccaneer Bay," Quinlan said. "There are canvas hammocks below. The galley's not much, not by our standards. Salted meat stewed with carrots and onions, and hardtack."

A few groans arose at this, and Quinlan grinned.

"Don't knock it," he said. "The average sailor in those days ate so poorly at home that he'd *gain* weight on a voyage with those rations."

He left them, and weighted silence dropped like an anchor.

This, Karl knew, was the hardest part. None of them had any idea who the others really were, what they were like, who could be trusted to keep their word and who'd turn coat in a heartbeat. There hadn't really been a need to bother with it until now, when they could look around at the five other faces they'd be stuck with.

First impressions . . . as far as Karl was concerned, Dale and Jimmy would be the main physical competition, but Dale was a grinning idiot and Jimmy was a punk. Angie had a bossy, abrasive air about her that set his teeth

on edge. Calliope affected an ethereal, otherworldly manner, and some might miss the shrewdness in her eyes. Letitia was warm and matronly, but she was the least fit and could cost them some competitions.

They were making the same judgments on each other and on him. Nobody wanted to be the first one to talk now that they were here and *could* talk freely. More or less freely, of course; their camera escort was in constant attendance.

Karl's money was on either Letitia or Dale breaking the silence, and it was money he would have lost. Jimmy did it.

"So, hey," he said, twisting a heavy silver ring he wore on his right hand. "We need a plan to whip those *Maracaibo* asses. I can do about anything they throw at us if it's climbing and swimming and stuff, but we've got to work as a team."

"I think we've got the edge," Dale said cheerfully. "We got the young studs and they got the old guys and the skinny little girl."

All three women turned on him, sisterly solidarity right off the bat, and Karl stifled a groan. If they let this turn into a guys-vs.-dolls from the get-go, they were doomed.

"We've got the best ladies, too," Karl said, not sure about it but no harm could come from a small lie made in a good cause. "We're going to be hard to beat."

Dale thrust out his hand, palm toward the deck. *"Tortuga!"*

One by one, the rest covered his, stacking them up and then stacking them up again. *"Tortuga!"* they cried in unison.

"What I think we need to do," Letitia said, "is start strong and stay strong. We need to be organized, look out for each other, make sure nobody gets too sick or weak."

"I've got it already figured out," Angie said. "Look, we know they're going to dump us on a beach, right?"

"We do?" Jimmy asked.

"Didn't you read the stuff they sent you? Didn't you pay attention at pirate camp?"

"Some of it." He shrugged. "Most of it was just history, with some survival tips and a list of what we're not allowed to eat. Like monkeys, we can't kill the monkeys."

Angie groaned. "They wouldn't have provided us with information about the island unless we were going to be spending time on the island, would they, Einstein? And it's supposed to be just the six of us, not all these other people." She waved around at the sailors.

"Hey, I read enough of it," Jimmy said.

"We're probably going to have to make our own shelter, take care of fire, find our own food, boil our own water. That's going to be a lot of work and everybody will need to do their share."

"I'm sure you can count on that," Dale said.

"I'm just saying," she said, pinning him with a look that spoke volumes about what she thought of him doing his share, "that I'm not going to carry any slackers."

"No one's going to slack," Karl said. "We're all in this together."

"There are a few things I'd like to make clear right from the beginning," Calliope said, her voice ethereal but strong. "I won't be a party to hunting, fishing, or anything else that harms any animals."

They goggled at her.

"Then what are you going to eat?" Jimmy finally asked.

"The island will have fruit, roots, other alternatives. Healthier alternatives, and kinder too."

"Oh, boy." Dale pinched the bridge of his nose.

"Lord knows I could stand a healthier diet," Letitia said, patting her hips, "but we're also going to need to keep our strength up. We're going to need protein."

"She's not saying that *we* can't hunt and fish," Angie said. "Only that *she* won't."

"I don't think the rest of you should either."

"No way," Jimmy said. "The book said there were pigs on the island. Boars. Like in *Lord of the Flies*. I'm going to make me a spear and go pig-hunting first thing."

Letitia chuckled. "Going to paint yourself and run naked?"

He was less than half her age and immediately went crimson, mumbling and rubbing at the snake tattoo on his forearm.

"Well, just so we understand each other," Angie said to Calliope, "I hope you don't expect us to live by your rules. And I hope you don't expect us to go picking extra fruit for you when we're eating barbecued pork."

"Or fish," Karl said. "I can fish."

"Good man," Letitia said. "I picked up some spices in town. Anybody think to get matches?"

There was an awful pause.

"For Christ's sake!" exclaimed Angie. "Nobody brought any matches? Nobody smokes? You don't smoke?"

Jimmy, whom she was pointing at, got huffy. "Yeah, everyone in my *gang*

does, when we're not knocking over convenience stores, tearing through town in our lowriders, and carving each other up with switchblades."

"Easy, son," Letitia said.

"We can make fire," Karl said. "It won't be a problem. A couple of sticks, and there you have it."

"That's nowhere near as easy as it looks," Dale said. "None of us wear glasses, either. I have contacts. I didn't think to bring my back-up specs; we could have used the lens."

"We'll work it out." Karl looked at the crystal around Calliope's neck. "That might do the trick."

She grasped it protectively. "It disturbs the aura if anyone else handles it."

Letitia jumped in as Angie was on the verge of saying something heated. "If that's so, maybe you'd be able to start us a fire. It's going to get chilly here at night."

Indeed, it already was. The light in the west had faded to a smear of burnt-orange, where a single pale speck glittered.

"I'm going to see about this galley," Jimmy said. "Then find one of those hammocks Quinlan was talking about. I don't know about the rest of you, but I didn't get much sleep last night."

The consensus was that he had a good idea, and they trooped off together. Only when they entered the galley and the camera escort came in after them did Karl realize that it was working already. Through that whole little spat, not once had anybody looked their way or seemed concerned by the fact that this might well wind up being broadcast to millions of American homes. Edited to bring out the worst of them.

The food in the galley was as bad as Quinlan had warned. To drink, they could choose between water, tea, or watered 'rum' – in the interest of network guidelines, they couldn't have real rum but the non-alcoholic stuff was a reasonable substitute.

"You know the funny part?" Dale said. "In a couple of weeks, we could be looking back on this as a luxury, just like those old-time sailors."

The same could be said for the hammocks, which were in a hold that had actual portholes and was quite a bit nicer than the one they'd been in a few hours before. The hammocks were slung between beams, rocking gently with the motion of the boat. Down here, the roar of the engines was louder.

Karl got into his hammock easily, though it had obviously been made with a shorter man in mind. He lay back waiting to see if the rocking would make him lose his supper. It would be a shame because he suspected Dale was right. The pickings might be slim in the days and weeks to come, their talk of fruit, fish, and pig-hunting notwithstanding.

Rather than being outraged, his stomach felt like a warm, full pillow. It liked the salt beef and vegetable stew much more than his mouth had. The lethargy of digestion combined with the long and rough day they'd put in – heck, the long and rough several days, since leaving home to begin this jaunt – took their toll and one by one the crew of the *Tortuga* nodded off.

*   *   *

Chapter 6

Edith Creighton didn't get worried until she put the food on the table. Alice was already there, having changed out of her "buy a flow'r, missus" dress in favor of jeans. She'd washed the smudges from her face and combed her hair, and plopped down at the table to reach for the plate of hamburgers.

"Not so fast, young lady," Edith said. "Where's your brother?"

"Dunno. Where's Dad?"

"I don't know."

"Well, their loss." Alice snatched a toasted bun, opened it, and picked up the serving tongs with her eyes on the char-broiled patties.

"Fine, go ahead." Edith wiped her hands, turned off the oven but left the fries in to keep them hot, and went into the living room.

The four members of the Creighton family shared a tiny apartment on the second floor of Dagget Central. It wasn't much space, wasn't nearly as much as they had at home in San Bernardino, but they made do. The kids had an entire pirate town to play in as well as the lounge downstairs, so they weren't always underfoot. Their apartment had a modest kitchen and living room, a bathroom of their very own with a shower almost big enough for Wallace to turn around in, a master bedroom, and a smaller bedroom with bunk beds.

Wallace was one of Dagget's sound men, responsible for coming up with the theme music and editing. He was also a special-effects nut, and loved nothing better than creating convincing explosions, thunder crashes, and eerie unidentifiable animal howls to put the players on edge. Edith worked for *Pirate Adventure* too, as head seamstress in charge of the costumes. Alice, at eleven, was the youngest participating actor in Rum Town, while Sean had been, in his words "dragged along on this dumb thing."

She sighed, hoping that he would be in a better mood now that the game was actually underway. He had agreed to wear the clothes and play with only 'period' toys when outside, restricting his video games and action figures to indoors, but the complaints were enough to break eardrums. He was only eight, an age at which he resisted and resented any change in his routine.

The door from their living room opened onto a hall that ran the length of the second floor. The other private apartments belonged to Burt Dagget, his daughter, and the higher-ranking members of the team. The elevator was at one end, near the cafeteria. The stairs were at the other. As she stepped out onto the sturdy indoor-outdoor green carpet, the elevator dinged and Wallace emerged.

Her husband had been a big man when they married and had gotten bigger since, victim of a desk job and a hearty appetite for pizza. When she was in an affectionate mood, she called him her "big huggy teddy," but ever since poor Larry Burlingame had dropped dead of a heart attack, she found herself looking at Wallace with a more worried eye. They weren't teenagers anymore, either of them. They were only two years from being the parents of a teenager, and if that wasn't daunting enough to make anyone's pulse skip, she didn't know what was.

"Hello there, beautiful," he said. "Is that our dinner I smell?"

"Yep. Is Sean with you?"

"Last I saw him, he had a box of his toys and said he was going to play at the creek. He's not here?"

"Would I be asking if he were? It may have escaped your notice, huggy-teddy of mine, but there's barely room to swing a dead cat in our apartment. I couldn't have missed him."

"Well, he'll be back."

"He should be back by now. It's dark out."

They entered the living room and Wallace went to the window. Dagget Central didn't have many, and most were very narrow, like arrowslits in some castle tower. "I see that."

"Do you want me to go look for him, Mom?" Alice asked around a mouthful of hamburger. She had a splotch of catsup on her chin.

"No, that's all right. You and Dad go ahead and eat. I'll find him." She took a light jacket from a hook by the door. The evenings got chilly fast at this time of year. "For someone who didn't want to come here in the first place

and says there's nothing to do," she added sourly, "he sure keeps busy."

Wallace kissed her on the cheek and patted her on the fanny. Alice made the face pre-teens do when their dorky old parents were being lovey, and returned to the kitchen.

The fortress was alive with the noises of a day's ending. The clatter of dishes came from the cafeteria, where the Creightons took breakfast and lunch most of the time. Dinner, though, Edith was determined to keep as a family event. They were blessed to have a kitchen, miniscule though it was, and she meant to use it.

She stopped along the way to ask several people if they'd seen Sean, and got the same answers. Those who had remembered him headed for the creek, which came into Rum Town under a small arch of a bridge and entered a brick-lined canal that channeled it between the buildings before spilling it in a six-foot waterfall to the beach.

The night, though getting cooler already, was pleasant. The sunsets had been picture-perfect every day that it wasn't raining, and even the storms had their own savage charm. Rain was something of a stranger in San Bernardino, coming a few times a year in sudden sheeting downpours, but those were nothing compared to the wind-furious beating they got from tropical storms.

At night, carefully-hidden electric lights illuminated the streets of Rum Town. Most were deserted now, everyone headed back to the fortress for the night. The only exceptions were the teams with the two ships, Leslie Beaumains' assistant Trip tracking them with the chopper to get the dramatic aerial shots, and the teams waiting at the beaches for the shipwrecks.

In town, no one was about but Tyler Brookstone, sweeping the porch of his "Bloodletter and Chiurgeon" office. It looked primitive and crude from the outside. Even a glimpse through the window didn't inspire thoughts of advanced medical care, since the town designers had set up a shallow false interior showing shelves of leeches and the medical instruments of the era. These could have been taken from a torture chamber, all manner of pinchers and pliers and hideous-looking tools.

Inside, though, it was the equal of any small-town hospital. Doc Brookstone couldn't handle anything too complicated, so if anyone needed surgery they'd have to go to Kingston by helicopter, but he could deal with broken bones and most other emergencies.

They exchanged greetings, and then Doc headed inside while Edith continued on her way, calling for Sean. She went over the bridge and followed the beaten dirt path that paralleled the creek into the encroaching jungle. It was quiet except for the stealthy night-sounds of birds and animals, normal noises, not the spooky wavering howls that Wallace could produce with a flick of his synthesizer.

The largest critters out there were the boars, dangerous enough as Arnold Warwitz could testify, but they would leave humans alone unless provoked. There weren't any indigenous predators on the island. Offshore, there were sharks and moray eels and the like, but even those tended to keep to themselves.

"Sean! Sean, it's dinnertime."

The cawing birds hushed, then one twittered scoldingly at her.

"Sean! I mean it! Now!"

Something rustled in the bushes. A boar-sow, scuffling in the roots.

"Sean, I'm not calling you again." She used her this-is-your-last-warning voice, which usually brought swift obedience from kids that weren't even her own.

Still no answer except for the birdies and the beasties.

"Do I have to count?" God, she hadn't used that one since Sean was four. Back then, it had been effective as a whipcrack.

This time, it didn't work. There was still no answer.

The first threads of fear unspooled along her nerves, but Edith tried to ignore them.

"Okay, but don't you expect any dessert, mister," she said in a low tone, and walked deeper into the jungle.

The shadows edged the path like black lace. The lights of Rum Town didn't reach this far and the moon was barely up yet. She heard the slow burbling of the creek as it flowed over the partial dam that the kids had built, blocking off part of it into a muddy-bottomed pool.

Her foot struck something that skittered, then splashed. She could see the shape of it against the water. It was a carved wooden ship, one of Sean's toys. Other toys lay on the ground in front of her.

"Sean?" She sounded frightened, and hearing it made it suddenly so. A cold tingle turned her skin pebbly with goosebumps. "Sean, it's Mommy. Answer me."

Something was in the water. A shapeless, indistinct dark blob.

It couldn't be Sean. She had never worried about letting him play alone by the creek because he was an expert swimmer, better than Alice. And the pool wasn't even that deep. Four feet toward the center, maybe.

"Sean?" Barely a whisper now, and it seemed to Edith that she heard a hollow, evil laugh from somewhere nearby. Or maybe from somewhere inside herself, where some cold and malignant truth lurked.

Panic seized her. She jumped into the pool, sending up a huge splash and almost falling as she floundered her way across. Her feet sank in the gooey

mud, silt rising to obscure her legs. Then she was there, reaching out, feeling the stiff, clammy flesh.

A wail tore from her throat, ripping her like shards of glass. She turned Sean over. The darkness wasn't complete enough to hide his pallor, or the bulging eyes and gaping mouth. He floated limp in her arms, not a boy but a boy-doll, in waterlogged britches that clung to his legs.

Screaming, helpless to stop, Edith struggled to the side with Sean in her arms. She fell back in, lost him, shrieked in anguish as his head went under again, fished him out, and got him to the bank. Weeping through her screams now, her tears scalding against the colder water that drenched her, she fell clumsily to her knees and pushed on his back. Water gushed from his mouth but no air went in.

Edith rolled Sean over, his arms loose and boneless. She was about to begin rescue breathing when she heard a step.

"Quick, go get Dr. Brookstone," she sobbed. "My son . . . he's hurt."

Another step. Closer. And she heard the laugh again. This time, she knew it didn't come from inside of her, couldn't have come from inside of her, not the Edith Creighton who had a prized collection of *Calvin and Hobbes* books and still watched *Winnie the Pooh* though both her children claimed they were too old for it.

She turned, wanting to see who could be so cruel as to laugh like that.

The curved blade, heavy at the end and with gems winking from its golden hilt, swept down.

Her new scream was cut off as soon as it started, turning into a grunt of pain. She felt what she thought was an electric shock where her shoulder met her neck, then a boiling wash of what she dimly accepted was her own blood. But more than the pain, more than the blood, more than the immediate and sure knowledge that her poor little Sean had been murdered and the knowledge that she'd never see Wallace or Alice again, more than any of those things, she was struck by a horror so severe that her sanity was torn free of its moorings and swept away like a boat in a typhoon.

The cutlass came down again, on a sideways slice this time that cleaved almost entirely through Edith's neck. Her head flopped onto her shoulder, a pose that might have been coy if not for the terrible red and pumping wound.

Edith fell forward over Sean. She was dead by the time her body was nudged with a foot, pushed into the water. A scarlet rill, looking black in the deepening dusk, flowed over the dam and away toward town.

* * *

Chapter 7

Heather Moss couldn't sleep.

She knew she should. She knew it would be a good idea to grab as much rest as possible while she had the chance. But it was all too weird.

How had she ended up here, anyway? Thousands of miles from home, thousands of miles from the peaceful and remote observatory in the Rockies. That was where she belonged. With her telescopes and her camera equipment and her star charts. Nobody around. Just Heather, and the endless crystal-clear blackness of the star-spangled night.

The hammock rocked and swayed. She could hear the creak of timbers and the flap of sails over the engine-rumble. Closer, the breathing-sounds of her companions were what was probably the main cause of her wakefulness. She hadn't shared a room with anyone since college, and that had been a single roommate. A single *female* roommate.

Now here she was with three men, two of whom were old enough to be her father. Three men, and two other women. Both younger than her, though Heather was aware that she looked like a teenager next to Connie and Tala.

The others all seemed to be sleeping, or at least no one else was letting on that they were awake. Someone was snoring gustily, probably B.J.

She had tried to use her knapsack as a pillow but the lumpy objects in it — a brass spyglass in particular — rendered it uncomfortable.

If she was this badly off now, what would happen when they were on

the island? Would they have hammocks or would they be making beds out of palm fronds on the ground?

The ship rose and fell on the waves. She was no judge of sailing but thought that they weren't moving very fast. Only darkness showed through the portholes.

Heather had to pee but couldn't bear the embarrassment of getting up and feeling her way in the dark to the chamber pots that Mr. Beaumains had pointed out to them. Couldn't bear dropping her pants, pitch-black as it was in here, and squatting. The splashing noises would echo, a deluge, Noah's flood, and even if everybody else was asleep it'd surely wake them up.

Thinking of splashes and deluges and Noah's flood only worsened her cramping bladder. But she had made it through twelve years of public school, a year of junior college, and four years at university without ever once having to get up in the middle of a class to go to the bathroom. She could last.

She had her glasses on although there was nothing to see. They were hooked around the back of her head with a stretchy cord so she couldn't lose them. There wouldn't be a handy Lens Express out here if she needed a new pair. The cord made a crimp in her hair, but better that than to grope her way myopically through the next three months.

Assuming I even stay that long, she thought. *I'll probably be the first one sent home. Made to walk the plank. They'll get rid of the useless ones first.*

Well, if she had to go home she had to go home. She didn't know what had possessed her to apply anyway, or what had possessed them to accept her. Better to just walk the plank than to be put through some sort of grueling physical challenge and *then* get eliminated. She had zero delusions about her abilities when it came to those sorts of ordeals.

She'd watched every episode of *Old West Adventure* and knew that the mind of Burt Dagget, a man whose idea of fun was to drag people behind horses, feed them buffalo testicles, and make them race along the tops of runaway locomotives, would be able to come up with plenty of miserable things for this show. Maybe it'd be literal keelhauling. Maybe they'd have to eat weevils, or rats.

Heather groaned silently at the thought. Best to hope for walking the plank.

Tears threatened, and she blinked them away. She'd cried enough for one day. The others already thought she was a hopeless wimp. The fact that they were right didn't help, either. She had cried, and she had thrown up. All it'd take to make the day complete would be to wet the bed.

The door opened and a thin line of light from an oil lantern pierced the

room. It reminded her of a Poe story, but the beam didn't fall on the cataract-filmed eye of an old man. It illuminated the silvered beard of Professor Charles, touched briefly on Tala Greywolf's serene face, lingered on Connie's taut rump, and came toward Heather.

Closing her eyes, she steadied her breathing. Why she was bothering was beyond her. The camera probably had special film and had caught her peering around in the dark.

Her eyelids went red as the beam passed over. When it had gone, she risked a peek and saw Ambrose, his yellow *Maracaibo* bandanna askew on his tight cap of hair. Then on to B.J., his mouth agape as he snored.

The light winked out. Heather hadn't been able to see who was behind it and now saw only the green streaky dazzle of afterimage. But she heard a low whisper, a question, and then a hushed reply.

Then, clearly: "Let's do it."

The door clicked shut.

Dagget's people. Something was about to happen.

She rolled onto her side and slid her arm through the strap of her knapsack. Her ears strained for sounds, for clues. She could hear footsteps, lots of them. The engine died.

Moments later, the ship shook in a grinding, shuddering crash. The hammocks yawed crazily. Heather, tense, was flipped out of hers to the wooden floor, her knapsack tangled in her arms. Ambrose let out a startled yell as he, too, slid out of his hammock.

A huge jagged chunk of the wall fell in, landing tilted against a beam. Connie screamed. B.J. shouted in alarm. Charles' querulous demands to know what was going on wove among the din.

The gap in the hull revealed dimly moonlit water and an inkblot of island. As the ship tilted, the sea rushed in, salty and cold as it doused Heather and Ambrose.

"Shipwreck!" came a bellow from the deck. "We've run aground. Shipwreck, man the longboats, all hands, to the longboats!"

More water. Heather had to pee worse than ever but she struggled to her feet. The floor was slanted and the slope was steepening. The others were fighting their way out of the hammocks. Ambrose flailed around, sputtering, and found a beam to cling to.

"What the hell is this?" Connie shrieked. "Are we sinking?"

"It's part of the game," Tala said. She sounded totally calm. "You can see the seams where they weakened the wall of the hull."

"Fire in the galley!" someone called. "Galley's on fire!"

"We'd better get out of here," B.J. said. "Everybody grab your stuff."

Heather already had hers, but the door was up and at an angle. "How do we get out?"

"There!" Ambrose pointed. A longboat was lowering on ropes outside the hole in the hull. He slung his knapsack and waded deeper, an expression of abject horror on his face.

"What's the matter, son?" Charles asked, grimacing as he stepped into the seawater.

"I don't swim very well."

"Oh, that's just great," said Connie. "Just perfect."

"Abandon ship!" someone on deck ordered.

They had light now, the leaping orange of flames from the fire in the galley. Smoke rolled, gritty and hot, a contrast to the chilly water that was up to their thighs and rising. Shadows raced around, the rest of the crew, hurling objects over the side.

"In you go!" B.J. and Ambrose had reached the longboat, and the burly grey-haired man seized the much smaller Ambrose by the belt and the back of his shirt. "Up and over."

He heaved, and Ambrose went sprawling into the bottom of the boat. Tala, moving gracefully, tossed her knapsack in and followed. Heather floundered after, the lenses of her glasses spotted with droplets. She had just grasped the edge of the longboat when she was elbowed aside by Connie and fell to her knees. Her head went under. She gasped in surprise and sucked in a mouthful of the briny blue.

A strong hand grabbed the nape of her neck and hauled. She came up choking and spitting. B.J. manhandled her into the longboat, then boosted Charles. Ambrose had found the oars but clearly had no clue what to do with them.

B.J. climbed in last, and his weight almost tipped the boat. He plunked down, dripping, on the middle bench and took the oars away from Ambrose.

"Wait," Tala said. She leaned out, and came back with a tin marked 'Flour.' "We might need this."

Various flotsam was bobbing in the water all around. Ambrose and Charles managed to lift in a wooden crate, and Connie caught another tin. Heather, still spitting seawater, tried for a jar but it sank just before her fingers touched it.

The longboat lunged away from the distressed *Maracaibo* as B.J. put his back into his rowing. They could see the deck now, backlit by flames.

"There's the island," Ambrose said.

"Let me help you." Tala, rising and stepping among them lithe as a doe, sat opposite B.J. and reached for the oars.

"I've got it," he said.

"Save your strength. We can help." Tala beckoned to Heather. "Sit by me and take that oar."

"This sucks," Connie said, watching the receding ship. "This really sucks."

Heather got up, feeling the boat teeter and knowing, just *knowing* that she was going to overbalance and fall in. She was already soaked head to toe, her clothes hanging and her hair plastered to her cheeks and forehead. Above, whirring almost silently in the night, a helicopter tracked them.

She sat where Tala told her and took hold of the oar. She and Tala rowed with B.J., pulling when he pushed, pushing when he pulled. They swerved in a circle until Heather got the hang of it.

"Sorry," she muttered, blushing.

"You're doing great," Ambrose said. He was huddled on his bench, knapsack hugged close, peering dubiously at the water.

"What are you even doing here if you can't swim?" Connie asked him.

"I *can* swim," he said. "Just not very well."

"*I* was varsity swim champ," she said.

B.J. grunted. "You've got better floatation devices, missy."

No one laughed. No one quite dared.

The island grew larger as they left the *Maracaibo* behind. Mr. Beaumains had told them it would be a few hours until they reached Dead Man's Cove, their destination, but it had already been longer than that. The moon soared higher, painting the surf with frost, and they were still a long way from shore.

*   *   *

Chapter 8

"Edith?"

Tyler Brookstone paused at the boundary of town and forest. The black bag containing his emergency first aid kit dangled at the end of his arm. He carried it everywhere and was by now so used to its weight that when he wasn't holding it, he listed to the other side out of the habit of compensation.

"Edith!" He tried again, louder. "Anyone? Is anyone there? Sean?"

He'd heard a cry as he'd been about to lock up his medical facility for the night. Like Dagget Central's fortress, the "Bloodletter and Chiurgeon" building left the 17th century at the door. Inside, it was bright and clean and as well-equipped as any self-respecting doctor could desire. He had a spare bedroom in the back, too, where he could sleep if he got too busy with his work or too fed up with the crowded conditions in the fortress.

A cry. Yet the more he thought about it, the more he was sure it had sounded like a scream.

His initial impulse had been to dismiss it as the call of a bird or a monkey. There were plenty of both on the island, and they could make a godawful range of noises. But then, as he'd been on the freshly-swept porch with the key in his hand, he'd remembered Edith Creighton.

"Edith, can you hear me?"

She'd come by, looking for her son. He'd seen her making for the bridge, which was now behind him. If she had returned, he was sure to have spotted her. Or heard her, berating Sean for being late for dinner.

Tyler was late for dinner too. Those who dined in the cafeteria would already be sitting down, and the first reports on the shipwrecked contestants would be coming in. By now, they'd be paddling for their assigned beaches. He was eager to hear what the production team thought.

But a troubling sensation was nibbling at his mind, and he couldn't get rid of it.

When he reached the creek and saw the grisly surprise waiting there, Tyler froze in stunned disbelief. His hands relaxed and his black bag fell to the soft, damp earth. Things clinked and jingled inside of it.

"Edith? Sean?" His voice was a weak whisper.

Then, shaking himself and forcibly coming to his senses, Tyler remembered who and what he was. He bent, snatched up the bag, and ran the rest of the way. He knew better than to believe they were still alive, oh yes, he was quite familiar with the face of death. He'd seen it settle like a mask onto Larry Burlingame when they'd failed to revive him. He'd seen it in med school and in many of the hospitals in which he'd worked before signing on as Dagget's staff physician.

He saw it now, on Sean and Edith. There was no hope for either of them. Edith would have been dead within seconds of the blow that had almost severed her head, even if she hadn't fallen face-first into the creek. Sean must have been dead for hours.

Tyler didn't let that stop him. He pulled the boy from the water and felt for a pulse, then pushed on Sean's back to empty his lungs. No good. And Edith . . . it was futile to even try to find her pulse. Her carotid artery had been sliced clean through. It would have pumped the life out of her in hard jets, killing her almost instantly.

As he sat back on his heels, shaking his head and feeling sick in the pit of his stomach, not so much from what he'd seen as what he knew it would mean to the remaining members of the Creighton family, a slinking and terrible thought occurred to Tyler.

Edith had been murdered. Sean's death might have been an accident, but near-decapitation like that was surely the result of a deliberate attack.

Someone had killed her.

That someone might still be nearby.

Tyler's breath snagged in his chest. He reached slowly for his black bag, eyes widening as he tried to glean every detail from the surrounding glade. If there'd been footprints, he had trampled them into oblivion by now. If anyone *was* there, watching him, he or she was hidden too well.

The skin on the back of his neck prickled. He could all-too-easily imagine

the murder weapon poised to swing at him. Something bladed and heavy and sharp. An axe, maybe, or a machete.

He whirled, not meaning to move but seized by a sudden panic. The killer would be right there, teeth bared in a manic leer, the blade already launched, and all Tyler Montgomery Brookstone would have succeeded in doing was turning to take the edge full in the face.

No one was there. Even the birds had quieted.

Under the circumstances, he found that decidedly ominous. An urge came to him, a compelling one. He would go back to Rum Town, lock himself in his little apartment, and wait for dawn. Wait for somebody else to deal with this.

But he couldn't do that. Even if Edith and Sean had been strangers to him, he couldn't have done that. His job, his very nature as a physician, demanded that he try to help. Or, if helping was impossible, that he at least not abandon them.

He turned to them again, the boy so small and pitiful amid the litter of his carved wooden toys. Tyler's heart wrenched to think that Edith must have found him here, that the cry he'd heard had been a mother's anguished wail.

If Edith had been at all like his ex-wife, in some way it might have been a relief to her to die so soon thereafter. When his and Ruth's only child had fallen victim to SIDS so many years ago, Ty thought Ruth would have rather been struck dead herself before having to see the tiny, stiff body in the crib that had been her grandmother's.

The discreet lights of Rum Town glowed through the underbrush. Tyler made for them, with many a glance over his shoulder, his steps as quick as reasonable stealth would allow. His hand was curled around his walkie-talkie but he didn't dare use it for fear of being heard. And wouldn't it be just too ironic if someone chose now to try to reach him on the channel they reserved for emergency medical matters?

As he hurried quietly toward the fortress, still hunched against the expected slash of a blade, Tyler thought of his earlier, unsatisfactory conversation with Burt Dagget.

Another incident. Another death.

And this one was no accident.

*   *   *

Chapter 9

"What do you think is the matter with the camera people?" Dale Sheffield asked in an undertone.

"Who knows?" Jimmy Hernandez matched his tone, both of them pitching their voices low and looking like they weren't doing anything more than basking in the shade in the humid heat of the day.

One camera crew was over by Angie and Calliope, who were having an argument near the area they'd set up as a kitchen. Letitia was trying to mediate, but the conflict between their nurse and their psychic advisor was going to make for juicy television.

Karl had gone a ways back toward the jungle, his cutlass swinging in one hand, his Nordic-blue eyes scanning the treetops for coconuts. He had stripped down to trousers and boots, with his red *Tortuga* bandanna rolled into a rope and tied around his tanned, bulging upper arm. The other camera crew was following him.

It had been three days since their miserable shipwreck and landing at Buccaneer Bay.

Jimmy still grimaced as he remembered the hectic scramble to get off the ship, the effort of rowing ashore in the longboat, and the way they had all staggered up the beach and then collapsed from exhaustion. The next morning had found them itchy from dried saltwater and sand. Their possessions and what little they'd been able to pluck from the water were strewn around on the beach.

The wreck of the *Tortuga* had still been there, a broken-open shell of the ship a few hundred yards out in the gently-rolling surf. Jimmy remembered the six of them standing around looking at it, all nonplussed, while their assigned camera teams said nothing and concentrated on getting good close-ups.

Finally, Letitia and Karl had gotten them moving. They reasoned that they were allowed to salvage whatever they could from the wreck, and that first full day had been spent rowing back and forth, stripping the ship and hauling what they could back to their little slice of paradise.

It *was* paradise, Jimmy admitted that much. He had grown up in one of the driest, dustiest parts of Texas and never imagined he'd be on a tropical island, living on a cove of bone-white beach backed by lush greenery, with a waterfall tumbling into a pool nearby and brightly-colored birds twittering and shrieking in the foliage.

Calliope had discovered the skeleton. Her scream had come just as the three guys were trying to hoist a sheet of wood into a juncture of tree-branches – the makeshift *Swiss Family Robinson* thing had been Dale's idea and would probably turn out to be more hassle than it was worth. When Calliope screamed, they'd dropped the wood and narrowly missed turning themselves into human pancakes under it.

She had gone looking for a likely spot to dig a latrine trench. They reached her, the young and fit guys easily outdistancing stocky Angie and matronly Letitia, as Calliope came racing out of the jungle with her beads jingling and her long hair streaming back.

That must have been great on film, too. She was mortified when they followed her back and she realized what had been immediately apparent to the rest of them.

The fake skeleton had been propped against a tree in a sitting position, under a weathered sign that read 'Buccaneer Bay.' Old Bony, as Dale nick-named the skeleton, was nailed in place by a cutlass through its ribcage. A ragged eyepatch covered one eye socket, the shreds of clothing hung from its bones, a faded and tattered scarlet sash identical to theirs was looped around its neckbones, and in the bent twigs of its fingers was a rolled sheaf of parchment.

Jimmy had caught the camera teams snickering at Calliope's fright. Dale squatted beside the fake pirate skeleton and pried the parchment loose. Unrolled, it proved to be a map of the island.

That map was now tacked to a tree in the middle of their chosen camp-site. It showed their beach – Buccaneer Bay – as well as Rum Town, and

Dead Man's Cove where the other team would be living. Various other sites with warm and fuzzy names like Maroon Lagoon, Hangman's Hill, Widowmaker Peak, and Blackbeard's Beach were also marked.

"They're not laughing now," Jimmy said quietly to Dale.

Dale nodded. He gave every outward appearance of taking a casual rest, something both of them did during the worst heat of the afternoon. "Conserving our strength," he'd told Angie.

"Lazing around while the rest of us are working," she'd shot back.

"You're a nurse," Dale had said. "You know about dehydration and exhaustion and things like that."

"I also know," she had said, withering him with a look, "that people who don't pull their own weight are the first to go."

"I wonder what happened," Dale said now, turning over and propping himself up on his elbows.

They had done a decent job in three days, setting up their camp. The scuttled ship had yielded up a few crates of foodstuffs and supplies, some lanterns and oil, hammocks, yards and yards of rope, a modest assortment of tools, sailcloth, and plenty of wood. While their result didn't look much like the treehouse that Dale had first envisioned and sketched in the sand, they had adequate shelter from the elements. Lots still needed to be done, but there'd be plenty of time for that.

The weirdness with the camera crews had started on their second day. They never talked to the players even when questioned or spoken to directly. They rarely talked to each other within earshot, and did their best to act invisible. But it was obvious that something was wrong. They'd been too quiet, withdrawn and ashen-faced, stressed over something.

"Maybe Dagget chewed them out," Jimmy said. "Maybe it's not going like he wants."

"How could it not be? We've got enough drama already around here."

"It could be the other team."

"If something was seriously off-kilter," Dale said, "they'd let us know. We've got other things to worry about. Our first challenge must be coming up."

"Good."

"Good? You bored already?"

"No, but I want to see what they've got for us. It'll be a break from working on the camp."

"And a step closer to the money." Dale rubbed his hands together in a caricature of miserly greed, making Jimmy laugh. "Half a million dollars in

solid gold . . . set for life, baby! What I'd do to get hold of that cash, you wouldn't want to know."

The argument at the kitchen had ended. It hadn't been settled, but Calliope had stalked off in a huff and Angie was chopping up salt pork with her mouth set in a thin line. Each whack of the cleaver, shearing through the tough meat and into the plank they used as a cutting board, reverberated up and down the beach. Letitia was headed toward Jimmy and Dale, shaking her head. Her hoop earrings kicked off twinkles of golden sunlight. The camera team tailed her.

"You boys get any more comfortable, you'll sink right into the sand," she called.

"Tish!" Dale hailed heartily. "Pull up a patch of shade."

She did so, sighing as she lowered herself onto a flat-topped rock. "Best not to go near Angie right now."

"Yeah," said Jimmy. "Not while she's got the cleaver out."

They sat in the shade, not talking much. Jimmy watched Angie for a while, but then his gaze drifted out to sea. Their bay was shallow and blue, without much surf, and the water was amazingly clear. Karl had been fishing last night and hadn't caught anything, but reported that the fish were so thick that they wouldn't have to worry about running low on food. If, that was, he ever made good on his boast to catch some.

"Where'd Calliope go?" Dale eventually asked. He had gotten up long enough to fetch a wood-knife and was attempting to whittle something out of a chunk of the wreckage of the *Tortuga*.

Letitia rolled her eyes. "Gone to light some incense or something."

"She make any predictions?" Jimmy had hardly been able to believe it upon learning what Calliope did for a living. "Like, for instance, that she's going to be the first one out of here if she doesn't lay the hell off?"

"You can't really blame her," Dale said, hissing as the blade slipped and nicked his thumb. He sucked at the tiny cut. "Stuck on an island with all us carnivores."

"It was her decision to sign up," Jimmy said. "Where's she get off, though, trying to make the rest of us live by her crazy beliefs?"

The cameraman shifted, and sun-wink off the lens flashed briefly across Jimmy's face. He blinked and wished for sunglasses, but they weren't allowed. Not period, according to Dagget. This wasn't one of those wussy shows that let you bring an item from home. Even if it had been, sunglasses wouldn't have made the cut. Far too useful.

The sun-wink, though, reminded him of the presence of the camera.

This was all going on tape. This might end up in homes all across America. Calliope herself would end up watching it and hearing what he was saying about her. He flushed.

Meanwhile, Dale was asking Letitia what a nice lady like her was doing in a place like this. "I've got the rest of us figured," he said. "On our crew, anyway. But what made you do it?"

"Mostly," Letitia said with a merry laugh, "because everybody who knew me never thought for a minute that I actually would."

"What do you mean, you've got the rest of us figured?" Jimmy asked.

"Sure," Dale said easily, giving up on his woodworking project and stretching out, folding his arms behind his head. "Angie's looking to prove some militant feminist thing, Karl's an adrenaline junkie, you probably did it on a bet, and I'm a greedy, money-grubbing pig looking for a springboard to fame and fortune."

"It wasn't a bet," Jimmy said. Then a reluctant grin broke through his indignation. "It was a dare."

"Either way," Dale said, smiling and shrugging.

"Then what about Calliope?" asked Letitia.

"Well, okay, I admit I'm a little stumped about that. Maybe she saw it in her tea leaves."

"Hey! *Tortuga!*"

The shout made them all sit up and look around. Karl was jogging toward them, sweat shining on his muscular chest. The cutlass had been slung at his waist. He was carrying a netted sack full of coconuts in one hand and a roll of parchment in the other. It looked like the same kind as their map.

"Woo, mail time!" Dale started singing a song from that *Blue's Clues* show Jimmy's little nephew used to watch.

"What is it?" Letitia called, ignoring Dale.

Karl puffed to a stop and handed it to her as Alice came over to join them. Letitia unrolled it. Jimmy moved close to read over her shoulder.

"Letter of Marque," she said, reading aloud.

Dale interrupted her. "Should we wait for Calliope?"

"She can see it when she gets back," Angie said brusquely. "If she wants to go off on her own, she's S.O.L."

Letitia cleared her throat and started over. "Letter of Marque: all crewmen will report to Blackbeard's Beach at the start of the Fourth Watch. Laggards will be flogged."

"Our bony friend was holding it," Karl said. "That must be where we get our instructions."

"The Fourth Watch." Jimmy looked at their crude approximation of a timepiece.

In pirate camp, they'd learned that their days would be divided into six four-hour Watches, midnight to four a.m., four to eight, etc. Among the supplies they'd salvaged from the *Tortuga* were a number of thick tallow candles, each marked with red lines to show the passage of time.

"I make it about two-thirty now," Karl said. "That gives us an hour and a half to get to Blackbeard's Beach."

"Or be flogged," Dale said brightly.

"Flogged is bad, *amigo*," Jimmy said. "Flogged is getting your ass beat with a whip."

"If it's the right pirate doing it, I might not mind," he replied with a waggle of his eyebrows.

"And to think, your mother's going to be seeing this on TV," Letitia said.

Jimmy went to the map. They hadn't done much exploring of the island, being too busy setting up. "Looks like Blackbeard's Beach is midway between the camps," he said.

"There's no scale on the map," Angie said. "We should get moving."

*　*　*

Chapter 10

CNN was on but it was all too depressing.

Trip Galloway picked up the leather satchel he carried everywhere and headed for the door, leaving a morbid silence in the rec room.

A few people had board games laid out on tables before them, but their play was desultory and their attention mostly fixed on the television screens. A correspondent was reporting on the latest in an escalating series of terrorist attacks. This one was a suicide bombing in Grand Central Station that had claimed an as-yet-untold number of lives.

"See you've got your man-purse," Robby Willets said. His arm was still in a sling and Doc Brookstone had cautioned him to stay off the booze, which only made him cranky.

"Yeah," Trip said.

He'd given up trying to explain to the likes of Robby that men carried satchels like this in Europe all the time. It wasn't a sissy thing. Trip, who'd been star of his high school baseball team, planned to join the Air Force, maybe become an astronaut someday if he wasn't too busy playing for a major league team, should have been the last one anybody would consider a sissy.

A knee injury when he was nineteen had put an end to most of those dreams, but at least he still had his flying. It had gotten him a chance to see the world, scouting locations for producers like Burt Dagget. One of the other pilots he'd worked with had been an Austrian who swore by his satchel, *der zak,* he had called it, or something like that, and after witnessing for himself

how much more convenient it was than being limited to the contents of a wallet, Trip was convinced.

He took the elevator up and put on his sunglasses as he emerged from the rooftop access door of Dagget Central, glad that the pilots were spared having to dress like 17th-century sailors.

The two helicopters waited on the roof, twin visions of sleek black insectile beauty. In keeping with the theme, Leslie Beaumains had christened them the *Anne Bonney* and the *Mary Read,* after two famous female pirates. The names were scrolled on their sides in white lettering.

No one else was up here yet. Trip paused to savor the silence and the fresh breeze cutting through the sticky heat.

The mood around Rum Town was as black as the paint job on the choppers, and spreading like a pall over the island. Trip, normally carefree and not given to brooding, couldn't escape it himself. How could he, when he'd been the one to take the Creightons to Jamaica?

What an awful flight that had been. The bodies of the woman and her little boy had been wrapped up and loaded into the *Mary Read's* cargo compartment, the man and girl slumped in their seats staring out the windows with glassy, dead eyes. Donna Vespucci, one of Doc Brookstone's medical assistants, had gone with them to personally deliver Doc's report to the hospital in Kingston.

That had been a hell of a thing, a hell of a thing. Murder. It had to be murder. No way it could have happened by accident. Yet no weapon had been found, and nobody on the island would have any reason to want to kill Edith Creighton.

Reason or not, the lady was just as dead. And Trip knew that plenty of people on the island were criticizing the way Dagget was handling it. They didn't have any police force out here, only a chief of project security, and Dagget had been adamant about not wanting to involve the local government officials. Some wondered if that was because he had something to hide, had maybe done it himself, but he'd been in full view of more than a dozen witnesses all that afternoon. There just wasn't enough privacy on Veradoga to let anyone get away with much.

Still, they had a murderer loose in their midst. Trip wasn't the only one who'd taken to locking his door at night, for the first time since they'd come to Rum Town. It seemed like everyone had his or her own wild theory, but sooner or later, the talk always came back to the curse.

He wished he could laugh it off as easily as Dagget did. But it was all adding up. The equipment malfunctions, the number of people who'd gotten

sick, the injuries, Larry Burlingame's heart attack, and now this. An amazing run of bad luck for such a short period of time.

The rooftop door opened again and Francie Abbott came out with her camera on her shoulder. Her partner, Pete Carter, was right behind her. They were both dressed for the heat in khaki shorts and tank-tops, both so tanned and fit they looked ready to go on a photo safari in deepest darkest Africa.

"Showtime," Francie said, seeing Trip. "The boss man wants some good panorama shots of the first challenge."

"Think it's safe to take her up?" Pete asked. He was a kid, a grad student, and puppy-dog eagerness was warring with apprehension as he gazed at the chopper.

"Why wouldn't it be?" Trip asked, nettled. "You think I can't fly her?"

"No, hey, I know you can," Pete said. "I'm just . . ."

"Just what?" Francie narrowed her eyes at him suspiciously.

Pete's laugh was forced. "You know. People are saying stuff's been going wrong with the computers, the cameras . . . all the electronic gear. What if the helicopter has problems?"

"Then we die in a hideous fireball," Francie said sourly. "Get your butt in there."

"You can't be serious," Trip said to Pete. "You're really worried about that? About . . . curses? Ghosts?" As if he hadn't just been pondering along those very same lines.

Pete was squirming. He mumbled something that neither Trip nor Francie caught, and when Francie told him to speak up, it was only barely audible. Something about Friday the 13th.

Baseball players and pilots had a tendency toward superstition, and Trip's gut gave a nasty wrench when he checked the day and date windows in his watch and saw that Pete was right. Francie, however, uttered a derisive laugh that made Pete cringe and turn red.

"You want bad luck?" she said. "Try telling Dagget that he's not going to get what he wants because you've got the heebie-jeebies."

"It's going to be fine," Trip said, mentally reaching down inside himself and strangling the whiny nervous coward lurking in there.

It wasn't so much the thought of Dagget as it was the thought of Leslie Beaumains that gave his nerves a boost. He wanted to impress her. Not by bragging and showboating like Skyhawk did, because he'd seen right away that she wasn't going to be impressed by that sort of behavior. He wanted her to notice that he followed orders, flew a good flight, and didn't go around strutting like a rooster.

Francie climbed in, and after a moment's hesitation, Pete did the same. Trip got up front and watched as they strapped in. Francie attached her camera to the long elbow-arm that she could control by a joystick without having to leave her seat.

The *Mary Read's* blades and rotors whirred to life. Trip glanced back and saw Pete's hands clenched into white-knuckled clamps on the armrests. That nervous flutter was still in his stomach, larger now. The joy and inexpressible sense of freedom he usually felt when taking off was absent for the first time in his life. That sense of loss, of being robbed, made it worse.

Not even the beauty of the scene helped. Normally, Trip loved the sight of Veradoga, its verdant rain forests and rocky peaks, the edging of white-gold beach like lace trim, the way the water darkened from aqua to turquoise to a deep indigo. Against that setting, the Caribbean-style town with its fort looked perfect, much better than any high-rise resort hotel with unnaturally blue swimming pools and landscaped grounds. He had overflown the island plenty of times since the location had been chosen, most of the time with Francie and Pete or one of the other film crews, getting scenic footage that would be pasted into the show to emphasize the raw natural splendor of the island.

Trip flew over Dead Man's Cove, getting a good view of the ramshackle shelter that the *Maracaibo* team had constructed. Part of the wrecked ship still rested aslant on its sandbar, stripped and hollow. They soon left it behind and were approaching Blackbeard's Beach, where Kelly Dagget would be conducting the first challenge of the game. Kelly's ship, the *Adventure,* was moored a goodly distance offshore. Closer in, Trip could see the structures that had been erected. Tall masts, and rigging—

The *Mary Read's* engine cut out. With no warning. None of his lights came on, there wasn't so much as a cough or a hiccup, but all at once they were dead in the air.

*   *   *

Chapter 11

The rocky stretch of Blackbeard's Beach was sheltered by two curving arms of stone that embraced the cove. The footing was treacherous, shifting and threatening a twisted ankle with each step. The closer they got to the water's edge, the more tide pools, washed-up kelp, and broken shells appeared amid the glistening dark stones.

Ambrose Matthews paused with his legs braced against two sizeable boulders. The muscles in his calves and thighs were already aching from the hike, but he didn't want to let on. He shaded his eyes against the sun and made a show of studying the arrangement that Dagget's people had constructed.

A familiar ship, the *Adventure,* was anchored in the deep denim-blue waters about four hundred yards offshore. Closer in, jutting from the rocky beach, were twin piers extending out over the water. Rope bridges swayed between the piers and a dozen mock-ups of mainmasts, complete with rigging and crow's nests.

He could see moving figures emerging from the jungle at the other end of the cove, their bright red bandannas marking them as the crew of the *Tortuga.* They were picking their way along with just as much care as the *Maracaibo* crew, and even as Ambrose watched, one of them slipped and went hard to one knee.

Connie laughed. She planted her fists on her hips, swaggered with her shoulders, and Ambrose nearly took a fall of his own, missing a step while staring at the way her enhanced breasts bounced. He looked away fast, not

wanting his parents to see him looking at Connie that way.

Their camera teams followed, making their way over the tricky surface with enviable, practiced ease. In the distance, a helicopter buzzed over the treetops.

Eventually, at the cost of a few skinned knees and abraded palms, the sweating but anticipatory players reached the wooden planks and spread out in two loose groups before Kelly Dagget.

Ambrose saw right away that she wasn't her usual perky-sadistic self. Something was clearly on her mind, by the distracted way she chewed on her lower lip. But she collected herself, summoned up a cheery grin, and waved expansively at the structures behind her.

"Avast and welcome to the first of yer challenges," she said. "Behind me ye'll see twelve masts, each with a crow's nest at the top. In each crow's nest, ye'll find flags. When I sound my ship's whistle, ye'll race across the rope ladders and up the rigging. The first crew to have their colors flying from each mast will be the winner. But be warned — no matter who wins or loses, *both* crews will then join me for the Captain's Court to discipline one of yer own."

At her direction, they took their spots on the piers, each in front of a rope bridge. Ambrose looked uneasily at the water seething below. It wasn't like their beach at Dead Man's Cove, shallow and clear. Here, he couldn't see the bottom. Anything might be lurking down there. Sharks . . . though if there were sharks, wouldn't the fins cut the surface? So, maybe not sharks, but the sea was full of plenty of other biting or stinging things. Jellyfish. Sea urchins. Moray eels with rows of needle-sharp teeth.

He wished he was back at Dead Man's Cove. It had been easy to see how the place had gotten its name, what with the skeletons sprawled around the bottom of a leaning signpost, rusted weapons half-buried in the sand as if they'd died in a terrible battle. All fake, Ambrose knew, but it had been a creepily convincing touch.

They'd done a good job bringing in stuff from the wreck of their ship, and mostly thanks to B.J. had put together a decent shelter. For those first three days, it had been like being castaways for real, with nothing to worry about but the basics of survival. They'd gathered food — Tala had demonstrated great skill in fishing — and firewood, and built a nice firepit ringed with stones. It wasn't the Holiday Inn, but it was a lot better than Ambrose had been dreading.

But they weren't here to lounge on the beach all day, eating fish baked in a wrapping of wide tropical leaves and picking fruit right from the trees.

They were here to compete.

Captain Kelly raised her arm high and brought her ship's whistle to her lips with the other hand. As she inhaled to blow, the noise of the helicopter's engine suddenly stilled. Heather and the motherly-looking black lady from the other crew cried out in alarm and dismay.

The whistle fell from Kelly's lips, dangling on its cord. She, too, stared in thunderstruck horror as the obviously-stricken helicopter fought to remain in the air. The residual downbeat of its whirling blades was preventing a steep plunge, but through the bubble of glass at the front, they could see the pilot's frantic efforts and the horrified gapes on the faces of the onboard camera team.

An eerie silence held the beach as they watched, helpless, waiting for the moment when the craft would nosedive into the ocean. It dropped lower.

"Come on, Trip," Kelly Dagget whispered. "Come on!"

The engine coughed, then roared. The instant before it would have hit, the helicopter soared high again. It made a slow circle, then headed back the way it had come.

Kelly's sigh of relief was echoed by the rest of them. She turned, a little shakily, and removed her plumed hat to wipe her brow. Her voice quavered as she asked, "Crewmen ready?"

Ambrose wasn't the only one to gawk at her. They'd just nearly witnessed a helicopter crash and she still wanted them to climb that damn rigging? But Burt Dagget's philosophy, expressed in every interview and article Ambrose had read about him, was that the show must go on. At any cost, the show must go on.

They resumed their places. The rope bridge looked no sturdier, the water beneath it no more hospitable, and the masts seemed higher than ever.

The whistle's shrill blast, although he'd been expecting it, still made Ambrose jump. He saw B.J. to his left and Tala to his right both start out across their bridges, B.J. with slow and careful steps, Tala moving swiftly and easily.

He stepped onto the bridge and it dipped sickeningly. The smell of salt water and kelp was all around him. The bridge had no railings, just boards. If he strayed too close to one side or the other, it'd tip. Too much of that, and he'd be flipped headfirst into the sea.

Setting his sights determinedly on the mast, Ambrose concentrated on putting one foot in front of the other. He didn't let himself look around to see how his crewmates, or worse, the competitors, were doing. All that mattered was getting across, and then the climb.

The platform at the base of the mast was small, but it was at least solid,

motionless. Ambrose spent a moment there, readying himself, all but hugging the mast. Then he looked up.

Heights didn't normally bother him, but the crow's nest seemed miles in the air. He grabbed the rough ropes and started climbing. The ropes had been coated in places with tar or tallow against the moisture, which lent them a singularly sticky and disgusting feel.

His shoulders started to burn right away. His sister Rachel was the athlete of the family, not him. She had been ever since they were kids, with gymnastics lessons and girl's soccer, while he was in the school band and the art club.

But he was the one who was here, and he didn't want to be the first one disciplined. He didn't really expect to win the grand prize, he'd just wanted to do something different, a once-in-a-lifetime thing. He had to give it his best shot.

He climbed, climbed, looked down once at the water he'd fall into if he let go, and that gave him the strength to keep going even though it felt like his arms were being pulled out of their sockets.

Someone screamed in victory. He held tight and risked a look. A brilliant red *Tortuga* flag was snapping in the breeze, and Karl the fireman was pumping his fists triumphantly in the air.

Ambrose threw himself at the task. Other people reached their goal – Tala, then Jimmy and Dale at almost exactly the same time. Captain Kelly was shouting out the score, *Maracaibo* one, *Tortuga* three. Then B.J. got to the top, nearly lost it, and toppled into the crow's nest with a thud that shook ripples all down the rigging he'd climbed. A moment later, his yellow flag rose on its line and Tala uttered a war-whoop.

Heather, even shorter and skinnier than Ambrose, swarmed up the last few yards like a squirrel and made it a tie. On the *Tortuga* side, Angie lost her grip. She fell into the sea with a splash. The others were leaning way over, urging Letitia and Calliope on.

Then there was a splash by the *Tortuga* pier as Charles went in. He had vehemently refused to answer to Professor, especially once Connie had started in with the jokes about how she got to be Ginger, B.J. was the Skipper, Tala and Heather could draw straws for Mary Ann, and that left Gilligan to Ambrose. As Charles fell, Connie's mocking laugh rang out again even though she was clinging less than halfway up her mast and making little progress herself.

Ambrose reached up and his hand touched wood, the crow's nest. He was amazed but wasted no time scrambling up and in and raising his flag two seconds before Calliope raised hers. Now they were tied, each with one in the

water and one still on the ropes, but Letitia was climbing better than Connie despite being twice her age and forty pounds heavier.

Angie beat Charles up the ladder at the end of the pier, but when she tried to run across the rope bridge, she did what Ambrose had been afraid he would do and tipped the works, taking another header into the water. Charles stopped on the pier long enough to shoot a smoking scowl at Kelly Dagget, as if she were single-handedly to blame for his loss of dignity.

Letitia's flag went up and she loudly praised God and added, "Devon, Rickie, I love you!" at the top of her lungs. The *Maracaibos* went nuts, yelling for Angie to hurry. She emerged from the water again and crossed the bridge with more deliberate care. She and Charles reached the bases of their masts at the same time and started up.

"Get your butt up here, dammit!" B.J. hollered at Connie.

She was hanging three feet below the bottom of the crow's nest, but let go long enough to flip him the bird. Then she climbed, flashing everybody a spectacular view of her thonged backside as she swung her leg over and in. Her flag went up.

It was down to Angie and Charles. Ambrose joined the rest of his crew in calling Charles' name – except for Connie, who screeched, "Yeah! Go, Professor!"

Angie reached the top and lunged in head-first like B.J. had done. Charles still had five feet to go when her red *Tortuga* flag was raised.

Kelly's whistle blasted again. "Victory for the *Tortuga!*"

The descent was worse, Ambrose found, than the climb. Not only because he had to look down at the dizzying drop to place his feet, but because the weight of having lost their first contest was like a stone slung around his neck. The others looked like they felt the same way. They regrouped sullenly on the pier while the other crew hooted and hugged and high-fived each other.

"We climbed very well," Tala said. "Today wasn't our day."

"It could have been," Connie said. "If the Professor here hadn't fallen off."

"You were sure taking your sweet time, though," B.J. said.

"It's a foolish competition anyway," Charles said. "Physical prowess isn't half so important as mental ability."

"But we lost," Heather said, meekly, as if she expected everyone to yell at her to shut up. "Doesn't that mean it was important?"

"Other facets will prove to be more so, later on." He drew himself up self-importantly. "I am, after all, a professor of history. My knowledge of the

era and customs will —"

He broke off as Kelly beckoned both crews. "*Tortuga*, here's yer booty. Well done."

She tossed a sack in the winning crew's direction. Dale caught it, beamed at the hearty clink of coin.

"Tomorrow," Kelly continued, "Ye can make the trek to Rum Town and spend yer gotten gain. For now, 'tis time for the Captain's Court, where discipline will be meted out."

A pair of longboats tied off under the piers, waiting for them. Ambrose groaned. On top of everything else, they had to row out to the *Adventure*.

Kelly got into a third longboat with the camera teams, a pair of sailors manning the oars, and Mr. Quinlan. They cast off, the lenses of the cameras angled back to catch the receding view of the weary and in some cases waterlogged players.

"Now?" Heather asked. "We have to go and vote now? Don't we even get to discuss it?"

"I guess not," Ambrose said. "Come on. Let's get it over with."

*   *   *

Chapter 12

"There we go," Trip said as he unbuckled his safety harness. "Safe and sound."

Francie Abbot, who had damn near lost her lunch when the *Mary Read* made like a brick instead of a bird, didn't know whether she wanted to slap Trip for making light of what had nearly happened to them, or hug him for bringing them back to the helipad in one piece.

Pete, the poor kid, was still white-knuckle on the armrests of his seat, his complexion ghastly beneath his tan. He *had* lost his lunch and the interior of the helicopter reeked of used pizza. He had spent those precious seconds that might have been their last living ones on earth howling that they were going to die. He'd kept it up even after Trip had gotten the engine started again, kept it up until Francie leaned over and let him have it sharply across the face.

The rooftop door slammed open and Leslie Beaumains was there, eyes flashing like black diamonds. "What the blue fuck was that all about, Galloway?"

"Engine failure," Trip said. "No biggie. Any landing you can walk away from, right?"

"No biggie?" Leslie's voice was a purr that the unwary might have considered sexy, if they hadn't heard the steel underneath. "I expect that sort of shit from Skyhawk, not from you. And costing us aerial footage of the first challenge, too? Dagget's going to have your ass on a skewer."

"Leslie, I didn't do it on purpose! The engines cut out on us, just died for

no reason. I was able to get us started again. We were lucky."

"We were cursed," Pete said in barely more than a mumble. "Friday the 13th and a curse to boot. We should be dead."

Francie rounded on him. "You will be if you don't shut up, kiddo. I'm tired of hearing that garbage."

"What's he talking about?" Leslie asked.

"We had a scare," Trip said. "That's all. It was an accident."

"Accident."

"Come on, Leslie, you know I wouldn't pull something like that. I know my job. There was a malfunction."

Leslie raked her fingers angrily through her hair. "All right, get a mechanic team up here to go over this bitch from one end to another. Pete, you get to clean her out. Francie, think of something to say to Dagget."

Pete, still green around the gills, emerged unsteadily from the helicopter. He saw the way Leslie Beaumains was looking at his stained shirt and shuffled his feet, but spoke anyway. "It wasn't any ordinary malfunction. I felt it. Something . . . something was trying to kill us."

"Oh, Jesus," Francie said. "Knock it off, will you?"

"Sure, don't believe it," Pete said. "That's the way it always goes, right? Nobody will believe until it's too late, but there is something *wrong* on this island. We're not alone here. It killed Larry Burlingame, it killed Edith and Sean Creighton, and we could have been next."

"Cholesterol killed Larry Burlingame," Leslie said. "As for Edith Creighton, it wasn't any curse that took her head most of the way off. It was a person, a living, breathing person. Got it?"

The kid nodded dolefully, unconvinced. Francie exhaled in what was almost a snort.

"Look, Pete," she said, trying to sound gentle because she did like the guy even if he was too exuberant and often a pain in the ass. "Dagget's got Security looking into what happened to Edith. It's no picnic to think that one of our own people is a murderer, but there's no one else on this island. No one but us. You'll see."

"I don't know," Trip said. "He may be onto something."

"Not you, too." Leslie groaned. "What is it about this place that turns men into superstitious nutcases? It must be something in the water."

"I'm just saying that it wasn't normal, the way we lost power." Trip was turning bright red beneath the combined gaze of Leslie and Francie. "What with everything else that's gone on, with the electrical equipment and the cameras, it's worth thinking about."

"I'll agree with that," Leslie said briskly. "But it's got nothing to do with haunts, for crying out loud. The manufacturers might have screwed us over, or there's a weird magnetic glitch around the island, or sunspots, atmospheric disturbance, any number of things. No haunts, no curses, no ancient evil reaching out to seize us in the bony grip of death. Okay?"

"Okay," the guys agreed, but Francie thought they sounded pretty reluctant.

Francie reached back inside to retrieve the camera. "We got some good shots before, anyway. Of the *Adventure* and the rigging set-up. We just didn't get the action."

"It'll have to do," Leslie said.

"Maybe Jason and Arabella had better luck," Francie said.

"It's film editing's problem, and Dagget's problem, not mine." Leslie strode to the door and they followed her into the dim, cool recesses of the fortress. "My problem is keeping those birds in good working order. C'mon, Trip. I want you to tell the boys in the machine shop exactly what went wrong."

They parted ways, Francie heading to the fourth-floor control room to review her footage while Pete went off in search of a bucket, rags, and cleaning supplies to take care of the mess.

Burt Dagget was waiting for her. Behind him, the rows of monitors showed various views of the island, as well as the action that Jason and Arabella and their teams were capturing of the contestants rowing out to the anchored *Adventure,* scaling the ladders, and milling about on deck as the sunlight slanted golden and gorgeous across the waves.

"I understand you had some trouble," he said.

Francie didn't think that Dagget ever slept. Not when he was on location, at least. Maybe he hibernated the rest of the year, storing up energy for each new season. He had a bearish enough build for it, and a bearish enough glower when things didn't go his way.

Like now. He was looking stonily at her, as if it was all her fault, and a hasty excuse rushed out of her against all her good intentions.

"It was the helicopter –"

"Yeah, yeah. Let's see what little you were able to get." He opened her camera, pulled out the tape, and plugged it into the playback unit.

A field of diagonal blue squiggles filled the screen. Squinting at what little slices of actual picture showed between them, Francie could just pick out the jungle, the cove, and a brown blob that might have been the ship. The muffled beat of the blades and their voices were drowned out by a hissing sound that

sent a shiver up her spine.

"No," she said. "No, it was working fine."

"This is all you got?"

The Drones, as Dagget's computer boys were generally known, were in the room. Francie didn't know their real names and didn't think anyone else on the team did either. They kept to themselves, usually talking in a rapid jargon that made as much sense to Francie as Swahili. Now one of them raised his hand like a schoolboy, and waited until he had their attention.

"You should listen to this, Mr. Dagget." He had headphones on and had evidently been running the tape through a digital enhancer. His eyes were wide, bugging out of his head to give him an unfortunately fishy resemblance.

His cohort, or maybe his brother for all Francie knew, was frowning intently as he pushed the headphones closer to the sides of his head and fiddled with a knob.

"Turn it on," Dagget said, indicating the speakers.

The Drones did as directed, and the hissing sound swelled to fill the room. It was low and somehow nasty, almost like the asthmatic laughter of a dying miser chortling over his revised will.

"Now this," the first Drone said, and turned a dial.

The sound changed. It *was* laughter. Faint, but chilling. And then a voice. It said a word, hushed and indistinct, with a long "i" sound.

"It says, 'die,'" the first Drone said.

"No, 'knife,' I heard it say knife," the other said. "Kniiiiiife."

Dagget's brow hunched down in terrible bearish disgruntlement. He shot Francie a sideways glance as if to ask her opinion, but she backed up a step and waved her hands, no thanks.

Because to her, what she'd heard when they turned up the volume, was neither 'die' nor 'knife.' What she'd heard had sounded like a name.

Smythe.

* * *

Chapter 13

Kelly Dagget felt much better as she faced the two crews awaiting the Captain's Court.

A radio message from Leslie Beaumains had eased her mind about the helicopter. Eased it a little, anyway. Another malfunction wasn't good news, but Trip and Francie and Pete had made it safely back to the fortress. Nobody had been hurt.

When she'd seen the craft faltering, a whirlwind of terrible images flashed through her mind. She'd been so sure that they were going to crash, that the helicopter would break open like some shiny black egg and splatter its contents over the waves. On top of the other tragedies and misfortunes that had plagued them ever since setting foot on Veradoga, she didn't think she could handle any more bad news.

But disaster had been averted, and the matter at hand was only bad news for the players. It was discipline time.

She slapped her short cat-o-nine-tails into the palm of her gloved hand and surveyed the twelve, who stood in a loose semicircle on the deck of the *Adventure*. A couple of camera teams slid surreptitiously around them, and the sound guys had suspended microphones in the rigging.

They were a sorry-looking bunch. Some were nursing rope-burns, and the two who'd gone into the drink were grimacing as the brine began to dry on their skin. Three days of island living had worn the new out of their costumes. Most of the men had stubble on their chins, or boasted the cuts

that came from trying to use a straight razor. The women had no make-up. All of them had hair limp from humidity and the harsh soap that had to serve them as shampoo, laundry detergent, and an all-purpose cleanser.

Each wore a crew kerchief somewhere about his or her body, and they had their pouches with their fate chits tied to their belts, tucked in their pockets, or held in their hands as they watched her warily.

Tony Vespucci, kid brother of one of Doc Brookstone's assistants, served as Kelly's cabin boy. He was thirteen, dusky and cheerful, and at her nod he went among the players and provided each with a slate board and a chunk of chalk. Steve Quinlan, dashing in his first mate's outfit, stood by Kelly with an earthenware jug that had the *Pirate Adventure* logo painted on it.

"The time's come to discipline the crews," Kelly said. "Mr. Quinlan will pass among ye with the jar, and ye're to each drop one chit into it with the fate ye'd like to see yer crewmate suffer. Note that the color of the chits matches yer flags. When that's done, ye'll each inscribe the name of yer chosen crew member on yer slate."

Steve stepped up to Jimmy Hernandez, who was at the end of the line. He waggled the open mouth of the jar in front of him until Jimmy, after pawing through the heap of chits in his palm, selected one and dropped it in. It clicked hollowly against the bottom. Steve moved on.

One by one, they cast their chits. The jug rattled when Steve shook it again. He moved to Kelly's side, where a table had been bolted to the deck.

"Now the slates," Kelly said.

They always hated this part. It might have been easier if they'd been allowed to do it in private, anonymously, but Kelly's father liked the drama that resulted when they had to reveal their choices in full view of everyone else.

Chalk squeaked on slate. She noted that some of them were writing like kids taking a test, arms curled, boards tilted, trying to prevent anyone else from seeing. When they were all done, boards held against their chests so that names were concealed, Kelly read doubt and worry in many of the faces.

"*Tortuga,* ye'll be first. And . . . now."

The slates were flipped over, and the red-kerchiefed crew shot their gazes quickly from one to the next. The same name was written on three of the boards. Karl, Jimmy, and Dale had chosen Angie. Letitia's and Angie's bore Calliope's name. Calliope had written Letitia's.

"Have ye anything to say for yerselves?" Kelly asked, affecting a stern, scolding tone.

Dale, blithe spirit that he was, nodded and appeared undaunted. "She

fell. That could have lost us the contest."

"She's a fine cook," Karl added, "but we need physical strength."

"I could knock you on your ass any day of the week," Angie said, her voice nearly a venomous hiss. "If anyone isn't pulling her weight on this crew, it's Miss Cleo Calliope over there."

"The slates have been written and set," Kelly said. "It stands final. *Maracaibo?* What's yer decision?"

The six of them turned their slates over.

"Three and three," Kelly said. "A tie. B.J., why Charles?"

She asked him because she'd seen how startled the others had been, and knew that the five of them had agreed among themselves to deal with Connie first. Yet both B.J. and Heather had changed their minds and put Charles' name down.

"I don't like to do it," B.J. said. "But he lost us the prize, and frankly his spouting off about history's been getting on my nerves. Who cares about Henry Morgan and all that? He's the guy on the rum bottles, that's all I know."

"Heather?"

The thin astronomer quailed and adjusted her glasses. "I . . . I . . . what B.J. said. He doesn't do much hard work, either."

"Like Connie does?" Ambrose asked, and then looked surprised at himself for blurting it out. "All she does is sit and preen for the cameras."

"Tala?" Kelly inquired.

Silver-grey eyes met hers forthrightly. Tala's voice was low, soft-spoken, but carrying. "I believe that Charles, with his learned background, will be of more use to us later on."

Kelly didn't invite Charles or Connie to speak. She summoned Tony, who hurried up with a wooden box in his arms.

"We have a tie," she said. The box opened to reveal two old-fashioned pistols resting on crumpled velvet. "And on *Pirate Adventure,* ties are settled by a duel. Ye were taught how to use these in pirate camp. They fire paint pellets. Ye'll stand back to back, and on my mark take ten paces, turn, and fire. The one who takes the most lethal blow is the one who'll face discipline."

Connie, with a contemptuous sneer, picked up one of the pistols. Charles rather dubiously took the other. Kelly ordered the deck cleared in a wide circle around them and they placed themselves back to back at the center of it.

"And . . . mark," Kelly said.

They marched ten paces, Tony counting them off. As he reached ten, Connie and Charles spun around, the exotic dancer with catlike speed and grace, the professor wobbling. The pistols cracked. Smoke puffed from the

barrels. Connie's paint pellet struck Charles in the chest, spurting bright pink across his shirt. Charles' shot went wild, hitting the mast four feet above Connie's head.

"Yes!" Connie cried.

Tony retrieved the pistols and Charles, glum, joined Angie in front of the table where Steve Quinlan had totaled up the chits. Steve grinned rakishly as he prepared to give them the bad news, and Kelly didn't miss how Arabella zoomed in for a close-up on that grin.

A twinge of jealousy pierced her but she fought it down. She'd know if anything was going on between them. On an island this small, and a group of people as close-knit as those who worked for her father, there wasn't much room for secrets.

Still, it bugged her.

"Mr. Quinlan?"

"Aye, Captain."

"What's the verdict of the Captain's Court?"

"The crew of the *Maracaibo* has chosen their crewmate to walk the plank," Steve said. "And it's to be keelhauling for the crewman of the *Tortuga*."

Angie bit back a retort with visible effort. Kelly shook her head at her.

"Yer fate's been decided, Angie."

The workers had, the moment Steve spoke, rolled the plank into place. It poked out over the water, and the only thing missing was a ring of circling shark-fins underneath. Not a problem; Kelly knew that they had ample shark footage which would be edited in later.

Everyone on board lined the rails as Angie strode onto the plank. Her head was held high and her chin thrust out, but furious, frustrated tears gleamed in her eyes. She took a deep breath, then jumped off like she was doing a cannonball from a diving board.

A speedboat would be waiting to fish her out and take her to Rum Town, where she'd spend the night. Then to Jamaica, and she'd be on the next flight home. Kelly promptly forgot all about her and turned her attention to Charles.

"Charles, ye've been sentenced to keelhauling," she said. "That means ye'll be facing a difficult task. In this case, a literal keelhauling. In pirate times, yer punishment would be to scrape ye against the barnacles, and rub yer skin raw. But we'll do it a little different. Ye'll be strapped into that harness and pulled along those ropes."

The ropes, to which she pointed, were arrayed on a system of pulleys and vanished into the water on either side of the ship.

"We've attached a number of flags to the underside of the hull," Kelly went on. "Ye'll pass under four times, and ye must retrieve no less than five flags in order to stay in the game. But here's the tricky bit – some of the flags are red, and some are yellow. The majority of the color ye get determines which crew ye'll rejoin. If ye fail to bring back the minimum number of flags, ye'll be sent home. If the colors prove to be a tie, ye'll be allowed to choose yer crew."

None of the players seemed happy with this, Charles least of all. He only nodded, touching the pink paint on his shirt and rubbing it between his fingers. He did not give the impression of a man who thought his chances were good.

"Man," Ambrose said as the workers led Charles to the rail and began strapping him into his harness. "I'm glad that's not me."

"But you're wishing it was me," Connie said.

"It was supposed to be," Tala said, looking at Heather and B.J. with one upslanted, inquiring eyebrow.

Heather bit her lip. "B.J. said –"

"He's going to be pissed if he makes it through this." Connie smirked. "I hope he does, so you'll have to listen to him go on and on about it."

Charles was secured, facing the ship with his feet pointing at the water. He was ashen now and his eyes were anxious, and the sunlight touched on the silver in his hair and beard, making him look even older. Kelly was pleased at how it would come across on television. These people had condemned a dapper educated man to this. She hoped he made it, because she privately agreed with Connie. He would be pissed, and they would never hear the end of it.

"Remember, grab the flags. Ye have to get at least five." Kelly nodded to the men standing by.

"You can do it, Charles," Tala said.

Kelly blew the whistle. The sailors hauled hard on the ropes and Charles plunged feet-first into the water. She knew that there were divers down there, in case he needed rescuing, and also an underwater camera team who had slipped over the side in their wetsuits the moment the fate was revealed.

The rest of the players stampeded across the deck to peer over the rail, at the water where Charles would surface. He wouldn't actually be scraping the bottom of the ship, but Kelly had personally tested each of the keelhauling punishments and knew that it wasn't pleasant down there. The flags were vividly-colored plastic with lead sinkers at the ends to keep them from fluttering too much, but they were slippery, hard to hold.

Charles exploded out of the water, upside-down, coughing, and flailing in his harness. His hands were empty. A few of the players cried out in disappointment. He was allowed time for a few quick breaths and then the sailors yanked the ropes the opposite direction and he went in head-first.

Back to the other rail. Kelly had to move quick to get out of their way, and bumped into a jovial Steve Quinlan.

"I'd say all's going rather well, wouldn't you, Captain?"

"So far, so good."

This time, Charles came up with a yellow flag, and the crew of the *Maracaibo* cheered for him. He disappeared into the sea again. On his third reappearance, he had two flags, one of each color.

"Only one more pass!" Heather was wringing her hands, which Kelly didn't think she had ever actually seen someone do in real life. "He'll never make it."

When they hauled Charles up, him coughing and spraying salt water from his mouth, he had a grand total of three. Two red, one yellow. Not nearly enough.

*   *   *

Chapter 14

They would not take warnings, not even those that were writ in blood.

Smythe had expected as much. They were too mad with greed, too hungry for gold. They wanted what was his, and would not leave until they found it.

His prize. His treasure. That which he cherished above all others.

He had his knife and his cutlass. He had the power to reach out and interfere with their hellish machines. Yet they persisted. They would not go.

He had the skulls.

They rested around him, ivory domes in the sand on the floor of the cave, ivory domes with wide, empty sockets and what teeth there were dark with decay. He knew their names. Many Johns, many Williams, many Edwards and Henrys. Good, solid names. Good, doughty men.

His men. His crew. Loyal even unto death and beyond.

He reached out with one thin hand and saw it shaking. The ring that he wore, that Luisa had given him, was loose on his finger. The heavy signet slid around so that he could only see the band. It almost slipped off and he curled his fist around the weight of gold.

The cutlass with which he'd slain the intruder woman was near the mouth of the cave, its stained blade point-down and its hilt leaning against the rocky wall. His knife was at his hip where it belonged, riding in its sheath on the cracked leather of his belt.

If they would not heed his warnings, they would be made to pay.

This was his place. His home. His refuge.

He would defend it with what remained of his life.

With this resolve firmly in mind, he rose from his resting place. His movements were careful, so as not to disturb the woman and child. They stayed as they were, her arms cradling the infant, its head nestled on her breast.

No one would take them from him. He would not allow it to happen.

Smythe picked up his cutlass and left the cave.

Dusk had turned the sky a rich twilight-blue. The raucous day-song of the birds was giving way to the night calls of the jungle. In the distance, yet nowhere near distant enough, the lights of the intruders sparkled through the leaves.

Closer, far too close, he heard voices and detected movement.

A man and a woman.

Young lovers out for an evening tryst? Such was his first thought, soon dashed as surely as relentless waves ever dashed a ship against the shore. They were moving with purpose, swinging the beams of their lights this way and that.

Searching.

Searching for him.

It had been a mistake to leave the others where he'd killed them. He had hoped at the time that the deed would be taken as a warning and the rest would abandon their greedy plans for his island, but all it had done was make them determined to find out who'd dealt the deadly blows.

He would not make the same mistake this time.

As quiet as they were, Smythe was quieter. He crept up on them and hunkered down to watch.

Yes, a man and a woman. Both of them tall, the man weathered of face and stern of demeanor, the woman fair-haired but cold-eyed. He had seen them before, when he had observed from concealment the great excitement and to-do that had come with the discovery of the bodies. They'd lit the area with daylight brightness, scoured the earth so diligently that Smythe was glad he'd had the forethought to sweep away his tracks.

Now here they were again, these two. Dangerous people. It was in the way they held themselves, the alert stance and posture. It was in the weapons they carried. They expected trouble.

They had no idea how bad it could be. But they were about to learn.

They were all about to learn.

*   *   *

Chapter 15

The Calico Jack was doing a brisk business in early lunch. Rum Town was open and fully staffed today, expecting the afternoon arrival of the crew of the *Tortuga*. Burt Dagget sat at one of the tables on the tavern's upstairs terrace, enjoying a flawless island day and a hearty meal of stew.

Kelly sat opposite him, picking at her plate of fruit. They'd both make themselves scarce before the players arrived, but seeing Rum Town in action was hard to pass up.

At the blacksmith's shop, Mike Glass' ebony skin gleamed as he hammered. Sarah Parkins, who had been Edith Creighton's assistant but recently promoted to head costumer, was hanging garments for display outside of the clothier's shop. The various actors portraying merchants were busy getting their stalls ready.

"We got some good parting shots this morning," Burt said. "From the two who left."

"There weren't any problems?"

"With the choppers? Nope. Skyhawk flew to Kingston this morning with his passengers. Before they went, we gave them each a few minutes in front of a camera to speak their piece."

"That's always fun," Kelly said. "Any interesting last words?"

"Guess."

"Hmm." She chewed on a bit of lime that had been macerated in sugar-water. "Charles got huffy and said they'd be sorry later, when we started

quizzing them on historical data."

"Bingo. And Angie basically blamed the rest of her crew for singling her out on account of her sexual orientation."

"Did they even know? I mean, that stuff's in the profiles, so we knew ahead of time, but I don't think she said anything about it to the other players."

"Not that I've seen," Burt said. "But you know how people are. It's never their fault. Everyone's ganging up on them for one reason or another. I love the drama."

Kelly nodded and went back to eating. Burt eyed her.

"What?"

"What do you mean, what?"

"What is it? Something's bugging you, Kelly. And not just you. I'd swear a pall is hanging over this whole damn town. We got some great stuff yesterday, punkin. Great stuff. That keelhauling, damn, but that was good. I don't even care anymore that we missed the aerial shots."

"Trip'll be glad to hear that."

"Mr. Dagget?"

Burt looked up. "Dan, hi. Join us?"

Unlike the people in the streets and shops, who wore middle- to lower-class 17th century garb, Second Security Chief Dan Harper was neatly attired in a period soldier's uniform, as if he'd been appointed to his office by the governor and did his level best to keep up appearances.

He declined with a shake of his head the offer of the chair that Burt pushed out. "Mr. Dagget, we may have a problem."

The expression in Kelly's eyes, at once fearful and knowing, exasperated Burt. He exhaled a hard puff of air.

"Oh? What is it now?"

"Baxter and Phillips didn't come back last night. They're . . . they seem to be missing."

"What?" Burt brought his fist down with a thump. Harper had been pitching his words low so as not to be overheard, but the jump and clatter of crockery on their table instantly made them the center of attention. "What do you mean, missing?"

"They went out yesterday evening," Dan Harper said. "Looking for something, anything that might point us toward whoever killed Mrs. Creighton. Their last check-in by walkie-talkie was at quarter after nine. Nothing after that."

"It's a big island, Mr. Harper," Burt said. "It'd take more than a few hours to do a thorough search."

"But they would have radioed in. With all the static and reception troubles we've been having, it might be that they tried and failed, but I can't say for sure."

"Well, until you *can* say for sure," Burt said in a warning tone, "I would prefer it if you didn't go around starting a panic."

"Shouldn't we look for them?" Kelly asked. "I know Joe and Beverly. Responsibility's their middle name."

"If they're not back by sunset, fine," Burt said. "But wipe that look of dread off your faces, both of you. I won't have anybody leaping to conclusions."

"Like what?" a new voice broke in. It belonged to Robby Willets, whose modern sling and plaster cast looked out of place against his rough seafarer's garb.

The Calico Jack was one of the few places that stocked alcohol, though it was kept in a locked cabinet and only Ann Parkins held the key. Doctor's orders to the contrary, Willets had a glass of rum clumsily held in his other hand.

"Like maybe something happened to them?" Willets went on. "Like maybe they're hurt, or dead?"

"We don't have a single scrap of proof that anything's happened to them." Burt stood to face him eye to eye. "They'll show up soon enough, and with luck they'll have figured out who's responsible for Edith Creighton's death."

A stirring of unhappy conversation followed this. Burt felt his temper fraying and wanted to yell at them, demand to know what was the matter with everybody, had they all taken leave of their senses? They were jumping at shadows, stringing together coincidences, and whipping themselves into a panic over nothing. There *was* luck, good and bad, and he'd experienced both of enough in his forty-nine years to know that. But he drew the line at curses and ghosts, thank you very much.

Tony Vespucci showed up, out of breath from running with the news that the crew of the *Tortuga* had been spotted. They were on their way to town.

Burt thanked the boy and finished his stew in three long gulps. He and Kelly returned to the fortress, taking the elevator to the control room. From there, they could watch through the many cameras strategically placed around Rum Town as the players did their shopping.

*　*　*

Chapter 16

Beverly Phillips was losing her mind.

First her sight, then her mind.

And the worst of it was that she *hoped* so. She would rather believe herself insane than have to believe in a world in which things like this could happen.

Her eyes burned. No, not her eyes. The places where her eyes used to be. They had been burned out with a brand, the length of wood heated in the fire until its end was all orange heat-glow beneath a whitish-grey chaff of ash. It had been the last thing she had seen, the last thing she would ever see, coming closer and closer as her eyelids strained against the thin slivers that propped them open.

And behind the advancing, smoking wood . . .

No. She couldn't think about that.

The pain had been enormous and terrible, the brand pressing into the defenseless staring orbs of her right eye, then her left. She had heard it through her muffled, gagged scream. Heard the pop and sizzle of her eyeball boiling away.

She'd lost consciousness then, initially believing that she was dying from the pain and almost welcoming it. After witnessing what had happened to Joe, the torture he'd been put through, she would have counted herself lucky to die so fast.

Luck had not been with her.

In the soupy fog of her recovering daze, she remembered how she and Joe Baxter had been prowling the island. Joe was a hard-headed ex-cop from Los Angeles. He didn't think that the Creighton woman had been killed by anybody on Dagget's team, because something like that couldn't be hidden in a group this size and a place that afforded little in the way of privacy. He thought, and Beverly had been inclined to agree, that there was someone else on the island.

How right he'd been, but not in the way that either of them had expected.

Beverly remembered a sudden tingle of apprehension and had just been starting to turn around when something swung and connected with the side of Joe's head. He'd been knocked down but not out, groaning as he tried to get his legs under him. Beverly whirled to glimpse someone in a tattered frock coat, the nodding plume of a hat, and then a colossal starburst erupted in her head.

She had come to hours later, judging by the darkness overhead. She'd been bound to a post, hands behind her, wrapped shoulders to knees in rope that looked old and slimy and smelled like rot. Joe had been tied in similar pose, on the other side of the fire from her.

The fire had shed enough light to let her see her surroundings, when she'd still had eyes with which to see. They were in one of the many small, sheltered coves that made up the coast of Veradoga, but she didn't know which one it was or how they'd gotten there. The beach was negligible, a spit of sand and then rocks, walled in by rugged cliffs that were streaked white with seagull guano. The waves only came in dispirited laps.

Joe had died when the sun started to rise. He'd walked to his own death, compelled by the point of a cutlass against his back. A slit had been cut in his belly, and a loop of gut carefully extracted and nailed to the post.

Then Joe had been made to march around and around, leaving a growing coil of himself as he went, and blood running down his legs nowhere near fast enough to kill him quickly. She could only imagine what it must feel like, the awful slithering unraveling of it and the knowledge that he was doing it to himself.

When he finally collapsed, possibly dead as much from revulsion as from the shock of his injury, it had been Beverly's turn. By then, she was weeping and would have begged for release if not for the gag in her mouth. She had never wept, never begged in her life, but in madness all things were possible.

And it had to be madness, given who their captor was. This couldn't be real. It had to be an insane dream or hallucination.

Once her eyes had been put out, and cauterized at the same time, she didn't have to see any more. But she could still hear, and still feel. Could hear the voice, whispery and coarse at the same time, telling her that she was going to die. That she deserved to die, they all deserved to die, they had come here uninvited and would not leave even when it was made clear they were not welcome.

She cringed when she heard the steely hiss of a blade leaving its sheath. She waited for the slice of pain at her waist, trying not to imagine what it would be like to have part of her insides drawn out into the open air. There had been sounds as she stood tied to her post, staring into the scorched darkness of her sight. Sounds she couldn't quite identify.

A tugging, and the ropes parted. They unwound and fell around her feet. The bindings at her wrists were cut next and she flexed blood back into her numb fingers. Her arms ached and felt leaden from their long hours pinned behind her. She was in no shape to run or fight even if she could have seen what she was doing.

It was still day. She knew that much from the sun on her face. Gulls cawed and she could imagine them, white and grey against the sky.

She stepped away from the post when she was nudged, and almost fell to her knees. A cold, terrible hand closed on her arm to steady her. She shied away from it but the grip was strong as an iron clamp.

Stumbling, steered by the arm and with the cutlass point pressed between her shoulderblades, Beverly went where she was led. The sound of the water grew louder and the surface beneath her feet changed from gritty rock to loose sand.

Her captor stopped. Beverly did too, stifling a whimper in her throat.

"Down here," the voice whispered, icy and soulless.

Still gagged, she couldn't answer, couldn't ask what that meant. She found out a moment later when she was pushed, and took a big step down into someplace clammy and cool.

Wet sand. She moved, and bumped into a wall of it.

Then Beverly understood.

She was standing chest-deep in a hole that had been dug at the edge of the small beach.

"On your knees," her captor commanded.

Beverly shuddered, knowing what would happen if she obeyed. She lunged for the side of the pit instead, groping with her tingling, half-asleep arms and kicking footholds in the sand.

Stars exploded around her again. She sagged, crumpling to her knees

while her head seemed to pulse in and out on flares of light. Grains of sand stuck to her cheeks, her forehead. Heaps of it fell with damp thumps beside her.

The hole. The hole was filling up. And the hole, Beverly knew, was below the high tide line that would swamp this little cove.

The sand was up to her hips now. Up to her waist.

Above, the gulls cawed and shrieked.

The sand was up to her shoulders. Her neck.

She heard the rushing and receding of the waves. Closer. Closer.

Water surged against her chin. She sucked in air through her nose, smelled the salt. Panic thundered in her blood.

Sticklike fingers brushed against her face. They pulled at the gag, removed it.

Beverly screamed. The gulls echoed her, mocking.

She screamed again, but the next wave spilled foul water into her open mouth and her scream became a choked gasp. She writhed her body in its prison, but the wet sand molded to her, weighed her down.

The salt water forced itself up her nose and stung the seeping black holes that were her eyes. She vomited, coughed, spat to clear her mouth.

"Please," she said. "Ple–"

The next wave swallowed her up.

*   *   *

Chapter 17

Murder. He had done it. Committed murder.

Oh, they wouldn't call it murder. After all, it wasn't like a pig was the same as a person. That's what they would say. What they always argued. People who should have known better. They couldn't rationalize away a moral wrong no matter how they tried.

Down deep, they knew how heartless and unnecessary it was. Human beings could survive perfectly well on a vegan or vegetarian diet. Proteins and fats were the big dietary problem but those could be provided through nuts and legumes, and naturally-occurring oils.

Selfishness got in the way. They liked the taste of meat and that's why they continued the cruelty. Chickens living out their entire miserable lives in cages too small to even let them turn around. Cows likewise imprisoned. Slaughter-houses . . . anyone who actually went to a slaughterhouse and witnessed the bloody carnage would certainly think twice before ordering another hamburger or plate of pork chops.

That was what Calliope Glenning had always believed, anyway.

She definitely would have said that if faced with the prospect of having to skin and dress their own meat, people would have been even more willing to subsist on fruits and vegetables. Having to be right there, up close and personal when the pig's steaming entrails plopped onto the sand, that should have left all of them sick to their stomachs.

Yet her fellow crewmates had watched, happy and excited, as Jimmy proudly displayed the pig he'd run down and stabbed with a spear. How it had squealed! Calliope had been able to hear it even from the beach, where she'd been doing her morning yoga.

The commotion had drawn the members of *Tortuga* from all points of the camp. Calliope had known what she would see when they burst through the bushes, and it was as horrible as anything she'd ever experienced. Jimmy, in breeches with his belt slung crossways on his chest like a bandolier, held a red-stained spear in his hand as he planted a victorious foot on the still-heaving side of the pig.

"Um . . . it's not quite dead," Dale had pointed out.

The pig, its coarse dark hide matted with blood, had been panting and scrabbling its legs feebly, as if to get up and get away. Calliope had seen its eyes, rolling and panicked but utterly aware. The eyes of a creature in torment.

"Can't you see how it's suffering?" she had said, fury rising in her like a clear column of flame. "Look at what you've done!"

Jimmy placed the sharpened wooden tip of the spear under the pig's ear and threw his weight against it. There was a wet punching sound and a gout of dark red blood, spattering his legs as well as those of Karl and Letitia. The pig shivered, snout wrinkling, and then went still.

"You bastard!" Calliope surprised herself by shouting. Her morning calm was shattered for the day, perhaps shattered for the rest of her stay on this barbaric island. "You didn't need to hunt. We have everything we need right here. We have fruit, and shellfish –"

"Screw it, I wanted some *meat*," Jimmy said. "It'll make us strong."

"You bought meat in town," she reminded him.

And it was true, they had. With their prize winnings from the rigging-climb contest, they had elected over her objections to buy three chickens as well as a substantial supply of rice, flour, beans, and spices. The chickens, already beheaded and plucked so she couldn't object too much, had been turned over to Letitia that same night and she had chopped them up, breaded them, and fried them for a victory dinner that Calliope had taken no part of.

"That was two days ago," Jimmy said. "I'm hungry for something solid and we'll probably get hit with another challenge tomorrow or the next day. We need to be ready."

"Eating that pig will be the worst possible way of getting ready," Calliope had argued. She could tell it would do no good, since her crewmates were saying nothing while their eyes measured the poor dead pig into ham, bacon, pork chops. "A meal of greasy pork, especially when you've been living on healthy food, will cramp your stomachs and give you the runs."

"I'll chance it," Jimmy had retorted. "Nobody's going to make you eat it."

She spun away and stormed off, but not before she heard Dale crow something about it being luau time. She had ended up on a rise of stone protruding into the sea, upwind so she wouldn't have to smell it as they cooked Jimmy's kill.

If that was how they wanted to be, fine. She knew her words weren't going to change their bad habits. Let them spend the next several hours running for the latrine. That'd serve them right.

One of the two camera crews assigned to Buccaneer Bay had followed her. She had grown used to them now, and glanced into the shiny eye of the lens.

"It's hard being the outcast," she said, scooping her wind-blown hair back from her face and tying it with her red kerchief. "I'd be gone already if Angie hadn't fallen off the mast. They say I'm not a team player, but if being a team player means that I have to go against my own convictions, so be it. I do my share. It's Dale and Jimmy who kick back most of the day. And now Jimmy's gone and killed himself a pig, oh, the mighty hunter, chasing after a defenseless animal, terrorizing it and stabbing it to death. I suppose he thinks that makes him a man."

The breeze strengthened and she closed her eyes, tipping her face into it to inhale deeply. As she did so, something intangible brushed her. A chill, a prickle on the back of her neck. When she opened her eyes again, the bright afternoon seemed shadowed, though the sky was as cloudless as ever.

Her hand went reflexively to the crystal pendant she wore around her neck. She held it, seeking comfort and not finding any. A sense of foreboding, heavy as lead, pressed down on her.

She looked down at the beach, at their shelter made from salvaged parts of the wrecked ship. A line of laundry flapped in the breeze. The volleyball court that Dale had erected – one of the few times he'd done much real work, useless though it was – was empty except for the ball that they'd made from stuffing a sewn cloth sack with leaves. She could just see the four of them by the fire, the pig hollowed out and hung over a spit, and the two additional figures of the other camera team taking it all in.

To her eyes, a dark fog seemed to surround them like an omen of onrushing doom.

"This is bad," she said. "Something bad is going to happen. I can feel it. There's danger coming. Someone's going to be hurt. Maybe even..."

Calliope stopped herself. She wasn't even looking at the camera but didn't have to be to see the looks the two members of Dagget's staff were exchanging. They were loving this, soaking it up, and they'd probably edit it to make her look like a complete idiot and pain in the ass.

Saying nothing more, she sat there until the barbecue was apparently over and the sun was descending toward the line of the horizon. Dale and Karl were batting the makeshift volleyball over the net by the time she returned. Jimmy and Letitia were by the fire, attacking the remains of the pig with Karl's machete and the small hatchet they'd retrieved from the *Tortuga*, dumping the bones into their one big kettle.

The stink of it hung in the air, an invisible pall of grease and charred flesh. Calliope's gorge rose but she wouldn't give them the satisfaction of seeing her reaction. She ate her solitary dinner of fruit and didn't join the others around the fire. Letitia and her boys, just kicking back and having the time of their lives. Like a more grown-up version of Never-Never Land, one fiftyish Wendy and three Lost Boys.

The weather turned troublesome overnight, and they woke to rain. Their shelter had the chance to prove itself, but the grey light muted the brilliant, vibrant colors of the island. Calliope wondered if this might have been what she'd felt, up on the rocky outcrop. Not approaching danger but a storm, a change in pressure and humidity that she'd mistaken for a genuine premonition.

Her mood wasn't helped by the fact that the other four were unaffected by the cramps and diarrhea she had predicted. Jimmy made a point of strolling past her many times, munching on a sort of sandwich he'd made by rolling shredded pork into a piece of flatbread.

Calliope did her best to ignore him, to ignore all of them. The rain deterred much solo wandering, except for Dale heading off to see if any messages were waiting in the dead grip of the skeleton.

He came back at a run, bounding through the rain. "It's today!" he called. "I think we get to blow stuff up!"

Dale was proved right a few hours later when they arrived, soaked to the skin, at Blackbeard's Beach. The site had undergone some cosmetic changes since last they'd been here, but the *Adventure* was anchored in the same spot and the piers were still in place, stretching out from the rocky shore.

Where the masts had been, plywood mock-ups painted to resemble galleons rose from the water. On the piers themselves, in deference to the weather, oilcloth canopies had been hoisted on poles to shelter cannons, piles of cannonballs, kegs of powder, and the various accoutrements that went along with them.

Kelly Dagget was waiting and her smile was fiendish. The crew of the *Maracaibo* arrived, just as drenched and looking as though the past few days had been tense ones at their camp, too. Dissention. Bitter words exchanged.

But the bickering and angst of the other team was not for her to worry about. She had resigned herself to the fact that she wasn't going to be around much longer. Probably not even longer than today, and at any rate not long enough to see what happened when the diminished crews were brought together.

"Ye each have fourteen cannonballs," Kelly Dagget told them. "In order to win yer prize, ye must be the first crew to put a hole through each of the five ships on yer side of the pier. Ye'll have to work as a unit and remember what ye were taught in pirate camp." She blew the whistle.

Dale leaped right in and took charge. "Okay, Karl, you and I will swing the cannon around and aim it. Jimmy, cannonball. Calliope, you're in charge of the powder – charge, ha, get it? – and Letitia, you'll strike the flint for the fuse." He didn't wait to see if anyone was going to disagree, and none of them did.

On the other pier, the yellow-kerchiefed crew were shouting much the same instructions at each other. They all rushed to their cannons, cudgeling their minds for the instructions they'd been given. Pirate camp seemed long ago, and real life even longer than that.

The *Tortuga* crew got theirs loaded and lit first, but the shot plunked into the water three yards short of the target. Dale made an aggravated noise and they tried again. The hollow booms of the explosions shook the misty air, sending sea birds winging with screeches of protest.

Their next shot tore smack through the middle of one of the galleons. Kelly declared it a solid hit, and they moved on to the next one. On the *Maracaibo* side, one of their cannonballs got dropped by the skinny girl with glasses, missing pulping her foot by a hair's breadth and then rolling over the side, splash, and gone.

The moisture in the air got the gunpowder damp and made it hard to fire. Letitia was having a hard time striking a flame. Karl and Dale almost pushed their cannon off the edge while trying to reposition it to take a shot at their last target, and Jimmy did fall in while helping them push it back to safety. He climbed back up, but by then the other crew was touching fire to fuse. Their cannon bellowed, jerking back, and a round hole appeared dead-center in their last galleon.

"*Maracaibo* wins," Kelly said, tossing them their booty. Then, with a solemn but I'm-enjoying-this smile, she gestured to the longboats and the waiting *Adventure* for their second Captain's Court.

*　　*　　*

Chapter 18

Dan Harper leaned against the only wall of the control room that wasn't covered with monitors, electronic equipment, or computers. In the shifting, uncertain blue glow that came from the screens, everyone in the room looked like corpses under the water.

Corpses. He grimaced, not liking the thought.

From where he stood, Dan could see two different views of the deck of the ship as Kelly Dagget conducted the ritual of discipline. It all looked and sounded perfectly normal, until he let his gaze stray again to the pale, blue-tinged faces all around him.

Too many hollowed eyes, too many worried looks. Skittish glances in the direction of Burt Dagget. Everybody knew that something had to be said, and nobody wanted to be the one to do it. So they talked about it among themselves instead, privately, nervously.

Dan, who said little and listened more, knew that the consensus among the majority of the production crew was to quit now. Abandon the island. Apologize to the contestants but explain to them that too much had gone wrong. Too many people had gone missing or been hurt, and those who remained were jumping at shadows, seeing death and destruction in every single little snag or glitch.

He wasn't sure what he personally believed. The disappearance of Joe Baxter and Beverly Phillips had been a nasty blow. Not a sign of them except for a few tracks. It was as if they'd vanished into thin air. Then, when Dan's

searchers hadn't had any luck, Robby Willets had decided to take it upon himself. He and a couple of buddies had gone out searching.

Now the three of them were gone, too.

Five people missing. Three people dead. A near miss with one of the helicopters. A raging epidemic of sickness for which Doc Brookstone had not been able to determine any cause. Problems with the security cameras. Problems with the vehicles.

And now, the thing with the food.

Dagget liked to call Ann Parkins the quartermaster. She was in charge of all the island's mundane supplies, everything from food to toothpaste to toilet paper. Annie kept everything running smoothly in the town and fortress alike. She had their weeks here planned down to the final detail.

Last night, though, Annie had gone down to the storage rooms behind one of the false fronts of Rum Town. She'd opened the door on a seething torrent of furry bodies and naked tails.

Rats.

A horde of rats, squeaking and scattering every which way as the light flooded the room. They left a mess of gnawed sacks and boxes behind. Spilled food. Droppings. Ann, reacting on impulse, had plowed into their midst, wielding her clipboard like a weapon. She'd been bitten twice in the frantic melee of escaping rats, but was more distraught about all her careful planning than she'd been about the possibility of contracting rabies.

So now food was in shorter supply. They weren't going to starve, but rations would be slimmer and offering less variety until the emergency shipment that Dagget had ordered this morning – grumbling all the while about yet another delay and expense – arrived with a fresh store of supplies.

Rats in the food. Dan hadn't been able to figure out how they got in, or where so many of them had come from. Oh, they knew there were rats on the island, it was all part of Dagget's amusement to see how the contestants dealt with the local wildlife and vermin. But this many? This bold?

Dagget looked to be totally absorbed in the action unfolding on the screens. The two players up for discipline were beside Kelly. The tall, thin woman with the long blond hair and the ethereal aspect looked unsurprised, as if she'd expected this. The other one, the short scrawny girl with the enormous glasses and the weak, timid eyes, looked both astounded and hurt to the point of tears.

But Marcus Adamson drew Dan's attention away from the screens. Marcus' main job was overseeing the challenges put before the players. He was always happiest whenever testing his latest test or fiendish contraption. He'd been

overjoyed when he got to play with the cannons and pistols, and should have already been eagerly anticipating the upcoming obstacle course.

At the moment, though, he was at the center of a small cluster of people, all of them leaning close to a television screen that was tuned to one of the satellite news channels. Adamson's face was a ghastly mask.

Curious, Dan drifted that way. He barely heard when Kelly proclaimed the fates of the disciplined crew members, because as soon as he got close enough to see what had captivated Marcus and the rest, the bottom fell out of his stomach.

Letters scrolled across the bottom of the screen, repeating in terse sentence fragments what the shaken news anchor was saying.

A nuclear attack. Someone had finally gone and done it. The world had been steadily hellbound over the past few years, but up until now no one had gone nuclear. Now the worst had happened. Pandora's atomic box had been opened.

"Where was it?" Dan asked in a whisper.

Adamson turned to look sickly up at him. "Washington."

The strength ran out of Dan's legs. He fell into a chair, the casters squalling on the floor. "No."

"The fuckers nuked D.C."

"They're saying it was just a little one," Arabella Agliera said. She kept rubbing her hands up and down her arms, hugging herself. "A backpack nuke. Took out a quarter of the city. A hundred thousand people dead or injured."

Dan couldn't move. Could barely breathe.

He had been aware of the worsening global situation, of course he had. Who could avoid it in this day and age? Terrorist attacks, hijackings, bombings, a canister of weapons-grade nerve gas released in the New York subway tunnels, riots in Los Angeles and Chicago, the Middle East awash in blood and fire . . . it was impossible to turn on the television without running across some act of war.

Yet no one had really seemed to seriously, honestly believe that it would come to this.

"We have to stop the show," Arabella said. She was trembling all over. "We have to go home. I . . . I have family in Virginia."

"We've all got family all over the place," Marcus said. "So do they, the players. And they don't even *know*."

"They have to know," Dan said.

Marcus shook his head. "No news, no contact from the outside world.

This is the late 17th, early 18th century, remember? The boss man wouldn't tell them if Earth got invaded by aliens or an asteroid was about to flatten the planet. Not until he brings in their visitors from home. That'll be a couple of weeks still."

"It's crap. I mean, it's fine under ordinary circumstances to keep them uninformed, but . . ." Dan waved at the screen. He looked at Arabella. "They might have relatives in D.C., too."

"The show must go on." Marcus laughed, and the sound of it turned Dan's skin to goosebumps. He'd heard laughter like that before, when he was working security at a mental hospital.

"Well said, Mr. Adamson."

The group gathered around Marcus twitched and whirled like guilty schoolchildren. Burt Dagget was there, his hands folded behind him. His pose reminded Dan of something and a moment later, as Dagget began to pace, he got it. Either General MacArthur reviewing his troops before an engagement in which they were outnumbered, or an old sea captain. Ahab, maybe, or Queeg, determined to press on no matter what the cost and any man who disagreed would find himself getting a harpoon suppository.

"I am not, *not*," he said, "ending this show. Not for superstition, not for terrorists, not for the end of the world if it comes to that. We've all put too much into it. Our time, our money, our very creative life's blood. People are counting on us. Not least of which are our sponsors, and those ten individuals still out there on the island."

"But –" Arabella dared.

Dagget silenced her with a sharp look. "We have a responsibility to carry out. If we turn tail and run at the first little setback, then we're letting them win."

"Little setback?" Dan echoed, incredulous. "The nation's capitol is so much glowing rubble. I'd hardly call that little."

"I wasn't talking about that." He flapped a hand irritably. "I was referring specifically to the way half of you are ready to believe there's some vengeful ghost haunting the place, siccing the Caribbean version of the Plagues of Egypt on us."

Arabella's chin quivered. "I have family in Virginia," she said again. "I have to find out if they're all right. I have to go home."

A couple of murmurs seconded her statement, and Dagget's lip curled in disgust.

"So you want to cut and run, is that what you're telling me?"

"You wouldn't understand. You wouldn't care. Your daughter's the only

family you have and she's right here with you. If the world does end, you'll be together." Arabella blinked rapidly, as if willing herself not to give Dagget the satisfaction of making her cry.

"The world isn't going to end." His thick finger stabbed at the screen, where the picture had shifted to a news anchor whose face was a stunned, wooden rictus. "Yes, that was a horrible event, a tragedy, and it's got to be answered for. But it was the act of one small group of fanatics. It's not World War III."

Dan rose, and squeezed Arabella's shoulder. She had her head down, hair hanging to hide her face, and he thought she had lost the battle against breaking down.

"Mr. Dagget, come on," he said. "Please. This is . . . we can't just carry on like nothing's happened. It's only a game show."

Dagget went rigid. His lips pursed into a white little knot. He drew in a long breath through his nose. Everyone else, even Arabella through her tears, looked at Dan like he'd just committed the most unpardonable of offenses. They even edged away from him. Like God was going to smite him dead with a lightning bolt for his effrontery.

God might or might not have been listening, but if looks could kill, Dagget's would have laid Dan out on the floor faster than a round from a .357 Magnum.

"That isn't the sort of team spirit I expect from people who work for me, Mr. Harper." He spoke in an icicle of a whisper that nonetheless carried to every corner of the room. "A game show. *Only* a game show."

Dan realized, with dawning dismay, that he'd been worried about Marcus Adamson laughing like an escapee from a lunatic asylum when the person he should have been worried about was Burt Dagget. Perfectionism was only obsession wearing a prettier mask.

No one said a word. Dan wished valiantly for someone to speak up, support him. It *was* only a game show, dammit. There were more important things to think of.

If only Kelly were here. She out of all of them might be able to talk sense into her father, get him to be reasonable. But she was out on her ship, unaware.

"I'll have you know, Mr. Harper," Dagget went on in that same cold, deadly tone of voice, "that this is far more than a game show to me. This is my life, and I'd bet that plenty of people, plenty of *loyal* people, feel the same way. If you can't see clear to that, I'm afraid I'm going to have to ask you to leave my employ."

His eyes, narrowed to slits, swept the room.

"That goes for anyone who feels like running away," he said. "Anyone who wants to put other concerns ahead of what we're trying to accomplish here. You're free to go. Now, tonight, if that's what you want. I'll radio down to the boat and they can be ready to leave in an hour. Of course, you'll be forfeiting your pay, and I can personally guarantee that your careers in this business will be at an end, but far be it from me to keep you here against your will."

Dagget looked from one person to the next, his left eyebrow raised in a silent, "Well?" that carried a weight of challenge.

For a moment, the room was silent and nobody moved.

Arabella raised her head. "I'm going," she said softly. "I'm sorry, Mr. Dagget, but I have to."

Three other people followed her out, avoiding meeting Dagget's eyes. They did not so much walk as scurry, heads down, ashamed.

"Spread the word, then!" Dagget shouted after them. "Let everyone know, so they can make up their minds too. Go on. The rest of us will manage fine without you."

The door closed. Dagget, breath snorting in and out of his nostrils like that of a maddened bull, turned to Dan Harper.

"And you?"

He thought about it. The freedom of leaving the island, getting away from Dagget's irrationality. Then he thought about Joe and Beverly. His friends. He couldn't leave without finding out what had happened to them. And there was still the matter of Edith Creighton's killer.

Damn my sense of duty, he thought.

"I'll stay," Dan said. "I'll stay."

*   *   *

Chapter 19

The crying girl was going to be great on television, just great.

"Don't they even *watch* the show?" Jason Washington wondered in an undertone to his partner. "I mean, why are they always so shocked when they find out how they've been used and suckered?"

"It's human nature to want to believe the best in everyone," Samantha Dressler said with a shrug.

"Not my nature, it isn't."

"You've been working in this industry too long. Now shut up and get in close. The big man will want to wring every drop of reaction out of her."

Jason saluted with one hand and hitched the camera higher on his shoulder. He moved with the stealth that Dagget's "just think of us as part of the scenery" camera people practiced, and zoomed in on Heather Moss's face.

She was blotched and runny, her eyes huge and defenseless without the shield of her glasses. They were held in one hand while she wiped futilely at a steady leaking of tears from the other. Her breath came in stuttering hitches, and every third or fourth exhalation came in the form of a sob.

Not far from Heather, and as different emotionally as night from day, Calliope Glenning stood at the prow of the motorboat, motionless as a figurehead, her hair streaming back from her temples. She looked like an oracle, a Cassandra who'd known this was coming and accepted it with resignation.

"I can't believe it," Heather said, the words broken into fragments by her

crying. "He tricked me. He was in with her all along. I thought B.J. and Connie didn't even *like* each other! They were always arguing."

At the rear of the boat, hand on the tiller, was Steve Quinlan. He affected a look of stony indifference, keeping an alert eye ahead as they skimmed through the placid, deep-green waters of Maroon Lagoon. The rain had stopped but dripping from the dense foliage made ripples flow across the surface, playing in intricate patterns with the wavelets caused by the boat.

A fence rose ahead of them, chain link set twenty feet from the shore of the island at the center of the lagoon. Water plants clung in the diamond-pattern of its links, and fallen strands of moss adorned the top. Steve pressed a button and a gate, triggered by remote control like a garage door opener, slid to the side with a metallic grinding.

The opening was wide enough for the boat with not much room to spare. Jason panned away from Heather, past Calliope, and focused on the island. It wasn't much, maybe the length of a football field from tip to tip and less than half that distance crossways, but it was lush with fruit trees and the cottage nestled among them looked like the sort of thing that a vacationer might rent for a getaway. The roof was thatched, the wraparound porch screened with netting to let in the air but keep out the bugs, and a generator provided power for the welcoming lights in the windows.

"Here we are, ladies," Steve said. "Maroon Lagoon. You'll find a mod-estly-stocked kitchen, running water, electricity from your very own genera-tor, spare clothes . . . most of the comforts of home. No radio or TV channels, of course, but there should be enough books, board games, and video cassettes to keep you occupied."

A tentative sort of hope had blossomed on the maroonees' faces as Steve outlined the amenities. After six days of living rough, they looked glad of a respite. But Steve hadn't quite finished with them yet.

"The catch being that you're not allowed to leave," he said. "Here you'll remain, you and any other crew members who end up sharing the same fate. There are camcorders in the cottage for you to record your personal thoughts, but you won't see another living soul. Not until the final Captain's Court, when you'll be called back to sit in judgment."

He skillfully pulled the boat up to the small dock, to one side of the tiny but pleasant beach in front of the cottage. Jason hopped out first and backpedaled down the dock, getting the reactions of the two women as they picked up their knapsacks and disembarked.

Heather was still sniffling, but the relief on her face said she'd expected marooning to be much, much worse. She brushed at her hip, where a drying

splotch of bright-pink paint told of the near-miss that had nonetheless lost her the duel and broken the tie. Two votes for her, two votes for Connie, and poor Heather tricked into wasting her own vote on Ambrose because B.J. told her he and Connie were going to vote that way.

That, Jason reflected with a grin, had been a good twist. Of course, he had known about the pact between B.J. Nathans and Connie Berkwelter, the blue-collar ex-Marine and the stripper young enough to be his daughter. Heather Moss found out the hard way that she couldn't trust anybody in this game. For all the good it would do her now.

A few thin streamers of sun broke through the clouds. Birds in the tree-tops twittered. Some of Dagget's precious parrots screeched from their wicker cages on the porch, beating their clipped wings in a flurry of scarlet, emerald, and yellow.

Calliope led the way up the whimsical path of stepping stones leading from the beach to the cottage steps. Jason swung aside to let her pass him, then loped up the steps once Heather had followed her inside.

The cottage was as Steve had described. Most of the comforts of home. Rattan furniture with cushions in bright tropical prints filled the central living room. Half a dozen small bedrooms and two baths opened off of it, and one wall was taken up with a kitchen.

Steve doffed his hat. "Farewell, ladies, and good luck. You'll note the telephone, but do be aware it is a direct line to the fortress, in case of emergency. No long-distance calls."

The three of them, Steve, Samantha, and Jason, returned to the boat and left them to their own devices. Jason patted the side of his camera.

"That was good," he said. "The look on her face when you read the results, just terrific."

"I did feel a little bad for the poor mite," Steve said. "She was blindsided."

The gate opened for them and closed once they'd passed through. Another dock waited at the far shore of the lagoon. Steve made for it.

Samantha started. "Hey, did you see that?"

"What?" Jason asked.

"Someone's out there. Hey! Who's there?" she called, raising her voice.

Fronds and bushes rustled where she was pointing. Jason had a brief impression of a figure ducking away and out of sight.

Steve cut the motor and the boat slowed as momentum carried it toward the dock. They waited a few seconds, Jason adjusting his telephoto lens at the spot, but nothing else came into view.

"Who do you think it was?" he asked.

As soon as he did, an ugly thought leaped into his mind. He saw it mirrored on Steve and Samantha.

"You know, I've heard people saying," Samantha said quietly, "that it could have been Joe Baxter or Bev Phillips, or both of them, who murdered Wally Creighton's wife."

"Couldn't have been Joe," Steve said. "He was on the *Adventure* the day Edith died."

"Beverly wasn't, though," Jason said. "She was in town. I remember seeing her at lunch."

Steve frowned. "I can't believe that either of them would have done it. Whoever was behind that has to be a stranger. We've all worked together much too long. We'd know if one of us had gone up and over the high side."

"We should go look," Jason said. "If we can catch him, if we can even just get him on film, then we'll know who it is."

"And if he cuts your head off?" Samantha asked.

"Nobody's going to cut my head off."

"Famous last words, old boy," Steve said.

The boat bumped into the dock and Jason was first out again. "Come on. Let's move before he gets too far away."

"We can't go charging off into the jungle after a crazed killer," Samantha said. "What if we never come back?"

"Then at least Dagget will have the whole thing on tape, assuming he recovers the camera."

"That will be a great comfort if we all die," Steve said dryly. "Still, if you're right and we can find out something, we owe it to our lost colleagues to give it a go."

"Wait, wait." Samantha got around in front of them on the dock and stood with her hands on her hips. She was a big woman, not fat but buff, Amazonian, and looked capable of knocking them both into the lagoon. "Am I the only one who thinks this is nuts?"

"Not at all," Steve said. "It is nuts, most assuredly."

"Then why are we doing this?"

"It'll be fine," Jason said, impatient, itching to get going.

Each second wasted arguing was a second in which their quarry got further away. He loved his job but this was his big chance to get noticed, to shoot film that could make him famous. Apprehension of a murderer, all caught on camera. He gauged his chances of getting around Samantha and didn't like the odds.

"I am armed," Steve said. He touched the butt of the pistol thrust through

his sash. "This isn't a useless antique, but only looks like one. Don't worry. The safety's on."

Samantha and Jason stared at him.

"Where'd you get a live gun?" Jason demanded.

"Security had a few on hand, and after that unfortunate incident with Arnold Warwitz and the boar, Dagget thought it'd be wise if a select few of us carried weapons."

"Oh, yeah, brilliant idea," Samantha said. "How did he know that he wasn't giving a gun to the killer?"

"Never mind, never mind, let's just go," Jason said. He took advantage of the step back that Samantha had taken when Steve mentioned the pistol, and was past her before she realized he meant to move.

"Jason, don't be a jackass!" she called after him.

"The leopard can't change his spots," Steve said. "We'd better tag along."

The dock was near one of the access roads that the initial set-up team had carved out of the island's heart. Never seen during the completed episodes of the show, these roads connected the behind-the-scenes workings. Jason left the road and plunged into the dense jungle.

He could hear Samantha behind him, telling him he was being stupid, that it had probably only been a monkey or a boar anyway. Steve brought up the rear, walking easily but warily. Jason could hear him calling in a report to Central – the phones were working for once, wonder of wonders. Steve's other hand never strayed far from the gun.

They came to the place where the bushes had moved. Jason stopped, sucked in a breath.

"Look! No, don't step on them." He caught Samantha's arm as she made to go around him.

The ground was bare here and soft from the rain, and the impressions were clearly defined. Tracks. Footprints.

Jason aimed the camera at them. The tracks were fairly large, and while he was no outdoorsman, no hunter, not an inner-city kid like him, he guessed them to belong to a man. The heels made rounded, deep depressions in the earth, depressions slowly seeping full of water.

"There *was* someone here," Steve said.

"This way. He went this way." Bent low, keeping his lens trained on the ground, Jason followed the marks. He was barely aware of the change in the terrain as the jungle floor became soupier, only noticing it insofar as it made the tracks harder to see.

"Hold up there a bit, Jason." Steve was picking his way along more

cautiously, and now Samantha was in the rear.

"Yeah, yeah," he mumbled. He had to sweep fronds out of the way with his free hand now and they were wet from the rain, soaking his sleeve, sometimes flicking him with water. His feet squished and squelched.

Something moved up ahead. Something man-sized and quick.

"Gotcha!" Jason broke into a run.

"Jason, no!" Steve yelled.

The camera bounced all over the place. He knew he was getting the sort of hectic, jerky film that Dagget hated, but it'd all be worth it when —

He ran onto a patch of palm fronds and his leading foot went through into a gluey, clammy substance that sucked at his leg like cold oatmeal. His arms pinwheeled. His body pitched forward. More fronds gave way and he was falling.

The camera flew out of his hands. Secured by its strap, it swung up and back and hit him in the face — immediate, dazzling pain. He twisted, landed on his side, and more of that cold clamminess engulfed his shoulder, his arm. Liquid grit splashed into his mouth.

Inner-city kid or no, he identified quicksand with a sudden flash of horror and insight. He surged up, but only drove the lower half of his body deeper into the muck. He howled for help, forgetting every single thing that they'd been taught about island survival.

Steve and Samantha were both shouting his name. Samantha caught Steve by the collar hard enough to rip it, preventing Steve from joining Jason in the quicksand.

"Jason, hold still! Hold still," she said.

He heard, but couldn't. It was dragging him down and he was going to drown in it, drown in the vile gritty mud. He flailed, heaved, and got his arms up . . . and his head went under.

"Grab hold of this, Jason." Steve extended a branch. Samantha had him by the belt instead of the collar, holding him as Steve leaned out over the pit of quicksand.

Spitting out a mouthful, Jason floundered toward the branch. He reached, missed, reached again, caught it. Steve pulled. Jason slipped. His face went under again. He brought it up, rivulets of muddy water running from his hair, and the branch banged into his already agonized nose.

His hands closed around it in a death-grip. Steve pulled again. Jason's body slid toward the edge, the quicksand clinging to him, not wanting to let him go. At last he was close enough that Samantha could reach him. She hauled him out and he sprawled on the driest patch of land he could find, dry-heaving.

"I lost the camera," he said when he could talk. It turned out to be a mistake, not only because Samantha gave him such a disgusted look that he thought she might kick him back into the pit but because his entire face exploded in pain when he did.

"Bloody hell," Steve said. He held up a quicksand-coated palm frond. It drooped soggily from his hand. He looked at Samantha, then down at Jason. "This was a trap, my friends. This was a deliberate trap."

*　　*　　*

Chapter 20

"You're the only one who can talk to him," Tyler Brookstone said.

Kelly Dagget, rubbing her temples in a futile effort to forestall a truly monumental headache, lifted her hair out of her eyes long enough to peer at the doctor. "Me. Right."

"He'll listen to you."

"No, he won't."

"He has to."

The lounge of Dagget Central was empty but for the two of them. The floors above were filled with sleep, though not as filled as they had been three days ago. Too many people were gone. Too many people had, as her father saw it, bailed out. Abandoned him, turned their backs on the show, and gone running home. Leaving those who'd stayed having to pull double duty in order to keep everything running.

She didn't blame the ones who'd gone. If she'd had any family besides her father, anyone else in her life that mattered, she would have been on the boat too.

They weren't able to get the news so much anymore, and it was almost a relief. What they could was worse and worse each day. The Cold War might have been over, but all that meant was that instead of the two powerhouse nations duking it out, every dictator and cult leader with the capability was getting into the game.

Her father had been wrong. It *was* World War III, not between two sides

but a melee free-for-all that would probably be even worse.

"They need to know," Tyler said. "It's wrong to keep it from them, you know that. And . . . Kelly . . . we've got to face facts. There might not be a home to go back to if we stay here too much longer."

"Don't we have enough problems without this?" she groaned. "Steve's convinced there's some lunatic loose on the island, we're operating with a skeleton crew that can barely keep things running, and Dad's . . ."

She couldn't finish it.

"He's losing it," Tyler said.

A defensive urge flared up in her even though she knew he was right. Why did she keep wanting to stick up for Burt Dagget after all the times they'd clashed? He still treated her like a child and an employee rather than an adult in her own right, yet she bristled whenever anyone else dared say what was on her mind too.

"Is that your professional diagnosis, *doctor?*"

"Would you rather I put it in clinical terms? I can, and I will."

"He'll get better. Everything will get better. We have one more challenge tomorrow, and then we combine the crews. They'll all be in one place so we won't have to spread the camera teams so thin –"

"Kelly, stop. It's over. The game has got to be over. We need to tell them what's happening in the world and let them go home. And hasn't it occurred to you that there might not be an audience left for the show, assuming we did stick it out to the end? What good is half a million dollars going to be to the winner, if there's nothing left to spend it on?"

"It couldn't really come to that, could it?" she asked.

Steve Quinlan came into the lounge. He was pale and looked sick, and when he sat down beside Kelly he tossed a portable radio onto the table. "It could. I caught part of a broadcast just now and they're saying that Los Angeles is gone."

"No. Gone? It can't be –"

He clutched her hand. "Gone, Kelly. Washington, New York, Chicago, Seattle . . . most of the major U.S. cities have taken a hit one way or another. We sent Angie and Charles home just in time, didn't we? Sent them home to die."

"You don't know that."

"London, too," Steve added in a hushed voice. Kelly looked at him sympathetically.

"We have to leave, Kelly," Tyler said.

"That might not be as easy as you make it out." Steve's eyes were hollow,

dark. "They've shut down the airports. There won't be flights anywhere. It's the biological agents, isn't it? The plagues. As if the bombings and nerve toxins weren't enough. Every country's shutting their borders. We may well be trapped here for a good while."

Tyler sank into a chair opposite Kelly and Steve. "But we've got the choppers. We can fly to the airstrip on —"

Steve solemnly shook his head. "Do you honestly think we'd get landing clearance? Or be able to catch a flight out even if we did? The helicopters can't carry enough fuel to make it anywhere else, and we'd have to load them to capacity to get all of us off the island."

"This can't be happening!" Kelly slapped a can of Pepsi off the table. It rolled, foaming and fizzing. A terrible laugh escaped her. "But if it is, I shouldn't waste some of the last soda in the world, should I? Steve, we can't be trapped here. What'll we do?"

"Now, wait, stop," Tyler said. "None of this is certain."

"Isn't it?" Steve looked at him bleakly. "Listen to the news, mate."

"You said it yourself, we're only getting bits and pieces. The reception's been fouled up."

"Maybe it's the electromagnetic pulse," Kelly said. "Or radiation in the air. Fallout. The sunsets, the sunsets have been so gorgeous . . ."

Her self-control shattered and she buried her face in her hands. The enormity of it was too great to comprehend. She had felt this way when she was just a little girl and came in from playing to find her parents watching the news of the *Challenger* exploding. Or that fateful September day in 2001 when she'd gone for an early-morning jog and found the streets almost empty, the few people she saw all wearing the same look of horror, until finally she'd asked someone what was the matter.

Steve put an arm around her. She leaned into him, not crying but feeling like she might fly apart into a million pieces.

The phone rang, the strident sound slashing the air and making them all jump. It hung on the wall, one light blinking red. That line was for the control room extension, but no one was up there, not even the Drones. They had both left with Arabella Agliera, Marcus Adamson, the Vespuccis, and many others. Kelly's father had regarded their defection as the unkindest cut of all, and the only thing that could have gone further to make him feel betrayed would have been if Kelly herself had gone.

On legs that felt like stilts, she went to the phone. There weren't that many people it could be. Barry and Samantha were covering Buccaneer Bay. George and Pete were at Dead Man's Cove. But either of those teams would have

used the walkie-talkies before the phones in the SUVs. Everyone else should have been asleep.

She picked it up. "Hello?"

A whisper came back. "Hello, please, is anybody there?"

"Heather? Is that you? What's wrong?"

"You've got to send somebody." Still whispering. "The lights went out and I think there's —"

The line went dead.

"Heather? Heather, talk to me. It's Kelly Dagget. What's going on? Heather, I can't . . . ah, fuck!" She slammed the useless receiver into the cradle, then snatched it up again and punched in the number that was supposed to connect her with the cottage at Maroon Lagoon.

Nothing. Not a ring, not a busy, nothing.

Kelly turned to Tyler and Steve.

"We have to get out there," she said. "It's the killer. I know it is."

*   *   *

Chapter 21

The time had come to use the skulls.

Many of the intruders had left, but those who stayed behind were of the most stubborn of sorts. Traps and warnings would not sway them. Only death. Only death would keep them from his cherished treasure.

For this, he needed his crew. Loyal to a man. They had fought for him. Died for him. And now, even with the flesh long since rotted from their bodies and their bones grown brittle with age, they would serve him.

"Your captain has need of you, my fine lads," he breathed, placing his thin hand upon the dome of each skull in turn. "Rise up."

One by one, they did. The pale and smoky forms had faces as familiar to him in death as they had been in life. Most of them looked young and hale, though with the marks of their violent ends still visible. The lipless, ragged slash of a cutlass-mark here, the gouged black hole of a bullet wound there.

They walked, these dead sailors of his. When they reached the waters of the lagoon, they headed across without slowing, and did not sink beneath its surface. When they reached the fence, they passed through it. The diamond-shapes cut lines in them that filled in with a few paces.

Smythe followed by longboat, the oars dipping almost soundlessly and leaving few ripples. He came to the gate as the others reached the shores of the small island. He reached up to the lock, wrapped his bony fingers around it, and the lock sparked. A whiff of lightning-scent puffed up. Smythe pushed the gate open, rowed through, and closed it again.

His crew surrounded the cottage, waiting for their captain to lead them. He circled to the rear of the building, where a fiendish machine hummed and emitted a foul-smelling gas. A touch of his hand and it faltered. The dim light that had glowed from one window winked out.

All was still. Smythe bade his crew advance and led the way, his boot heels thudding on the wooden planks of the porch.

He heard movement within. Frightened movement. He could taste the fear of the women who cowered in the dark. A voice whispered but he could not make out the words.

Then, candleflame. And a tall, slim woman with hair bright as Spanish gold. She emerged from a room and stopped when she saw him. The candle trembled.

She was going to scream. Smythe struck her across the head with the flat of his blade and sent her spilling to the floor. The candle spun away, guttered, and went out.

"She is yours," he said to his crew.

They descended on her, pallid forms in the curtain-filtered moonlight. The woman sat up, saw them, and bolted to her feet. She ran for the door, clawed it open.

Smythe ignored the chase. He knew how it would end. He listened to the whispering, followed it, and found another woman crouched in the corner with something held to her head and something else in her lap, a dark and bulky something that made a whirring noise.

He touched one object, then the other. Each made the spark and the storm-scent. The whirring noise stopped. So did the tinny squawk of a living voice from inside the smaller device.

"Hello? Hello!"

The woman fell silent. She was a small, and scrawny thing. Her arm lowered and her head turned and she beheld Smythe.

A shrill scream came from outside.

Her eyes did not so much as twitch in response to the scream. They had gone blank behind her spectacles, as blank as the eyes of a clubbed fish. A wetness spread beneath her as she voided her bladder. Her hands fell limp at her sides and she slouched in her corner.

"It is mine," he told her although he knew that she could no longer make sense of words. "You shall not have it."

He wore a loop of cord through his belt and removed it. The cord was just the right length for the job of woolding. It fitted nicely around the woman's head. He grasped the ends and twisted, twisted, winding the cord tighter and

tighter. She did not react except to blow a bubble of spit from her slack lips. Her eyes bulged. Her spectacles fell off.

Tighter. Twisting.

Her eyes. The pressure. The strain.

Just as they'd bound ropes around a mast.

Bone cracked. A low gibbering noise came from the woman. Her eyes bulged more, until it seemed they would burst from their sockets.

He heard the other one scream again, along with splashing. Had she escaped them?

Twisting. A muffled, mortal cracking, a sudden sense of *give* as the plates of the skull caved in beneath the constricting pressure of the cord.

The woman was dead.

Smythe shook her free of the cord and left her where she fell. He went to the door and looked out. Yes, the other woman had escaped the sailors. Her garments were shredded into rags and the bruises of their dead hands marred her white skin. She had escaped them into the lagoon, wading, water up to her hips.

They went for her, on the surface of the water while she stumbled through it. She looked back once and saw them, and amid her weeping she shrieked for help. She hurried. Fell once, emerging with her glorious golden hair molding around her shoulders, her breasts. Then, seeing her attackers closer, she threw herself full-length and swam.

She reached the fence and Smythe could see, even at such a distance, the way she clung to it in gaping disbelief. It penned her there as the sailors advanced, their mocking laughter like the dry crackle of dead leaves.

The woman lunged at the fence and commenced to climb, toes and fingers poking through the diamond-shaped gaps.

She hadn't gone halfway when they caught her and bore her kicking, writhing form back to the beach.

*   *   *

Chapter 22

Dan Harper leaned forward, trying to see as the dark island rushed past beneath the helicopter. His eyes felt grainy from the restless four hours of sleep he'd gotten before Kelly Dagget's alarm roused the fortress. But tired or not, he was alert.

Beside him in the pilot's seat, Leslie Beaumains wore a flight jacket over surprisingly feminine emerald satin pajamas. She guided the chopper with smooth surety toward the lagoon.

She flew low. In the back compartment, Doctor Brookstone and Steve Quinlan had their heads pressed to the windows and were doing like Dan, staring down into the black jungle. Dan spotted the mirror-like expanse of the lagoon and the moonlit glitter of the chain link fence, then the cottage.

"There, down there," Dan said. The sour taste of dread filled his mouth. He'd seen something at the water's edge, a shape against the sand. He hoped it wasn't what he feared it was.

Leslie circled. A spotlight beam stabbed from the underside of the helicopter and pinned the shape, throwing it into stark relief.

A body. Calliope Glenning's body. Naked and battered.

"Take us down now," the doctor said. "Quick. She might be alive."

The helicopter descended rapidly, beating the lagoon into churning waves. They barely had clearance to land inside the perimeter of the fence. Steve Quinlan was opening the side door the moment the pontoons touched water. He leaped out, landed knee-deep, and turned to offer assistance to Doctor

Brookstone.

"Wait for me," Dan said. He unbuckled his safety harness and joined them as they waded to shore.

Calliope didn't move as they approached. The closer they got, the more their flashlights showed what had been done to her. Dan felt sick.

Steve Quinlan turned away. Leslie Beaumains looked at the woman, her expression an unreadable mask.

"Is she dead?" Steve asked with his back turned.

"Yes," Brookstone said.

"What about the other one?" Leslie asked, gesturing at the cottage.

"I'll check," Dan said.

"None of us should go anywhere alone," Steve said. "Whoever did this might be nearby."

Leslie bared her teeth. "I hope the son of a bitch is. If I get my hands on him . . ."

"You stay with the doctor," Dan told Steve. "You brought your gun, right? Good. Leslie, come with me."

"Are you certain —" Steve began.

"With Joe Baxter gone, I'm acting chief of security," Dan said. "That means I'm in charge here."

It was apparently good enough for Steve, because he didn't object. He stayed where he was, one of the peculiar pistols that had been designed to look old-fashioned but were really custom jobs by Smith & Wesson made specifically to Dagget's orders in his hand.

Dan and Leslie skirted Calliope and went to the cottage. It was ominously quiet. Too quiet. As they reached the porch, Dan saw why. The half-dozen parrots and parakeets were at the bottom of their wicker cages, their chitinous feet curled into stiff claws.

"The birds too?" Leslie asked of no one in particular.

The cottage's windows were dark. No sound came from within. Dan stepped through the door and his nose wrinkled. The living room stank of urine, blood, and something else that he couldn't identify. He swept his flashlight around. No signs of a struggle —

"Oh, God!" Leslie gagged and put a fist to her mouth.

He moved to her, then saw what she'd seen.

Heather Moss was behind one of the long rattan sofas. Her posture suggested she'd been hiding, but had been found all the same. The cottage's cordless phone was on the floor beside her, along with her eyeglasses. One lens was cracked. One of the small camcorders that the maroonees were

supposed to use to record their private thoughts was in her lap.

But the worst of it was her head. Her skull had been crushed. Tacky blood matted her hair to her scalp, and her eyes were on the verge of popping out.

"Don't touch her." Dan grabbed Leslie's wrist as the woman reached out.

"The camcorder. Maybe she got film of whoever did it."

"Good idea. But I'll get it. Stand over there and don't touch anything."

She did, and Dan bent down to gingerly pick the camcorder out of Heather's lap. Some blood had trickled over it, and the sticky still-warm feel of it on his hand made him want to retch.

"What did that to her?" Leslie asked.

"It looks like someone wrapped something around her head and . . . and squeezed it," Dan said. "Squeezed until her skull just . . . just split."

"Wouldn't you have to be super-strong to do that?"

"Not if you twisted it right. We'd better tell Doctor Brookstone."

"The gate was shut. How'd he get in and out?"

"With our own boat, probably."

When they got back outside, Steve was walking around and sweeping his flashlight beam in arcs. Doc Brookstone straightened up.

"The other girl?"

"Dead," Dan said, and described what they'd found.

"This one was sexually assaulted and strangled," Brookstone said, striving to sound clinical.

"What's Steve doing?" Leslie asked.

The doctor cleared his throat uneasily. "Looking for . . . there aren't any tracks. Well, her own, you can see them, over here and leading down to the water. But there aren't any others that could have been left by her attackers."

"He's right," Steve said, returning. "By the look of it, she was running from something or someone, but hers are the only tracks I can find. The ground's soft, so there should be something, but . . . ."

"That's impossible," Leslie said. "There must be tracks."

"None that I can see."

"Could they have been cleared away?" Dan asked.

"That completely?"

"Okay, forget it. Let's find something to transport the bodies in —"

"Move the bodies?" The doctor frowned at that. "What about an investigation? We have to call in —"

"We don't have that luxury," Steve said. "You saw the news. We're not

going to be able to fly in a team of forensics experts. We're on our own, old chap, and I agree with Dan. Best to get back to Central and decide what to do from there."

Dan held up the camcorder. "This may be able to tell us who we're after, too. We can't look at it here because these don't have a playback feature. We have to hook it up at the control room to see what's on the tape."

"Yes, all right," Doc said. "We'll take the bodies back with us. There should be sheets and blankets in the cottage. We can wrap them up. Not the best, but it'll do."

They went to work, raiding the cottage's linen closet for sheets and turning the dead women into bundles. Once their faces were covered, and their bodies were less readily identifiable, the job got a little easier.

"What about the birds?" Leslie asked.

Dan explained to Steve and Doc, pointing out the parrots and parakeets. "If we took a couple back, do you think you could figure out what killed them, Doc? None of them are bloodied."

"Pardon me if I'm more concerned about people than parrots," he said.

"I'll bag them up," Steve said, getting a pillowcase and dropping a few of the birds inside.

Between them, Steve and Dan were able to carry the bodies to the helicopter without dunking them in the water. It was a relief to climb inside and shut the door. Dan tucked the camcorder into the elastic net on the back of his seat and buckled himself in.

Leslie started the engine. The blades revolved, slowly and then picking up speed, the whickering of their passage turning into the familiar whup-whup-whup that roiled the lagoon.

"*Anne Bonney*, this is Central," Kelly Dagget's voice said over their headsets. "Please reply."

"We hear you, Central," Leslie said, sounding steadier now that she was back in her element.

She started to tell Kelly about the gruesome discoveries at the cottage, and was interrupted by uproar and Burt Dagget's bellowing. It sounded as though everyone left at the fortress was crowded into the control room, all of them babbling at once. Leslie winced. Dan held his headset away from his ears.

"Central, we're coming home," Leslie shouted over the din. She turned the volume to its lowest level, reducing the chaos at the fortress to background noise.

"He's got to quit now," Brookstone said. "This is a disaster. Two players

dead and the world about to end. He's got to quit."

"I'm sure he'll see that," Steve said.

Dan wished he was as confident as Steve sounded. He wasn't even sure if *Steve* was as confident as Steve sounded.

The *Anne Bonney* rose above the treetops and banked around in a U-turn. Leslie tipped the chopper forward, increasing their speed. The lights of the fortress at Rum Town guided them. Looking to his left, Dan could see a tiny ember that would be the camp at one of the beaches. He grimly wondered what the contestants would say when they found out about the pitiful cargo that the *Anne Bonney* carried. He was glad that would be Dagget's job and not his.

The smell hit him first. A thick, musty stench of something that had lain long beneath the earth and should have been left there. It couldn't be the bodies, which weren't even fully cold yet, much less decomposing.

He swiveled in his seat, saw that Steve was wrinkling his nose too and looking around for the source of the vile stink.

"What is that —" Brookstone said.

Leslie Beaumains jerked in her seat and uttered a short, sharp cry abruptly cut off. Dan turned back to her and a yell of shock burst from his throat. His first thought was that she was having a seizure of some sort, epilepsy maybe, but then he realized that she was struggling with something he could barely see.

The helicopter yawed and pitched as if caught in a hurricane. The pallid figure bent over Leslie had her by the neck. Dan thought of the livid strangulation marks Doc had pointed out on Calliope Glenning.

But what he was seeing couldn't be real.

"Shoot him!" Steve Quinlan said. "Shoot him, Dan, for the love of God!"

Steve saw it too?

Leslie's face was plum-colored. She made a series of thick, glottal noises that might have been words. Her hands ripped at the arms that pushed her, drove her, held her pinned against her seat. The joystick of the *Anne Bonney* dipped to the right, sending them into a steep curving dive. The air was suddenly filled with unsecured items taking wild flight.

Dan fumbled for his gun. His fingers felt oversized, overstuffed, meat-gloves that didn't belong to him. He drew and aimed, then hesitated for fear of sending a slug through the windshield's bubble.

Her eyes decided him. They rolled helplessly up, exposing the whites, and she went limp in the grip of the stowaway.

He fired. The shot was a thunderclap, the range was all but point-blank.

It tore through the pale side of Leslie's assailant, passed completely through, and let in the wind through a jagged hole in the Plexiglas.

The helicopter plummeted out of the sky, spinning crazily. Dan fired again, but the tossing of their wild flight threw his arm just as he pulled the trigger. The bullet plowed into Leslie's thigh. Her blood splashed over the instrument panel, spotting the dials and readouts.

Another buck of the stricken chopper made Dan lose his grip on the gun. He saw the trees racing toward them and held onto the armrests of his seat.

"We're going to crash!"

The others were screaming too, but Dan couldn't make out what they were saying. All that mattered was the leaves slapping against the sides as the helicopter dropped, the crack of thin branches breaking, the squeal of thicker ones on metal. He could see the ocean and if they could just clear the island, they might have a better chance . . .

Dan had never flown anything more complicated than a kite but he'd seen movies. He grabbed for the joystick and pulled back hard. The *Anne Bonney* barely budged from her deadly course. The top of a tree snapped off. A second one snagged in the undercarriage and all at once they were tumbling sideways, blades shredding the jungle canopy. The tail section wrenched off and air howled through the interior.

There was nothing Dan could do. He threw his upper body forward, hugging his calves and pressing his head into his knees. His parents' faces flashed through his mind, and then the shattering impact ended all thought.

*   *   *

Chapter 23

Trip Galloway charged up the stairs to the roof. He didn't care about the panic that reigned in the control room, everyone plunging around in a blind frenzy as they tried to figure out what had gone so wrong, so fast.

All that he cared about was what had come over the speakers in those last few seconds. Screams. Gunshots. Dan Harper's voice, loud and clear: "We're going to crash!" And then the shearing and crumpling of metal, followed by a bray of static.

Leslie. He was intent on Leslie Beaumains.

She was all right. She had to be.

And the others, too, of course . . . but it was the thought of Leslie that dominated his frantic mind.

The door burst open and he was on the roof, but he wasn't alone.

Skyhawk was beside the *Mary Read,* and Trip could see half a dozen other people in there. Jason Washington with his nose splint and his puffy raccoon eyes, Francie Abbot, others whose faces he couldn't make out. Skyhawk was boosting the last of them – Ginger Warwitz – inside and was about to get in himself when Trip called to him.

"What are you doing?"

"What does it look like?" Skyhawk, rangy and hard-featured, strafed Trip with a scornful look. "We're getting the fuck out of here and if you're smart, you'll come with us."

"The other chopper just crashed. We've got to stage a rescue op."

"Forget them. They're dead, or as good as."

He wasn't aware of crossing the rooftop tarmac, but the next thing he knew, Skyhawk's forearm was in his grasp.

"We have to help them."

The other man tried to pull away. He was older than Trip and stronger, but couldn't free himself without prying at Trip's fingers one by one.

"Kid, we're leaving. This place is cursed, and everyone who stays here is dogmeat."

"You're . . . what about the people you left downstairs?"

"They won't all fit."

"What about Leslie?" Anger boiled up inside Trip. "You're going to run out on her?"

"I'm going to save my own ass. Let go of me."

The pain in his fingers was too severe. Trip let go, but promptly seized Skyhawk by the front of his leather jacket. Zippers jingled, rabbit's feet swung.

"Get away from that helicopter. You are not taking it anywhere."

"Oh, yes I am." Skyhawk shoved him.

Trip stumbled back but kept his hold. "Leslie needs help!"

A fist looped out of nowhere and smashed into Trip's mouth, squashing his lips against his teeth. Trip tasted blood. His fingers slipped. He went to one knee.

The people in the helicopter watched, but for all the concern they showed, it might have been some stunt show. Not real. Not anybody they knew.

Skyhawk doubled his fists and raised them, pausing for a split second. Maybe it was to savor the moment, maybe it was because he was having doubts, maybe he was making sure he had judged the angle just right so that when he brought his arms down he would hit Trip exactly where he wanted. Trip didn't wait around to find out. He dove forward, scraping his palms on the roof. His bad knee flashed white-hot with pain.

He heard quick footfalls. But instead of kicking him in the ribs, Skyhawk ran past Trip and scrambled into the helicopter. Trip tried to rise. His knee wouldn't hold him, spilling him to the roof again.

The *Mary Read's* blades started turning. Trip crawled, dragging his leg.

"You can't do this! Damn it, Skyhawk, you can't do this." One of his teeth wobbled. He pushed at it with his tongue and it came out, rolling into his mouth with a trickle of blood.

Dispassionate eyes watched him through the windows. Skyhawk flipped him the finger as the blades sped up and their downdraft flattened Trip.

The helicopter lifted off. It soared over Rum Town, fast and graceful,

115

heading northwest. By the time Trip got to a sitting position, the black body of the craft had been swallowed up by the night.

Gone.

* * *

Chapter 24

Someone was pleading for help.

Steve Quinlan fought his way up through fathoms of darkness. His head throbbed. In fact, every part of him hurt.

Alive. At least it meant he was alive.

His eyes opened. The world was at a funny angle. No, he was the one at a funny angle, still strapped into his seat in the rear of the *Anne Bonney's* cabin. The helicopter was tilted forward and down, nose into the ocean.

And sinking.

Water coursed through the ruins of the Plexiglas front bubble. Steve's elevated, angled position had kept him dry so far, but a third of the cabin was submerged. Leslie Beaumains was bent forward from the waist. Her arms floated. Her dark hair fanned out around her head. She was face-down, unmoving except where her limbs were pushed by the waves.

He had no idea how they'd ended up like this.

"Stuck . . . help me, I'm stuck."

Steve turned his head.

Tyler Brookstone was pinned in his seat by folds of metal. The right side of the helicopter had caved in like a crushed aluminum can. Dan Harper, who'd been sitting in front of the doctor, was gone. Or very nearly so . . . he and his seat had apparently been torn in half. Everything of Dan from the chest up had been thrown clear. Blood tinged the foam that eddied through the interior of the craft. It had sprayed all over everything including Steve himself.

"Steve," Tyler croaked. His hand, shaking, stretched out.

He took a breath to reassure himself that he still could, and let it out in a groan. He felt along his limbs, probed his head. Nothing broken. So he hoped.

Water lapped at his feet. He yanked them back, somehow superstitiously sure that once the sea got a taste of him, nothing would do but to finish the meal. The level was rising, gurgling as more spilled in through the place where the bubble had been.

"Hang on, Tyler," he said. "Hang on, we'll get out of this."

His buckle was latched. He couldn't work it. The water was coming in faster, and he could no longer keep his feet out of it, but the buckle stubbornly refused to budge.

It let loose when he wasn't expecting it to. Steve fell against the back of Leslie's seat. His movement caused the sinking helicopter to list to the left. One of the bodies in the back came free of its restraining straps and fetched up against the curved wall.

"Help me, Steve. I can't . . . I'm stuck."

A part of Steve wanted to flee, escape with his own hide intact and the Devil take anyone else. He'd be stupid to risk his own life. All he'd accomplish would be to save neither of them. They'd both drown.

But his better self overruled. He picked his way carefully to Tyler, setting his feet on whatever seemed most solid, crouched and walking slant-ways to avoid hitting his head on the ceiling.

The doctor's seat had been bent at its support base by the crumpled metal. Steve couldn't see Tyler's arm or leg on the right side. He didn't know how in the world he was supposed to get the other man out, with no tools and no help.

Tyler saw it in his face. The knowledge aged him fifteen years in the blink of an eye.

"Don't leave me," he said with surprising strength, and clutched Steve's collar. "Don't leave me here to die."

"I'm not about to," Steve said. "But how badly are you hurt? I don't want to make things worse."

"Things are going to get as bad as they can be if you don't get me out of here," Tyler said. "Forget the rest, just get me loose!"

"You're the doctor."

Steve worked his hands into the wreckage, feeling for the seat belt. He popped it open but Tyler was still pinned. Groping his way along, he discerned that Tyler's leg was the most severe problem. It was bent in unnatural

angles, and when he touched it, Tyler screamed. Broken. In at least three places, Steve guessed. And the ankle might as well have been caught in a bear trap. Serrated teeth of metal had it in a death grip.

"You only seem to be bleeding from the ankle and a few scrapes," Steve said. "The flow's not terribly fast, but . . ."

Tyler's breathing was quick, a rapid panting. He didn't answer. In the uncertain moonlight, his skin had a ghostly cast.

Shock. He was going into shock.

"I'm going to try and move the metal that's holding you," Steve said. He cut his finger as he forced his hands under, and strained with all his might.

Nothing.

The metal wouldn't budge. And the water was higher. Only floating hands and a few strands of hair could be seen of Leslie. Her fingers rode the ripples and seemed to Steve almost to be waving a sorrowful farewell.

"We'll have to do it the hard way," he said, and wrapped his arms around the doctor. He pulled.

Tyler Brookstone shrieked as his body came most of the way out of the seat. His right arm flapped bonelessly but his leg was still caught. Steve heard a cracking noise, felt it reverberating through Tyler's body. His knee, maybe, but more likely his hip dislocating.

Rising water. Mixed now with gas and oil as well as Dan Harper's blood. Churning in and out of the cleft-open cabin. Horrible images assaulted Steve. Metal striking metal. A spark. Then a blazing inferno. Death by fire and water.

With a final heroic yank, he wrenched Tyler Brookstone the rest of the way out. Tyler had passed out and after one look at his leg, Steve thought that was a mercy.

The side door was jammed. The *Anne Bonney* let out a bubbly sigh and rolled, more water flooding in through the gap at the front. Steve was soaked, treading water, doing his best to hold Tyler's head above the surface.

He didn't have much choice. The only way out was straight ahead.

Sucking in a deep breath, he curled an arm around the unconscious doctor and dove for the opening. The inrushing flow slowed him, fought him, but he kicked with both legs and used his free hand to grab the broken edge of Plexiglas. It slashed his palm but he was able to pull himself and Tyler through the gap. He swam hard to avoid being sucked down. A series of bubbles rose and burst around him, the last of the cabin's air.

The tail end stuck up, mangled into something that looked more like a segmented scorpion's tail than the aft section of a helicopter. It was sinking with a queer sort of grandeur.

Steve looked wildly around. He couldn't remember the final few seconds of their flight, couldn't remember the crash itself – like Tyler's unconsciousness, he considered it a mercy – and had no recollection of leaving the land behind. They might be half a mile out to sea, which would be a sure death sentence for the both of them.

But the island was right there, only a few dozen meters away. Steve maneuvered Tyler's body into a lifeguard's hold and started stroking, one-armed, toward shore. He saw a cove and made for it, not wanting to take his chances with the waves that dashed themselves against the high, barren cliffs that made up this part of the coastline.

Luck was finally with him. The current carried him into the cove, and just as he felt his strength flagging and knew he couldn't go much further, a gentle swell picked him up and bore him in. His feet touched the sandy bottom. Kelp twined around his legs. He half-lifted, half-dragged Tyler as he stumbled up the beach.

He'd almost made it to dry land when his foot struck something buried in the sand. A stone, maybe. It tripped him and he went down with a grunt. Tyler went sprawling. A final wave scurried up the beach at them as if meaning to draw them back into the sea, into the depths. Steve lunged away from it.

Dry sand. He crawled across it and bumped his shoulder into a tree trunk. He looked up.

Not a tree trunk. A post. And something nailed to it.

The moonlight was bright enough to illuminate the dead man's tortured features in harsh clarity. The gulls had been at him, gouges in his face and gaping sockets where his eyes had been. His torso was laid open, hollowed out but for some hanging strands and strings.

Steve bit back a cry.

Joe Baxter.

And, as his gaze swept the beach eager to find something, anything other than the mutilated corpse of the former chief of security to look upon, he noticed the half-buried stone he'd stumbled over. Which wasn't a stone at all. It was a head, a human head with sand-caked blond hair still clinging to patches of scalp and empty, black holes where the eyes should have been.

He recognized this one, too. Beverly Phillips.

The grotesque scene, on top of everything else he'd experienced this hellish night, threatened to unhinge Steve's sanity. He grimly forced himself to stay strong, to not give in to an almost overpowering urge to just curl up in the sand and let his mind drift away. If he did that, he knew that Joe's and Beverly's wouldn't be the only corpses to decorate the cove. His, and Tyler

Brookstone's, would join them. As would whatever washed ashore of Leslie, Dan, and the two women they'd retrieved from the lagoon.

Tyler was still out cold, though breathing in great uneven gasps. Steve went to him. The leg that had been broken in the crash had been further mauled in their escape from the sinking chopper, and it stretched out stiffly to one side, seeming to have developed several askew and additional joints. Blood was still oozing from the torn flesh of the ankle, and pale bone peeped through.

Steve stripped off his shirt and made a bandage. He was freezing despite the balminess of the night, a reaction to his immersion but more to the repeated horrors of the evening. Emotion leached the energy from him. He hauled Tyler further up the beach, above the high-tide line. When there was nothing more he could do for the doctor, he patched himself up as best he was able.

"They'll find us," he said, though no one but himself was able to hear. "It shouldn't be long. They'll come for us."

His gaze went to the ocean, where only the crippled tail rotor of the *Anne Bonney* poked out of the surf. The rest of it had been entirely taken by the hungry waves. Including, he realized with dismay, the walkie-talkie that had fallen off his belt at some point, as well as the camcorder that Dan Harper hoped had captured the image of the killer.

Dive for it?

In the dark, with no gear? And in the shape he was in? He'd be lucky not to kill himself. It'd be pointless to throw his life away for a videotape that was probably already ruined.

He sat down beside the doctor, their backs to the wall of stone that cradled the cove, and waited for rescue.

*   *   *

Chapter 25

"Why, that dirty old man," Barry Lee said.

"Shh." Samantha Dressler shushed him. "They'll hear you."

"This is voyeurism, plain and simple," he whispered as they crept through the dense vegetation. "Not to mention pornography. It'll never get on the air."

The camera, equipped with high-resolution film and a light-amplifying lens that took advantage of even minimal light, picked everything up in shades of crisp grey. "We just have to be artistic in staging the shot," Samantha said.

"And him a married man. With kids."

The prudish disapproval in his tone made her smile. But it was a hard-edged smile, a cynical one. Barry was fundamentally a decent guy. Some of the production team teased him for his habitually polite manners, inherited from his mother. It had to rankle at him to be sneaking through the night trying to film lovers on the sly.

The setting for the sleazy little *affaire de coeur* was a clearing not far from the *Maracaibo* beach camp. It wasn't much of a romantic spot but it did boast a large flat-topped boulder, upon which had been spread a layer of leaves covered with a blanket.

No, not much . . . but Samantha supposed it beat the back of a compact car, or a quickie standing up in an alley. At least they were making themselves comfortable. And just coincidentally, conveniently, providing a perfect view for the camera.

Benjamin "B.J." Nathans was already naked, sitting on the boulder with his broad, hairy back to them as he watched Connie Berkwelter hang her clothes on a branch. She was down to a thong and a miniscule bra that did not look anywhere near capable of holding up her titanic breasts, but thanks to their own silicon-filled firmness, they stuck straight out like those of a comic-book superheroine. The tattoo on Connie's back, a blue-flowered vine, undulated as she moved.

"Do we have to do this?" Barry hissed in Samantha's ear.

She couldn't see him blushing but she could practically feel it, baking off him like a fever. Poor guy.

"You know what Dagget would say."

"I know, I know. They gave up their rights to privacy when they signed the forms."

Connie moved to stand in front of B.J., her fingers teasing at the front-hook of her bra. "This what you want?"

"I sure do." He reached up with both hands, big callused construction-worker hands that Connie batted away.

"How about a lap dance?" she purred. "It's what I do for a living."

B.J. nodded vigorously, then laughed. "But I don't have any dollars to tuck in anywhere."

"We'll find something to tuck in somewhere." She swayed, jiggled, and danced for him.

In the bushes, Barry covered his mortified face and left the filming to Samantha. She patted him consolingly on the shoulder.

The dance went on, Connie rubbing her body all over B.J., and taunting him all the while about what would happen if *this* was on the show, what would his wife think when she saw it on television. B.J. only laughed harder and said that it would serve her right, the frigid old cow, and all his bowling league buddies would give him a standing ovation.

Samantha wondered if Connie had seen them. Did she know? Was that why she was making such a production of it? Or was that just the way she was?

Either way, it didn't matter. Dagget was going to love this. It might even bring him out of the black mood he'd been in lately. It might cheer everyone up. When she and Barry had left the fortress just after supper, along with George Parkins and Pete Carter who had the night duty over at Buccaneer Bay tonight, the mood of the team had been dark and bitter as coffee grounds, thick enough to slice with a knife.

Some good dirt and scandal, that was what they needed. Some titillation,

emphasis on the first syllable.

B.J. leaned back on his elbows. Connie straddled him, standing on the rock, shaking her hips, then lowered and slithered along him like a snake. She ended up kneeling at his feet, her head going up and down in his lap while he latched one hand in her hair and guided her.

The appetizer was giving way to the main course, Connie kneeling astride B.J.'s lap, when the phone clipped to Samantha's belt made its nasal ringing beep.

"Shit!" Samantha slapped it, silenced it, but the damage was done.

"They're taping us!" B.J. bellowed. "You fucking perverts!"

Barry yelped, broke and ran for the beach. Connie screeched with mirth and Samantha knew that her earlier speculation had been right on the money. Connie *had* known, and was loving every minute of it. B.J., meanwhile, was not. He lurched up off the rock, roaring like a maddened grizzly. Samantha backpedaled, trusting that B.J. would stop rather than pursue with his defenseless nudity leading the way through the underbrush.

It was a near thing. B.J. showed every sign of giving chase until a branch that Samantha's butt had bent snapped past her hip and whipped him smartly in the nuts. He bellowed again, this time in pain, and staggered back cupping himself.

Samantha turned and hotfooted it after Barry. The commotion had wakened Tala and Ambrose, who stared in astonishment as their camera team pelted down the beach, Samantha unable to control a fit of snickering.

They stopped near the fire. Barry kept a watchful eye back the way they'd come.

"He's going to kill us. He's going to get dressed, come down here, and twist our heads around until they pop off."

"No, he won't. It's in the contracts they all signed," Samantha said. "No interference with any member of the production staff."

She unclipped the phone, brought it to her mouth, and it sirened its call again, right into her ear, startling her. She fumbled it, juggled, caught it again, and answered the call.

"Dressler here. What?"

"Samantha? This is Kelly. We have . . . oh, God, we have problems."

"Do we?" It was hardly news to her. Jason Washington had busted his nose falling into a quicksand trap just the other night, and while Samantha was no closer to believing that there was a curse on the island, but she did believe that someone was running amok, sabotaging things. Thus, she greeted Kelly's announcement with a complete lack of surprise. "What's hit the fan now?"

But when Kelly proceeded to tell her about the helicopter crash, four of the team missing and no one knew if they were dead or alive – and there was more that Kelly was purposefully not mentioning, Samantha could tell by the hesitant, yet portentous weight to her words – it surpassed her expectations.

"You're kidding me! Steve, Leslie? Doc Brookstone? Dan?"

"We lost contact with them on the west side of the island. Nearer to you than to George and Pete. Can you take one of the Excursions and go look? I'm on my way, but you're closer."

"We're on our way," Samantha promised. She thumbed off the switch and looked at Barry. "Let's roll, my friend."

"But –" He gestured vaguely at the camp, at the two players still staring at them, and off in the direction from which they could now hear the approach of a presumably-dressed B.J. and Connie.

"Orders from Central. You going to argue?"

"No, I guess not."

They reached the camouflaged shed where some of Dagget's monstrously huge Ford Excursions were stored. Kelly weighed in again with the news that Skyhawk and several of the staff had absconded with the second helicopter.

"Has everyone gone insane?" Samantha demanded of her as she jumped into the driver's seat.

"Maybe. I've called Pete and George, telling them to come back to Rum Town," Kelly said. She sounded awful, near tears but holding herself together by sheer grit.

Samantha, like practically everyone on Veradoga except for Steve Quinlan himself, knew exactly how Kelly felt about the Brit. Same way that Trip Galloway felt about Leslie Beaumains. The two of them had to be going out of their minds with worry. As if that wasn't enough, Trip had been punched out by Skyhawk.

And, as Kelly told them once they were well away from Dead Man's Cove where there was no chance of being overheard, the two players who'd been sentenced to marooning were dead. Their bodies were presumably amid whatever remained of the helicopter.

It was just shaping up to be a wonderful night all around.

*   *   *

Chapter 26

"You're going too fast," George Parkins said, holding onto the handle above the passenger-side door of the silver Excursion with one hand while the other was braced against the dashboard.

Pete Carter didn't slow. "It's not like there's going to be traffic."

"But you might miss the –"

He'd no sooner said it than Pete did it, missed the turn. They went rocketing down a bumpy side road, sending a troop of monkeys bounding out of their path. The monkeys squealed and chittered angrily after them.

"Slow down, you're going to bust an axle or something," George said.

Pete applied the brakes. By the time he brought the large vehicle to a full stop, the road had narrowed until it was barely more than a path of two wheel-ruts heading toward Widowmaker Peak.

"Okay," Pete said. "This slow enough?"

"Ha, ha. Turn us around, wiseguy."

"Actually, I don't know if I can." Pete looked dubiously out the windows at the encroaching jungle. "We'd get stuck for sure."

"And I know whose fault it would be." George sighed and unbuckled his seat belt. "Tell you what. I'll walk and give you directions, you steer. We should be able to find a spot big enough to turn this baby around."

"Sounds like a plan."

George got out and slammed his door. It didn't seem like all that great a plan to him. He was never going to like the tropics. Too many shadows, too

much stealthy movement, too many weird noises. Bird calls that sounded like babies crying. Monkeys that could scream like people. The urgent snuffling of the wild boars. And of course, the snakes. Couldn't forget the snakes.

This is the last time I let Mom talk me into this, he swore to himself as he walked up the road searching for a wide spot. *The absolute last time.*

Trouble was, he'd made such oaths before. Mom and Sarah always got so excited at the prospect of each new exotic location. In his bleaker moments, he even suspected Mom of having something going on the side with Burt Dagget. She was always able to wheedle him into signing on for yet another of Dagget's Magical Mystery Tours.

Now here he was, bathed in the white glare of the headlights, hoping not to step on a snake or walk into a spiderweb complete with fat, venomous spider poised in the center. Pete inched the Excursion along, his window rolled down and his head hanging out exactly like that of a dog, delighted to be going on a ride. All he needed was to have his tongue lolling.

"Okay," George said, holding up his hands with the palms out so Pete would stop. "This looks good. Be careful, though. If you go in the mud, we'll be a long time waiting for a tow truck."

Pete giggled and began the delicate process of backing and filling. The Excursion worked its way around, headlights leaving the road to cut a swath into the jungle. George paced alongside, cautioning Pete whenever he got too near a muddy patch, telling him when to quit backing up.

He caught sight of something. In the glow of the headlights, off among the trees. A sparkle as of something metallic. He was squinting, trying to make out what it could be, and consequently Pete backed straight across the road. The rear wheels went into a shallow creek, and the rear bumper banged into a tree.

"Hey!" Pete cried. "What are you doing out there? You're supposed to be directing me."

"Sorry." George barely heard, answered by rote.

"George, Earth to George."

"I think I see something," he said. "Look out there. See it? Something shiny."

"So?"

"So, let's check it out."

"No way, Jose! We've been ordered back to the fortress. Besides, there's nothing out that way but Hangman's Hill."

"I'm going to look anyway."

"Wait for me, then."

Pete turned off the ignition and joined him, pocketing the keys. He had brought a flashlight from the glove compartment and George took it, aiming the beam at the spot where he'd last seen the metallic twinkle.

They set off, pushing through the thick curtains of leaves, earning more scoldings from monkeys and birds. George took the lead with Pete on his heels.

"What is that?" Pete asked, looking at the twinkle.

He was whispering, and George was about to ask why when a sense of being watched swept over him. Every instinct he had told him that they weren't alone, and that whoever was out there wasn't friendly.

The flashlight's bright disc grew smaller and more centered as they neared the source of the gleam that guided them. It was a belt buckle, and George's first thought was that Lester Silverman had one like that.

Then he realized that he was looking at Lester Silverman, or what was left of Lester Silverman. He dropped the flashlight.

It landed at an angle, throwing its light across the tableau.

Hangman's Hill got its name from the single spreading tree that grew from the top of an otherwise bald dome of dirt. George, who divided his time between the camera team and the challenge team, had been here before, though not by this route. He'd been here helping set up last week.

Six barrels that would be filled with gunpowder were placed equidistantly on leveled spots around the tree. The players would have each been given a small bag of powder to lay a line, which they'd then light by means of flint and steel. The first one to blow up his or her barrel would have won.

Five of the barrels were undisturbed. The sides of the sixth were smoky and charred, some of the slats only barely held by the bands. The lid had been opened, and something black and lumpy poked out of the top. Something black and lumpy with a glint of metal where a waist would have been. Lester Silverman. Burned to a charcoal husk that barely resembled a human being.

"Jeez," moaned Pete Carter, pinching his nose against the sickly stench. "What did that?"

"I remember reading something in one of Dagget's reference books," George said. He bent over without taking his eyes from the crisped corpse, and retrieved the flashlight. "How pirates would make people stand in barrels full of powder, and hold lit matches over them to make them tell where they'd hidden their money. If a person wouldn't cooperate, they'd drop the match."

Pete grabbed his shoulder. "Let's get out of here. Right now, what do you say?"

"I know him. That's Lester. See the buckle? Harley Davidson logo, big as a plate?"

"He was one of the guys that went with Robby Willets, wasn't he? Searching for Baxter and Phillips."

"That's right. Lester, Robby, and Doug Fogarty."

"So where . . ." Pete looked around, and his grip on George's shoulder turned into a vise. "Up there. The tree."

He aimed the flashlight up the hill. A body hung from one of the lower branches, not just noosed around the neck but encased in some sort of cage of metal hoops that resembled a picture of a medieval torture device.

The body was entirely black, and George's first assumption was that whoever it was had, like Lester, been burned alive. But as his feet led him closer of their own volition, Pete protesting as he followed along unwilling to let go of George's shoulder, they saw that the dead man in the cage had been coated head to foot in tar.

"This was in the books too," George said, fascinated despite himself.

"Screw the books!" Pete tugged at him. "Back to the car. Now, huh?"

"We have to find —"

He tripped over Robby Willets, stubbing his toe on the hard plaster cast that Robby still wore on his arm. George sprang over the body in an ungainly leap, Pete's fingernails ripping his shirt and peeling what felt like four feet of skin from his arm. He didn't want to fall on Robby, who was slimy with decay and alive with seething maggots.

Pete was hyperventilating. He stuttered something incoherent, pointing at Robby.

George was only glad they'd found him by night. By day, his rotting flesh would have been buried under a humming drape of flies, and the stink rising in the humid heat would have been unbearable. As it was, he had to fight not to throw up.

"— out of here —" Pete choked.

"In a second." He did not want to look closer, yet he had to. Had to see if he could determine how Robby Willets had died.

"I'm going back. I've got the keys. If you're not there in two minutes, I'm leaving without you."

The circle of light swept along the body. It was hard to tell what had been done by animals, but George thought that the long slashes were the work of a blade. A machete, maybe, or a cutlass.

He was dimly aware of Pete blundering off. Holding his breath, George crouched and examined the side of Robby Willets' head. The skull was deformed. He might have been shot. Shot in the head at close range. Then hacked apart.

The full realization of what he was doing hit him then. Studying a body like he was back in biology lab and it was nothing more important than a frog or a cat laid out on the dissection table. This was a person, someone he'd known, someone he'd shared meals with and slept down the hall from. His signature was among the scribbles on Robby's cast.

This wasn't a book. This wasn't an illustration. This was real.

These people were dead.

He took three steps away and bent double, spraying the contents of his stomach into the dirt. It seemed as though he'd never be done, retching and retching until he was bringing up nothing but acidic spittle. He was dizzy from the force of his vomiting fit, hazy spots swimming in front of his eyes, and he had to drop to his knees beside one of the untouched barrels and hold onto it or else fall flat on the ground.

George sucked in a deep breath, but the wind was wrong and it was full of the burnt-pork stink of Lester Silverman. He went into another series of dry-heaves, his throat feeling abraded and half-dissolved. His ears rang so loudly they drowned out the sounds of the island, though he did hear a distant boom like a far-off clap of thunder.

Pressing a bandanna from his back pocket against his face, he tried again to breathe. Better. Not much, but a little. He could still smell it and thought that he always would. Wasn't the act of smelling the same as taking in particles of the item? That meant tiny bits of Lester and Robby were *in* him, adhering themselves to his nasal passages so he might never be rid of them.

The thought made his gorge rise again. He worked his tongue around to summon up a mouthful of saliva, and spat to the side.

The bandanna did help, though. He got up, his insides all loose and trembly from the puking. He was drenched in cold sweat.

"Pete?" he called. "Hey, Pete, you still around?"

No answer. He hadn't heard the Ford's big engine turn over, though he hadn't exactly been listening for it while he was emptying his guts. Had two minutes gone by? He had his watch but he hadn't looked at it when Pete delivered his ultimatum.

"Pete!"

Still nothing. The chickenshit was probably sitting in the driver's seat with the windows all rolled up and the CD player going, watching the clock in the dashboard and counting down the seconds.

The flashlight. He'd lost the damn flashlight. It should have made its location known but either he'd unknowingly turned it off or it had broken when it hit the ground. George wasn't about to retrace his steps. They could

take it out of his salary.

He headed for the road, and that feeling he'd had, the one about not being alone, returned. It had vanished, or he'd been too busy with other things, while he'd been looking at the bodies. Now it was back, tickling along the back of his neck like spider's legs.

The headlights beamed a beacon through the dark jungle. He followed it, wanting nothing more than to be safely locked inside and speeding away from this death-place. He would not say a word to Pete about driving too fast. The faster, the better.

His abused, recovering nose detected a whiff of smoke on the air. Powder-smoke. Gunpowder. That strange scent so evocative of childhood Fourths of July before fireworks had been outlawed almost everywhere.

The windows were down, as they'd been while he was directing Pete's attempt to turn around. The Excursion was still crooked, perpendicular to the road with its back wheels in the muddy ditch. Pete hadn't made any effort to bring it the rest of the way around.

George went to the passenger-side door. He stuck his head through the open window, having to go on tiptoe to do so.

Pete Carter was motionless behind the wheel, his hands limp in his lap and his head down so that his chin was to his chest. His seatbelt was cinched, keeping him from slouching forward onto the wheel.

The odor of gunpowder was stronger.

"Pete?"

Even as he said it, he wished he hadn't because he was suddenly sure that Pete would raise his head and turn it toward him, exposing the mortal soot-ringed hole in his forehead where the pistol ball had gone in. Not a bullet, George knew. A pistol ball. That clap of thunder he'd thought he'd heard hadn't been thunder at all.

Pete did not move. By the glow of the interior lights, George could see the rill of blood that had dribbled down his front.

The keys were cupped loosely in one of Pete's hands, but George barely gave them a second glance. To get in and move the body out of the driver's seat would be bad enough. But to take the keys from fingers that would still be pliable and warm . . . he couldn't do it.

Bushes rustled.

George gave in to the panic that had been building in him. Without a look back, he fled down the road in the direction of the turn-off to town.

*   *   *

Chapter 27

Smythe was well-pleased with this night's work. Many of the intruders were dead, and the rest were terrified and demoralized. As for his crew, their morale hadn't been so hearty in a long while.

Next would be the town. The sacking of the town.

He knew now that they had little in the way of proper loot, and not much else that he would have once upon a time looked for. No bales of cotton or silk, no rum, no tools for carpentry or navigation. No gold, no silver plate. The riches of the New World that had abounded on the Spanish Main had dried up, or so it seemed.

But his purpose was not the acquisition of wealth. It was merely an old habit that died hard, as hard as Smythe himself.

No, his purpose was to defend what was his, and punish those who would seek to take it from him.

If that meant slaughtering the intruders to a man, so be it. If that meant killing women and children, what of it? Hadn't he done it before?

He would have their town, and destroy it.

Then the island would be his once more. The island, the cave, and the precious treasure it contained.

*　　*　　*

Chapter 28

"They said we'd get so used to them, it'd be like they weren't even there," Dale Sheffield said. "That was true enough, I guess. So how come it's so freaking weird when they're gone?"

"What made them go, that's what I wonder," Karl said.

Letitia added some wood to the fire to drive back the dark.

It was still the middle of the night, and the beeping signal of the phone followed by the abrupt departure of their two-man camera team, had sufficed to wake them all.

"Maybe they're not really gone," Jimmy said.

In the flickering firelight, with his scarlet kerchief tied around his head and his longish black hair streaming from under it, Dale thought that he looked every inch the pirate. All he needed was to borrow one of Tish's gold hoops, and it'd be perfect.

"What do you mean?" Letitia asked. She sat on the log that Karl had dragged down from the jungle to serve as a bench, between Dale and Jimmy.

"I see what he means," Karl said. He was on his feet, swinging his cutlass in idle arcs, which was why the rest of them chose to be on the opposite side of the fire pit. "It's part of the game. To see what we'll do when we really think we're unobserved."

"Like what?" Dale scoffed. "What could we do that they haven't already seen us doing? I had to pee on my own leg thanks to that jellyfish, and what about when Tish got food poisoning?"

"Don't remind me," she said with a sour face. "That's the last time I let you boys handle the cooking."

"They've already got us on tape plotting against Calliope, butchering a whole pig, and taking dumps," Dale said. "About the only thing they haven't got is somebody boffing somebody, unless I missed that part. Did you guys hold the orgy without me?"

"Orgy? Get real," Jimmy said.

"Why, thanks, sugar," Tish said dryly. "A lady always likes to know she's attractive."

"The point is, we do act differently when we know we're under observation," Karl said. "It doesn't matter how used to the cameras we are. We still know they're there. It's always in the backs of our minds. We had a documentary film made at my station once and it was the same thing. We always knew."

"So they might want to see what we're really like." Jimmy made a show of stretching and craning his neck, looking around for hidden cameras.

"Oh, very subtle," Dale said. "Hey, do you think maybe something big happened at the other camp? If one of the *Maracaibo* crew got hurt, Dagget might want to get lots of different angles."

"Maybe that's where our other team's been," Tish said. "There used to be four of them, two sets of two, and these past few days we've only ever had the one pair at a time."

"Is it just me," Jimmy said, "Or have they been really out of it too?"

"It's not just you." Dale got up, brushing sand from the seat of his shorts, and went to their stores of food. "Wish we had marshmallows. I could go for some s'mores right about now."

"Not period cuisine," Tish chided. "How about some toasted coconut?"

"If I never eat coconut again . . ."

"It's barely been a week, Dale. You better toughen up or you'll never make it," Karl said.

"Maybe it's not anything to do with the game," he mused as he rummaged through the supplies. "Maybe there's an industry strike and they're doing a work slowdown. I hope not. I don't want any delays standing between me and my half million."

"Dagget would kick their asses." Jimmy came over to help him look for something suitable for a midnight beach snack.

"They'd tell us if something was seriously wrong," Tish said. "What we should be thinking about is the next challenge and who we're going to discipline."

"That's gonna suck." Dale decided on fruit and went back to the log. "I like you guys too much to get rid of anyone else. Not that I wouldn't happily sell your souls to the Devil for the prize money, you understand."

"Let's plan this out," Karl said. "We only have to get through one more before they bring the crews together, and we want to go into it with numbers and a strong bond, right?"

"Right," the rest of them said together, nodding.

"So we agree to pick one of us and keelhaul him."

"I don't want to get dragged under that ship," Tish said.

"It might not be the same thing next time," Dale said.

"But it's always a physical task," Karl said. "That's what they told us at the beginning. So what I propose is that we agree right now to have me do it."

"You? Why you?" Jimmy demanded.

"Because I'm in the best shape."

"Oh, like we're chopped liver."

"Settle down, Jimmy," Tish said. "Nobody's calling you a weakling. Karl, are you sure you want to do this?"

"It's our best chance of holding our crew together," he said.

"I can do anything he can do," Jimmy grumbled.

Dale laughed. "Well, sure. So can I. But do you *want* to? If they're going to hang us by our thumbs from the yardarm, and Karl's willing to suffer, I say let him."

"When you put it that way, it doesn't sound like such a good idea after all," Karl said. "But I still think it's what we should do."

"And I doubt they'd try the same thing," Tish said. "They were not happy with each other at the end of the last Captain's Court. That would give us four against three."

"So, what do you say?" Karl asked, looking from one to the next. "Do we go for it?"

"Why not?" Dale stuck out his hand. "*Tortuga!*"

They joined him. "*Tortuga!*"

*   *   *

Chapter 29

"Dad, I can do this. You don't have to –"

"Shut up, punkin."

Kelly Dagget closed her mouth so fast she pinched the inside of her cheek between her teeth. She had heard her father angry before, raging about sponsors and censors, delays and the weather, about anything that went beyond what he could control. But he'd never sounded quite like this. Flat. Scary.

She glanced over her shoulder. Mike Glass was folded into the middle row of seats. He was so big it looked like an optical illusion, even with the size of the vehicle. He met her gaze somberly and didn't say a word.

Her father was hunched over the wheel, scowling. His eyes ticked ceaselessly back and forth, making her think of those horrible clocks shaped like Felix the Cat. Somehow, Kelly didn't have the feeling that he was looking for signs of the helicopter half so much as she had the feeling he was looking for someone to blame for this latest fiasco.

Pirate Adventure was over. They couldn't go on, not after all this. They only had a handful of people left on the entire island. Sixteen, assuming that the four in the *Anne Bonney* were still alive.

It was a wild assumption, pure wishful thinking, and Kelly knew it. They'd heard it over the speakers, those last few terrible moments of gunshots and screaming and then the agonizing screech of metal. All they picked up after that was the idiot static of null space. The radio had been pulverized, and it stood to reason that the occupants of the cabin had been pulverized too.

Including Steve, and she'd never summoned the nerve to ask him out.

Kelly berated herself for thinking primarily of Steve. Why weren't her thoughts on Tyler Brookstone, who had been one of her family's closest friends for years? Or Leslie Beaumains, with whom she'd gone to college? Or the poor doomed women who had called for help too late, and whose bodies were now tangled in the wreckage?

But it was Steve her mind stayed fixed on. She vowed she wouldn't cry until she knew for sure, and it was a vow she was determined to keep even though her chest ached, her eyes burned, and a tension constricted her throat.

"Dad —"

"Don't start with me, Kelly."

"I wasn't!"

"You were, don't give me that. You were going to start in about how I should have stayed at the fort and let you handle this. In case you've forgotten, this is *my* show and I am not too old to take care of things that go wrong. I don't need you filling in for me."

"Dad, I —"

He shot her a crafty, sidelong grin. "Though you'd like that, wouldn't you? Half the country thinks it's your show already because you host it. They forget who's behind the scenes calling the shots. They forget, and I think you have too."

Mike remained silent as a graven idol, but Kelly sensed his stern disapproval. She was glad that he was along, and not just because they might need his strength to rescue any survivors.

What was she thinking? That Mike would protect her? From her own father?

That was crazy. She was Burt Dagget's daughter, and while they had never been all that close emotionally, he wouldn't do a thing to hurt her.

That grin, though. That crafty, cunning grin. And the way he was talking. Like she was conspiring against him or something. Trying to steal his show out from under him.

"You get the spotlight, and it goes to your head," Burt said. "You start thinking that you know better than your old dad. You think I'm going to give up, don't you?"

"No, Dad."

"And then you can pick up the pieces and come out the hero," he went on as if he hadn't heard her. "Burt Dagget can't control his own show, that's what they'll say. He's too old, past it, time to retire and hand everything over to his daughter. That's what you've been waiting for. I wouldn't even be

surprised if I found out that you knew all along who was behind the prob-lems we've been having."

Kelly blinked at him, not able to believe her ears. He was *accusing* her. Was it possible for someone to turn paranoid overnight? Because that's what this sounded like. Total raving paranoia. He'd been under strain, they all had, but . . .

"There," Mike said, leveling a finger nearly as thick as Kelly's wrist toward the windshield.

The headlights touched on a shredded patch of brush, and a single heli-copter blade embedded in the ground like a spear. The treetops here looked like a giant had gotten clumsy with a weed whacker. Bits of mown leaf littered the ground in green confetti.

The path of destruction was easy to see. It led toward the west coast of the island, the rocky and inhospitable area that Kelly hadn't seen except on maps. They couldn't drive any further, even with four-wheel drive.

She was afraid that if she suggested her father stop, he would take it the wrong way and say she was ordering him around. His spate of accusations had quashed her thoroughly.

Mike rumbled low in his chest as if about to speak up. Another pair of headlights, these ones oncoming, appeared ahead of them. The two groups met by the blade. Samantha Dressler and Barry Lee got out, joining Burt, Kelly, and Mike.

Samantha knocked her knuckles on the blade. "Lordy," she said.

"This way." Burt led the way, arming aside branches before they could hit his face.

Kelly went behind him, then Samantha and Barry. Mike was last, with the first aid kit from the store of emergency gear in the Excursion's rear cargo space dangling like a child's toy at the end of his arm.

The path proved as easy to follow as it was to see. Kelly found herself recreating what the crash must have looked like, a tree-shredding, metal-splitting tumble. Her imagination insisted on adding body parts flying out of the cabin in a grisly pinwheel.

The underbrush ended in a stretch of barren stone. Pieces of helicopter and long scrapes on the surface of the rock showed them in more detail than Kelly needed how the *Anne Bonney* had landed here, slid and rolled, and gone plunging off the edge into the sea.

She pushed past her father and broke into a run. He swore, snatched at her, missed, and ran after her, puffing from either anger or exertion or both.

Kelly reached the edge and stopped, heart in her mouth. The clouds had entirely cleared and the moon sent a shimmer over the waves. The tail of the

helicopter stuck up, the smaller rotors bent in all directions. Flotsam surged and receded. She saw a blanket-wrapped bundle that might have been a body, but no signs of life.

"Steve!"

His name burst from her, torn with such anguish that it broke the dam holding back her tears. She covered her face, sobbing.

"Kelly?" It was a weak reply, but the real thing. No trick of the wind and surf.

A sob lodged in her throat. She spun around, looking desperately across the water, seeing nothing.

"He's down there!" Samantha cried. "On the beach, I see him."

On the beach. Kelly saw the little cove, and a waving figure. She vaulted down the steep slope like a mountain goat and seconds later was throwing her arms around Steve Quinlan.

*   *   *

Chapter 30

Tala Greywolf did not want to believe what she was seeing.

She closed her eyes – the eerie silver-grey eyes that her grandmother had told her were spirit-eyes attuned to sights not of this world – and willed the vision to disappear.

The inner serenity that she'd been able to achieve since she was a little girl had abandoned her. Not even thinking of her precious baby daughter helped. Instead of summoning up feelings of peace and contentment, the image of Mai's soft round face only filled Tala with an unformed, chilling dread.

Unnerved, she hastily opened her eyes to the camp again.

There was neither peace nor serenity to be had at Dead Man's Cove this night. Ever since she and Ambrose had been wakened by yelling to find B.J.'s and Connie's sleeping-spots empty, nothing had been right.

B.J. stalked up and down the beach, alternately swearing how he was going to sue the hell out of Dagget's people for invasion of privacy and steaming in high blood pressure silence. It hadn't taken long for Tala and Ambrose to figure out what had been going on, not that it had been any real surprise.

They'd figured it out at the last Captain's Council. Instead of going along with the agreement that Connie would be next to face discipline, B.J. had tricked Heather into voting for Ambrose, while he and Connie wrote Heather's and made it a two-way tie with one vote left over. And of course Connie, who to give her credit was a decent marksman, had pegged Heather in the

tie-breaking pistol duel.

Poor Ambrose, innocent that he was, hadn't gotten over the shock yet. He'd been looking up to B.J. as a leader, and had been fully taken in by B.J.'s professed dislike of Connie. Tala had too, though she had noticed B.J. casting ogles Connie's way from their first day on the island. This, she had attributed to nothing more than typical male lechery. They'd look, even if the woman in question was blatantly disinterested or an absolute bitch-on-wheels, they'd look. As long as the woman had a good figure, men could hardly pry their eyes away.

The disruption made it unlikely that any of them were going to get much more sleep. B.J. paced, Connie sat on a rock and preened like a mermaid, combing out her wavy bronze hair and smirking. Ambrose had wandered down to the foamy line of the surf, where he stood with a handful of pebbles to toss into the water.

Tala looked at the face of the moon and saw a skull.

She looked at her crewmates and saw them wreathed in black.

"I wish we had a mirror," Connie said.

No. That was the last thing Tala wanted. With a mirror, she could view her own visage. And if she saw the black aura around herself . . .

"Something is wrong," she said.

"Yeah, Big Brother flew the coop." Connie shook her hair down her back and crossed her legs, giving Tala a smug look as if she'd won some undeclared contest. "We're all on our lonesome."

"It is more than that."

"What, you think we've offended the spirits of the island?" Connie asked in a sarcastic, sneering tone. "Ooh, they're going to come and get us, suck our souls out in our sleep."

Already wishing she hadn't said anything, Tala fell silent. She rose from her perch on a sling chair that she'd rigged with ropes and a section of sail. The sand went from cool, loose and dry beneath her bare feet to cool, packed and damp as she reached the waterline.

Ambrose greeted her with a nod and tossed another pebble. It plinked into an oncoming wave. "What are we going to do?" he asked. "It's them against us, isn't it?"

"Yes, if you and I stick together."

He quailed. "I'd understand if you clubbed in with them. Once the crews were combined, the others would pick B.J. and Connie off pretty quick, I bet. You could go far."

"I would not side with them, not for a million dollars." She collected a

few pebbles of her own and rolled them together in her palm. They clicked and grated in a way that was oddly comforting. "But if you want to, I wouldn't mind. This isn't an adventure anymore. It's gone sour, and I don't know why."

"I know. I keep thinking about my mom and dad. I tell myself I'm homesick. I've never been this far from home, never been away from them this long." Ambrose made a little noise of self-deprecation. "Rachel, my sister, thinks it's pathetic that I'm still living in their house. She can talk. She's good at everything. It's because of her that I'm here, but . . . I shouldn't be. This isn't for me."

"Do you want to leave?"

"Kind of." He threw six pebbles in a scatter. "But I'd hate to see one of *them* get the money."

"I agree with you there. Can we stop them?"

"We'd have to name B.J. next time. He does all the work and Connie doesn't do anything, but if it came down to a duel . . ."

"Yes, we know Connie can shoot. B.J. was in the Marines, so I guess he can shoot too."

"Thirty years ago, maybe," Ambrose said. "I was watching him when we were at pirate camp, when they gave us lessons. I think he needs glasses but he's too proud to admit it. One of us might have a better chance against him than Connie."

"Which means we'll be stuck with her." Tala picked another pebble between her thumb and forefinger and held it, thinking. "The other crew consists mostly of men. She could use that to her advantage, but if she wasn't careful, they'd realize they were being played. It's probably our best chance."

"Okay. Do we give him the plank?"

"That's probably best. He might make it through the keelhauling, and we wouldn't want him to come back at the end after marooning. It should be the plank."

"You think so, huh?"

They whirled at Connie's voice. She had come down the soft sand without a sound, and regarded them with a steely glint.

"Let me clue you in on a few things," Connie said. "You get rid of B.J., or me, and the other side will pick the rest of us off one by one. We have to work together."

"Oh, yeah, you say that now," Ambrose said.

"I suppose you were planning to keep us around, then, by that same reasoning," Tala said.

"That's right."

Ambrose looked like he believed her, or at least wanted to believe her, but Tala wasn't fooled. The quickness of the answer, the defensive shift of Connie's eyes, gave the lie away.

"So you want us on your side," Tala said. "Until, that is, you can find a new sugar daddy over on *Tortuga*. When you'll cast us, and B.J., aside faster than a horse can run."

"What, you think you've got a better chance with them? I've seen the way you parade around here, just biding your time."

"Tala? Parading? That's crazy," Ambrose said.

"Well, I'll tell you something, sweetheart," Connie said to Tala, ignoring Ambrose. "The unattainable ice-princess thing isn't going to work for shit. As long as there's no cameras, I can tell you exactly the way it is. Men are led around by the dick. That's where their brains are. You control the dick, you control the rest of them. And to control the dick, you've got to put out."

Tala smiled. "*Whore Your Way to the Top*, a self-help book by Connie Berkwelter. Sure to be a best-seller. You won't even need to win the half-million."

Until this very moment, she had not made a single confrontational remark to anyone in the game. That it leaped out of her now, all full of cat-claws and ire, surprised her nearly as much as it did the two of them. Ambrose goggled.

"Bitch!" Connie spat.

Her hand snaked out meaning to slap Tala, but Tala ducked under it. She was terrified by what she was seeing around Connie, the bilious red-black shot with green of hate and envy, and all at once the premonition of danger she'd been trying to deny all night struck her full-force.

Connie slapped again, over-swinging. Tala sidestepped, crouched, and swept her leg around in a graceful arc. The move knocked Connie's feet from under her, dumping her to the sand.

"Ah! Hey, don't," Ambrose said. "Don't fight."

"Oh, I'm going to get you," Connie promised, flinging her hair furiously out of her face. "I'm going to kick your ass all the way back to Jamaica."

"What the hell's going on down there?" B.J. thundered, in exactly the same tone he might have used to quell the kids in the rumpus room. The voice of Father, the voice of God.

Tala glanced that way for the barest of seconds, a costly mistake. Connie, still on her back, pistoned both feet at her.

Connie's heels, so hard from dance-calluses that she could have been

wearing leather soles, collided with Tala's shins. Tala hit the ground in a spray of sand, winded. Connie sprang on her and the catfight was on as Tala tried to defend herself. They rolled down the beach and into the surf, not scratching and hair-pulling but punching and kicking for all they were worth.

Ambrose hopped around them from one foot to the other, bleating at them to quit it before someone got hurt, and B.J. was shouting other commands as he ran. Tala paid no attention. She clipped Connie under the chin with her elbow and that should have ended it, but Connie got a knee into Tala's midsection at the same instant. They flew apart, Tala wheezing, Connie spitting blood from a bitten tongue.

"Get her, Connie!" B.J. hooted with laughter. "Tear her up."

"No, make them stop," Ambrose rounded on him. "Make them stop!"

"Shut up, junior. Let's see some skin!"

Connie lashed out, caught the collar of Tala's blouse, and ripped it to her belt. B.J. cheered. Tala caught her wrist, yanked Connie's arm out straight, and then, unable to believe that she was doing this, drove the heel of her hand against Connie's elbow and forced it the wrong way. The scream of pain was at once gratifying and awful.

As Connie staggered back, cradling her arm and yowling, B.J. threw his big arms around Tala from behind and lifted her feet off the ground. She could smell sweat and grime, could feel his excitement pressing against her ass like a bar of iron. It seemed impossible that things had gone so wrong so fast, gotten so deadly earnest.

"Let *go*." She rocked her head back as hard as she could.

The back of her skull met B.J.'s forehead. There was a sound/sensation like a mallet whacking a ripe pumpkin, a dull pulse of light that generated from inside her head, and the next thing she knew she was on her hands and knees, dizzied, seeing stars.

"Tala!" Ambrose offered his hand to help her up.

Taking it, she did not so much stand as weave to her feet. Nausea clutched her guts. She leaned on Ambrose, kitten-weak.

B.J. was laid out flat on the beach, arms and legs splayed like he was making a snow angel in the sand. His eyes were open but vacant. For one horrible moment Tala thought she'd killed him, but then she saw his chest heave.

"You bitch, you fucking bitch." Connie, her right arm tucked against her chest, pointed at Tala. "This isn't over."

"Yes, it is," Ambrose said. He sounded six years old and scared to death. "What's the matter with you people?"

"What's the matter?" Connie's voice took on a syrupy, dangerous sweetness. "I'm going to kill her, that's what's the matter. Walking the plank isn't good enough. You better watch your back, Pocahontas."

"Connie—"

It was no use. Her head was reeling, swimming, caught in a whirlpool. If Ambrose hadn't been holding her up, an heroic effort on his part because she was three inches taller, she would have collapsed like a marionette with no strings. Whatever she might have said to defuse the situation spiraled away into her dazed mind.

"Fuck you," Connie said. Bent over her arm, her eyes wild, every trace of her beauty was gone and she was haglike, hateful. She kicked sand at them. "Fuck you both. Next time I see you, I'm going to rip your faces off."

Ambrose led Tala up the beach, casting frequent frightened glances back as if he expected to see Connie running at them with a chainsaw. But she stayed put, near B.J., watching them go with cold reptile's eyes.

"I hope Dagget's people get back soon," Ambrose said, puffing from exertion as he finally lowered Tala to a seat. He hurried around the camp gathering up all the sharp tools and knives. "Because I really think she means it."

* * *

Chapter 31

"Central? This is Barry Lee. Central, is anyone there?"

"Hardly," Ann Parkins said into the phone, from the main console of the otherwise-empty control room. "Sarah's down in the infirmary with Trip. George and Pete haven't reported back in yet. What's the story out there?"

"Bad," Barry said. "We found Steve Quinlan and Doc Brookstone, but it looks like they're the only ones who made it. The others went down with the chopper. It crashed into the ocean and sank. Only the tail's sticking up."

Ann sat back in her chair, trying to make sense of it. Leslie, dead? And Danny Harper, dear, polite Danny?

"There's more," Barry went on.

"More? Steve and Tyler, they're all right, aren't they?"

"Steve's more or less okay. The doc is in bad shape. But . . . they found Joe Baxter and Beverly Phillips. What's left of them, anyway."

"God." She ran her hands up the sides of her face. "This has to be a nightmare. This can't be real."

He rambled on, giving her the salient points that she barely heard or cared about. And to think, only a few minutes ago she had allowed herself to be distracted by the undue concern that her daughter was showing Trip Galloway. Sarah's combined urges to play Florence Nightingale and to take his mind off Leslie, not to mention the fact that she'd had eyes for the handsome young pilot since they first met, had been preying on Ann's mind. She liked Trip well enough but didn't think he was right for Sarah.

That hardly seemed to matter now. The missing and dead on the island were almost outnumbering the survivors. They had no way to leave, and the last thing she should be worried about was her daughter having an affair with a helicopter pilot.

Barry told her that the Daggets were headed back with Steve Quinlan and Doc Brookstone, while he, Samantha, and Mike stayed at the cove. Mike wanted to try diving into the wreckage, hopefully to bring back the bodies for decent burial and possibly to recover a camcorder that Steve said might have captured the face of the killer.

"At first light," he said, "we're bringing in the players, both crews. The game's over."

"Did Mr. Dagget give that order?"

"Kelly did."

Annie sucked in a breath. "Brave girl. He's not going to like that."

Barry hesitated, and she could sense his discomfort radiating across the airwaves.

"Anyway," he said, "we're going to need to know what our supply situation is like."

"I can have a detailed inventory ready by morning," she said. "I'd have one now, except those damned deserters helped themselves to whatever they could carry. I'll get right on it."

She signed off and sat for a moment in the dark silence of the control room. The banks of monitors around her were mostly blind and black, showing nothing. A few still showed scenes of the lifeless streets of Rum Town, or the abandoned deck of the *Adventure*.

"We can get through this," she said to the empty room.

We can get through this. It had become her motto, her mantra, during the rough years after Frank had run off with Annie's own hairdresser and left her to raise three kids on her own. It had helped her cope when Nellie, the oldest, had died in a stupid, senseless Prom Night car accident.

She had gotten through those times and she could handle this. They *would* get through it. She had Sarah and George to think about, not to mention the others who'd become like an extended family to her. Burt Dagget would need her more than ever. They would all need her. She would be their rock, their anchor.

The silence of the control room extended throughout the fortress. Ann made a quick check of each of the rooms on her way down. She saw signs of hurried flight everywhere – scattered clothes and toiletries, drawers askew, closet doors open. Those who'd gone with Skyhawk hadn't had much time

to pack, grabbing whatever they could stuff into a duffel bag and heading out the door.

Her work was cut out for her. Everything would need to be collected, organized, listed, rationed. They might be here for a while, since there was no real way to leave and no one was likely to be able to come for them in the foreseeable future. Not with everything else that was going on.

They might even be stuck here forever.

She thought of her house. It wasn't much, wasn't fancy, just a three-bedroom rambler in Glendale that she'd finally scraped up the money to buy. Sarah and George had grown up there. Nellie had spent the last two years of high school there. A lot of memories, good and bad, were stored within those walls. Now she might never see it again.

But the house, and their accumulation of possessions, weren't important. Her children were here with her. They were together, they had each other, and she felt a swift stab of pity for everyone else. Burt Dagget had Kelly, but the rest were on their own. With loved ones scattered all over the suffering world, and no way to contact them.

Trip and Sarah were in the infirmary. Unlike Doc Brookstone's small-scale but complete setup out in Rum Town, the infirmary in the fortress was little more than a school nurse's office. Its main purpose was to provide Band-Aids, aspirin, ice packs, and Ace bandages for minor injuries and ail-ments. Trip was stretched out on the bunk, a blanket covering him from chest to mid-thigh. His leg was elevated and one knee was snugly wrapped. The dried blood from his split lip had been washed away, his mouth had been packed with gauze where he'd lost a tooth, and the lower half of his face was swelling.

Not exactly conducive to romance, Annie thought with a small measure of relief.

Then it occurred to her – if they *were* stuck here forever, that was going to severely limit the dating options. Sarah might have a hard time doing better.

Hardly something she needed to be thinking about. She turned to Sarah, who was fussing with the cold remedies, antacids, and other over-the-counter goods on the shelves of the white metal cabinet. It struck her that Sarah, just-turned-twenty, looked just like Nellie would have, had Nellie lived through her teens. She was wearing a 17th-century frock even though she'd gone off-duty hours ago. The dress-up and play-pretend aspect of this had always been what appealed to her the most.

"Iff aihr ah-hee oos?" Trip hitched himself up on his elbows, searching Annie's face hopefully.

Having seen George through six months of having his jaw wired shut, courtesy of a mishap on the high school football field, she understood.

"There is news, but I'm afraid it's not so good." She sat on the padded stool with its rolling casters and trundled it nearer to Trip, beckoning to Sarah as she did so. She put an arm around Sarah's waist and held Trip's hand as she told them what Barry had relayed to her over the radio.

"Oh, gaahh," Trip groaned. He squeezed his eyes shut and an errant tear slid from the corner of one. "Eshyee."

Sarah reached out, perhaps meaning to offer a sympathetic touch, but Annie intervened gently.

"They'll be bringing Doctor Brookstone to his office," she said. "I want you to go over there and make sure everything's ready, honey."

"Who's going to take care of him?" Sarah asked. "Both his assistants are gone, and it's not like he could do it himself."

"We're all going to have to do the best we can. Everybody will help out, but we all need to do our part. We can get through this, Sarah."

The old adage brought a wan smile to her lips, which quickly faded. "I don't want to go over there, Mom. I don't want to go out."

"Sarah, honey, what's the matter?"

"Mom! Go out by myself? After everything that's happened on this damned island?"

She had a good point. Ann parted the slats of the vertical blind and looked down on Rum Town, its streets as deserted as any gold-rush era ghost town. Only the rats made themselves at home there. The rats. Slinking from shadow to shadow.

Ann shuddered in remembered revulsion. Opening the storeroom doors on a horde of them . . . nasty and skittering, their hunched brown bodies and bare pink tails, their eyes like little drops of oil, stupid but cunning in a savage, hungry way. The sharp pain of their savage little teeth, tearing her flesh. She rubbed at the scabbed-over bite marks.

The rats owned Rum Town. If she sent Sarah out there, alone and defenseless, Ann suddenly knew what would happen to the girl. The rats would come for her. They'd swarm out of the darkness, surround Sarah, and attack. Never mind that rats were cowardly creatures. Not these ones. These ones would be bold. They'd run under the hem of Sarah's skirt to gnaw at her ankles. When she tried to run away, she'd fall and they would flow over her, biting with their snaggled yellow teeth. Going for her eyes, her throat, the soft tissue of her face.

"You're right," she said. "We'll wait here for them. I'm sure everything's in

order over there anyway. Doc Brookstone runs a tight ship."

A door downstairs slammed open with an echoing bang. Sarah and Ann jumped, instinctively throwing their arms around each other. Trip sat up too fast, his cry of pain smothered by the gauze in his mouth. He clutched his leg and fell weakly back onto the cot.

"Somebody, hey, somebody, help!"

"George?" Annie called.

"Mom? Mom!"

"Second floor, infirmary." She pried loose of Sarah and went down the hall, stopping at the top of the stairs when she heard George's clattering feet as he ascended.

He appeared, filthy with mud and soot and green jungle stains. His hair was so mussed that it looked like it was standing on end. A large wet patch spread across the front of his pants and a bib of caked vomit covered his shirtfront.

Ann involuntarily stepped back as he raced to her. She corrected herself at once. This was George, this was her son, Sarah's brother. He might be a mess and stink to high heaven but he was her son.

She held him and made soothing crooning noises as he leaned against her. He was panting and shaking, and she remembered a dog they'd had when the kids were little. Boris, his name had been, a gigantic mixed-breed that could have doubled for a hellhound if he'd learned how to snort fire and brimstone from his nostrils. But Boris had been terrified of loud noises, and whenever there'd been a thunderstorm, he would shake and pant and huddle so closely against her that it was as if he were trying to meld physically into her and absorb her confidence.

Sarah looked out of the infirmary. "Mom? Is he okay?"

"What is it, honey?" Ann asked, stroking the disheveled tangles of George's hair. It was as fine as her own, and just like hers, had been platinum blond when he was a baby but dimmed to a mouse-brown as he grew up.

"Pete." George forced the word out. "Pete Carter. He's dead."

She crushed him closer. "Okay, all right, take it easy. We can get through this."

"Pete too?" Sarah cried shrilly.

"They shot him," George said. "They put a pistol ball in his head while I was looking at the bodies. They're all dead. Robby Willets, Lester Silverman, Doug Fogarty. All dead."

Ann ushered him into the infirmary. Trip was sitting up, his back propped in the corner, his complexion a chalky grey that made the puffed bruise on his

lip look bigger than ever. George sat on the end of the bunk, elbows on his knees, hands clasped but dangling, head down.

"They shot Pete," he said. "I ran. If I didn't, they would have shot me too. Or worse. Like they did to Robby and the others. Pirate torture. It's all in the books."

"Help me clean him up," Ann said to Sarah.

Together, they got George out of his clothes. He mumbled the whole time about gunpowder and hanging cages and bodies dipped in tar. Sarah wrung out a warm, wet towel and Ann used it to wipe away the worst of the mess. Trip took off the blanket and draped it over George's back.

The story came out of him in mixed-up pieces, but Ann was soon able to figure it out. He and Pete had gotten the call to return to Central and been obeying, when they missed the turn and had to try and get pointed in the right direction. Then they'd seen something, investigated, and found the three who'd gone out looking for the missing Baxter and Phillips. Pete had gone back to the car, and by the time George got there, Pete was dead behind the wheel with a gunshot wound to the head.

"I couldn't get in," he said, steadier now. "Pete had the keys but his blood was all over the seat, and I would have had to move him. They might have come back while I was trying to turn the car the rest of the way around. Then they'd shoot me, too. So I ran all the way back."

"You're safe now," Annie said, holding him and hoping she wasn't telling him a lie. "Sarah, pour a capful of Nyquil."

"Mom, that'll knock him out. You know he's got no tolerance for that stuff."

"I think he could use the rest, don't you?"

"Oh. Oh, yeah. Okay." Sarah fetched the bottle with its green-black, licorice-smelling liquid and poured a hefty dose.

George, who had vigorously objected and complained his whole life at having to take any medicine, even orange-flavored baby aspirin, downed it without a word. His features contorted and he shuddered in response to the powerful taste, but he drained the plastic cup. On an empty stomach – and judging by his clothes, Annie knew it would be empty all right – the Nyquil would hit him like a runaway semi.

Trip plucked the wad of gauze from his mouth. It was saliva-soaked and blotched with blood, and he regarded it with a pucker of distaste as he dropped it into the plastic-lined wastebasket. "He can have the cot," he said, his words only slightly slurred.

Sarah moved quickly to support him as he limped on his bad knee. "What

about you? You've had such a shock —"

"That's no excuse. Who hasn't?" He sounded bleak under a layer of false bravery, but Annie's estimation of him went up a couple of notches all the same. "If I can get over to the doc's, he's got crutches in the closet. I can't afford to sit around, not when we all need to pull together."

"I'll help you," Sarah said, her fear of having to cross Rum Town in the dark evidently forgotten.

Annie started to protest, thinking of the rats. As she was about to speak, she heard an approaching engine and parted the vertical blinds again. One of the SUVs was coming into town. It stopped in front of the shop with the sign reading "Bloodletter and Chiurgeon," and Burt Dagget emerged from the driver's side door.

"There they are," she said. "Okay, Sarah. If they need you to help out, do, but if not, come back here. We're going to have to start making an inventory."

"Yeah, Mom." The girl wasn't listening, concentrating instead on Trip Galloway.

She let them go, trying to ignore the misgivings that still griped and nagged in the back of her mind. "How are you doing, George?"

"Better," he said sleepily, hoisting his eyelids to half-mast to look at her. "I'm gonna take a little nap now."

"You do that." Ann rolled the stool beside the cot and sat down, holding his hand until she felt it go slack in her grasp. Moments later, a slight snore issued from George's half-open mouth.

*   *   *

Chapter 32

Mike Glass waded into the sea, breathing canned air from the small tank on his back. The weight of it was negligible, and his main concern was whether the mask would stay in place on his head. The scuba gear hadn't been designed for people of his stature, and the mask fit him as well as a child's swim goggles might have pinched the face of an adult.

Each of the fleet of Excursions had a stash of emergency gear in the rear compartment. Tool kits, first aid kits, scuba equipment, bottled water, granola bars, flashlights, anything that could be compactly and conveniently made to fit. Burt Dagget, the good Boy Scout, believed in being prepared to a fault.

Trouble was, Mike thought as the water closed over his head, there were some things for which you couldn't adequately prepare. The inexplicable, for instance.

He didn't talk much, and he knew that led people to believe that his brains were on the slow side. His brains, as it happened, were just as quick and keen as anyone's. The problem was his stutter. The bane of his early childhood, it had caused such teasing that Mike had determinedly thrown himself into strenuous physical workouts from the time he was twelve years old. His body had cooperated marvelously, shooting his height to nearly seven feet and layering him with muscle.

His build, and the threatening glower he could put on when he wanted to, had served their purpose. Nobody teased Mike Glass about his stutter. But he knew they still made fun of him behind his back, when he couldn't

catch them and pound them.

The only answer had been to give them no ammunition. So he stopped talking. Like someone had thrown a switch. A word or two, here and there, enough to get his point across. The rest of the time, he cultivated the strong and silent image.

But he never stopped thinking. He'd been a voracious reader all his life — yet another source of teasing from other kids, hailing as they did from a neighborhood in which the height of literature was expressed in neon-orange graffiti. So he had ideas, many ideas, about what they were dealing with on Veradoga.

Proof of it might well be on the tape in the camcorder that Steve Quinlan said was still tucked into the elastic netting on the back of Dan Harper's seat.

The flashlight beam brought the night sea alive with darting, flickering fish. They flocked to the light, silvery shimmers against the indigo-black background.

Mike leaned forward and swam, his powerful legs propelling him toward the *Anne Bonney*. There were more fish here, schools of them, and they wheeled away as he drew near. A moment later, he understood what had attracted them here. They'd been nibbling on the tendrils of flesh that wavered up like strands of kelp from the corpses strapped into their seats.

The sight was pitiful and horrible. Mike couldn't let himself react, knowing that it was too late for Leslie and Dan but not too late for the rest of them. There'd be time enough for grieving later.

He worked his bulk through the shattered Plexiglas bubble, trying to keep his breathing regular. He was no big fan of confined spaces, and the possibility of getting trapped in here was a very real danger. He'd seen as he closed in how the helicopter was precariously poised on a ledge, beyond which the sea floor dropped sharply away into pure blackness.

Steve, lucky for him, hadn't seen it and therefore had been blissfully unaware of how easy it would be for one wrong move to send the *Anne Bonney* sliding off in a long, silent plunge.

A cloth-wrapped bundle drifted near him, one pallid hand floating from it like that of a woman in a desperate plea for help. Mike heard the Darth Vader rasp of his breathing, much too fast, and paused to calm himself down. He took hold of the wrapped body and pushed it through the hole, out into the open water. It bobbed there, neither rising nor falling, just the right amount of air trapped in the folds of the blanket to keep it from sinking to the depths, or floating to the top.

The other one, the smaller one, had ended up at the very back of the

cabin. Mike moved deeper, startling a large yellow fish that startled him in turn as it shot past him, tail beating. Its cold scales brushed briefly along his arm.

He got the other body out too, and looped a length of cord around them both. The other end of the cord ran back to shore. He tugged on it twice, paused, and twice again. At that signal, Samantha Dressler and Barry Lee began reeling in the sorrowful catch.

Mike reached behind Dan's seat, not wanting to look at the bisected body of the security agent but unable to help it. Dan had been torn in half at an angle, and where the rest had ended up, Mike didn't even want to guess. He was just glad that enough time had elapsed between the crash and his dive to have let the blood drain from the body and dilute. He wouldn't have fancied swimming through a dense cloud of bloody water.

How long until sharks caught the scent and came to investigate? Mike didn't want to be here when that happened. He sped up his groping search of the cabin.

His hand touched something squarish and solid. He withdrew the camcorder from the elastic netting. It was miraculously all in one piece, though whether it still worked would remain to be seen.

The many pockets of his khaki pants were roomy enough for the camcorder. He stashed it.

The helicopter tipped as more of the shelf supporting it gave way. Mike didn't realize he was holding his breath until his lungs started to burn.

Time to get out of here. No more dawdling.

He undid the seat belt and freed Leslie Beaumains' body. He saw her face briefly in the glow of the flashlight, beautiful in a flowing frame of dark hair, beautiful with the customary contemptuous chip-on-the-shoulder sneer gone.

That left Dan. Mike wasn't even sure how to begin. What would he do, tote him by the ankle?

As he deliberated, the *Anne Bonney* leaned further, with an unsettling sensation of crumbling and vertigo. She was going over, Mike knew it, and without further thought he pushed off from Leslie's seat. He shot through the gap in the Plexiglas, scraping a long ladder down one arm, and kicked for the surface with Leslie's wrist manacled in one huge hand.

Beneath him, the helicopter heeled over and tumbled, with silent grandeur, into the depths.

Mike's head broke the surface. He spat out the regulator and breathed fresh air, then stroked for shore towing Leslie's body.

Samantha and Barry had completed the equally grisly task of digging up

Beverly Phillips. Her sand-clotted body lay stiffly beside the cloth-wrapped bundles. Mike deposited Leslie there, a heap of four dead women, and went to help Samantha and Barry finish unwinding Joe Baxter from the pole where he'd met his ugly demise.

*　　*　　*

Chapter 33

Burt Dagget called it the War Room. This was where he held his planning sessions with the challenge team, where they designed the feats that the players would tackle. It was a windowless room smack at the center of the second floor.

The long oval table was surrounded by chairs. The corkboard walls were covered with sheets of paper that looked like storyboards for a movie, sketches of cannons and rigging and treasure maps. A water cooler squatted in the corner, next to a counter that held a coffee machine.

He gathered his people in the War Room at six the next morning. That had afforded all of them a few hours to grab some sleep, those that *could* sleep. He suspected that most had, like himself, lain wakeful and braced for the next catastrophe.

Ten. He looked around at ten faces. Ten left out of the dozens that had initially comprised his production personnel.

Well, he thought, *look what Christ did with just the twelve.*

Kelly was in the right-hand seat. She was sulky. He hated that sullen pout, remembering it far too well from her childhood. She always knew how to use it to good effect on Margaret, sulking until she got her way. Once it had just been the two of them, he'd made it abundantly clear that such theatrics cut zero ice with him.

Uppity little brat. Trying to wrest control of his show away from him. Giving orders that directly contradicted his wishes. She knew it, too. Knew

she'd been caught. Hence the snotty, pooched-out lip and arms crossed tightly over her chest.

He'd have to remind her, and the rest of them, who was in charge. Who had created this show from the ground up. Burt Harrison Dagget, that was who.

The Parkins family took up the next three seats, Annie making sure that her children's chairs were drawn close to hers. George had a Nyquil hangover. He'd been rousted from a solidly doped sleep for the meeting and it was all he could to do keep from nodding off. Sarah was being far too attentive to Trip Galloway for her mother's tastes, as Burt could tell by the rigid set of Annie's features.

Trip looked like he'd come out the loser in a barroom brawl, with his split lip and wrenched knee. An aluminum crutch from Doc Brookstone's supply leaned against the wall behind him.

And speaking of Tyler Brookstone, he was at the end of the table oppo-site Burt, the chair that normally went there having been moved out of the way to make room for a wheelchair. Tyler hadn't had much rest, spending the hours directing Kelly and Barry Lee in the finer points of bonesetting and applying plaster casts. His left leg was only fractured, but the right was splin-tered, and his right arm was dislocated at the shoulder as well as broken above and below the elbow.

He needed surgery, but that was beyond them. Until and unless they could get some help from Kingston, Tyler was going to have to make do with a collapsible wheelchair and all the codeine he could suck down.

Steve Quinlan was seated across from Kelly, on Burt's left. Much of the cocksure bravado had been beaten out of him in the crash. He had a glorious black eye and a cut on his cheek, and the uninformed observer might have thought he'd been in the same barroom brawl as Trip.

How had Burt ever approved of him? Steve was an opportunist, a sweet-talker relying on a passing resemblance to previous versions of 007. He was probably waiting with bated breath for Burt to screw up, so he could take over. He and Kelly. In on it together.

Mike Glass, as imperturbable as ever, sat beside Steve in a chair that didn't look capable of supporting his massive frame. The only outward sign he gave of the anxiety and tension that filled the room was a creasing of wrinkles on the mahogany slope of his brow.

The last two seats were taken up by Samantha Dressler and Barry Lee, a mismatched couple if ever there was one. The Amazon and the diminutive Oriental, one a brash loudmouth and the other soft-spoken to a fault. They

kept checking their watches, as if painfully aware that day would be breaking over the beaches where the players made their camps, and no cameras were on hand to record any of it.

Burt surveyed them. The last vestiges of the Dagget Productions empire. Everyone else had deserted him like cowards, or died.

He took a deep breath that wanted to become a yawn, and exhaled what wanted to be a roar of frustration at how quickly and cruelly Fate had turned against him. Everything had gone wrong, whether by accident or sabotage or even — and he was only willing to allow brain-space to the idea because he was so damned tired — three-hundred-year-old pirate curses.

George Parkins had just finished describing, in a slow, befuddled voice, what he'd found at Hangman's Hill just before the death of Pete Carter. Steve Quinlan went next and told of the discovery of Heather Moss and Calliope Glenning, and when he faltered, Samantha related what had apparently happened to Joe Baxter and Beverly Phillips. Burt had seen those ones for himself, rotting grotesques that they were.

"Someone," he said when Samantha finished, "has been doing his homework."

"What are you talking about?" Ann Parkins asked.

"It's the books," Sarah said. "Like in Charles Johnson's essays, or that other one, *Under the Black Flag*. The way they all died, George said, was like how pirates would execute their prisoners."

"Right," Burt said, nodding. "Every one of them could have come straight out of one of those books. They're full of accounts of pirate atrocities. The Moss girl, they called that 'woolding' and would twist a cord or piece of rope around the head until the skull cracked and the eyes popped out. Hanged men would sometimes be dunked in tar to prevent them from decaying as fast, and suspended in iron bands as a warning to others. There's a reference to a French pirate captain who would extract a bit of gut, nail it to the mast, and make the victim dance until he'd danced himself into disembowelment."

"Dad, please!" Kelly broke in. "We've seen the results. We don't need to hear every gory detail."

"I think you do," he said, lancing her with a glare. "Because someone on this island, and maybe even someone in this very room, is a murderer. Someone with access to those books."

They all looked warily at each other.

"I don't believe it," Samantha said after several weighted seconds had passed. "None of us would do anything like that. If it was someone on the team, it must have been someone who left. Maybe whoever it was knew that

they couldn't get away with it, and ran while they had the chance."

"Then who shot Pete?" George Parkins blinked owlishly and peering at her. "That happened after the other helicopter left."

"And it doesn't explain the crash of the *Anne Bonney,*" Kelly said. She leaned over, focused on Steve. "Can't you remember anything?"

"Nothing, sorry love," he said. "We were heading back to the fortress, we had the bodies in the rear of the compartment, and the next thing I knew, the doc and I were caught in the wreckage and Leslie and Dan were both dead."

"Tyler?" Burt said, hoping to prompt some involvement from his old friend.

Brookstone, whose skin was so white and waxy that he might have died in the crash too and just been putting on an unconvincing charade of life, shook his head. His movements were slow and filled with a pain that even his best drugs couldn't erase. "I don't even remember taking off," he said carefully, feeling his way from one word to the next.

"We heard you shouting for Dan to shoot someone, Steve," Kelly said. "Over the radio. You yelled, 'shoot him, for the love of God, shoot him,' or something like that."

"No, there's nothing," Steve said, after a pause in which he knit his brows and seemed to be cudgeling his memory.

"It's the shock of the event," Tyler said. "Loss of short-term recall."

"But was there someone else on the helicopter?" Kelly asked. "If there was, and he was the murderer, where'd he go?"

"It couldn't be," Sarah Parkins said. "Because what about Pete? How could the murderer escape the helicopter crash and get all the way to Hangman's Hill in time to kill Pete?"

Mike Glass spoke slowly, his voice a bass rumble. "More than one."

"Oh, come on!" Samantha slid down in her chair and gripped handfuls of hair on both sides of her head. "Isn't one psychotic killer bad enough? Now you're saying we've got a spare? Or an army of them, how about that? Why make it easy?"

"They don't travel in packs, like hyenas," Ann Parkins said. "It's got to be one or two people."

"Mike's got a point, though," Steve said. "How could just one man do all the things we've seen done? It wouldn't be a simple task to coat a man in tar and hang him from a bloody tree. Not a one-person job. Especially when you factor in that Robby Willets' bunch was a trio. What would the other two have been doing while our madman was working on one? Not stood about,

I'll tell you."

"They might have been killed first, shot like Pete was," Barry suggested. "And the rest of it arranged after. Without an autopsy, we can't know for sure."

"Doc?" Kelly had to repeat it to get his attention. Brookstone's eyes had glazed over from the medication. "Doc, you said that it looked like the Glenning woman had been assaulted by multiple people, didn't you?"

"Yes, that's how it seemed," he said. "But as Mr. Lee points out, we'd need a much more thorough autopsy to say one hundred percent. And even if I were capable, we lack the facilities."

"What about the camcorder? The one you found with Heather Moss?" Kelly asked.

"No good," Mike said, shaking his head. "It's wrecked."

"Damn!"

After Kelly's outburst came a long and thoughtful pause.

"I can't believe it'd be any of us," Samantha said.

Sarah sat up straight. "Maybe it was one of them."

"Them who?" Burt Dagget asked.

"Them, the players," Sarah said. "That one, the history professor, re-member how he was always going on about how we'd gotten this wrong and that wrong? I bet you anything that he'd read all those books too. He would have known about the pirate atrocities."

"Charles Lowell," Kelly said. "But he went home after failing a keelhaul-ing, at the very first Captain's Court. It couldn't be him."

"He could have told the others," Sarah persisted. "The rest of his crew, or even all of them when they were at pirate camp."

"They were covered by cameras the entire time," Barry said. "We'd have known."

"We haven't reviewed every tape," Burt said. "And in case you haven't noticed, three-fourths of my camera teams are gone. Just because none of you witnessed it doesn't mean that it didn't take place."

"So it could be one of the players," Ann said, with a measure of relief. "Not one of us, then. That's good."

"No," Kelly said. "Is everybody forgetting Edith and Sean Creighton? That was on the first day of filming, and both crews were covered nonstop. For that matter, how could someone be sneaking away from camp often enough and for long enough to do all this? When would they have had a chance to learn the island, and set everything up? We've been here for weeks and there's places that even we haven't been to. It's impossible that it could be

one of the players."

"Too true," Steve sighed. "Which brings it back to being one of us, unless we're willing to entertain the possibility that someone else has been here all along."

"I'd rather think that than think it was someone in this room," Ann said.

"And why?" Sarah asked. "Why would anyone want to do this?"

"Maybe there *is* a curse," Trip Galloway said.

Burt hammered his fist on the table. Most of them jumped, and two or three cried out. "There is no curse on the island! If we start thinking like that, who knows where we'll end up? Leaving out saucers of cream for the wee people and looking for omens in sheep guts, that's where."

"Curse or not," Kelly said, "we are in danger. So are the players. We can't continue the game. For their safety, for our safety, and logistically as well."

"Kelly —"

"Please, Dad. I know how you feel, I really do. I'm not trying to steal your thunder or make you look bad or anything. But think about it. How can we go on? We don't have the manpower. Even if we split up, which I don't want to do, we couldn't run everything. The cameras, the challenges . . . it's too much. Dad, we can't do it."

"Can't isn't a word in my vocabulary," he said. "Can't didn't get me where I am today. It didn't get you where you are either, Kelly Pauline."

She flinched.

"Burt, there's no cause to –"

He rounded on Steve Quinlan. "Shut the hell up. I know you're just siding with her so you can get into her pants, so hear this right from my mouth to your ears: if you ever so much as touch my daughter, I'll kick your ass from here back to merry olde England."

"Dad!"

"You've both been against me all along. Don't think I'm not aware of it. Well, it's not going to happen, do you understand me? I am not about to let you ruin everything I've worked for."

"Stop it!" Ann shouted, then mellowed her tone. "Burt, stop. No one's against you. But Kelly is right. It's not possible to keep the game going. Not this time. There'll be other chances. Other shows."

In that instant he wanted to grab Kelly and Ann by the napes of their necks and knock their heads together a few times. They, more than anyone else in this room, knew what he had riding on this. They knew how deeply in debt he was, how the sponsors were breathing down his neck, how the budget had already far exceeded expectations. Now he'd have to arrange for

new helicopters and hire additional staff to make up for the ones who'd chickened out.

And the lawsuits! Two players and umpteen of his own people dead. The lawyers would rake him over the coals, signed releases or no signed releases.

If he didn't have a completed season of episodes to show for it, he was as good as done for. Not to mention the hell this would play with the plans to turn Veradoga into a theme resort getaway.

Kelly was loving this. She might be wearing a mask of daughterly concern, might be pretending to be hurt by his accusations, but he could read her all too clearly. She liked throwing it in his face that they didn't have the manpower to do a good job. She knew that *he* knew that she was right, and how much it galled him.

Because they didn't have the manpower. Not with the eleven people in this room. Doc wasn't fit for his own duties, let alone taking on anything extra. Even if he could field adequate camera teams, that didn't leave sufficient people to set up the challenges.

"It takes a big man to admit when he's been beaten," Burt Dagget said, the words not coming gracefully to his lips. "So for now, all right. The game's off. But only until I figure out who's behind these problems."

"What about the players?" Kelly asked, oh-so-innocently as if she wasn't gloating on the inside. "We can bring them in?"

"I suppose we'd better," he said, just waiting for her to bring up that other garbage about World War III and how there wouldn't be anyone left to watch.

He knew better. It'd blow over. America had stood tall and fast through disasters in the past, and life had gotten back to normal soon enough.

And what helped life get back to normal, boys and girls? Why, everyday things. Like television. Like game shows.

*   *   *

Chapter 34

Morning came pearly with fog to the beach at Buccaneer Bay. The red *Tortuga* flag flapped damp and dispirited on its pole. Letitia stirred the fire to life and started a pot of water for coffee, and another for the lumpy gruel that she called porridge, Karl called oatmeal, and Jimmy called spackling paste.

Dale jogged up as the water was beginning to boil. Jimmy, scratching his ribs and running his tongue around because it felt like the insides of his mouth were coated with fuzz, gave him a nod.

"Yo. Any mail?"

"Nothing," Dale said, dropping onto the log beside him. "Old Bony's just like we left him. I'm tired of sitting here. My money's getting lonely for me. I can hear it calling. 'Dale! Daaaaale! Come and spend me!'"

"It's got to be today," Jimmy said. "The next challenge. We're overdue."

Karl paused in the act of chopping fruit. "And they're still gone?"

"Affirmative." Dale shrugged. "I looked all over for cameras, and if they're there, they're better hidden than I could see."

"It is strange," Letitia said, stirring both pots with ambidextrous skill.

The harsh scent of coffee – in keeping with the theme, it was coffee as it would have been available in the 17th century, coarse and bitter and so loaded with caffeine that the smell alone made your heart skip – overpowered the salty sea air. Tish poured each of them a cup, and passed around the raw sugarcane that made it barely bearable.

"We're all agreed on the plan, right?" Karl asked.

"Right, right," Jimmy said. "You don't have to tell us again."

"Believe me, Karl," Dale said, giving Jimmy a chummy, conspiratorial bump with his shoulder, "it'll be a bona fide pleasure to keelhaul you, buddy."

The fog lifted as they ate their breakfast. The sun drove the lingering night chill away, and the breeze picked up with the promise of another gorgeous day on Veradoga. Jimmy washed up the dishes, since it was his turn, and then offered to go check for a new Letter of Marque.

He was itching for the next challenge, itching in general figuratively as well literally. He wanted to win the booty, and use his share to buy a change of clothes in Rum Town. Despite their attempts at washing, the ones he had were stiff with salt and their only crude soap was not exactly laden with fabric softener.

"I'll come with," Dale said.

"You said you'd clean up your mess today," Letitia said, raising her eyebrows and nodding her head in the direction of Dale's strewn belongings.

"I will, I will. Jeez, Mom. Clean your room, stand up straight . . . you won't boss me like that when I've got a half a million in pure gold in my pockets."

"Hush, now," she said, brandishing a ladle at Dale threateningly but smiling as she did so.

"When I get back," Dale promised. "Come along, James, my good man."

"We can use some more firewood," Karl called after them.

Jimmy detoured and grabbed the wood scuttle Dale had made out of a piece of sail, some rope, and a couple of sticks.

"Do you think they'll come to our camp, we'll move to theirs, or we'll all start over somewhere new?" he asked Dale as they walked along. "When the crews combine. That should happen today, too, I bet."

"Then I guess Mama Tisha has a good point and I'd better clean my room. We've got to come here. We've got the best beach."

"You haven't even seen the other beach."

"I just know."

Jimmy looked askance at him. "Sure, you do."

"Who do you think'll be left from *Maracaibo?* That big guy, B.J., he could cause us some trouble."

"Yeah, I can see him wanting to run things," Jimmy said. "If he's calling the shots, he'll still be here after the Captain's Court. I'd bet he'd be trying to get rid of Ambrose."

"Why? You getting some racist vibes off of him?"

"Some, but they did get rid of a couple of white folks first. No, I think it's because of the chicks."

"Chicks? Tish hears that, she'll swat you one."

"The ladies, excuse me. He's keeping the babes for himself. His own little harem. He won't like having three young studs like you, me, and Karl around, cutting in on his action. Connie's hot but she seems like a bitch. Tala, though . . ." He finished with a wolf whistle.

"Well, best of luck to you, Casanova." Dale punched him in the arm. "For me, I don't expect it'll be a problem."

"Why, you gay or something?"

"Yep."

Jimmy faltered, then laughed. "Good one, man."

"I am."

"So who's this Cindy you've been talking about, then?"

"Sid-ney," Dale enunciated. "My boyfriend."

"You're shitting me," Jimmy said, eyeing Dale closely. "It's a joke, right?"

"No joke. You're not going to go all homophobic on me, are you?"

"Who, me? Nah. No. It's no big deal. So what? So you're gay. Great. For you, I mean. It's your life and everything. None of my business."

He walked a little faster and edged to the side, increasing the distance between him and Dale. Up ahead, he could see the clump of trees that served as Old Bony's resting place.

"Jimmy."

"What? Let's check for messages, huh?"

"It's not like I've been keeping it a secret. I thought you already knew. Tish does."

"Look, man, it's none of my business, okay?"

"I wouldn't have said anything if I knew you were going to freak out on me."

"I'm not freaking out."

Dale made a sort of hopeless gesture with his hands. "Whatever you say."

They came to Old Bony, and Old Bony wasn't alone.

*　　*　　*

Chapter 35

"Are you sure we should be leaving your dad?" Samantha Dressler asked. "Because frankly, Kelly, I think he's a burger short of a meal deal."

"We're not leaving him alone." Kelly felt absurdly like Linda Hamilton or Sigourney Weaver, or one of those other old-time action movie butt-kickers from twenty years ago, loaded for bear with one of the modified flintlocks riding on each hip, a survival knife strapped to her leg, and a sock filled with buckshot stuffed into her pocket.

All I need is a grenade launcher, and maybe a chainsaw, she thought. *As if any of this is going to help.*

Which was sort of a strange thought to have. Why wouldn't being armed to the teeth help if she ran up against a nutball serial killer?

Then again, Joe Baxter and Beverly Phillips had both been armed. So had Dan Harper. For all the good it had done them. Even Robby Willets and his friends had taken what weapons they could scrounge, machetes and knives and a stout police baton that Lester Silverman usually carried in a sheath across the back of his motorcycle jacket.

They were all still just as dead.

"— in such bad shape and all," Samantha was saying.

"What? Huh?"

"I said," she repeated, "that I don't know if it's such a good idea, your father staying here. Doc Brookstone is the only one who can talk sense to him besides you, and with Doc in such bad shape and all . . ."

"I think you're underestimating Annie Parkins," Kelly said. "She can keep him cool."

"I hope you're right." Samantha was packing as much weaponry as Kelly, but somehow on the taller, tougher woman, it looked much more appropriate. Samantha seemed like she could pull the limbs off any would-be attacker as easy as a kid de-legging a centipede.

They were at the outskirts of Rum Town, beside a large building with a façade of fake balconies made to resemble a brothel. Kelly remembered, with a bitter sort of nostalgia as if it had taken place long, long ago, some of the guys on the production team good-naturedly begging her father to hire a bunch of extra actresses, or maybe swimsuit models, to work there.

No dice. The warehouse sized building was a garage, housing the fleet of Excursions, smaller vehicles, and motorcycles as well as the machine shop. A wide ledge circumnavigated the interior about where a lofty second floor would be. It held tires, tool boxes, leftover wood and materials from the construction, and various other odds and ends.

The automatic door jerked, and rolled upward. An Excursion drove out with Steve Quinlan behind the wheel, closely followed by a second driven by Mike Glass. They pulled up alongside Kelly and Samantha as the garage door began closing.

"How do we want to do this, then?" Steve asked.

"We're not going to split up," Kelly said. "Bad enough we have to take two vehicles to fit everyone in. We'll go to Dead Man's Cove first, all of us, and load up the *Maracaibo* bunch. Then we'll, all of us, head for Buccaneer Bay."

"So we all get killed together," Samantha said. "Fun."

"If you have a better idea, I'm listening."

"No, no. Brad Pitt canceled our lunch date, so I had nothing else on my calendar for today."

"I'll ride with Steve. You go with Mike."

"There's a surprise." Samantha winked. "Sure you want all the muscle in one place?"

"I believe I resent that," Steve said.

Kelly wanted to scream at them. Jokes? Humor? At a time like this? She understood that for some people, it was a stress release, a defense mechanism, but her nerves were so jittery that she felt like she might just explode any minute. And they were cracking jokes.

"Just go with Mike."

"Aye, aye, Captain."

"And quit with the Captain shit, okay?" That came out louder and more histrionic than intended, causing both Samantha and Steve to recoil and Mike, over in the other car, to raise his eyebrows. "Sorry. I don't know how we're going to explain this to these people, I hate having to deliver bad news, I absolutely *hate* it."

The driver's door opened and Steve got out, putting his arm around her. "There, now . . . I remember during *Old West Adventure* when you had to tell Lucy Rennault that her husband had been in that car smash. You handled that like a champ."

"This is a little more than that," Kelly said. "He only had a few broken ribs. How do I tell them about Washington? And L.A.? And everyplace? How do I tell them that we don't know anything about their families and there's no way to find out more?"

"We'll have to muddle through." He bent down, pressing his forehead against hers so he was peering directly into her eyes. "You're not on your own in this. Hear me?"

"Yes. Thanks, Steve."

"Anytime. Now, shall we hit the road?"

Mike and Samantha stayed close behind as Steve led the way. Although it wasn't the most direct route to Dead Man's Cove, he took the road that brought them to the spot where George Parkins said he'd left Pete Carter.

Pete was still there, stiff behind the wheel. He was pale, and Kelly knew from watching the occasional crime scene show that by now the blood in his body, except for the little bit that had leaked out of his perforated skull, would have settled into his butt and lower legs.

It had been quick, she could at least be thankful for that. He probably hadn't even had time to realize what was happening to him. She could envision it in her mind. Pete, waiting and watching straight ahead for George to come back. The killer coming up stealthily alongside. Maybe at the last minute, Pete heard something, or simply sensed it, and turned his head.

Pow.

Oblivion.

Dead and gone before he had time to be scared.

The more she thought about it, the more Kelly wondered if that was a good way to go, or not. Surely it was better than the lengthy torment that the others must have endured. Beverly Phillips, being allowed a tantalizing gasp of air between each wave, until finally the tide covered her. Or Joe Baxter, dying slowly and horribly by unraveling inches.

Yet Pete had died without knowing it was coming. He hadn't had a

chance to reconcile himself to it. Kelly wasn't sure whether she believed in God or not, but it'd be nice to be able to make peace with *something* before the end. If she was going to die – and with every hour ticking past, the possibility became one she was having to explore more closely than she wanted to – she would like to have long enough to try and prepare herself for saying goodbye to the world.

Nobody asked whether they were going to bring or leave Pete's body. Mike silently unrolled a canvas tarp, and he and Samantha lifted Pete out of the vehicle, bundled him up, and stashed him in the back of their Excursion.

Kelly didn't know if she could have done it, marveled at their equanimity in being able to touch and handle the corpse. They'd done the same for Joe, Beverly, Leslie, Heather, and Calliope. She sometimes, in her darkest black-humor moments, imagined writing a glowing letter to the company about the cargo capacity for hauling bodies.

"What about the ones George saw?" Samantha asked. "Do we bring them, too?"

George's vivid description flashed across Kelly's mind. One burnt to charcoal, one caked in tar, and the last a flyblown mess. They were people, people she'd known and more-or-less liked, but now they'd become objects of horror.

"I don't think I can cope with more death right now," she said. "I mean . . . what I mean is . . . we should get to the players and make sure they're safe. We've got to look after the living first."

She didn't want to look like a squeamish little girl in front of Steve, and couldn't look at him while she spoke. But he nodded, as if he really did understand.

They rolled Pete and George's Excursion off the road and continued toward Dead Man's Cove. Kelly wondered what had ever made them give it such a foreboding name. But they couldn't have known. Nobody could have known.

The roads had been cut through the jungle with care, so as not to be visible from the camps or the spots where the challenges would be held while still allowing them relatively quick and easy access to most of the island. They reached the nearest point to the beach and got out.

The climbing sun had chased away the early fog. Except for bird calls and the noise of the surf, all was quiet.

Feeling suddenly like she'd been being a coward, Kelly insisted on taking point. She led their small group down a hillside, brushing leaves out of the way. Steve was right behind her. He should have been back at the fortress,

resting after his ordeal, but he'd insisted and Kelly was glad. Glad, even if it meant getting more grief from her father.

What had that been about, anyway? Her father liked Steve, had often joshed that he and Kelly would make a cute couple, that they'd breed cute grandkids. Then this complete one-eighty and he was threatening to kick Steve's ass? Where had that come from?

The *Maracaibo* main dwelling was a long wooden shelter with a roof layered in palm fronds. A line of laundry swayed in the breeze, and a thin thread of smoke rose from the center of the firepit.

Several large crabs scuttled on the shore, and Kelly knew something was wrong. Food was always a premium; even if the players had won all the challenges and been able to buy whatever they needed, they wouldn't turn down free food. Particularly protein. Those crabs should have long since been boiling in the big iron pot, and the sea turtle she saw wallowing in a tide pool should be well on its way to becoming a hearty soup.

"Where are they?" Steve asked quietly.

"Oh, don't," Samantha said, pushing up beside him to look at the camp. "Don't say they're not there. Don't say the killers got them."

"No bodies," Mike said.

"Unless they're in where we can't see them."

"Samantha, stop it," Kelly said. "You're the one saying we shouldn't talk like that."

"Then where are they?" she shot back.

"Come on. Let's have a bit of a look-see, shall we?" Steve started forward, then caught himself and bowed to Kelly, holding a branch out of the way. "Is it still ladies first?"

"Funny." She went past him, not quite drawing her flintlock but with her hand resting on it just in case. "Hello! Hello the camp, *Maracaibo*, anybody home?"

Laundry, swaying. Crabs, scuttling. Waves, crashing. No other movement. No answer.

Kelly cupped her hands around her mouth. "Benjamin Nathans, Tala Greywolf, Ambrose Matthews, Connie Berkwelter! *Maracaibo*, where are you?"

From behind her and off to the side, Samantha Dressler cried out in alarm. Kelly and Steve raced back to her, only to find her shaking her head in disgust at herself. Sprawled before her on the sand were human skeletons and rusty cutlasses, and rising above them was the post with its painted sign: Dead Man's Cove.

"I feel like such a moron," Samantha said. "Sorry, gang, false alarm. I saw

them and thought the worst, you know?"

"God, scared by our own props," Kelly said, laughing. "Smooth."

"Hoist by our own petard," Steve said.

"There's nobody," Mike said. He looked up and down the beach. "They're gone."

"Search the camp." Kelly's laughter withered and died.

She felt an oddly heavy responsibility for the players, greater than the one she felt for the rest of the production team. The production team worked for and answered to Burt Dagget, so the main responsibility for them was his. But to the players, although they knew that her father was the man behind the curtain, she was Captain Kelly. Figurehead boss.

They searched the camp, searched the beach, and found nothing.

The *Maracaibo* crew was gone without a trace.

*　*　*

Chapter 36

"Quit babying me, Mom." George Parkins twisted away from his mother's hand as she tried to hold it against his forehead to check for fever. "I'm not sick, so could you quit acting like I've got malaria or something?"

"After what you went through last night, I can't help but worry. I still think you should be in bed."

"No. Everybody else is helping out. Even Doc Brookstone, and him with half the bones in his body busted all to hell. So tell me what I can do."

Ann sighed. "I don't suppose you want to help your sister inventory clothing."

George made a face. "What else you got?"

"I need to go over the food situation again and see what the rats left us. Trip agreed to look in the machine shop and see what we have in the way of parts and tools. Barry's going through the building, turning off all non-essential appliances. If you're offering, you could go down cellar and check the tanks for the generator. We'll need to know how long we can maintain power."

"Okay." He got up and clipped a walkie-talkie on his belt. "Mom?"

"Yes, George?"

"We're stuck here, right?"

"I'm afraid so."

"For how long?"

"I wish I knew. It might be a long time."

"Are we ever going to be able to leave?" he asked, trying not to show

how nervous he was.

"Someday, I hope. That's the best I can do."

"But if we have to stay here, a long time, I mean, we can. Right? We're not going to starve?"

"No. I promise. We have plenty of food and fresh water. We may have to ration it, and we may have to think about starting some gardens and greenhouses if it looks like a long stay, but we're not going to starve."

"What about the electricity?"

"That's another story." Ann shook her head. "We came here prepared to run Rum Town and the fortress for a good five months. With less than twenty people on the island, and since we don't need to have the cameras going 'round the clock or use up a bunch of gas tracking the contestants and events, we can stretch the fuel a lot farther than that. The freezers and fridges are the only things we really need to keep running."

George felt a hollow bleakness in his stomach. His mother smiled at him, as if trying to lighten the mood.

"Look at it this way, George. There's not going to be anything on TV anyway."

"That's not very funny, Mom."

"We've got to make the best of this," she said. "Whenever I think of what's going on out there, it makes me heartsick. I worry about your grandparents, about our friends, but there's nothing we can do for them. All we can do is take care of ourselves and hope for the best."

"What's the use, though? We're going to die anyway."

"Don't talk like that."

"It's true. We're going to die. Like Pete did. They're going to kill us."

"We're not going to let that happen. Whoever's behind all this will be found, and stopped."

"Maybe. But what then? If we're stuck here? We're still all going to die eventually."

"That would be the case no matter where we were, honey. It's the way it works. We can live just as well here as we could back home."

"Easy for you to say. You've got Mr. Dagget, and Sarah's got her pilot, but what do I have? Nothing. No girlfriend, nothing to look forward to."

Her mouth fell open and he could tell that he'd flustered her. "There isn't anything between Burt Dagget and myself except for a professional business relationship."

"Uh-huh."

"Are you going to check the fuel tanks or not?" she said crossly.

"I'm going, I'm going." He took one of her ever-present clipboards and a pen.

"Me and Burt Dagget," Ann huffed as George left the room. "What on earth would give anyone that idea?"

He could hear her in there as he went down the hall to the elevator, and grinned despite himself. Got her. Got her good.

His grin faded as he thought of the rest of what he'd said. It was true. If they all did manage to get through this – Mom's motto – without being painfully murdered, and they were stranded on the island for the rest of their lives, what was he going to do? The guys seriously outnumbered the girls, and George had no illusions about his prospects against the competition.

The elevator descended to the basement level. Only as the doors opened did it occur to George that if they were so set on conservation and making their supplies last, the elevators should be the first things to go. The fortress had stairs.

What would it be like, not having the use of all the gadgets that made life comfortable? They'd have to be careful with the batteries, so no phones or walkie-talkies or flashlights. No music – he thought of the rack of CDs in his room with longing. No video games or DVDs, unless they devised some sort of reward system for very special occasions. A movie a month, maybe.

At the opposite end of the hall from the elevator were two doors. One, George knew, led into the laundry room with its banks of six each washers and dryers. There was something else they could kiss goodbye. It'd be hand-washing and line drying.

Jeez, he signed on to *work* on the game show, not fucking *live* it.

He proceeded to the other door. This one was locked and had a dia-mond-shaped placard set into the door. A similar one was on the machine shop, warning that there were explosive liquids and corrosive materials. Gasoline and batteries, in other words.

The door opened onto a flight of stairs disappearing into cavernous blackness. The generator's noise was a barely-noticeable but constant hum on the upper floors. Down here, it was a gravelly drone, the snore of a sleeping giant.

George flipped the light switch and three bulbs strung across the room came on. He could see the network of pipes running along the ceiling, some carrying water, others with bundles of electrical cables concealed inside. The body of the generator hulked at the far end, the sleeping giant itself.

He started down the steps, clipboard in hand. As he reached the bottom, he caught a strong smell of gas. It really stank. Not eye-watering bad, but he

coughed and then scowled as the fumes seemed to coat his throat and nasal passages with a thin, oily rime.

"Yuck," he said.

Was it supposed to be this bad? Or . . .

Or did they have a leak?

Oh, that would be just perfect, wouldn't it? On top of everything else that had hit the fan.

The floor wasn't wet, at least not over here. But it wasn't level, either. It sloped at a barely perceptible angle toward the tanks. Maybe gas was pooling over there.

Call Mom on the walkie-talkie? No, he could take care of this himself. Each of the tanks had a wrench hooked to its release valve with a bicycle chain. If there was a leak, he could shut it off and be a hero instead of a kid who had to ask his mommy's advice on every single thing.

The three bulbs didn't shed much light at this end of the room. The fumes got steadily thicker as he approached the tanks.

Something moved in the shadows.

"Barry?"

The figure stepped into view.

It was a man, or had once been a man. He was all dried skin stretched so tight over a framework of bone that the skin tore in places. He had deep eye sockets in which dull lights like embers glowed. Strands of long, lank hair fell from beneath a black hat to the tattered collar of the coat that enveloped the skeletal body. The coat might have once been red as heart's blood, now faded to a rusty color. Breeches flapped around legs thin as broomsticks, and the bare bones of tibia and fibula disappeared into boots with the cuffs folded down. The cracked leather belt sagging off the hip bones supported a holstered pistol so old it looked ready to crumble into dust at a touch.

His hand, the bones of the knuckles showing ivory through splits in the skin, held a nicked and rusty cutlass.

George couldn't draw a breath.

Other figures appeared out of the darkness. These were smoky and translucent but no less terrifying for their apparent insubstantiality. All wore rough seaman's garb not unlike the stuff Sarah and Edith Creighton had made to outfit the production team and sell to the players. They carried pistols and knives and bottles. George saw a peg leg, eye patches, a hook where a hand should have been.

He reached down, touched the walkie-talkie, unclipped it. His lips were dry, and his scalp tickled as if his hair was trying to crawl out by the roots.

The dead pirates – Captain Smythe and his crew – advanced and fanned out to circle George. He tried to keep an eye on all of them at once but couldn't. They came closer, close enough that he could make out details of their faces. Their greedy, cruel smiles of anticipation.

What was he going to say? That he was down in the basement, the fuel tanks had sprung a leak, and he was about to be attacked by ghost pirates?

He brought the walkie-talkie closer to his mouth. As he inhaled to speak, he coughed again on the dense fumes. The men around him weren't bothered, and why should they be? They were already dead. When he joined them, he wouldn't care either.

George pressed the Send button on the walkie-talkie. As he did, that tiny spark of electrical connection met the layer of gas fumes that had risen around him. The fumes ignited in a sudden whooshing rush. His clothes in flames, George was hurled backward. The air was sucked out of his lungs as the world exploded around him.

* * *

Chapter 37

Dale and Jimmy drew up short, their conversation cut off by the expected sight of the fake skeleton and the unexpected sight of his very real company.

The woman, Tala, looked like she'd gone a few rounds with Tyson. Her yellow *Maracaibo* kerchief had been impressed into service as a bandage, swathed around her head in shocking contrast to the long tangles of her blue-black hair. She was leaning on Ambrose, but pulled herself erect as the two *Tortuga* dudes appeared.

"What the hell happened to you?" Jimmy asked, before Dale could formulate a similar question.

"And what are you doing *here?*" Dale asked a heartbeat later.

They had their knapsacks, and Ambrose was dragging a bag that seemed to have been hastily stuffed with food, blankets, and supplies.

It crossed Dale's mind that maybe this was part of the game, a last little twist before the two crews were brought together. He and Jimmy would be sent to Dead Man's Cove, maybe, or maybe Tish and Karl were already on their way and the camp at Buccaneer Bay would be empty when they returned.

Then he took a closer look at their weary, haggard faces and reconsidered.

"We want to join you," Tala said.

"Tala, I don't think that's allowed," Ambrose said nervously, but with a

tired air as if he'd repeated the same thing all throughout their walk, to just as much effect.

"It's some sort of trick," Jimmy said, but as wary as he was, Dale didn't miss the way his gaze avidly took in Tala's long legs and striking silvery eyes. Even messed up as she was, she was something.

"No," she said. "We can't stay with our crew. I won't."

"She and Connie had a fight," Ambrose said.

"A fight?" Dale studied Tala's bruises. Not 'fight' in the way Angie and Calliope had used to fight, then. An actual knock-down drag-out punching match.

"Are you okay?" Jimmy asked. He chivalrously stepped up to carry Tala's knapsack for her. "Maybe you better sit down."

Tala looked around and frowned. "They're not here, either, are they?"

"You mean yours are gone too? Your camera teams?" Dale asked.

"Last night," Ambrose said. "They left in a hurry. I thought it was because B.J. was threatening them, but they got a call, an emergency, and they took off."

"Ours too," Jimmy said. "What do you mean, B.J. threatened them?"

"It seems," Tala said, lowering herself onto a rock with a grateful sigh and bending to massage her bruised shins, "that they were filming B.J. and Connie doing something that B.J. didn't want to see end up on network television."

Dale and Jimmy swapped an incredulous glance.

"After they split," Ambrose said, "Tala and I were discussing our strategy, and Connie overheard us. It got . . . well . . ."

"Unpleasant," Tala finished. "Then violent. Connie attacked me, and then B.J. decided to help."

"Tala head-butted him." Ambrose's eyes lit up. "It was beautiful. Bonk! And down he went, flat on the beach."

"We were afraid to stay after that," Tala said. "Ambrose rounded up the various knives and sharp things, and hid them, but by the time it started to get light and neither of us had slept a wink, we decided that we had to get away from them. I don't trust what they might do without having the risk of evidence caught on film."

"That's amazing," Dale said, sitting down cross-legged in the sand. "Head-butted him, huh?"

"Bonk, and down he went," Ambrose reiterated.

"And nobody was there, none of Dagget's people?" Jimmy asked.

"None. If they do have hidden cameras," Tala said, echoing what they'd

been talking about at their own camp that morning, "they're invisible. And I would think, hope, that someone would have intervened if they'd been witnessing it."

"So you came here," Dale said. "Well, now what?"

"I don't know." She touched the back of her head and grimaced. "But we don't want to go back and give them another shot at us, and we had to go somewhere."

"The problem is," Ambrose said, "I don't think we're allowed to . . . to . . . jump ship. We can't just up and decide to join the other crew, even if they'd have us."

"Let Kelly Dagget tell me that herself, then," Tala said. "Let someone in authority do it. They can be the ones to deal with B.J. and Connie."

"Look, Tala, Ambrose," Dale said. "It's not really up to us. Letitia and Karl are still back at camp, and even if they say it's all right – which they might not, us being rivals and everything – in the end it's up to Dagget. But . . ."

"But we think something's seriously wrong on this island," Jimmy said. "It's weird that they'd take off and leave us on our own. If they want drama and conflict, you can bet they would have wanted to be there to see a fistfight. I don't think they are filming us on the sly. I think they're gone, and something bad's going on."

"It doesn't feel right anymore," Tala said, nodding. "It doesn't feel like a game. The stakes have gotten too high and the rules seem to have disappeared."

"They'd tell us, wouldn't they?" Ambrose wondered. "If the rules changed, they'd have to tell us."

"We're not going to solve this sitting here," Dale said, getting up. "Let's go down the beach and see what Karl and Tish think. Maybe a hike to Rum Town is in order. If we don't get any Letters of Marque today, or if the cameras don't turn up, that's what I think we should do."

The astonishment on the faces of Karl Werner and Letitia Jackson were priceless as Dale and Jimmy trudged down the beach, each of them burdened with *Maracaibo* knapsacks and toting the sack of supplies between them while Ambrose continued to support Tala. That was a job that Jimmy probably would have preferred, and in the short while it took them to get back to the beach he was going out of his way to act all buff and macho. Showing off for Tala, that was part of it, but Dale now realized that his casual revelation about his personal preferences had thrown Jimmy for a major loop.

Too bad. Dale would have broken it to him easier, except he'd honestly

thought that everybody else already knew. It wasn't like he'd kept it a deep dark secret.

"What are *they* doing here?" Karl shouted when they were still a hundred yards from camp. He was holding his cutlass like he thought they were being invaded.

Dale explained, with interjections from Ambrose and Tala. Letitia took charge at once, leading Tala into the shelter and seeing to her injuries. Karl surveyed Ambrose with narrow-eyed suspicion, really rolling out the red carpet, and when Jimmy offered to show Ambrose around, Karl took Dale aside.

"You believe this story of theirs?"

"I didn't at first," Dale said. "Thought maybe Dagget had sent them and we were going to have to reshuffle the crews, or maybe they were trying to scope us out before the next challenge, but once I heard what they had to say, yeah, I believed them. Tala didn't beat herself up, and I don't think Ambrose could tell a lie if his life was on the line."

Karl pondered that, scowling. At last he relented. "At least you considered the possibilities."

"I'm not an idiot," Dale said. "But you've got to admit, nothing is normal around here anymore. Until we hear different, I'm inclined to let them stay and see what comes next."

"We keep an eye on them, though," Karl said. "We don't let them in on our plan."

"Obviously."

"Fine. I don't like it, but I'll go along for now."

Dale clapped him on the back. "Good man."

They regrouped around the fire, the social center of life on Buccaneer Bay, and despite everything else, it was nice to have some company. New faces, new people to talk to. It was funny how fast a person could get cabin fever, stuck with the same companions.

And these two seemed okay. Tala and Tish hit it off right away, preparing a snack together and chatting like old friends in no time. Ambrose was quiet and shy, and with his slight stature all too clearly felt physically intimidated by the other guys. Dale was getting mixed signals off him. Either he was this uncomfortable around women because he was uncomfortable around everyone, or he was uncomfortable around women because he was so deeply in the closet that even he didn't even know it.

The jeering shout startled them all.

"I thought we'd find you losers here!"

Karl was up and reaching for his cutlass again. He placed himself between the rest of them and the newcomers to their beach.

Connie, who had been the one to shout, gave him a scornful look. She was favoring one arm and looked like she'd had just as rough a scuffle as Tala. "What are you going to do with that, jerk?"

B.J. ignored them both and leveled his finger at Tala and Ambrose. "You two. Get your asses back to camp where you belong."

He had an enormous purple goose egg on his forehead, the twin to the lump on the back of Tala's head. Dale caught Karl's eye and dipped his head in a significant nod. *See?* he tried to convey. *Looks legit to me.*

"Get off our beach," Karl said. "You're not welcome here."

"They," B.J. said, "are cheating. So are you."

"They're a pair of weasely, cheating traitors," Connie said. "Come crying to the other crew, Tala?"

"Hasn't it gotten through your thick head yet that the rules seem to be on hold?" Dale asked. "Take a look around. Dagget's people are gone, we don't know why, but –"

"But nothing," B. J. said. "It's all part of the game. A trick. They want to see what we'll do. I know all about that son of a bitch, Dagget. He's always saying how he'd love to do a show where the people on it didn't even know they were. That's us. That's this."

"It doesn't matter anyway," Connie said. "Those two are on *our* crew and we want them back."

"You don't own them," Letitia said, fists on her hips. "So don't you come in here spouting off like that, girl."

"I'll say whatever I damn well please."

"We're taking our crew and we're going back to our camp," B.J. said. "You can make your pacts against us once we've merged, but until then, Ambrose, Tala, no treating with the enemy."

"We are not going with you," Tala said. "Not after last night."

"Aww, baby can't take a spanking," Connie said. "Did I mess up your pretty face, princess?"

Calmly, Tala turned her back on Connie. This gesture, more than a double-birdie flipping off, more than a biting of the thumb, drove the blonde into a frenzy.

"Don't you show me your back, you cunt!"

The word was like a gunshot, stunning all of them. And stupid though it was, though he knew better, Dale's first instinctive reaction was to look around guiltily for the camera because she couldn't *say* that on television!

Tala stayed as she was, back to Connie and ramrod straight. She was as motionless as if she'd been carved from wood, except for a fluttering tic at the corner of her mouth.

Connie snarled and stepped forward. Karl raised one hand, palm out in a stopping signal. His other arm was down at his side, the cutlass blade along his leg.

"I'll take that sword away from you and shove it up your —" B.J. said.

"Hello! *Tortuga!* Hello, the camp!"

The yell came from the jungle, followed moments later by the appearance of Kelly Dagget, the hunk who'd been introduced as Mr. Quinlan, a giantess from one of the camera teams, and an even larger black giant.

The tableau on the beach was halted in the barest instant before combustion. No one moved.

Something was different about Kelly Dagget, and as she hurried toward them, Dale got it. Gone was the outlandish frock coat with its gold shoulder braids, the wide sash, the plumed hat. She had on denim cutoffs, low-topped hiking boots, and a khaki shirt. And she was weighed down with the contents of a small armory.

Out of breath, Kelly stopped and looked from face to face. "*Maracaibo,* you're here. Thank God. We thought you must be dead."

"Dead?" Letitia asked. "What?"

"Kelly, love," Quinlan said. "Perhaps you'd best let me —"

"No, Steve." She waved him back. "I'll do it. It's my job."

"These two are cheating!" B.J. said hotly, pointing at Tala and Ambrose. "They snuck over here in the middle of the night to make deals with the enemy."

"That's not true!" Ambrose said. "They —"

"Would you just forget all that game bullshit?" Kelly cried. "Forget it, all right? The game's over."

"No cameras," Dale said. "And you guys have got guns. What is all this?"

Kelly pressed the heels of her hands to her temples, briefly lifting her reddish-brown hair before letting it fall in uncombed disarray. "Oh, hell. This is harder than I thought it was going to be."

"Maybe we should get back to the fortress first," the tall camerawoman-without-a-camera said. "You can explain it there."

"The only thing that needs explaining —" B.J. started.

"Shut up, B.J.," Letitia said. "Can't you see that something's wrong?"

"Okay," Kelly said. "This isn't easy to say and it isn't going to be easy for you to hear. You might want to sit down."

Still, nobody moved.

She inhaled deeply. "The game is over. Cancelled. Done. There've been . . . there've been problems. A lot of problems. People have been hurt. No . . . you might as well know now . . . people have been killed."

"An accident?" Karl asked. "A fire?"

"Murder," Steve Quinlan said when Kelly seemed unable to speak. "There's been a series of murders on the island."

"Good Lord," Letitia breathed.

"Murders." Dale sampled the word as if he'd never heard it before.

"Most of our people have left," Kelly said. "At first because, well . . . oh, shit, Steve . . ."

"Go on," he said.

"You haven't been able to follow the news while you've been out here," Kelly said. "But you all know that the international situation was getting pretty ugly. I'm afraid things have taken a turn for the worse."

"What are you telling us?" Tala asked. "Are we at war?"

"Bloody near everybody's at war," Steve said.

Kelly's blue-grey eyes were sunken and miserable. "It's bad out there. So bad that all of the airports are closed, all of the ports and train stations. Bombs, nuclear missiles, biochemical weapons, viruses . . ."

"World War III, you mean," Dale said. "You're saying that it's the end of the world."

"Not the way we used to think of it," Steve said. "Not global destruction in a nuclear firestorm launched by the two superpowers."

"No, because things have changed," Letitia said. "It isn't one big red button in the Oval Office and one big red button in Moscow. It's hundreds of little red buttons all over the place, isn't it? You're saying this is happening now? Right now? Sites have been hit? American sites?"

"We don't have much information," Kelly said. Her face was wretched. "We do know that . . . that most of the major U.S. cities have seen some sort of attack. Washington. Los Angeles. New York."

Letitia wailed and fell to her knees. Dale remembered her telling them all about her home in the Big Apple. His head spun with terrible mental images taken randomly from memories of newscasts and disaster movies. Landmarks devoured in tornadoes of atomic fire.

He was surrounded by people all trying to talk at once and be heard over the din of everyone else. They were begging to know about San Diego, Amarillo, Boston, Phoenix. Dale thought of Sidney and the condo they shared in Orlando and his heart felt crushed in a metal clamp.

184

"I'm so sorry to have to tell you this," Kelly Dagget said when she'd finished replying that no, they hadn't heard anything about San Diego, et cetera. "We have tapes of the newscasts back at the fortress. For now, that's where we need to go. Between what's going on out there and the problems here on the island, it's the safest place. We have to stay together and figure out what we're going to do."

"Oh, that's enough," B.J. Nathans said. He was the only one who hadn't asked about the fate of his hometown. "Enough already. What a steaming crock of shit. You expect us to believe that?"

"It's true, mate," Steve said.

"A murderer on the island *and* the end of the world? Don't you think that's laying it on a little thick? Wouldn't one or the other have been plenty?"

"Mr. Nathans, we're not making this up," Kelly said.

"I'm on to you, missy. You and your father. Dagget's done some low crap before but this takes the cake. You think a prank like this is funny, telling people that their homes are gone and their families are dead? Good drama, right? That's what you want, you fucking little vulture. And you, you –" He rounded on Samantha. "You getting it all on tape, Wonder Woman? Got your miniature spy camera hidden in your Wonder bra? Sucking up the reactions, playing games with us?"

"Mr. Nathans –" Kelly began.

"And the rest of you, falling for it." He snorted in utter disgust. "Falling for it. Giving that prick Dagget what he wants. Yeah, I know he'll see this on film, and hear what I have to say. Let him. Screw him. If he thinks putting people through shit like this is worth half a million, he can shove it where the sun doesn't shine."

"B.J.'s right!" Connie said. "That's the lowest damn thing I've ever heard of. You bastards would do anything for a good show."

"I told you, we're not making this up!" Kelly Dagget said. "People are *dead!*"

"Including some of your own," Steve Quinlan put in coldly, resting a hand on Kelly's shoulder. "We found Heather Moss and Calliope Glenning murdered at Maroon Lagoon."

"No, that can't be," Karl said.

"You're lying." B.J. said.

"Come back to the fortress and see for yourself," Steve replied. "Or if that's too far a walk for you, come have a look in our cargo space, where you'll find one of our cameramen with a bullet hole in his head."

"Steve, don't," Kelly said. "It's bad enough without . . . without throwing

it in their faces."

"We haven't the time to mollycoddle and coax them along, Kelly love. If seeing the bodies is what it'll take to convince them, that's what we'll have to do."

"I'm convinced," Jimmy Hernandez said. "Nobody would lie about that."

"You think so?" B.J. laughed bitterly. "I've read interviews with Burt Dagget. He's stated right out that he's not going to be satisfied until someone dies on camera. Why would he draw the line at messing with our heads?"

"Please, listen to me," Kelly said, skipping over B.J. and pleading with the rest of them with her solemn eyes. "This isn't part of the game. This is real, and terribly serious. Between those who've gone away and those who've been killed, we've got less than a dozen of our production team left. We're all in danger, and if you stay out here, you'll be in the most danger of all."

"Who's doing this?" Dale asked. "Who's been killing people?"

"We don't know. It looks like it's the work of more than one, though. And the ways they've died –"

"That hardly needs going into right now," Steve said to Kelly, low, an aside.

"I have to call my husband," Letitia said. She was still on her knees and clutched at Kelly's legs like a penitent. "I have to call Devon. And Rickie. He's away upstate at college. He's got to be all right."

"The fortress," Kelly said. "We can try from the fortress. Just grab your stuff and come with us. We've got a couple of cars parked on the road up the hill there, room for everybody. Once we're safely back, I promise, we'll –"

The thunderous boom of an explosion interrupted her. Dale, sure that this was it, this was the end, threw himself flat and covered his head with his crossed arms. Around him, he was aware of other bodies hitting the sand, doing the same thing. A vibration like the expanding ripple of an earthquake shivered through the ground.

Five seconds passed and they were still alive. Dale raised his head. No searing fireball, no whistling of incoming missiles.

Ragnarok? Armageddon?

Ten seconds. They weren't dead yet.

And now he could see something. A pillar of smoke and dust piling above the treetops. In the direction of Rum Town.

*   *   *

Chapter 38

Barry Lee stood in the middle of the darkened control room, unwelcome dread filling him. He had just finished unplugging all of the computers, the sound and video editing equipment, even the phones.

He wasn't looking forward to visiting the living areas on the lower floors. The apartments and dormitories with their occupants either fled or dead, the remnants of their lives strewn around. There might still be framed pictures sitting on nightstands, personal effects of a private nature, and other items that would make his mere presence feel like a violation of privacy.

The chore was necessary, though. With all but the barest of essentials turned off and unplugged, the generator would be able to power what was left for a lot longer.

Habit took him to the elevator. It wasn't until Barry was inside and had already pushed the button for the third floor that he realized what a dumb move he'd made. Here he was, trying to save energy . . . using the elevator. He'd be sure to take the stairs from now on.

He heard and felt the explosion simultaneously. Heard it in a gigantic roar, felt it as the elevator was slammed side to side in the narrow shaft. He was deafened, and flung into the corner hard enough to break both wrists on the arms he brought up to shield his face.

Barry knew what was happening, knew it as surely as if he'd been told. The fuel tanks.

The cables holding the car let go with a twanging that Barry could feel

but not hear. It plunged with him in it, plunged into the heart of the upswelling, roiling column of flame so neatly channeled and contained in the elevator shaft. The last sensation he had was of his own flesh cooking on the bone.

*   *   *

Chapter 39

The sweet taste of the nonalcoholic rum finally overpowered any placebo effect it might have had. Burt Dagget knew that he could drink a barrel of it and he wouldn't get drunk. Diabetes, he might contract diabetes, but he wouldn't get drunk no matter how much he wanted to.

He had no one to blame but himself, only his own policy to thank. There was an on-site bar, but the booze was kept locked in a safe to which only Annie had the key. He knew better than to even ask.

The Calico Jack was empty except for him. He found something disturbingly final in the unoccupied tables, the vacant bar, the cheery Caribbean-style décor, and the lingering echoes of scent — beer, tobacco smoke, hearty stew, and the spicy sausage that usually sent anyone brave enough to sample it running to Doc Brookstone for a dose of antacid.

No one would be gathering at the Calico Jack for an evening's entertainment. The card games and joking would not take place.

Burt left his half-filled glass on the table and went to the balcony, studying the town. It looked like what it was, a stage set. An illusion. He had tried, and wanted, to make something so close to reality as to be convincing, even indistinguishable. And look. It was a less obvious version of a ride right out of Disneyland, that's what it was.

It was done. It was over.

He had lost at his own game.

Reality had butted in, and proven to be more powerful than the fictional, substitute reality he'd so desperately wanted to create.

The only sign of life he could see was Sarah Parkins and her limping helper, Trip Galloway. They were moving around in the clothier's shop as Sarah inventoried and neatly organized the bales of cloth, spools of thread, cases of steel sewing needles, and pre-made garments that stocked the shelves.

Down the street, the façade of the "Bloodletter and Chiurgeon" building was marred by the propped-open door that showed a slice of gleaming white and chrome sterility. Tyler Brookstone would be in there, resting in his wheelchair as he no doubt perused one of his medical texts to see how bad the prognosis for his pulverized bones must be.

And there was the fortress. Dagget Central, his pride and joy, the nexus of his control.

Even as he looked at it, the fortress exploded.

Dagget jerked back from the rail, instinctively ducking.

The stone building jumped. The few windows, mostly on the second and third floors, blew out in gouts of lathe and glass. Cracks raced up the walls, met, and caved in.

The concussion wave sent Dagget sailing backward into the Calico Jack. Tables were bashed to pieces under the impact of his body. The bottle from which he'd been refilling his glass shattered and splashed him with sticky-sweet fake rum.

He couldn't seem to marshal his limbs into an orderly enough regime to stand, so he crawled fast as he could to the balcony again. The fortress, <u>his</u> fortress, canted to the left. Smoke gushed from the holes where the windows had been, and the cracks in the walls.

The front doors, made to look like iron-bound oak, were gone, blown all the way across the street and now so much planks and rubble against the front of the butcher's shop. More smoke, with licking tongues of fire, turned the doorway opening into a hellish maw.

Dust and debris flew in a hurricane. He saw one of the chairs from the War Room, intact but with the upholstered seat and back in flames, whirl away and splash into the harbor. He saw books take to the air, covers and pages flapping like wings.

Who had been in there? Who had still been inside?

Ann Parkins.

The bottom dropped out of his stomach. Annie. And George, her son. And Barry Lee, it had been because of Barry that Burt himself hadn't been in the control room. He'd left, unable to stand it, as Barry went about his Annie-appointed task of turning off all the equipment. Each flipped switch, each

unplugged plug, had felt like parts of himself being turned off.

Below him, Sarah Parkins ran over the cobblestones, screaming for her mother. Trip Galloway, the pain in his sprung knee seemingly ignored, raced after her and caught her a few steps before she would have reached the gaping mouth of the fortress door.

"No!" Burt raged, far too late even if denial and protest might have prevented this.

He swung his legs over the balcony rail, tried to estimate the distance to the ground, and decided it didn't matter. He pushed off and let go. One of his ankles gave a twinge but he otherwise landed unharmed. He ran toward Sarah and Trip. Out of the corner of his eye, he saw Tyler Brookstone fighting to get his wheelchair through the door of his office.

Trip was holding Sarah by the upper arms, his head lowered to be very close to hers. Burt could see Trip speaking but was too far away to hear. He could guess, though, when the pilot turned and, yanking the collar of his shirt up to cover the lower half of his face, charged into the seething red-black entrance.

Burt reached Sarah, and some fatherly instinct made him grab her arm in case she had any crazy ideas about following Trip in there. He would have done the same for Kelly, and knew that Annie would want him to look after her daughter.

Sarah struggled with him, straining toward the building and howling for her mother, for Trip. Burt pulled her away. He got her to retreat with him as far as the courtyard, where they had held the marketplace on days when the winning crew got to come to town to spend their booty – that now seemed like something that might have happened roughly a hundred years ago.

Tyler Brookstone freed his chair from the doorway and wheeled toward them, steering it with the joystick on the left armrest. The left was his off hand and he swerved like a drunk driver before braking near Burt.

"My God, Burt," he said. "My God, what now?"

"Mom!" Sarah screamed, but this time in discovery and not despair.

A staggering, soot-covered figure lurched out of the fortress. It was Ann Parkins, choking and gasping for air, a scorched clipboard held at arm's length in front of her. Most of her hair had been burnt off, just a crispy cap of ash left on her blistering scalp.

Sarah tore away from Burt and he let her go because he was already running to Annie. He got there first and would have swept her up to carry her to safety, but then he saw how badly she was hurt. Second degree burns covered most of her visible skin.

"Mom, oh, Mom!" Sarah's hands flexed as if she, like Burt, had no hint how to help.

The fortress groaned, beams buckling deep within the structure. More cracks, crevasses, really, split the walls.

"Get her away from the building," Burt shouted. "It's coming down!"

"Trip's still in there!"

"Go!" He spanked Sarah hard on the fanny. "Now!"

Shepherding Annie between them without touching her, they retreated. The fortress held its shape for a moment longer, just long enough for Burt to begin to hope that it wasn't collapsing after all, and then down it went.

The sight ripped him apart. He had suffered similar pangs that terrible, world-changing September, but in some awful and selfish way, this was worse. The loss of life was negligible compared to that tragedy, and the spectacular destruction of the towers had altered the landscape of a nation's conscious-ness, but he hadn't personally lost anyone to it. He had been a step removed.

This . . . this was *his*. The fortress was a symbol of the entire project. His brainchild, crumbling and sending up a great churning cloud. His ruined dreams, his life's work. Gone.

* * *

Chapter 40

The two Excursions, loaded with people and their quickly-collected belongings, sped into Rum Town and screeched to a halt.

Kelly Dagget was out before Steve had turned off the ignition. She only got a few steps before slowing, then stopping as the smoking devastation of the sight sank in.

The fortress was heaped rubble, beams and stones tumbled into the basement. The town around it had been peppered with flying debris. Insanely, she thought how it gave the place a look of authenticity – this was what it might have been like after Edward "Blackbeard" Teach or Henry Morgan launched a full-out attack with all cannons blazing.

Her eyes closed in a spasm of anguish. Dead, they all had to be dead, no one could have survived that blast. Her father and everyone who'd stayed behind. Dead. Maybe never to be found in big enough pieces to identify.

"Kelly!" Steve shook her. "Over there."

She looked, and saw Sarah Parkins emerge from the door of the doctor's office. Sarah, sobbing, broke into a run and threw herself at Kelly. Words mixed with her sobs, enough for Kelly to ascertain that Burt was alive, as was Doc Brookstone, and Sarah's mother. For now.

The others gathered around as Sarah wept out the story of how Trip Galloway had gone into the inferno and rescued her mother, but hadn't made it out himself. Neither had Barry Lee, or Sarah's brother George. Kelly saw belief register on most of them, though B.J. Nathans and Connie Berkwelter still wore those mulish, belligerent scowls.

"Where is my father?" Kelly asked.

"Calico Jack's." A flash of hate penetrated Sarah's tears, actual hate as sharp as a blade. "He took the keys from my mother and went for a drink. He didn't even try to help her. He said Doc and I would have to do that. He just . . . just left her."

"Still think they're shitting us?" Jimmy asked B.J. and Connie.

A matched set of sneers was their only answer.

Letitia had pulled herself together on the ride over, mostly thanks to Dale's constant soothing assurance that until they knew for sure, it was no good worrying herself sick over what might or might not have happened in New York. Kelly wanted to round on him and tell him to shut up, tell him that seeking solace that way wasn't going to do anybody a favor. But Steve had cautioned her with a look, and she'd kept her silence, too busy herself worrying about what they'd find when they got to Rum Town.

Now, drawing a deep and tremulous breath, Letitia said, "I'm a nurse. Maybe I can help some."

Sarah practically leapt at her. "Please . . . she's in so much pain, and Doc Brookstone's not in very good shape himself. If there's anything you can do, anything at all . . ."

The two of them headed off, and Kelly was torn between going with them and confronting her father. Then she heard Dale Sheffield, and turned back around.

"Where are you going, B.J.?" Dale asked.

"To talk to Dagget," B.J. said. "This is too much."

"No," Kelly said. "Leave that to me."

"The hell I will." He stalked toward Calico Jack's.

"They're not faking this," Karl said, interposing himself in B.J.'s path. "This is no act."

"You can believe it if you want but I'm not going to be suckered. I'm going to have it out with Dagget right here and right now. Then, I'm dropping out of this entire stupid goddamn show and going home. And I'm going to sue their asses off."

B.J. tried to pass Karl, and Karl moved to intercept him.

"Mr. Nathans —" Kelly said.

"Shut up. And you, Karl, get out of my way or so help me God, I'll knock you down and go over you."

"I'd like to see you try," Karl said, adopting a boxer's stance.

"Gents, if you please," Steve said. "We've got far better things to do. The

fisticuffs can wait. We've got to see what's gone on here and what we can still save. With the fortress blown up, our chances, not excellent to begin with, have taken quite a turn for the worse."

"What do you mean?" Jimmy asked.

"He means," Samantha said, "that every way of communicating with the outside world was in there. So were most of the supplies. Food, toilet paper, you name it."

"We're going to starve?" Ambrose asked. "Is that what you're saying?"

"And we can't contact anyone?" Tala's composure had taken a lot of blows, and now it was finally shattered. "There are no other phones, no radios?"

"Would you people just quit it?" B.J. said. "It's all a bunch of —"

"Don't." Mike Glass loomed over B.J.

"You'd best organize this, Kelly love," Steve said.

"Me? Why . . . never mind." She abandoned her objections, knowing he was right. As much as she might want to run away from it, or crawl into bed and pull the blankets over her head, she didn't have that luxury. Someone had to be in charge, and guess who won by default? Captain Kelly.

She pushed all the rest of it out of her mind. The recent events were too numerous and had happened too fast for her reactions to be anything but numbed. So many dead, so much up in smoke . . . she couldn't deal with it. Couldn't think about it. Not yet. Or else she would fall apart.

"Okay, everybody, stop!" she called. "Listen to me. We've got to get under control."

B.J. still looked ready to take on all comers, Mike and Karl and Samantha all at once if he had to, and anyone else who interfered. Connie was beside him, and the wild light in her eyes made Kelly think of Greek myths, of the Furies.

"I'm not going to play this game," B.J. said. "You don't want me to talk to Dagget, spoil your fun? Fine. But I won't stay around here and be more fodder for your network. Fuck you all."

"Where do you think you're going?" Tala asked. "Haven't you heard a word —"

"We've heard plenty," Connie said. "And we're getting out of here." She tucked her arm imperiously through B.J.'s, and the snotty look on her face made Kelly want to slap her.

She conquered that urge, though not without great difficulty. "Let them go, if that's what they want."

"It's not safe out there," Steve said.

"It's not safe anywhere, and we won't accomplish a thing with them here. We have to work together, be on the same page. We can't afford to waste time and breath on trying to convince them."

Dale waved at Connie and B.J. "See ya, wouldn't want to be ya."

"What about the killers?" Samantha asked. "We're just going to let those two idiots walk away and get murdered?"

Something in Kelly snapped. "I'm two short steps away from killing them myself, so I don't really give a damn what they do. Just get them out of my sight."

"You can't talk to us like that –" Connie said.

The gun was in Kelly's hand as if it had sprung there by magic. She stuck it in Connie's face.

Nobody moved or spoke. Nobody dared. Kelly saw Connie's pupils dilate, saw the color fade from her cheeks.

"Easy now," Steve said. "There's no call for that."

"That's not a real gun, so just cut the shit," B.J. said.

Kelly swiveled and fired. The sharp crack of the shot made everyone jump. Long splinters of wood flew from a post at the near end of the dock, exposing pale inner wood. She deliberately swung the weapon toward B.J.

"Anything else, Mr. Nathans?"

He opened his mouth but Connie elbowed him in the side. "No," she said. "No, we're leaving, like you want. Okay?"

"Good. You're free to come back when it's gotten through to you that we are not screwing around, that this is real and totally serious."

Connie dragged him away, neither of them apparently willing to turn their backs. Kelly saw the rest eyeing her warily, wondering if she really would have put a bullet in somebody if they'd kept it up.

She wondered, too.

When Connie and B.J. had vanished over the little bridge that led out of Rum Town, Kelly lowered the gun and re-holstered it. She looked at those who remained – Steve, Mike, Samantha, Karl, Jimmy, Dale, Ambrose, and Tala.

"I'm sorry," Kelly said. "About everything. But we've got to stick together."

"No arguments here," Dale said. "Just say the word. Tell us what you need us to do."

"We believe you," Tala said. "But, please . . . I have a little girl. She's staying with my mother. I have to know if they're all right."

Kelly gestured hopelessly toward the fortress. "Steve was telling the truth.

Everything was in there. The tapes of the news broadcasts, the satellite receivers, everything. We've lost both helicopters and the transport boat, so there's no way off the island."

"What about your ship?" Ambrose asked.

"The *Adventure?*" Steve shook his head. "She's a capable enough sailing vessel for trips around the island, but she was primarily made for show. I don't know if she could make the trip all the way to Jamaica."

"It sounds like even if we got there," Dale said, "we wouldn't be able to get anywhere else after that, if it's as bad as you say. Not that I'm saying it isn't, so don't get hasty with the gun again, okay? I'm only saying we might not get a very warm welcome."

"Better a not-so-warm welcome than to stay on an island with the murderers," Samantha said, under her breath but still clearly audible.

"First things first," Kelly said. "We've got to see if we even *can* stay on the island. We have to find a safe place, and gather whatever we can to survive. Nobody goes off alone, understood? Stay close, but start searching the buildings. Bring anything that might be useful, anything at all."

"What about you?" Steve asked. "Where are you going?"

Kelly sighed deeply as she looked toward Calico Jack's. "To talk to my father."

*   *   *

Chapter 41

Trip Galloway didn't know how much time had passed. His watch, supposedly waterproof, shockproof, impact resistant, and damn near indestructible, was broken.

He couldn't tell this by sight, since the total blackness swallowed him whole. He only knew from walking his fingers over the shattered surface, and not being rewarded with the luminous blue glow when he pressed the small button on the side.

Or maybe the watch worked fine, and he'd gone blind? And why was he preoccupied with his watch, anyway? He should be concentrating on finding a way out of here. Out of his prison, which was otherwise liable to become his tomb.

His satchel, good old *der zak*, rested beside him on the angled, jagged bed of concrete. He had a sports bottle in there, and maybe it was better that he was thinking about his watch instead of thinking about what it would be like to tip the plastic spout against his lips and squeeze out a drink. The water wouldn't be chilled, but it would be wet, and his parched mouth craved the liquid.

He hurt all over.

No, that wasn't quite true. His bad knee no longer hurt at all. Or maybe that ache was so minor as to be insignificant compared to the other pains.

A lighter was in his satchel, but he hadn't yet tried it. The air down here still stank of gas fumes. Bad enough he was trapped. It'd be far worse to

broil alive.

Worse than dying of starvation or dehydration?

But then, if it absolutely came down to a choice of how to die, he also had a Swiss Army knife and he thought – hoped – he had the nerve to open his wrists or stab himself in the throat if he had to. If nobody found him.

Was anybody even still alive? He remembered leaving Sarah and entering the fort, fire all around him, smoke stinging his eyes and choking him through the makeshift filtering mask of his shirt. The whole place had been falling in, heavy items crashing down through holes in the ceiling.

He'd found Ann Parkins huddled under a desk, in a pose reminding him of earthquake drills when he'd been in grade school in quaketastic southern California. He'd gotten her out from her hiding place and guided her toward the exit, and then the floor had given way underneath him.

That was the last of his recall until coming to, in this spot. Wherever it was. However long ago it had been.

A sip. Just a sip. He had to ration his water, but it wouldn't do him any good to deny himself the minimum needed to sustain himself.

He'd have one sip, enough to wet his mouth. Then he'd see if he could sit up all the way, and try to assess his physical condition. If he'd been bleeding badly, he was sure he would have died already.

He groped through the satchel, finding the curved surface of the sports bottle. It sloshed as he brought it out and the sound was maddening. Three-quarters full.

The first drop spread across his tongue in cool, wonderful relief. His arid tissues woke up and clamored, and before he could stop himself, Trip had sucked down a full mouthful. He could feel it working through him, trickling and revitalizing every cell it touched.

Stop, stop or you'll drink it all! he thought wildly.

His body didn't care. His body was more than willing to guzzle down the entire bottle. Willpower won out at last and Trip re-capped the bottle. Half full.

"No, no, that's bad," he moaned, and thrust it deep in the satchel, piling other things on top so it would be a chore to dig it out again.

But it had done the trick. Ponce de Leon's Fountain of Youth couldn't have been more invigorating. He felt renewed strength flowing through him, washing away some of the pain and clearing his head.

Trip laboriously sat up. Bones in his back creaked, protested. He was suddenly sure he was going to hear a breaking sound, and go numb from the waist down. But that didn't happen, and he was finally in a more or less

upright position. One arm held him up while the other felt along his legs, trying to judge by tactile impression how badly off he was.

Very badly indeed.

His searching hand started down his leg, anticipating the bulge of his knee beneath its snug wrapping of Ace bandage. Instead, he found stone. A solid block of it. On his leg.

He had no sensation below where his knee was supposed to be. No feeling of wiggle when he tried to move his toes. No pain, no nothing. All he could conclude was that the stone block had so thoroughly crushed his leg that the nerves were dead, useless.

His thigh was swollen from a backlog of blood. The veins and arteries would be compressed under the stone, crimped flat. It made its own tourniquet, preventing him from bleeding to death so long as the weight was there. But if he tried to get free . . .

How? He couldn't budge the stone, couldn't pull his leg out from under it. Even if he did, the moment that pressure was released, he'd bleed out from what had to be multiple compound fractures.

What did that leave? Amputation? Cutting his own leg off at the knee with his Swiss Army knife? And if so, what then? Tie on another tourniquet, using his belt? Cauterize the stump with his lighter? Neither of those would work . . . he'd be dead within seconds, even assuming he didn't immediately pass out from shock.

If he shouted for help, would anyone hear? And if someone did, would they be able to reach him? Was he going to run out of air, adding suffocation to the horse race of ways in which he was liable to die?

The string of questions running through his mind came to an abrupt end. The fear that the questions had been trying to forestall, in a last defense against panic, overwhelmed him.

He meant to call out once, then listen. But as soon as he voiced his first cry, he did panic and began screaming, screaming until his throat was sore and felt as if it might split. The hollow space around him bounced his cries back in a deafening discordance.

At last, when he could only manage a raspy croak, Trip regained control of himself. He wanted another drink, needed it to ease his burning throat, but wouldn't take it. He strained to listen instead, hoping to hear answering calls, the sounds of rubble being lifted and shifted, the sounds of rescue.

Nothing.

And then, a step. A scraping.

"Hey," he croaked. "Hey, over here, help."

Closer. Someone was coming closer.

"Who's there? I need help. I'm caught. My leg . . ."

He trailed off, struck with a vision of the rats that had infested the food stores and bitten Ann. Maybe what he was hearing was a rat, smelling him, helpless prey, slinking out to gnaw at him.

Trip grasped the strap of his satchel. The moment he felt the first brush of a furry hide, he'd swat it, kill it if he could. And he'd do the same to any other rats that got bold enough.

Eat them, if he had to?

He pushed that thought away, and with it the memory of the way Dagget's challenge team had plotted and laughed and shown the rest of them some of the vile stuff they were planning to make the players eat. Weevils in hard tack, and yes, rats.

All at once, Trip was beyond fear, beyond panic. He was in the grasp of a terror so complete that he could barely comprehend it, and he didn't know why.

"Who's there?" He spoke in a hushed breath, almost as if he didn't want to be heard, and was astonished to find that on some level, he didn't. On some level, he knew that whatever he was sensing there in the darkness was not rescue, nor rat.

No answer but the footsteps, coming closer, and a papery crinkling sound that he couldn't identify.

He reached into the satchel. Gas fumes or no gas fumes, he had to see. If he *could* see . . . if nothing had happened to his eyes.

But he hesitated when the lighter was in his fist. Did he have to look? Wouldn't he be happier not knowing?

His thumb flicked the striker wheel on its own. The reliable, efficient lighter shot up its flame, dazzling his eyes and making them water. He blinked, scrunched up his face, and braced himself for the fumes to go up in another deadly fireball, taking him along.

The fireball didn't come. The fumes must have been too weak, or burnt themselves out. He didn't know the physics of it, didn't much care.

Squinting carefully, he opened his eyes.

The lighter fell from his hand. It clicked on stone, fell into a crack, and wedged there without extinguishing. The flame wavered, that was all. It still shed more than enough light for him to see the source of the footsteps.

Nope, he wasn't blind.

Too bad.

He saw a dead man, walking skeletal remains in a captain's outfit, shuf-

fling toward him with a piece of paper in one brittle hand and a quill in the other. Beyond that apparition, the half-seen and insubstantial wraiths of sailors flickered in and out of view.

The fleshless jaw moved. A word hissed out. "Siiiign," it said.

Trip recoiled as far as his imprisonment would allow. He could read the large letters across the top of the paper, in a fancy calligraphy.

Articles of Agreement.

Below, lines of smaller script filled most of the page. At the bottom was a place for a signature.

"Sign," the skeletal captain repeated, more distinctly. He set the quill and the paper in front of Trip.

"No," Trip whimpered.

Suffocation. He had used up all the air and was suffocating. Or bleeding to death after all. This was a dying hallucination. Instead of his life passing before his eyes, he got this final nightmare.

The captain drew a pistol so cancerous with corrosion it seemed on the verge of falling apart in a shower of rust. "Sign, or die."

He took the quill. It felt nasty against his skin, the decaying feather dripping its ink that looked like blood. A drop fell onto the paper, spreading just as the water had spread across Trip's tongue. It covered some of the fine print but Trip wasn't reading anyway. He scratched his signature, or a scribble that vaguely resembled it, on the line. Then he threw away the quill and covered his eyes.

One of them touched him.

A cold, almost-not-there touch like a breath of wintry wind.

His eyes opened.

They were clustered around him, the ghostly forms with their hoop earrings and their tattered britches. One had a parrot on his shoulder, an albino-white bird that was eerily silent. Another bore a wickedly-curved hook where his right hand should have been.

But they weren't real. He could see objects on the other side of them, and sometimes two of them would pass through each other, rippling as they did like curtains of grey-blue gauze.

The one that had touched him, that deathly-cold touch, was bent over his knee. As Trip looked on, clinging fervently to the hallucination idea, this specter produced a tool.

A hacksaw.

The serrated blade lowered toward Trip's leg.

A fresh scream ripped from him. Oh, he felt that, all right! He felt the saw

shearing through his flesh, carving him like a Thanksgiving turkey, felt the shiver all through his body as the blade met bone.

Blood ran from him in a dark river. He heard himself babbling for them to stop, they were killing him, he was going to bleed to death, please, they had to stop.

Another upended a bottle and a freezing misty fluid spilled out, dousing Trip's leg with what felt like liquid nitrogen. The one with the saw continued his brutal work. The hacksaw squealed through bone while Trip flailed and screamed with untapped energy he hadn't known he possessed.

Then he was falling, tumbling backwards as he was released from the trap. His leg was a spouting stump, gone below the knee, part of him detached forever and so much useless meat underneath the huge stone block.

They caught him, held him. How could they hold him when they weren't there, when they weren't real? Their hands should have gone through him and yet he could feel their tight grasp. And now, here came one who had kindled a torch from the flame of the lighter that was still wedged upright and illuminating the entire unthinkable scene.

The phantom holding the torch might have had all the substance of an eddy in the fog but the fire was real. The pain as it was held to Trip's stump was real, encompassing, a blinding agony. He heard the sizzle, smelled himself cooking. When the blood stopped, he was looking at a gnarl of burnt tissue where he ended.

He smelled something new, a pungent odor that he couldn't instantly place. It came to him as a specter appeared with a bucket. Asphalt. Tar. The time they'd repaved the street out in front of their house, when he was a kid. And the stink, the way it had gone all through the house and his mother was frantic, sure that they'd never get rid of it, that it'd permeate the curtains and carpets and no amount of shampooing or air freshener would do.

Hot pitch. He saw what it was, knew what it was for, and scrambled helplessly to escape. The intangible hands nonetheless held him relentlessly down as the end of his leg was immersed in the bubbling black tar.

*   *   *

Chapter 42

"See?" B.J. Nathans jabbed a thick forefinger at a camera mounted on a pole. "Like I said."

"You don't have to convince me." Connie did note, though, that the camera wasn't moving. It didn't pan to follow them, only perching there on its post as robotic and anonymous as the highway cams the local news shows used to report on the daily commute. "So, where are we going? Back to our beach?"

He shook his head curtly. "There's got to be another way off this island. They must have a hidden cove somewhere with boats, maybe helicopters."

"Can you fly a helicopter?"

"Sure."

B.J. didn't sound all that convincing but Connie elected not to press him. They were in a bad spot for sure, kicked out of the game. At gunpoint, no less . . . that freckled little bitch had drawn a gun on her. A real one, with real bullets.

What an act! Connie stifled a spate of jealousy. If she hadn't known better, she might have really been taken in by it. Kelly Dagget was some actress. Better than Connie herself, irritating as it was to admit.

Her whole reason for coming on the show was the instant celebrity it'd garner. Next stop, the Playboy Mansion, and then the big screen. Take that, every drama teacher and casting director who'd liked her looks but told her she couldn't act her way out of a paper bag. They'd be sorry.

That had been her plan. Now it was wrecked. They'd be kicked out of the game for sure, and goodbye, stardom. No way Dagget would let them still be in the show, since they were on to his head games and manipulations.

The half million would have been nice too, but Connie had harbored no delusions about her chances at winning. They never would have let her get that money. All the women hated her, envied her. They'd have found some way to stop her from walking off with the prize.

"Where are we going?" she asked again as B.J. trudged on.

"Told you. We're searching the island. We're going to find a speedboat or a chopper and shake the sand of this shithole from our boots."

"I'm tired," she said.

He reflexively looked at his wrist, where the white flesh usually covered by a watchband had been more vulnerable to the sun's burning rays. The rest of his arm was darkly tanned, but for that red welt. With no watch to check, he looked up and around at the position of the sun and shadows. The sky was weird, a greenish hue, but Connie attributed that to the foliage.

"It's not even ten in the morning yet."

"Uh-huh, and how much sleep did we get last night? Not much, remember?"

"So what?"

"So I'm tired," Connie complained. "My arm hurts from that bitch Tala springing my elbow. I want a hammock and a nap, and maybe something to eat."

"I got something for you to eat."

"Ha, ha."

"You didn't mind last night."

She gave him a withering look. "The game's over, B.J. There won't be any more of that."

B.J. stopped. His expression slowly changed. "What?"

"God! Some men are so dumb."

"That was part of the game?"

"Part of my strategy," Connie said. "Worked great, too."

"*My* strategy. I was the one telling you how to vote."

"Oh, get real. You did everything just the way I wanted you to."

"You were using me."

"So? You were using me, too. Except I was using you to get ahead in the game, and you were using me to get back at your wife."

"Would've dropped me like a bad habit when they joined the crews, huh?"

Connie laughed. "No way . . . I would have snuck around with all those other guys. Behind your back, you know, so each of you would think he was the only one getting lucky. I would have played you off against each other. My strategy. I wouldn't have won the money, but all of America would have seen you guys being my little love puppets."

"And seen you being a slut."

"Oh, and when a man nails five or six women in a row, he's a stud? Fucking double standard. Shove it."

They walked on, following the trails and roads that Dagget's people had carved out of the jungle. Every so often, they'd find sheds where the SUVs could be parked, but no wheeled vehicle was going to get them off the island.

The wind picked up, rustling in the leaves. The sky was still greenish, strange. Dusty clouds skidded across it out of the northwest. Connie wondered if this was a precursor to a tropical storm, or maybe a tornado. She didn't know the first thing about the weather, but she did know she'd never seen anything like that before.

"Look at the sky," she said to B.J.

He did, shrugged, and returned his attention to finding an easy route to the shore.

"And the sunsets these past few nights have been amazing," Connie said.

"So what?"

"Well . . ." She let it go, knowing that what she was thinking was crazy, and nothing that B.J. would want to hear.

Yellow-green sky. Dirty clouds, like gouts of smog blown on a high wind. Sunsets that turned the western horizon into a blaze of scarlet and burnt orange.

They came out onto a rocky coast on the opposite side of Veradoga from the beaches where the crews had been shipwrecked. No gentle curves of sand here. It was all gravelly stretches and sea-sculpted rocks, and battering waves spitting foam high into the heavy air.

"This doesn't look like a good place to leave a boat," Connie said.

B.J. didn't bother to answer. He picked his way to the edge and shaded his eyes — not that there was much need, as the rapidly-moving clouds were dimming the daylight — to peer up and down the shoreline.

"I don't like this," she said.

"Would you for Christ's sake shut your yap?"

"Hey!"

"Hey, nothing. From now on, you do what I say."

"What's that supposed to mean?"

He came toward her, face flushed and angry. "It means that you do what I say. I'm going to get us out of here. Until I do, I'm the boss. Got it?"

"Like I'm going to take orders from you or anyone."

"You better."

"Or what?" Connie asked, challenged.

"Or you can go back and play with the rest of those assholes. I bet they'd be glad to see you."

"I can do whatever I want, whether you like it or not."

"Oh?" He crossed his arms. "And what's that?"

"What's what? I don't have anything in mind. I just want you to quit ordering me around."

The sky. A storm was blowing in, that must be it. The northwest was a smutty pall of grey-brown, with downward flickers of lightning made miniscule by distance. She thought she might have heard somewhere that changes in atmospheric pressure made people irritable. As if she and B.J. needed more reason to be irritable after all the shit they'd been dealt. First by those traitors, Tala and Ambrose, and then by Kelly Dagget and her bunch.

But . . . wasn't there something else she'd heard? Something having to do with sunsets and weather patterns after volcanic eruptions, and big forest fires?

B.J. had said something that she missed, and must have taken her silence for agreement because he'd turned away and resumed scanning for the hidden cove he had hypothesized.

"B.J.?"

"What?" he barked.

"Look at the sky."

"You already told me to and I already did."

"No, come on. Look."

He did again. "So we're going to get rained on. We can backtrack to one of their sheds if it gets too bad."

"Remember what they told us? About the bombs?"

"Yeah, World War III, nuke strikes and Armageddon viruses, that's what they want us to believe. You're not still thinking about that, are you?"

"The sky, though. The sunsets. Volcanic eruptions and big forest fires play hell with the sunsets, because of all the ash and crud they throw into the air. Nuclear bombs, too."

He snorted in disgust and walked away from her.

"What if they weren't lying to us?" Connie asked.

B.J. didn't look back.

"What if something really did happen?" She hurried after him. "Damn you, listen to me."

"Not as long as you're talking bullshit."

"But what if it *is* the end of the world?"

He spun and grinned at her. The grin was so toothy and unnerving that Connie fell back a pace.

"Then I guess," he said in a soft yet carrying voice, "we'd be stuck here. We'd have to rebuild. A strong man could set himself up to be a king, with his pick of the women all so thankful to have someone to protect and look after them. You might want to think about being nicer and watching that mouth of yours."

"Go to hell."

"I almost wish it *was* the end of the world," he said.

His eyes glittered, and for the first time, it occurred to Connie that B.J. was beyond angry. She felt a thin thread of fear weave through her, and quashed it.

"I don't need anyone to look after me," she said.

"No, you think the laws will do it. But those would be gone, wouldn't they? No more laws, no more sexual harassment complaints, no more feminists. Survival of the fittest. It'd be a real man's world, where real men would be in control. The way it was meant to be."

"Meant to be? Come on! I can do anything you can."

B.J. closed the distance between them. "You're smaller. Weaker. Can you hunt? Can you build? Can you fight off an enemy?"

She tried to retreat but he'd somehow cornered her against the edge of a bluff. The drop at her heels wasn't far, but the waves down there were choppy, slamming into the rocks.

"It's civilized society that keeps you safe," he said. "With that gone, with no fear of being caught and punished for it, what's to stop a man from just grabbing you and doing whatever he wants? If you're right and this is the end of the world, what's stopping me from fucking your brains out this very minute?"

"I'll rip your balls off," Connie said.

"Yeah? Let's see you try."

He lunged at her. Connie kicked, missed his crotch and struck his thigh. B.J. didn't miss a step. He punched her in the belly, and as she was gasping, bent double, he clubbed her in the side of the head with his fist. He picked her up, despite her struggles, and carried her away from the edge and toward

the shelter of the jungle.

"Let me go, you sick bastard," Connie coughed.

"Smaller," B.J. said. "Weaker."

She landed face-down over a log, driving her breath out again. Her usual costume included a yellow and black striped skirt cut in a handkerchief hem, with bikini bottoms underneath. B.J. tossed the skirt up and tugged her swimsuit aside.

"Stop it, B.J., this isn't funny!"

"See what I mean? Any man could have you. No laws to stop him. No police to call."

"Let me go —"

Her final word turned into a startled scream as he entered her, fast and rough.

"There," he grunted. "There. There." Each 'there' was emphasized by another thrust.

"B.J., damn it, stop, you're hurting me!"

Connie thrashed, but couldn't dislodge him. Her blouse had torn and her stomach scraped against the bark of the log. His hands dug painfully into her hips, holding her in place. He battered into her and she was dry, not ready, and it did hurt. More than the hurt, it was humiliating to be helpless like this, invaded. Furious tears squeezed out of her eyes. She clawed at the ground, hoping to find something to use as a —

Her hand closed over a stout length of wood. Pain blazed in her elbow but she didn't care.

"There," B.J. said. "There, you bitch, there, see what I mean? You'd have to have a man to defend you, keep the others from doing *this* —" with a particularly hard thrust, "— and you'd have to pay him with pussy. Just like caveman days!"

She waited, gripping the end of the stick so tight that her knuckles went white. She waited and endured his pounding, his frantic pace as he thundered toward his orgasm.

He had quit trying to talk and only grunted like an animal. Harder and faster, and then he strained against her and her abraded stomach scratched along the bark and bled. She felt him jerk and spasm inside her, shooting his load. Then he sagged onto her back, puffing hot breath against her neck.

"There," he said, conversational now. He withdrew and slapped her on her upturned ass. "See what I mean?"

"Yes," Connie said. She pushed herself up, legs trembling and feeling like she'd been reamed out with a broomstick. Two years of lap dances and g-

strings and occasional hooking on the side, bachelor parties and fraternity initiations for the most part, yet she'd never felt so used. "Yes, I see."

He helped her up, the bastard, actually offered a hand and helped her up. She took it, and as she stood she swung with the arm that had been out of his sight behind her body.

The fat end of the branch met his forehead with a solid thunk. B.J. let go of Connie and staggered sideways, clapping a hand to his head like he'd just missed an easy quiz show answer. She didn't wait for him to regain his balance but hit him again. Mashed his ear to the side of his head, bringing blood to his grey-streaked crew cut. And again, missing his head but getting his shoulder.

B.J. yelled. He tried to move away and stumbled. Went to one knee. Connie flailed at him with the stick.

"There!" she cried with each blow. Her injured arm was forgotten in a wild exhilaration. "There! There! How do *you* like it?"

He pitched forward onto his belly. Connie straddled him, bringing the branch down over and over and screaming 'there!' each time she did it until he wasn't moving anymore. His hair was matted with blood. More ran from his ears and his nose.

Connie wedged her toe under him and tried to flip him over. His weight was too great. She bent, seized his meaty arm, and dragged. He flopped onto his back, head lolling, eyes staring fixedly up at the seething brown clouds.

"One more for the road," Connie said.

She raised the branch in both hands, held it there at the apex of her swing for an anticipatory moment, and brought it down squarely between his eyes.

"There."

*　　*　　*

Chapter 43

Her father wouldn't speak to her, wouldn't acknowledge her presence even when Kelly got right up in his face and raised her voice. He did nothing but reps of elbow curls – lift the glass, take a drink, set down the glass. The potent smell of rum hung around him in a mist. He seemed to be making a concerted effort to drink himself into a coma.

Disgusted, Kelly gave up and left him with his bottle. But only the one. Her last order of business as she prepared to depart the tavern was to take up the ring of keys. Annie Parkins' keys, on a big brass hoop. She closed and re-locked the safe with the liquor in it on her way out.

Her blowup at B.J. and Connie had somehow served to clear her mind and allow her to organize her thoughts. She ran down a list in her head of what they'd need to do, what their options might be.

It was like something she remembered from eighth grade. The class had been divided into groups and told to make believe they were stranded on a desert island, crash-landed on a habitable planet, or whatever. What skills would they need? Who could they do without if someone had to be left behind? How would they choose the ingredients to help their society survive?

Those classroom exercises had never involved psychotic murderers on the loose as well. If not for that, Kelly liked to think that the rest of them might stand a reasonable shot at survival.

Thirteen of them. Lucky thirteen.

Plus her father. He wasn't going to be any help if he insisted on drowning

his sorrows in rum, but Kelly didn't know what else to do for, or about, him.

She had B.J. and Connie to worry about too. She wouldn't put it past them to come back and start more trouble.

So that made sixteen in all. Sixteen of them left alive on this island.

Rum Town yielded up a few boxes' worth of foodstuffs, mostly the hardtack, salt pork, beans, rice, spices and flour that they'd brought in to sell to the players when they won booty in challenges. They had bales of cloth, bound bundles of leather hides from the cobbler's shop, lanterns and flasks of oil, some rope, jewelry and baubles, and a collection of knives and cutlasses.

"No luck at the lagoon, love." Steve exhaled heavily, sinking down onto the low stone wall beside her.

They'd come up with the idea of making camp there, where they'd have power, running water, a decent store of food. Steve and Samantha had volunteered to go check it out.

Now, Steve's words, and his bleak tone, dashed hopes Kelly hadn't even known she'd been clinging to.

"What happened?" Kelly asked.

"It burned flat. Samantha thinks it was set, and I'm inclined to agree. Nothing to save. What we can find here is all we'll have."

They regarded the pitiful pile of goods together.

Kelly combed her fingers through her hair, wincing when she hit a tangle. "Almost all our supplies were in the fortress. We've got the Excursions, which all have gear in the back —"

"Also," Steve said, "three of the smaller cars, two motorcycles, three drums of petrol, and enough of the other assorted automotive accoutrements to keep them all shipshape for at least a year."

"We can't keep the vehicles in the garage," Kelly said. "Those drums of gasoline . . . we can't risk another explosion or another fire."

"Speaking of explosives," he said.

"What? Oh, God, what else?"

"The shed at Hangman's Hill. We'd taken six barrels of gunpowder out there, remember? I'm assuming one of them was used to dispatch Lester Silverman, but someone should check on the rest."

Kelly moaned. "There's gunpowder aboard the *Adventure*, too. We just *had* to have working cannons . . . had to make it all look good . . ."

"How are things here? Tyler? Annie?"

"Letitia's a good nurse, but she's no surgeon," Kelly said. "Annie's lungs took a beating from the smoke, and with the burns, she's almost sure to get an infection. Doc isn't saying much, but I look at his legs and I wonder about gangrene or who knows what else. If we can't get them to a proper hospital, they're going to die."

"*Could* we make it to Kingston?" Steve studied the *Adventure,* which was moored at the end of the dock. "She's got a good engine, and the sails aren't just for show. If everyone cooperated, I think we could man her. Dangerous, though. We have no way of contacting other ships or the harbor patrol, and, frankly, we don't know what it's like out there. Or what the weather will be like. I don't care for the looks of those clouds."

She followed his gaze and saw that the mare's tails had given way to scudding fish-scale clouds of a dingy rusty-grey against an unhealthy sky. The northwest horizon, visible over the ruins of the fortress, was a dark and ominous blur.

"Fallout? Will we have to deal with fallout, too?" A frustrated cry burst from her. "Aren't things bad enough?"

He slung a companionable arm over her shoulders. "There's not a bloody thing we can do about fallout, love, so I suggest you put it out of your mind."

"Until it starts raining glowing green," Kelly said. "Or acid. That would finish us off. Even if we took shelter, it'd strip the island bare and there goes our fruit, firewood, wild pigs, the works."

"Let's fret about that if and when it comes," Steve said. "Don't take on more than you have to."

"This from the guy who put me in charge."

"It's only natural. The players are used to you telling them what to do. So are those of us left on the production end."

"Because I deliver my father's orders. What if, when he wakes up, he wants to do something different?"

"Kelly." He waited until she was looking at him, into his serious eyes. "If it came to it, more of us would be willing to listen to you than to him. You're out here working, trying to do what's best, trying to help and do your share. He isn't. That's going to make a difference in the way people see him."

"Mutiny, Mr. Quinlan? I don't want it to come to that."

"No one does. I'm only saying 'if.' You'll have our support."

"Thanks, Steve. I guess."

"Now give me a smile, love. A real one. Better yet, a kiss."

Kelly blinked at him, not sure if she'd heard him correctly. "Excuse me?"

"Bad policy to not keep a professional distance between oneself and one's co-workers. Particularly the boss' daughter. But that's changed now,

213

hasn't it? We're off the clock. Possibly for good. Wouldn't you agree?"

"Um . . . well, yeah."

"I could do with a kiss about now, Kelly love, and I think you could, too. Unless I'm mistaken?"

She slid her arms around his neck and pulled his head down so she could press her lips to his. As they kissed, she felt him smile, and when they parted, he spoke softly into her ear.

"I take it I wasn't mistaken at that."

"No," Kelly said. "No, you weren't."

*   *   *

Chapter 44

Fools. Cowards. Traitors.

Burt Dagget, hungover but grimly determined, crept through the sleeping town.

The others thought he'd drunk himself into a coma, and that he would not move under his own power until well into the morning.

Fine. Let them think that.

He had a job to do.

His first stop was the garage, where he gathered the tools he'd need for the task at hand. Then, after a careful look around to be sure he was still unobserved, he crossed the marketplace to the dock and hurried to the gangplank of the *Adventure.*

The ship was silent and empty. It stirred with the gentle motion of the tide, a rising-and-falling like the breathing of an aquatic giant. Dagget knew the ship inside and out, like the back of his hand, and had no trouble making his way even in darkness to the lower level.

To the hold. To the engine room.

He hated to do it, he really did. The ship was a thing of beauty, another of the fruits of his creativity made real.

"Sometimes sacrifices have to be made," he said, looking over the complicated machinery for its vulnerable spots. "Sometimes, to save the whole, you have to give up a few parts."

Burt worked quickly, his hands sure despite nausea and a vise-grip of a

215

headache.

Leave the island? Give up? Cut and run?

Not Burt Dagget.

And not anyone else, either. He'd see to that.

* * *

Chapter 45

He had hurt them, hurt them quite badly indeed.

Smythe was pleased.

They were bound to leave now. They had to know that the island was no welcome refuge for them, only a place of suffering and death.

His treasure would be safe. He'd taken a new man into his crew, a crippled one but what of it? Many a ship had gone a-sea with a maimed cook or carpenter. This one, this living one, would serve to guard them while the spirits of the skulls rested. It took much to raise them, and he could not maintain them for long.

Nor could he keep up such a pace. He was not so young as once he'd been. The days of his hot-blooded youth were far and long behind. He felt an ancient weariness in his dry bones and wanted nothing more than to settle undisturbed in his cave.

The new man sat at the opening, his leg stretched out in front of him. The leather straps were old and worn, and the carved wooden peg they secured to the stump of his leg was weathered. Still, it would serve. The end was capped with good iron, and the man would soon have the knack of balancing upon it.

None of the others had been willing to sign. The Articles, a standard pledge among the brethren of the sea, were his to choose to offer or withhold as he saw fit.

For was he not the captain? His ship might lie in waterlogged disrepair at

the bottom of the island's deepest cove, the sails rotted away to shreds, corals and sea lichens growing along the hull and railings. His crew might be dead, and his proud black flag torn down, but he was still the captain.

He crossed the cave, moving slowly over the sandy floor and minding his steps that he not upset the semicircle of skulls. At the back, where the woman and the child were entwined, he lowered his frail body to a sitting position. The knobs of his spine leaned against the oak boards of the chest.

The new man would keep watch while the captain slept.

*　　*　　*

Chapter 46

Morning came sullen and murky. The grimy-looking clouds of the previous evening had thickened into a featureless grey-brown mass. No rain had come yet, but lightning flared in the distance and the air had a smoggy, unpleasantly humid flavor.

The heap of rubble where the fortress had been was still smoldering in spots. Karl had spent most of the previous day creeping over the tumbled stone walls, placing his feet with care because one wrong move might have set off an avalanche.

He knew it was dangerous, and probably useless as well. It went against his training because he shouldn't be out here attempting any sort of rescue without proper safety equipment and backup. But none of those things were forthcoming, and if there was a chance, however slim, that someone might be alive down there, he owed it to them to do his best.

When he woke to that fuming brown daylight, he lingered long enough to wolf down a quick breakfast of eggs and milk – they had to eat those first, Kelly said when she'd brought them over from the tavern's refrigerator, because otherwise they'd go bad and have to be thrown out – before resuming his futile search.

Dale and Jimmy, later risers, ambled over to see what he was doing.

"Stay back," he said. "It's tricky underfoot."

"We want to help," Jimmy said.

"You can help by staying back," Karl said. "Or find something else to do."

"There's nothing for us to do," Dale said. "Ambrose is helping Kelly and Sarah organize the stuff we collected yesterday, Tala's assisting Letitia with the patients, Mike and Samantha are hauling water, and Steve's fiddling around over at the garage. Something about gas tanks, and filling the small ones instead of letting the big one sit there and wait to be blown up."

"Yeah, by the crazy killer," Jimmy said.

"What about Dagget?" Karl asked.

"Spent the night passed out in the tavern and woke up nursing a head-splitting hangover, by the look," Dale said. He bent over and picked up an object from under a chunk of wall, and dropped it when he saw that it was a framed picture of someone's family.

"I think we ought to be making weapons," Jimmy said. "I haven't seen Captain Kelly or Mr. Quinlan there passing around the firearms to the rest of us, you know? If that killer does show up, I want to be able to fight back."

Karl pried up a section of interior paneling and looked at a pile of videocassettes, most melted into their black plastic cases, and trailing loops of shriveled tape like intestines. "Who's this killer supposed to be, anyway?"

"Sarah told me it's a ghost," Dale said. "The vengeful ghost of an English pirate captain who buried his swag on the island and then was shot to death by the Spaniards."

"Yeah, sure it is," Karl said.

"It could be one of them," Jimmy said. "We know it can't be one of us, since we were on our beach the whole time, but what if it's one of them? Who maybe just *thinks* he's a ghost. Or the reincarnation of the pirate captain. Or a descendant. That guy Quinlan's English, maybe it's him."

"Maybe it's Dagget himself for all we know," Dale said. "Not the point."

"There's a point?" Karl moved on gingerly. He could see the oblong box of what had to be an elevator car.

"The point is, we can sit here and blue-sky guess all we want and it won't make any difference. We've got to keep our eyes open and be ready."

"Which is why I'd be happier with a weapon," Jimmy said.

The elevator doors were closed, but the black rubber lips of them had run like tallow and left a half-inch gap. Karl inserted the end of the crowbar he'd requisitioned and pulled. He didn't think he'd be able to get it after all, and then the doors opened and something crispy fell out.

Dale shouted and jumped back. Jimmy kept his poker face, but he'd gone sallow. Karl tried to swallow past a click in his throat.

The dead man hadn't so much been burned as he'd been baked to beyond well-done. The metal elevator car must have been like an oven.

"Did we need any more proof that they weren't putting us on?" Karl asked, more to himself than the others.

"It's more than enough for me," Dale said in a weak voice. He sat down at the edge of the heap of debris and propped his head in his hands. "This is more than any of us bargained for."

"A half million isn't worth this," Jimmy said.

"Oh, hey," Dale said in sudden dismay. "You don't think the money was in there too, do you?"

"In here? In the fortress?" Karl asked. "If it was, it's gone now."

"No," Jimmy said. "It was supposed to be buried on the island. In a treasure chest, see? The winner'd get a map and have to follow it, dig up the prize. But who cares? What good is it to anyone now? The way Kelly's been talking, money's useless now. Even if we could get out of here, it's not like we'd be buying new cars and vacation houses in Malibu."

"It's gold, though," Dale said. "Half a million in gold. That's got to be worth something to someone somewhere."

The two of them seemed pathetically eager to have changed the subject away from the dead man in the elevator. Karl lowered a section of paneling onto the corpse and edged carefully closer to Dale and Jimmy. As he went, he crossed a sunken place strewn with half-charred books, charts, and pieces of paper. Letters of Marque that would remain undelivered, he realized. He picked up some to examine them.

The last one in the stack wasn't a Letter of Marque at all. It was a map. Purposefully aged and yellowed, then singed around the edges either by the same deliberate hand or as a result of the explosion.

"Something like this?" He held it out to Jimmy.

"Yeah, I bet this is it. See here? X marks the spot." Jimmy tapped it with his fingertip. "Right here's where the gold is."

"Let's go get it," Dale said.

"Weren't you listening, man? What's the use?"

"It's half a million dollars."

"That we couldn't spend," Karl said. "That doesn't belong to us."

"Are you telling me that you don't think one of the three of us would have won the game?" Dale asked. "Get real, Karl. It would have been one of us."

"That doesn't matter now," Jimmy said. "The game's done."

"I'll do it myself, then." Dale reached for the map and Jimmy whisked it away. "Give it over."

"Knock it off, Dale," Karl said. "Jimmy's right. What's the use? In case you haven't been paying attention, we're stranded on this island and the rest

of the world is going up in smoke. Food and water, shelter and defense, those are what's important now."

"Okay, fine, sheesh. It's just stupid to let it sit there."

"You got somewhere to go?" Jimmy asked.

"It's Dagget's money anyway," Karl said, seeing Dale start to pout. "Dagget's, or his sponsors'. They're not about to let you stroll off with it."

"Forget it. Forget I ever brought it up."

Kelly Dagget called their names. She was waving them over.

"Should we tell her about the . . ." Jimmy nodded at the elevator.

"I'll handle it," Karl said.

Jimmy threw the map aside and they joined Kelly and the others in the middle of what had once been Rum Town's market square. Even Burt Dagget himself had put in an appearance, holding his head as though he was afraid it would roll off his neck and splatter on the cobblestones like an overripe Halloween pumpkin. He was wearing a loose shirt that must have been made with Mike Glass in mind, for although Burt Dagget was a beefy man, it hung on him in drapes and folds.

Thunder rumbled, closer now, and a few spots of rain darkened the dusty ground. The raindrops looked greasy, more like runoff from a pan used to fry cheap meat than clean water. It smelled bad, too. A bitter, oily, foul smell. When a drop of it landed on the back of Karl's hand, it stung. He wiped it away with revulsion.

"Let's get inside, under cover," Kelly said.

"Acid rain?" Sarah asked, fearfully regarding the sky.

"Inside," Kelly said again.

They filed into the clothiers' shop, their ragged band of castaways caught in a game turned all too real. Burt Dagget was glowering silently at nothing, but when Steve Quinlan, the last one in, stepped through the door, Dagget's lip curled back from his upper teeth in a definite snarl.

Seeing that, Karl's adrenaline went on alert. Dagget either already knew or was just figuring out what the rest of them now knew about Steve and Kelly. And by the looks of it, the news didn't make him happy.

"As we all know," Kelly said, "we've got a serious problem here. We need to decide, as a group, what we want to do next. Do we stay on the island and make the best of things? Or do we try to leave?"

She laid it out for them with a frank honesty that at the same time somehow managed to be gentle. The supplies, the condition of the injured, everything.

"What makes you think we'll be able to get to anyplace better?" Ambrose asked. "Or if there's even anywhere to go?"

"We have to try!" Sarah cried, making Ambrose recoil. "If we don't do something, my mother will die! We can't stand here doing nothing."

"There is one more thing," Steve said. "When Samantha and I were out yesterday, we tried the car radio. Most of what we picked up was static and dead airwaves, but we did hear some broadcasts. Voices."

"Let's hear it," Karl said.

Steve obliged by bringing out a portable, battery-operated radio that had been in the back room of the doctor's office. He extended the antenna to its fullest and turned the radio on. A loud hiss of static made them flinch. He swiveled the knob slowly, moving the red line down the row of numbers.

As he'd said, it was mostly static and empty gaps of dead air. But here and there, surfacing through white noise like fat in a skillet, they could hear garbled, faraway voices. He stopped on the clearest one, a man jabbering urgently in rapid-fire Spanish.

Jimmy listened the most intently, his ear almost on the speaker. He scowled and chewed his lip, and finally straightened up. He had lost the vestiges of his tough-young-punk demeanor and was visibly shaken, upset.

"I couldn't get most of it," he said. "I think it was out of Florida, though."

"Florida!" Dale perked up. "An Orlando station?"

"I don't know. He was saying something about fires in the sky, and he sounded sick."

Everyone contemplated this in silence, and then Kelly spoke up again.

"From the news we got when we still had satellite hookup, it sounds like lots of people are getting sick out there. If there's plague, contagion, biological weapons . . . those things might not be able to reach us here."

"If they're talking about airborne viruses," Letitia said, "and they're blowing junk into the atmosphere with their damn bombs, we're not any safer here than we would be someplace else."

"But there are other survivors," Kelly said. "Other places that may be in good shape. If we were to load all our supplies onto the *Adventure*, we could theoretically make it as far as Jamaica or one of the other islands. We might find a hospital, get help."

Rational discussion ended at that point. Some were arguing in favor of prudence, of staying here where they were safe — relatively safe anyway — rather than risk bad weather, deadly plague, and the possibility of failure. Others wanted to try and go no matter the cost, blindly sure that if they could make it to their homes, they'd find their families all right.

Karl couldn't stand to think about that. San Diego, near so many military bases, would have been high on the list of targets once the nukes started

223

flying. He was divorced, his long and irregular hours having been too much for his wife to put up with, but she still lived nearby, with custody of their kids. He would have given anything to know that Karl Jr. and Katrina were all right, but what good would it do them to get himself killed trying to find out?

"If we're going to die anyway," Letitia said, raising her voice stridently, "better to do it trying to get home to our loved ones! I say we go. We pack up that ship and go. That way, if we do die, it'll at least mean something."

Sarah Parkins broke down in a crying fit. She beat her hands on the nearest counter, wailing that they were all going to die anyway, the pirate curse would claim them all.

Dale, who was nearest to her, patted her uncertainly on the back and sent pleading looks for help around the room.

Karl, seeing that no one else knew what to do, stepped up and smacked the girl sharply across the face.

Her tears and wails cut off as if he'd thrown a lever. She stared at him, enormous watery eyes and a trembling mouth, and a crimson handprint blotching her cheek. When her tears resumed, they were quiet, and she slid down the corner of the wall to sit huddled on the floor, hugging herself and weeping softly.

Letitia looked at Karl with a peculiar expression that both scolded him, and thanked him. She knelt beside Sarah and, murmuring soothing nonsense, gathered the girl to her ample bosom. Sarah clung to her and cried.

"Tish is right," Jimmy said. "We're screwed either way. We might as well try."

"How about we put it to a vote?" Kelly suggested.

"How about not?" Burt Dagget, who hadn't said a word since the impromptu meeting began, stood up from where he'd been leaning against the wall. His overlarge shirt flapped, and the scent of old rum hung around him like a wreath. "You haven't given me my say, *punkin.*"

"Dad —"

"We are not leaving this island. I've seen to that. We are not abandoning what we've worked so hard to build."

"Take a look around you," Tala said. "What you've built is in ashes. I have a little girl at home."

"Burt, it's for the best," Steve said. "We'll do no one any good by staying, and if we —"

"I've heard about enough out of you, Quinlan. You think I'm an idiot? A used-up old fool who doesn't notice what's going on behind his back? You and Kelly, you'd love to see me fail so you could take over. You're already

planning the publicity, aren't you? When you *rescue* —" He made the quote marks in mid air, a habit that Karl had always found loathsome and oh-so-Hollywood, "— all these poor people from Dagget's greatest blunder. You can't wait to tell the press how I endangered their lives and brought about the deaths of so many others, but you were able to save the rest."

"That isn't at all true, Burt."

"Dad, don't do this. No one is trying to make you look bad."

"Oh, I don't need any help in *that* regard, is that it?" He laughed and leveled a finger at Kelly. "*You* blew up my fortress. I understand now. You and him, in on it from the beginning. What a shame I wasn't inside, huh? I could have been out of your way once and for all."

Kelly looked like she, rather than Sarah, was the one who'd been slapped in the face. "Blow up the . . . I would never . . ."

"You and him. Arranging the whole thing. You're the killers, the two of you!"

"But he was with —" Samantha began.

"Yesssss, I'd expect their accomplices to back them up," Dagget said, eyeing her with crafty little rat's eyes. "You've done a fine job getting rid of everyone else."

"That's it, Dad. No more," Kelly said. "You don't know what you're saying."

"I know how to get back what's mine. Quinlan!"

"Yes, Burt?"

"We'll make this fair." Dagget bent his arm behind his back, under the loose shirt. A pistol was tucked into the waistband of his pants. He drew it.

The front room of the clothiers' shop was small, and yet somehow the dozen people found space to draw back against the walls, leaving a clearing in the middle. Dagget stood at one end of this space, staring at Steve Quinlan over the top of the flared barrel of the old-fashioned gun.

"A duel," Dagget said. "Ten paces, turn, and fire. Not with paint pellets, oh, no. Oh, no! This is the real thing, Quinlan."

"No!" Kelly sprang between them. "Dad, stop. You don't want to hurt Steve, and he doesn't want to hurt you."

"I warned him what would happen if he laid a hand on my daughter. That was bad enough. But this? This is mutiny! He's trying to take over what's mine. So are you, Kelly, but I'm more willing to give you a second chance. Outside, Quinlan. Now."

*　　*　　*

Chapter 47

Tyler Brookstone heard the commotion from elsewhere in town but it made as little impact on his thoughts as did the steady, thick patter of the rain.

The wheelchair, metal prison in which he'd be spending the short rest of his life, trundled slowly across the room. Both legs jutted out stiffly in front of him, leading the way. The left wasn't so bad. The right, well, that was another story.

He didn't need to see to know. The smell told him all. The pestilent smell of gangrene. It was in him already.

Amputation might have been able to forestall the inevitable. But the very idea was ludicrous. Trying to talk one nurse and a handful of untutored civilians through the procedure? It might have been possible on another patient. Not on himself. What would he do? Use his clumsy left hand to assist?

The morphine had already stopped taking the edge off of his pain. He wasn't entirely sure how long it had been since the helicopter crash, a few days maybe, not nearly long enough for the drugs to have lost their effectiveness or his body to build up a tolerance. The pain was too huge, and stemming from so many sources that it was impossible to manage.

The cabinet was ajar. Letitia had left it that way, given how many time she was in and out of there to fetch painkillers for Tyler and for Annie. Security didn't seem like such a big deal at the moment. Normally, of course, it would have been kept locked up tighter than an HMO's billing department.

He found what he was looking for, precisely where he expected it to be.

That part was easy. Juggling the vial and the hypodermic was another matter.

Eventually, though, persistence paid off. Tyler chuckled to find himself actually being mindful of air bubbles in the syringe. A bit silly, under the circumstances.

"First, do no harm," he said. He laid the syringe in his lap and toggled the switch to steer his chair to the bed holding Annie Parkins.

She was unconscious, mercifully. The burns were bad enough to be exquisite agony. Scarlet-red skin was all taut and shiny over swollen subcutaneous tissues. Blisters seeped and oozed clear fluid. The lightest covering, even a single sheet, would have been too much for her to bear.

Her hands were the worst, but, ironically, would cause her the least pain. Third-degree burns left the nerves as dead and black as shorted-out wiring. The fingers were hooked into claws around a no-longer-present clipboard, and swaddled in gauze.

Ann's breathing was slow and measured. A slight hissing came from the oxygen tank at the side of her bed. Clear tubing ran from the valve of the tank, branching to enter her nostrils. Another tube had been funneled down her throat, preventing her smoke-damaged trachea from swelling entirely shut and pinching off her air.

Her face was unfamiliar, a doll's face surmounted by a blistered scalp from which most of the hair had been burned away. A few singed strands remained, like parched desert plants.

His clumsy left hand wrapped around the hypodermic.

"This won't hurt a bit," he said, as all doctors did with the bluff and hearty assurance of being the one on the other end of the needle.

She didn't respond, not even when he slid the point under her skin and found the vein. He depressed the plunger halfway, only halfway, for this was potent stuff and he had another use for the rest of it.

No immediate change came over Ann. Her breathing remained steady for several beats, then quickened into a series of short gasps. Her eyelids, minus their lashes, fluttered but did not quite open. Then, with a sigh, she relaxed and was still.

Tyler removed the needle. He could have drawn a fresh one, but it was too much trouble. Like with checking for air bubbles, it seemed needlessly silly. Cross-contamination was the least of his worries. He didn't bother with swabbing the site with alcohol, either.

He prodded his left leg above the end of the cast, finding the femoral artery pumping away, pumping fast. Although outwardly he was sedate, maintaining the calm appearance that had seen him through many a challenging

surgery, he knew that on the inside, the excitement was running through his body.

Good. It'd speed the drug on its way.

Won't hurt a bit? That was a lie.

The silvery, piercing sting made him suck in a breath. His hand shook and wiggled the needle where it went into him. A bead of blood appeared, swelled into a glimmering ruby of surface tension, and then broke into a trickling roll down his thigh.

He depressed the plunger. The contents of the syringe mixed into his bloodstream. He pulled out the needle and let it fall to the floor, absently pushing with his thumb on the little entry wound.

Another silly precaution. Did it matter if he bled? He wouldn't bleed for long.

Soon, the drug he'd injected into his system would complete the course and reach his heart. He'd be . . .

*　*　*

Chapter 48

Connie Berkwelter, holding a wide palm frond over her head in an unsuccessful attempt to ward off the biting, stinging, dirty rain, stopped when she saw the tableau in the middle of Rum Town.

She was tired and hungry, and sore all over. Some places more than others. She'd spent a terrible night in the jungle. Her shoulders still hurt from swinging the branch, her stomach was all scraped, and she couldn't walk straight for the used and battered ache between her legs.

The scents of blood and sour sweat attracted bugs by the teeming hundreds. She swatted them, waved them off with the same frond she also held as a half-assed umbrella.

With the morning, if something so dismal could be called a morning, she'd known that she had to go back to the others. She'd think of something. Some story to tell them. They'd have to believe her and take her back in. She could tell them that B.J. had forced her to go along with him, against her will. She hadn't really wanted to leave.

Yeah. They'd buy that.

The rain began as she was walking toward town. The stuff was nasty. It tingled on contact, it tasted like coffee grounds steeped in battery acid, and it left discolorations on her clothes. She went on regardless, wanting a roof over her head and something to eat. The hardtack at which she'd turned up her nose back at Dead Man's Cove was now an image that made her stomach growl.

Now she'd finally reached the town, and instead of being inside out of the rain like sensible people, her former crewmates and everybody else were milling around in front of the clothiers'. Most of them were ducking under eaves or trying to find makeshift cover of their own, but one, a sturdy figure she recognized as Burt Dagget, stood stolidly in the middle of the street. He was holding something against his leg.

A gun?

Yes, it was a gun, one of those lame paintball dueling pistols. Another was in the hands of the dark-haired British guy, Quinlan. He was a specimen that Connie wouldn't have minded taking to bed, not that sex with anyone was much on her mind right now. And not that it would have been allowed. The terms of the contracts they'd signed said that relations between players was fine, encouraged even, but the staff was off-limits.

The redheaded bitch, Kelly Dagget, was shouting at her father but Connie couldn't hear her over the rustling of the rain in the leaves. She kept trying to get in front of Quinlan, but he pushed her aside and addressed Dagget himself.

Dagget waved the gun. His face was red, and with his stocky build he looked weirdly like B.J. for a second. Just another bull moose, another caveman, full of strutting macho bullshit and trying to prove his place at the top of the pack.

Connie worked her way closer, holding the frond over her head. Rainwater ran over her fingers, down her wrists, leaving stinging little trails. She was almost to the ruins of the fortress, almost to the garage. A half-open door in the latter beckoned and she stepped inside where she could keep an eye on the events unfolding in the street but also be out of the rain.

Such a relief just to lower her aching arms! The right one was pure torture, the elbow a stiff and swollen mass where Tala had driven it against the hinge of the joint.

The garage was a dry and welcome haven after the jungle. Connie leaned against the door jamb, cradling her right arm. The shadows would hide her from the others, while giving her a clear view of whatever the hell they were up to.

She found that out a split second later when Dagget fired. The report of the gunshot was far louder than any paintball toy, and the wetness that splashed in a fan from Quinlan's body was anything but fluorescent pink paint.

*   *   *

Chapter 49

Steve was faster on the draw, but Burt Dagget knew the Brit was a coward at heart when it came to pulling the trigger. Scheming behind a man's back was one thing, shooting him face to face was something altogether different. Something that took guts, that took good old all-American balls.

Dagget's shot tore flatly through the air. He experienced a sudden surge of vindicated satisfaction as the treacherous bastard danced backward, blood flying, the impact spinning him around.

Amid that satisfaction, shock and horror woke up deep in him. Had he really done that? Shot Steve Quinlan? He could hardly believe it.

A moment of sharp clarity cut through the haze of rum and paranoia, making Burt recoil. He would have dropped the gun, would have run to Steve to help him and apologize, but they moved on him. Mike, Karl Werner, Samantha. They moved on him, rushing him, and he knew that they wouldn't understand. There wouldn't be time for them to understand. They'd pummel him senseless and ask questions later.

So he brought the gun to bear on them. A traditional flintlock would have required lengthy reloading but these held ten-shot clips.

"Wait," he said. "Wait, I can —"

He fired again, into the sky, hoping to make them stop where they were. It worked, and the wariness in their eyes did him a world of good.

"Drop it, Dad," Kelly said.

"Kelly. Kelly, listen to me."

She was aiming her own gun at him. At *him!* His own daughter. Her face was white as a clown's mask under the spray of freckles. Her eyes were wide and frantic. But her hands were steady.

"Drop it right now."

"Kelly." He lowered his gun, though already that moment of clarity was fogging over again with his fury at her. She'd rebelled before, defied him before, but this! In front of his people!

Out of the corner of his eye, he saw Samantha make her move. She came in low, hands raised in some sort of martial arts pose. Dagget reacted instinctively and swept the barrel of the pistol at her face. He meant to clout her, lay her cheek open, but somehow he squeezed the trigger. Her pantherlike charge turned into a rag-doll tumble and she landed at his feet with half her head blown off.

"Back off! Back off, damn you." He shifted from her to Mike and Karl, both big targets. They were on Kelly's side, all of them, it was too obvious. He should have figured it out long before now.

"Don't, Mr. Duh-Dagget." Mike stepped toward him. His huge hands were spread, ready to grab.

"I'll shoot you, Mike, I will. I'd hate to, but I will if you force me." His voice was wound tight, on the breaking point. "This is my show, hear me? Mine. I'm not going to let anyone take it away from me, if I have to shoot you all."

His finger tightened again on the trigger.

He heard Kelly say, "God help me," and then heard the shot. Something that felt like a padded sledgehammer hit him in the chest and his feet flew out from under him. His back slammed down on cobblestones.

Rain, lukewarm and bitter-brown as dregs of tea, pattered onto his face. He could taste it. The taste of failure, of defeat.

Then Kelly was there, bending over him, crying, her clean salty tears mixing with the raindrops.

"Dad, no, oh God, I'm sorry!"

Funny how all it took was a little rain to wash away the fog. He saw everything, now that it was too late.

"Kel . . . ly . . ."

"Please, no! Dad!"

He wanted to speak to her. Had so many things to tell her.

But it was too much effort. He'd tell her later. First, he needed a nap.

Burt Dagget closed his eyes.

*   *   *

Chapter 50

"I can't. I can't. Letitia, I'm going to faint." Ambrose Matthews reeled at the sight of the blood, so much blood.

It was one thing to be told that people were dead. Or to see the after-the-fact injuries that the doctor and the supply woman had suffered. But to have to witness people shot right in front of him? Mere yards away? He balked. Down deep in his soul. He just flat-out *balked.*

"You need to help me or this man's going to die," Letitia said.

"Nonsense," Steve Quinlan said faintly from the ground. "I'm feeling quite chipper."

"Hush, now. You're losing a lot of blood. We've got to get it under control. Ambrose, you fold that up and you lean on it, hear?"

His head was light, his ears filled with a high-pitched ringing. The activity all around him — Mike and Tala attempting to subdue a hysterical Kelly Dagget, Sarah and Dale running toward the doctor's office, Karl kneeling by Samantha, Jimmy standing guard over Burt Dagget as if he expected him to revive like the star of a slasher film — seemed to be happening in the background, white noise, something taking place on a television that was tuned to a channel no one was watching.

"I can't —"

She pinched his ear, sudden drilling pain like the sting of a wasp. "You can and you better."

"Best do as she says, mate," Steve said. "I think she means it."

"You, I said, hush."

Letitia's capable hands snatched the cloth from Ambrose and folded it double, then double again, until it was a dense pad. She put the pad against the wound in Steve's shoulder. Taking Ambrose by the wrist, none too gently, she pushed his hand into place.

Ambrose tried to pull away. She wouldn't let go. He could already feel, or imagine he felt, the blood seeping through. Touching his skin. Maybe getting into him through the cuts and scrapes he'd gotten. Steve didn't look like he had weird diseases, but you couldn't tell, could you? No, you never could tell. Here they were with no gloves or anything. And Letitia a nurse, who should have known better. They could be infecting themselves right this very minute.

"Bullet went clean through," she told Steve. "Missed the bone, so count yourself lucky for that."

"I'm finding it rather hard to count myself lucky at the moment."

"You're alive, aren't you? We're going to keep you that way, too."

"Is Kelly all right?"

Letitia paused and looked over her shoulder. Ambrose automatically did too. Kelly was nearly lost in Mike Glass' tree-trunk arms, her feet held a good six inches off the ground to prevent her from throwing herself on her father's body. She had stopped the terrible keening caterwaul, and her struggles were feebler, but Ambrose still didn't think she could be called 'all right' by any stretch.

"She's doing fine," Letitia said. It was a nurse tone if Ambrose had ever heard one, so comforting that it was impossible to doubt.

A fresh scream, just as Kelly had quieted down, pealed from the direction of the doctor's office. It ended in the sharp sound of a slap.

"No more," Jimmy Hernandez said. "No more, I can't take any more . . ." He added something in street Spanish that might have been a prayer.

"Karl?" Letitia asked calmly.

"Yeah?"

His reply was equally calm, and Ambrose had a moment of fierce envy for them. They'd seen and done stuff like this before, trauma nurses and firefighters, people who hadn't spent their lives at home living in their parents' basements.

"What's her status?"

"Dead. Instantly. No chance."

"All right then. Leave her be, and go check on Sarah and Dale. I need that stretcher."

Steve mumbled something about being able to walk. He was fading, and now Ambrose knew that the damp on his hands wasn't rainwater, wasn't his own sweat. When he lifted his hands away, he'd see the blood staining the lines of his palms.

Karl rushed off. There was no need to ask about Dagget, who plainly didn't need a guard, but rather than come over and help, take over for Ambrose so he could run and scour his hands – maybe dunk them in bleach or disinfectant into the bargain – Jimmy stayed where he was and kept praying.

Mike brought Kelly over. Not carrying her, the way a little kid might carry a teddy bear, but shepherding her and using his body to block her sight of her father and Samantha. Tala trailed behind Mike, looking like a sleepwalker caught in a nightmare from which there was no waking.

"Tell me he's going to live," Kelly said. "Please, Letitia."

"I'm going to do my best, don't you worry."

"How did it come to this?" Kelly looked from face to face. "I never thought he'd really . . . but he did. He shot Steve, and he shot Samantha. If I'd been quicker, I might have saved her but . . . but he was my *father!*"

"You did what you had to do," Mike said, still preventing her from glancing at the bodies.

Steve stirred, and some focus returned to his eyes. "Kelly."

"Oh, Steve. I'm so sorry. I don't know what happened to him. He . . . he went crazy."

"Come down here a minute, love."

"Don't you take that pressure off," Letitia said to Ambrose.

The cloth was turning red, sopping with blood, but he nodded.

Kelly knelt opposite Ambrose. Steve's free hand, the one not attached to the shoulder with the hole in it, found hers.

"If you hadn't done it," he said, "more people would have died. You saved our lives. You made the hardest choice."

"That's enough," Letitia said. "Save your strength. Where is that stretcher?"

Karl appeared as if on cue, carrying a stretcher under one arm. He motioned for Ambrose to scoot around to Steve's head, and set the stretcher on the ground.

"Where are Dale and Sarah?" Tala asked. "What was that scream?"

"The doctor's dead," Karl said, his lips a grim line. "So's the Parkins woman. A mercy killing and then a suicide, it looks like. His hand was still on the syringe."

"Annie? Tyler Brookstone?" Kelly asked. "No, not them too."

Karl nodded. "The girl found them. Dale's with her. She's taking it pretty

badly."

"None of us are going to get out of this alive, are we?" Ambrose asked. "We may as well give up."

"I won't hear any talk like that," Letitia said. "We're still alive and we're going to stay that way. Including Mr. Quinlan, here. It's a shame, but the doctor knew his own condition better than anybody and if he thought there was no hope, he did the brave thing to spare himself needless suffering."

"I thought you were a nurse," Jimmy said. "What about valuing life?"

"What about dying with dignity?" Karl said. "We treat our pets better than our loved ones sometimes. When our dog was old and blind and failing, we had him put down. My grandfather spent the last four years of his life wasting away, not knowing who he was or recognizing any of his family, in pain all the time, and all they'd tell us was that we had to wait and let nature take its course."

"We can argue about that later." Letitia, who'd fallen all to pieces yesterday, was brisk and in control now that she had her profession to fall back on. "Karl, Jimmy, you take his legs. Ambrose, steady his head and keep that pad on his shoulder. When I count three, we're going to roll him to the right. Tala, you slip that stretcher under him as far as you can. Then we'll lower him back down. Ready?"

They took their assigned positions. Letitia counted, and when she reached three, they rolled Steve Quinlan onto his right side. The pad shifted but Ambrose pushed it hard against the man's shoulder, never minding Quinlan's groan. Tala put the stretcher in place.

"Easy as pie," Steve said, though his face was the color of curdled milk, with sweat standing out on his brow.

"We have to get him out of the rain," Letitia said. "The rest of us, too. I doubt it's very good for us."

"Is it poison? Radioactive?" Jimmy asked, swiping his palm down his arm and looking in revulsion at the murky streams that dripped from him.

Nobody had an answer for that one, not that they were willing to say. Under Letitia's direction, they got Steve's stretcher into the doctor's office. There, they saw what Sarah had already seen – the wheelchair-bound body of Doctor Brookstone slumped to the side, the lethal injection he'd self-administered still sticking out of his leg. In the bed, Ann Parkins was a lifeless mannequin. Sarah had her head buried on Dale's shoulder, crying her eyes out.

"Karl, could you wheel the doctor on out of here?" Letitia asked, laying out a suture kit. "We're going to need more space."

"What should I do with him?" Karl directed that one to Kelly.

"How should I know? Stash him somewhere, and put my father and Samantha with him." Her voice spiraled toward a shriek. "We've got more dead than alive on this damned island anyway. What do we do? Bury them all? It's the decent thing to do but right now I'm a little more concerned about keeping the rest of us in one piece!"

"We'll f-find a puh-place," Mike said.

He and Karl left, Karl pushing the wheelchair and Mike gathering Ann's body into his arms. After a moment's hesitation, Jimmy and Tala followed.

"You can go, too, Ambrose," Letitia said. "Thank you. You did fine."

Ambrose smiled wanly and hoped that they couldn't see through to his real reaction. He let go of the pad and turned his hands over. As he'd feared, a thick reddish smear obscured the lines of his palms.

"What about us?" Dale asked. He'd divested himself of the sobbing girl, but she followed him like an imprinted duckling. "Can we help?"

"Sarah, you know where everything in here is, right?" Letitia asked.

"Yes," she said, wiping her eyes. "My mom —"

"And you're a seamstress so you know your way around a needle. Can you help me stitch him up? I need you to be strong, girl, okay? Your momma's not hurting anymore, and she'd want you to do your best to help out."

"Okay." She sounded steadier.

Ambrose, meanwhile, had made a beeline to the sink in the corner. He scrubbed his hands until the suds quit coming up pinkish-red, rinsed them again and again under water as hot as he could stand. He might have done that for the rest of the day, if Kelly Dagget hadn't reached past him and turned off the tap.

"What's in the tanks is all we've got, and there won't be electricity to heat any more. We'll be able to make do with the creek and fires, but save what's left in the hot water heaters for them so they can get Steve patched up."

"Right. Sorry." Ambrose gulped and looked at his hands. They seemed clean, but . . .

"Are you okay?" Dale asked Kelly. "You look like hell."

"Okay? Why wouldn't I be? I just shot my own father! I feel like I'm cracking up, sure, you bet I am, but if I can't hold it together, we're sunk." She tittered, a laugh perhaps meant to reassure them but instead one that only sent shivers up Ambrose's spine.

"Take her on out of here," Letitia said. "Dale, Ambrose, go on. Sarah and I can handle this."

Dale grabbed a bunch of what Ambrose first took to be plastic trash can

liners from a large, flat, cardboard box. Upon closer inspection, they turned out to be white plastic bags with the red biohazard symbol emblazoned on the sides. He swiftly fashioned them into slickers and hoods. "We can use these like raincoats," he explained.

Ambrose felt like an idiot with a plastic bag draped over his head. The rain was all over them anyway. What was the saying? Closing the barn door after the horse ran off? Still, when the three of them stepped back outside, and he heard the drops striking the plastic without further wetting his skin, he was glad of the protection.

The bodies of Burt Dagget and Samantha Dressler were gone. Puddles on the cobblestones, rapidly diluting in the rain, showed where they'd been. A door was standing open next door, in the building billed as the "Apothecary." Ambrose knew that to mean roughly the same thing as 'pharmacist' or 'drug-store,' but on the one occasion he'd been in there, all it had stocked were 17th-century remedies. Including a jar of fat leeches and a booklet on their use. The wheelchair, empty now, stood outside the door. They could hear voices coming from inside, discussing how best to arrange the bodies.

"Ambrose! Hey! Ambrose!"

He turned, at first thinking it must be Letitia. Calling him back, wanting him to help with the messy job of sewing up Steve Quinlan. If that was the case, he was going to wear gloves. There'd been a whole shelf of them in varying sizes on the wall of the doctor's office. He might even double-layer them. Or triple-layer. He inspected his hands closely and didn't see any open cuts, just some scabs. But all it took was a pinhole for bacteria and infection to get in.

The voice that was calling him wasn't Letitia's, and came from another direction. He looked around and saw Connie Berkwelter limping toward him. Her clothes were in shreds, she was barefoot, and she looked like she'd been through a meat-grinder.

"Her again," Kelly Dagget said. Rather than angry, she sounded exhausted and resigned, as if she knew she wasn't done shooting people for the day.

"What do you want, Connie?" Dale asked, shouting not only to be heard above the rain but to let everyone else know that they might be getting a second helping of trouble.

"She looks hurt," Ambrose said. "And I don't see B.J."

Connie staggered closer. "He's dead," she said, starting to cry. "B.J.'s dead and the killer almost got me, too."

Kelly's hand, which had begun to stray toward her waist as if she'd for-gotten that she'd flung her gun away, paused. "You saw the killer?"

"He killed B.J.," Connie said. "Beat his brains in with a stick. I would have been next but I got away, fell down a cliff."

Dale's shout had drawn Mike, Karl, Jimmy, and Tala. They clustered in front of the drugstore-turned-morgue, staring at Connie's injuries. The preening pin-up, Miss Veradoga, was gone. What was left was a battered refugee.

"Who was it?" Karl asked.

"It was . . . it was her father," Connie said, averting her gaze and shrinking from Kelly as if she feared a physical rebuke. "Burt Dagget. Burt Dagget killed B.J."

*   *   *

Chapter 51

Smythe slept, and dreamed of times that should have faded into the amber mists of memory but remained as clear and vivid as if they'd happened but a few days before.

In his dreams, he was young and hale and whole again. His old life gone, to be sure, the life of wealth and privilege he'd known as scion of a prestigious family. Their line had fallen on hard times, been mistreated by a vindictive queen, and after his father had been beheaded in the Tower of London on unfounded crimes of treason, Elliot Smythe had taken to the sea.

He'd made it his own, going from a hired-on sailor to a first mate and finally, when he rallied the crew to defeat an attacking French barque after their captain had been shot through the heart by a pistol-ball, to a captaincy of his own.

He had preyed upon all ships with equal fervor and ferocity. It seemed more romantic in retrospect than it had been at the time. The veils of sleep hid the dreary and terrible parts that Smythe did not care to recall.

He did not dream of long days becalmed on a sea that shone like a mirror in the blazing heat of the sun. He did not dream of being adrift in a longboat, the men drawing lots to see who might be killed that the rest might drink of that sailor's blood and live. He did not dream of the failed mutiny near Madagascar.

No, he dreamt of his most glorious adventures. The sacking of towns, and pitched battles all cannons booming and cutlasses clashing on smoky decks.

He dreamt as well of the fateful day when a ship had been spied from

the crow's nest. A fine fat galleon, and their sacking of it had proved to be every pirate's greatest wish. A treasure ship, separated from its fleet by a hurricane. Gold and silver bound for Spain, but landing in the hands of Elliot Smythe instead.

How the crew had rejoiced! How they had anticipated spending their shares in the taverns and whorehouses, squandering a fortune in a few nights' wanton revelry. Rum and women!

Luisa moved through his dreams. Lovely Luisa . . . as he'd first seen her . . . with her dark hair pinned back and her face regal, fearless. She had been his from the start, never forced but always his willing wife.

Those happy dreams darkened into nightmare as he saw in his dozing mind the warship's sails on the horizon, putting an end to their plans of spending their newfound wealth.

He had put it to the crew. Hide their wealth, to return for it when they were free of pursuit? Or risk losing it?

The island . . . the cave.

Smythe knew the customs that dictated a man be left behind, shot dead so that his ghost would remain to guard the place. But he'd sensed even then that he would need each man of his crew alive, if any of them hoped to survive to ever reclaim their treasure.

The unforgiving eye of dream did not soften the images of that last, dismal battle. He saw his ship, holed by cannonballs and foundering over the deepest part of Veradoga's bay . . . the *Good Lady Jane* sinking amid bubbles and flames into the depths. He dreamed again and again of the pistol-shot that had pierced his skin and lodged itself in his kneecap.

They had escaped, some few of his men, as the Spaniards descended upon them with swords waving and pistols roaring. But escape had not proved their salvation. Their wounds or disease had taken them, one by one.

And Luisa, pretty Luisa, had lived only long enough to birth a son whose final breath coincided with her own.

In the end only he was left. Alone among the dead. A captain without a ship or crew. A husband without a wife, a father without a son.

The sleeping, dreaming Smythe shied away from those recollections. He did not want to relive his lonely years. He dreamt again of happier times, and sank into his sleep until he was motionless, unaware of anything but the world within his own mind.

He slept . . . like the dead.

*   *   *

Chapter 52

"It was Burt, then? Always him? Kelly, love, are you sure?"

Steve Quinlan was sitting up in bed. His color was good and his appetite, as proved by the way he was going through the bowl of seafood soup that Kelly had brought him, seemed fully restored. The white of his bandage stood out starkly against the bronze skin and crisp dark hair of his chest.

"It's what Connie says," Kelly said. "I guess that should make me feel better about what I did, but . . . it doesn't. He was still my father."

Sun, tepid and strange as if it was filtered through silty water, but sun all the same, fell through the open window. The rain had passed the night before, leaving Rum Town speckled with stains.

He set aside his empty bowl and took her hand. "Don't blame yourself, love."

"But I should have known something was wrong with Dad! Why didn't I see this coming?" Unable to bear even Steve's comforting touch, Kelly rose and paced the small room.

It had been Doc Brookstone's refuge, a tiny studio apartment at the rear of his office, a place where he could get away from the bustle and noise of Dagget Central if he needed quiet time.

The window showed part of a street and the balcony of Calico Jack's, but did not have a view of where the fortress used to be, or of the apothecary where they were keeping the bodies. Out of sight, but by no means out of mind.

"I knew what kind of stress he was under," she went on. "I thought he was just being temperamental. The classic Dagget stubbornness. Why didn't I *know*, Steve?"

"So you do think it was him?"

"He knew this island better than anyone. He nearly memorized all those books on pirate history. He had all the keys, he had access to the equipment and the helicopters and gunpowder and everything. Even if someone saw him doing something weird, who'd question Burt Dagget? Who'd suspect the big man? Sure, he *could* have done it. I know that in my head. My gut's what's having a hard time with it."

She sat down again. She'd barely gotten a wink of decent sleep the previous night. Whenever she closed her eyes, she would relive the moment in which she'd killed her own father.

Sometimes, when she did sleep, she'd dream the scene over and over, but be too slow. Or she'd miss. Then she'd stand helpless as he turned his gun on her, or saved her for last while he mowed down the others. She'd wake, gasping and doused in cold sweat, in the instant before the dream-bullet tore into her body.

Weariness wrapped around her like a heavy mantle. She was tired of it all. Tired of waiting for the next piece of bad news, the next death. But with Burt dead, that part was over, wasn't it? The murders were over.

"If it was him, that rather solves one problem," Steve said. "We don't have as pressing a reason to leave anymore. With poor Tyler and Annie dead, it isn't as though we have to reach a hospital."

"Except for you being shot, Mr. Quinlan."

"Letitia did say that a jaunt to the nearest emergency room would do me good," Steve agreed. "If it's feasible. But if it isn't, I'll live."

"What about Connie? She's pretty worked over," Kelly said. "What about finding out what's left of the rest of the world? Would we really want to stay here forever?"

He took her hand again, and this time she let him hold it. "There's no one I'd rather be stranded on a tropical island with, that's for certain. But we're not the only ones with something at stake. There are other people depending on us to help them get home."

She sighed and looked out the window. The sound of voices carried to her on the wind, but she couldn't see them. It sounded like Karl and Jimmy, continuing their salvage efforts at the ruins. They'd already found several passable or undamaged items, maybe not key to survival but good for comfort. Partly burned books and singed cushions, an entire case of sponsor-donated

Snickers bars that had come through the disaster squashed but miraculously unmelted, a box of crayons from the art supplies that had been fused into a single multi-colored wax brick, other odds and ends.

"I'll ask them again," she said. "I'll see what they want to do."

*   *   *

Chapter 53

Sarah had told him that the name of the rock was Lookout Point.

Unimaginative, maybe, but it served the purpose. Dale said he was going to sit up there a while with a telescope, scanning the sea for ships and the sky for planes. It was a good excuse. In reality, he was glad for any pretext to get away from Sarah and her clingy neediness for a while.

He felt bad for her, of course. She'd lost her brother, her mom, and the guy she had a crush on, all in a couple of days.

But she was acting like she expected Dale to step in and take care of her and make it all better. Whether he was filling in for the brother, the mom, the crush, or all three, Dale wasn't sure. Nor did he want to find out. A few hours of having her trail after him and not want him out of her sight had been plenty.

At last, she'd fallen into a thin, troubled sleep and he'd been able to slip away. She would probably come looking for him, wailing that he'd left her alone.

He scaled the steep trail and emerged onto a flat platform that had been fortified with a curved wall of mortared, rough-hewn stones. A security camera rose on a post from one corner of this little lookout. Dale had a great view of the town, the blasted rubble of the fortress, and the *Adventure*.

Their ticket out of here.

Kelly Dagget had put it to them last night. Stay, or go? She laid out all the reasons like she had before, the amended list this time, and put it to a vote.

Nobody was that shocked at the ultimate decision. They'd seen too much death here, brushed too close to it themselves. Even if they could only get as far as Jamaica, that'd be better than staying on this island. Too many bad memories.

So, they would leave.

Not today, probably not tomorrow, but soon.

Once they'd loaded all they could onto the *Adventure,* it'd be *adios* Veradoga.

"Come to Jamaica, mon," Dale said, for no particular reason, as he extended the telescope. He put it to his eye.

What he saw was not that inspiring. The sea was an inhospitable green-grey, the sky feathered with more of those nasty-looking brown clouds. The rain gave them an itchy rash, and he didn't like to think about what else it might be doing.

After a few cursory sweeps with the telescope, more to satisfy anyone who might have been watching him than because he really expected to see anything, Dale collapsed the brass tube in on itself and put it back in his pocket. His hand came out holding something else, something that crackled.

It was yellowed paper with singed edges, spotted with brown raindrops that had blurred some of the ink. Still, it was fairly legible. A map. The map. Dagget's final challenge.

He'd gone back for it in the aftermath of the Rum Town shoot-out, hiding it in with his clothes and personal belongings until he could find the privacy to give it a good long study. That time had come. Up here, undisturbed, he could decipher it and know for sure where the treasure chest had been buried.

Half a million in gold. Maybe it didn't mean diddly-squat to Karl or Jimmy, but it meant something to Dale, all right.

A consolation prize, call it. Hazard pay.

Gold was still gold, after all. A fortune would still be worth a fortune.

The others, as far as Dale was aware, didn't know he had the map. He hadn't mentioned it to anyone, and he didn't think that Karl or Jimmy had, either. Things had gotten pretty busy right around then. For all he knew, the two of them might have forgotten about it by now.

Dale had not forgotten. It had stayed on his mind throughout everything.

Half a million dollars.

Okay, so maybe it was no great shakes by the economy they'd left behind, when it would barely be the price of a decent house in Orlando. A star baseball player – Dale wasn't much of a fan of sports but he was a fan of hottie athletes – could make half a million by playing two or three ball games.

Bill Gates probably raked in that kind of dough just by switching on his computer.

But it sure wasn't chump change. Nobody in his right mind would turn up his nose at a cool half-mil. Least of all a guy who'd grown up a few steps removed from trailer trash.

Tract trash, that's what he and his brothers had called it when they were growing up in their grubby housing development home.

He traced his finger along the map. X marks the spot, and if he was reading it right, that X would be somewhere around the base of Widowmaker Peak.

"Is this seat taken?"

Startled, he crushed the map into a crumple. He caught himself too late to avoid looking guilty, and did his best to pass it off as surprise.

"Hey, Connie."

The greeting was cautious. He didn't know what to make of her. She'd cleaned up well from her ordeal, and dressed more sedately than ever before in roomy men's trousers and a long white shirt. Her brassy blond hair was tied back with someone's red kerchief, since *Tortuga* and *Maracaibo* no longer mattered.

Mostly.

Tala and Ambrose avoided her like the plague. Tala, having been on the other end of the catfight, was probably justified. Letitia took her cue from those two and treated Connie with cool indifference. Everybody else expressed varying degrees of neutrality, though Dale had caught both Karl and Jimmy giving her the appreciative eye around the old campfire last night.

The stunts she had pulled might have been spiteful and mean, but that had been in the game. The game was over now. After having witnessed B.J.'s death, Connie was a shadow of her former self.

Dale decided that she was okay. He wasn't about to trust her with his life or anything, but he wouldn't spurn her if she wanted to sit up on Lookout Point for a while.

He scooted over. "Nope, have a seat."

"Thanks." She lowered herself as if it hurt, blowing out a slow breath. "I wanted to get away from things for a while."

"I know the feeling."

"Can I tell you something?" she asked, after they'd watched the surf churn on the beach for a while.

"What?"

"I'm sorry."

"For what?"

"In general. I'm telling everybody, one at a time. I know you didn't have to put up with a lot of the crap that was going on, being on the other crew, but I figured I owed you each an apology."

"Well, uh, thanks. That's nice of you. But you'd do better starting with Tala."

Connie picked at the seam of her pants. "I'm working my way up to that, hoping it'll get easier as it goes along."

"Fair enough."

"I mean, we're all in this together. I was wrong to listen to B.J. This is a serious mess. He didn't believe any of it. I didn't *want* to believe it."

"Who does?" Dale took out the telescope again. "I never thought I'd be living through some slasher movie combined with a post-apocalypse gig."

"Do you think there's still anything out there? Any places that are all right?"

"I hope so. Guess we'll find out when we get there."

She drew up her legs, groaning a little, and rested her chin on her knees. "I hate that it's all been for nothing. So many people dead, we don't know what will happen next, and we won't even get to be on television. That sounds stupid-selfish, I know, but —"

"Nah, I'm the same way. This was going to be my stepladder to wealth and fame. High living. Expensive sports cars. Interviews, commercials, movie deals." He linked his thumbs and flapped his hands, a birdie flying away. "So much for that, huh?"

"And we never even finished the game and found out who'd win."

"Me."

She smiled. "Yeah, right. If it had come down to a choice between us two, maybe, since they all hate me and everyone likes you. Really, they'd probably give it to Tala or Karl or somebody."

They watched the waves some more, and while they did, Dale pondered. He didn't want to share the wealth. Sharing the wealth was what poor people said. Rich people said fuck that, keep it all!

But he didn't have a lot of time. And a half-million in gold was going to be heavy. He could use some help.

"Yeah, but I still won." He smoothed out the map and showed it to her. "What do you say? Up for a treasure hunt?"

*   *   *

Chapter 54

Sarah lay wakeful in the dark. She heard the others doze off one by one, murmured voices ceasing and the measured breath of sleep taking over. Every inch of her was plain bone-weary but her eyes would not close.

Through the gaps in the shutters, she could see the night sky alive with strange colors. St. Elmo's Fire, blue and pale green, danced on the *Adventure's* rigging. Flashes of heat lightning lit the lowest layer of clouds from above, giving the impression of dirty, demonic faces leering from the heavens. The thunder was distant and sounded like the growling chuckle of those selfsame demons.

The weather had gone as insane as the rest of the world. Sunset had been a violent splash of red. While they'd been eating their dinner from cans warmed in the embers, a water cyclone had spun into view between sea and sky.

And they were going to set sail in that madness? Tomorrow?

Sarah had sat like a lump all evening, picking at food that had less appeal than roadkill. It felt wrong to be eating. Felt wrong to be doing anything at all, including living.

She might have been all right if someone, anyone, would sit with her and tell her that it was going to be okay. Why didn't they see? Didn't they care?

Nobody cared. They were all stronger than her. They could get through this. Shrug it off and go on with what needed to be done. Kelly Dagget was so strong that she'd been able to kill her own father. That was a service, a gift, that Sarah hadn't even been able to do for her suffering, dying mother.

The thought had crossed her mind, oh, it had. Seeing her pain, how the lightest touch of a bandage or a sheet brought such terrible agony . . . what was a daughter for, if not to end a mother's misery? Sarah had contemplated turning off the oxygen, even putting a pillow over Annie's face and suffocating her . . . but in the end, she had chickened out. She'd been afraid that it might not work fast enough, that it might make things worse.

So Doctor Brookstone had done it for her, and robbed Sarah of the final deed she could have performed for her mother.

There wasn't even going to be a burial. The others had decided to leave the dead where they were. Just leave them to rot. Why waste time and energy digging graves, when they'd need to conserve their strength for survival?

No one would ever come and attend to those corpses. There wouldn't be any funerals, no priests with comforting words, no memorials with flowers.

She watched the skyshow through the unshuttered windows, the faces of the demons in the clouds, and tried not to think about her mother, her brother, Trip, everyone else.

The harder she tried, the more she did think about it. Would the rats find them? She remembered how her mother had screamed in rage and horror when the rats came teeming out of the food stores. She'd gone after them, whacking them with her clipboard, killing a few even as they bit her.

Was it revenge time for the rats? Were they even now slinking through the cracks in the apothecary shop's walls, advancing on her mother's stiffened, defenseless body?

All at once, Sarah couldn't stand it. She could not leave Ann to the rats. Burial at sea would be better than that, cleaner somehow. Or she'd set fire to the shop. Its shelves still held some medicinal remedies, rubbing alcohol and the like, that might serve as accelerants. A cremation. Consumed in cleansing fire, much better than being consumed by festering, disease-carrying rats.

She rose silently from her cot. No one else stirred. Not even Dale. There was only a motionless shape under his blanket.

A lump rose in her throat.

Dale had been so nice to her, so comforting. She'd instinctively known that he would take care of her and make everything right. Like Trip would have done. Trip had braved the flames to save her mother, a sacrifice that cost him everything and proved futile in the end. She had hoped that Dale would show the same chivalrous stripe.

Now he was ignoring her. He'd gone away while she was napping, after he'd promised to stay by her side. When she woke up, he'd been up on the

Lookout with Connie.

It was enough to make Sarah want to scream. Connie, of all people! Just because she had those huge boobs! Sarah had thought Dale was different. She'd thought he actually cared about her.

A lantern hung on a nail near the door, unlit but half-full of oil. A box of long-sticked matches sat on a shelf under it. Sarah took both and made her way out into the street. She'd splash the oil around, strike a match, and voila. Instant pyre.

A bobbing white beam stopped her in her tracks. She froze with the lantern still dark in one hand and the box of matches in the other. Wild notions of UFOs and will-o-the-wisps shuffled through her mind.

No, not any of those. A flashlight. Moving around by the garage.

A chill slid into her like a dagger. What if Burt Dagget hadn't been the only killer after all? What if he'd had help? And what if they were coming back to finish the job?

Sarah shrank into a pool of shadow and watched. She could hear, barely and when the fickle breeze blew in her favor, the clatter and clank of metal on metal.

The garage . . . if lamp oil and rubbing alcohol would do to give a fire a kick in the pants, surely gasoline would do it even better. Someone was sabotaging the garage, setting up a booby trap like the one that had blown up the fortress. Attaching bombs to the cars, maybe. She'd seen enough movies to know all about how dynamite could be wired to a car's ignition.

She wanted to yell, wake everyone up, sound the alarm. But if she did, whoever was skulking around by the garage would be able to run away and hide long before anyone could get out there.

It was all up to her. If she could get closer, see who it was . . . what he or she was up to . . .

Glad for any excuse to take her mind off her mother, Sarah crept in that direction. She left the lantern and the box of matches in the shadows.

Clattering. Clunking. Metal on metal. Then the sound of something rolling. Wheels.

A wheelbarrow came into view, illuminated by the weird, irregular pulses of storm-light. She saw someone pushing it, and almost laughed out loud.

Dale! She had nearly sounded the alarm on Dale.

Sarah trotted toward him, then stopped short as the flashlight came around the edge of the building. Someone else was carrying it, because Dale was busy with the wheelbarrow. In the beam's backsplash, Sarah easily recognized Connie.

That slut!

That bastard!

And she'd thought he was different. She'd thought he cared about her.

What were they doing, anyway? Sneaking off for a quickie? Sarah had heard all about how Connie and B.J. had been caught in the act by the camera crew. Now the bitch had gotten her hooks into Dale?

Didn't Dale know what kind of a person Connie was?

She was about to stomp over to them and give them both a piece of her mind when she paused to wonder what they were doing with a wheelbarrow, and a flashlight, and whatever those clunking metal things had been.

Neither of them had seen her, and Sarah was able to get close enough to hear them talking.

Arguing?

"Look, I'm not one of those guys who's too proud to ask for directions," Dale said. "Just give me back the map."

"I can read it," Connie said, tossing her hair haughtily. She trained the flashlight on a scrap of paper. "We want to head for the black mountain toward the middle of the island. Widowmaker Peak."

"Then what?"

"Why don't we worry about that when we get there? Let's make it quick."

"Be quicker if we took one of those," Dale said, indicating the SUVs with a jerk of his head.

"Too noisy," Connie said. "This is our secret."

"Fifty-fifty, you and me."

"That's the deal. But we've got to get it, first. And stash it on the boat to sneak back to civilization."

"No problem." Dale lifted the handles of the wheelbarrow. "Let's roll."

*   *   *

Chapter 55

Trip no longer paid much attention to his bodily needs. He knew that hunger and dehydration had combined to whittle the pounds off him . . . not counting, of course, the several pounds he'd lost in an instant when his lower leg had been severed. The addition of a wooden peg only added back a little of the weight.

But it just didn't seem to matter all that much. His mind felt scrubbed smooth. Washed clean. Erased, like a chalkboard.

His clothes drooped on his body like becalmed sails. He reeked of incontinence, sweat, and tar. His stubble of beard and uncombed hair gave him a crazed castaway's appearance. His satchel hung over his shoulder, its freight of water and snacks completely unnoticed.

None of this registered on his thoughts in a more than idle manner. All that mattered now was protecting the cave. That had been the order given him by his captain. That was what he would do.

A cutlass rested across his lap, an old and pitted thing with a handle wrapped in cracked, age-split leather.

The normal sounds of the jungle ceased, and Trip cocked his head to listen. He might have been reduced to a zombie, a robot, obeying one single instruction, but there was nothing wrong with his senses.

"I told you, you're reading it wrong." A woman.

"Part of it's missing. I'm doing the best I can." A man.

They sounded vaguely familiar to Trip. He got up, balancing on his

peg-leg, unmindful of the dull beat of pain radiating up from the stump. The cutlass was no longer in his lap but grasped in his right hand.

Light streamed in through the concealing screen of bushes. Not torch-light or lantern-light, it was a solid white gleam that half-blinded him. His eyes were accustomed to the cave, which was dim even by day. He squinted, not in pain as much as in annoyance.

Trip felt that he should have known what that steady glow was, just as he felt he should recognize the voices that were drawing nearer.

But that didn't seem important. They were too close. Close to the cave. Close to disturbing the captain's rest.

He moved toward the entrance, making sure to keep a rocky outcropping between himself and the approaching beam.

"I think we're on the wrong side of the mountain," the woman said. "Look at the map. It shows a valley. That's where the X is. In the valley."

"No, it's a cave."

"You didn't even look at the damn map."

"I'm not talking about the map. I see a cave. There. Right there, behind those bushes."

The light held stationary. From where Trip stood, he could see the pinprick glitter of ore in the roof of the tunnel, the elongated silhouettes cast by the rock formations.

"I think you're right," the woman said. "It does look like a cave. You think the treasure's in there?"

"It's perfect. Give me the shovel. You take the crowbar. Leave the wheel-barrow for now, until we see what's in there."

Rustling sounds, clanking sounds, then the rustling of leafy branches be-ing pushed aside. Trip held his position and waited. He saw their faces peer in. Again, he had the feeling he should know them . . . but it was overshadowed by the stronger feeling that it didn't make any difference.

They were after the captain's treasure. They intended to trespass in the cave.

"We have to go in there?" the woman asked, askance.

"Spooky-cool!" The man sounded delighted. "Leave it to Dagget not to miss a trick. Wanna bet we find some more of those fake skeletons laying around? Dead men tell no tales, fifteen men on a dead man's chest, and so on?"

"I don't care about fake skeletons. Let's just get the gold and get out of here before someone notices we're gone."

They entered the passage, drawing nearer to the cavern chamber itself

and Trip's hiding place. The light spread out, touching the rocks, and the sand, and the skulls.

The woman was in the lead. She stopped and made a revolted sound. "You weren't wrong about the skeletons," she said. "Look at all this. Son of a bitch."

The man looked over her shoulder, and grinned with boyish glee as he took in the scene. "Excellent!"

Trip crouched in the shadows. Another couple of steps, and they would be within reach . . .

The skulls on their ledges gleamed dull white, naked domes with gaping sockets and toothy jaws bared. The treasure chest itself sat half-buried in a heap of sand, its curved lid rising like the back of a breaching whale.

"They really went all out," the man said admiringly. He guided the woman's hand to shine the beam of light toward the rear of the cave. "How about that guy?"

The captain was there in all his glory, hat askew on his head, bony shoulders holding up the faded cloth of his frock coat. His spider-thin hand rested on the delicate bones of his wife, as if his final act before dying had been to reach out to her. The tiny skeleton of their son was cradled in the fleshless embrace of her arms.

"That is *too* creepy," the woman said. "Wasn't this supposed to be a family show? It looks like a damn horror movie!"

"Sweeps week," the man said, and nudged her. "Dagget, always pushing the envelope and tweaking the network censors. Come on. Let's see what's in the chest. I want that gold!"

As they moved forward, Trip lunged out of hiding and swung the cutlass in a low, flat arc. The blade met meaty substance, parted it. The high odor of blood and entrails filled the air.

The woman screamed. The light fell from her hand and shattered and went out, casting the cave into blackness.

*   *   *

Chapter 56

Dale Sheffield had a brief impression of a lurching, haggard-faced man coming at them. Then Connie screamed and staggered backward, clutching her stomach. Her cry rebounded off the cave walls. The flashlight fell, hit a rock, and broke.

Raw instinct saved Dale's life. He sensed a blow coming at him in the dark and dove flat. Something whickered through the air over his head. He hugged the sandy, pebbly cave floor.

A foot bumped his side as the attacker's follow-through carried him a step forward. Dale hurled his prone body against the leg. He felt the man topple over him, heard the explosive grunt of his landing as an undertone to Connie's ongoing, gurgling screams.

The man whipped about like a snake, clipping Dale's elbow with something that felt like a riot baton. A fist clenched in Dale's shirt, yanked him around, flung him onto his back.

Dale brought up crossed arms and the descending forearm of his assailant collided with them. The impact jarred loose something from the man's hand. It sliced past Dale's head, grazing his ear with a thin line of pain.

The man fell on him, grappling with him. Strong fingers closed around his throat. The thing that felt like a baton whacked him in the shin.

A fierce, strangling grip cut off Dale's breath. He bucked and thrashed. He tried to pry the fingers loose and couldn't. His lungs ached with the need for oxygen. His head was going cloudy.

He groped his way up the man's corded arms, over cloth that felt nasty and lice-ridden. Reached higher yet and blindly touched a bristly chin, a cheek. His finger poked into the man's mouth. Before Dale could yank it back, the teeth snapped down in a vicious bite.

Dale would have yelled if he'd been able to draw breath. He raked his other hand at the man's face. His thumb found an eye and gouged at it, twisting, corkscrewing.

The man drew back, his jaw and his hold on Dale's neck loosening for a fraction of a second. Twisting with his whole body, Dale wrenched away and rolled onto his stomach. He wheezed and sucked in air. His bitten finger throbbed and he was afraid to touch it for fear that he'd find it ended in a knob of bloody knuckle.

Something was pressing into his chest. He was laying on it, pushing it into the sand. It was maybe three feet long, curved, hard. Metal. The shovel? A sword? Yes, a sword . . . a cutlass . . . like the one Karl had been carrying around.

His attacker pawed at him, finding a handhold in Dale's belt. As he was pulled, sliding easily through the loose sand, Dale groped for the handle of the cutlass. He wrapped his hand through the guard and clutched the hilt.

Stabbing pain. A pointed blade sank into Dale's back. Not deep, but sharp, and he yelled.

He threw himself sideways, sat up, turned and swung in one convulsive motion. The cutlass made that whickering sound again, this time ending in an exclamation point of a hearty wooden thunk.

What had he hit? A table leg? A post? The treasure chest? He was all turned around in his mind, didn't know which way was which.

He yanked the cutlass free, every movement triggering fresh pain in his back, and swung again.

Swoosh. Missed.

It occurred to Dale that Connie had quit screaming. He wasn't sure when. But he could hear his own ragged gasps, and those of his opponent. Holding his breath, although it made his lungs pound, Dale tried to pinpoint the other man's location by sound.

To his left. Very close.

Holding the cutlass in both hands, he brought it around as hard as he could. It chopped into something that wasn't wood. A spray of hot mist hit Dale in the face. The man howled and fell over. Dale found him by feel, found him trying to crawl-scrabble-hitch away.

He hacked again and the sound was like when Jimmy had used the hatchet

to butcher the pig. Ah, back in those nostalgic, innocent days when their biggest concern had been getting through the next Captain's Court.

His back felt like he'd had a skewer rammed into it, deep, below the ribs. Kidney shish-ka-bob. Dale couldn't let that stop him. His only thought was that this guy, whoever he was, had already tried to kill him and might have done a better job on Connie – that silence was seriously unlike her – and if Dale didn't finish him first, he'd never leave this cave alive.

The man had stopped trying to fight was only trying to get away. Or get to another weapon. The whimpers and mewling noises he made were pathetic as he dragged himself along.

Pathetic or not, Dale couldn't let that stop him now. Life or death, no place for sympathy. No place for mercy.

He chopped with the cutlass again. The man bleated and kept crawling. Dale hitched after him, scootching along on his ass. He grabbed for an ankle and got a smooth, rounded length of wood.

A wooden leg? A peg-leg? Like a pirate?

Crazy, but true.

The man's other foot, the one that was still the original, hit him a glancing lucky kick in the wrist. Dale lost the cutlass, heard it fly off to rattle against stone. Too far away to find in the dark. He rose to his knees and fell full-length on the man. He got him by the hair, which felt every bit as greasy and nasty as the clothes, and plowed the man's face into the sand.

No good. He'd never knock the guy out this way. Might smother him, but the man was snapping his head side to side, snatching for breath.

With a heave of his body, he almost dislodged Dale, throwing him half-way off. Dale's forehead smacked into something curved and unyielding. He picked it up. The remains of the flashlight, its heavy casing intact, the batteries giving it a good heft.

Dale didn't stop to think it over, just smashed the butt end of the flash-light into the back of the man's head.

Again.

And again.

He did it until the man stopped moving, gave him a few more for good measure, and one to grow on. Only then, when the body under him was no longer struggling, did Dale stop.

Cautiously, not really thinking the guy was shamming but not fully believing his apparent unconsciousness, Dale retreated from the body. He felt the flashlight, hoping that it might have just gotten jarred into the off position when Connie dropped it. The end of the casing was gooey with blood and

hair. Possibly brain tissue.

"Oh, gross," Dale said.

He crouched and scrubbed his hand through the gritty sand. Moving like that sent a new spike of pain into his back and made him conscious of the blood soaking him from the waist down.

Shifting the flashlight to his left hand, he bent his right around behind his body to see how badly he was hurt. He encountered the handle of a pocket-knife still sticking out of him like a pin. The blade was sunk all the way into his back.

Stabbed, oh, jeez, how bad?

He thought of how far he was from Rum Town, and how nobody else knew that he and Connie had gone for a late night excursion. Even if their absence had already been noticed, how would help find him? Jimmy or Karl might remember the map but neither of them had looked at it long enough to remember any salient details.

Pull the knife out or leave it in? If he left it in, every time he tried to move he'd be doing more damage as it worked around in the hole. But if he pulled it out, he might speed up the bleeding.

How long was the blade? It felt like a fucking bayonet, a wonder the other end wasn't poking out through his abs.

"Connie?" he asked, not liking the hollow way his voice rang in the blackness. "Connie, are you okay?"

She didn't reply.

Dead? Out cold?

No, she was dead. They both were. He was alone in a cave, with no company but the dead and the faux skeletons that Dagget's people had planted here.

He shuffled a few steps and his foot hit something. Not a body. A bag, it felt like. Dale bent over again, the blade moving in him, slicing in him, and found a leather bulgy object. A purse of some sort.

Had Connie been carrying a purse? No, of course not, she hadn't had anything but her clothes and the stuff they'd stowed in the wheelbarrow.

Dale picked up the bag. He reached in, not sure what he hoped to find but getting a most welcome surprise when he touched a penlight. He brought it out, turned it on, and swept the fine beam over the sandy floor.

The man he'd beaten with the larger flashlight was face down, arms splayed out. One of his legs did indeed end in a wooden peg, as Dale had thought. His clothes were in such bad shape it was impossible to tell how they'd started out. The same could be said for his head. The back of it was a

pulpy mess.

"Killed him, I killed the guy," Dale said. He wasn't sure if he sounded nauseated or victorious.

Connie was beyond the fallen man. She had collapsed in a folded-over pose, partially on her knees with her side leaning against the wall near the cave mouth, her arms hanging in a loose cradling position by her waist. Her head was down, her hair obscuring her face, and Dale was glad about that.

He could see enough in the quick pass of the beam. She'd been disemboweled, the spill of her intestines in her lap. Pale and shiny.

Bratwurst, Dale thought, remembering a time that Sidney had taken him to a kitschy Bavarian-themed village for Oktoberfest. Oompah-bands, beer served in enormous steins, men in *lederhosen* and funky suspenders, blond-braided *frauleins* with apple-cheeked smiles, and bratwurst. Loop after loop of it. Greasy off-white until cooked.

He looked away fast but the sight was engraved in his mind. He leaned over – more tearing pain in his back – and tried not to throw up.

At last the urge passed and Dale was able to straighten up. He rummaged further in the purse-thing, finding a plastic water bottle, a few granola bars so crushed that they were crumbs in their foil wrappers, a paperback book, other stuff. Way at the bottom was one of the walkie-talkies that had been carried by Dagget's people.

"What's this?" Dale asked, only half aware that he was still talking out loud. "What the hell?"

He'd been going on the half-formulated assumption that maybe Burt Dagget hadn't been the real killer, but it had been some crazy hermit living in this cave all the time. The discovery of the walkie-talkie knocked that into a cocked hat.

Unless they'd been in on it together. Dagget and this guy. Hadn't they been saying that some of the murders would have been too much for one man to do?

Dizziness washed over Dale. He forgot about the purse and started worrying about his back again. The knife had to come out. If it hadn't diced his kidneys or sliced his spine yet, it would if he kept moving around.

He peeled off his shirt and walked his fingers around the place where the blade went in. It felt like an ordinary small pocket knife. One of those folding jobs, that's what he was hoping. No more than two inches long. Not enough to have impaled anything too vital.

After ripping a chunk of cloth from his shirt and folding it into a pad, Dale braced himself for what he knew he had to do. He reached around

behind his back again, wishing absently for that extra joint that women seemed to have in their elbows that enabled them to hook and unhook bra clasps.

The handle was slick with his blood, hard to get a good grip on.

"One, two . . . three," Dale said, and tried to draw it out in one swift, smooth move.

He squealed through gritted teeth. The knife came halfway out before he lost his hold. Blood ran down his back, not a gusher but more than a trickle. He tried again.

The knife came free. Dale took the folded cloth and held it against the gash, pushing as best he could given the impossible angle.

As he waited to see if the flow would stop, he played the penlight around the cave. The stage setting, when he avoided looking at the bodies of Connie and the guy with the peg-leg, was as properly piratical as he could have wished.

The skeleton in the captain's coat and hat was the crowning touch. That one even looked like it still had dried skin stretched over its bones, and strands of hair hanging from its desiccated scalp. A single key, green with corrosion, hung around its neck on a chain. Dale had no doubts that the key would fit the padlock on the chest that was half-buried in the sand, only a few feet from him.

"Nicely done," he said. "You sure could put on a show, Dagget, even if you did turn out to be a mad-dog psycho killer."

The bleeding had slowed, maybe even stopped, but Dale knew that any exertion on his part would immediately start it going again. If he tried any-thing strenuous, like, oh, say, digging up a treasure chest with the shovel that he and Connie had brought—

Was he still thinking about the money? Connie was dead, and so was her murderer. Dale had killed a man. Self-defense, to be sure, but shouldn't he be thinking about that instead of half a million in gold?

"Fuck it," Dale said, shining the light on the dried mummy-face of the skeleton in the captain's coat. "This only makes me deserve the cash more. I walk away now, and they died for no reason. Besides, this way it's all mine."

Among the junk in the leather bag, he'd seen a roll of black electrician's tape. He wound it around his torso, taping the crude bandage into place. It'd have to do.

He drank some water and munched a handful of granola crumbs. Am-brosia. He could feel his flagging strength returning.

"First, though," he said to the skeletal captain, "I'm going to help myself to your key and take a peek in yonder chest, my anorexic friend."

Dale crossed the cave, the empty stare of the skulls seeming to follow

him. Good special effects. They looked damned real. And the one with what appeared to be a baby in its arms, what was that about?

"They probably would have told us the story later on in the game," Dale said. "Filling us in on the legend and then quizzing us. But all that's done with, so I guess I don't need to know."

The captain skeleton had ancient pistols resting in its lap. A cutlass in even worse condition than the one that had killed Connie rested alongside its skinny leg.

Dale had to take its hat off to lift the chain and key over its head. Up close, he would have thought that the illusion would fall apart, but it was as effective as anything that had ever come out of a special effects creature shop.

"Thanks, Cap." He replaced the hat with its mangy plume, tilting it at an angle over one vacant eye socket.

Even up close, he couldn't tell it wasn't real bone.

The key fit the lock perfectly. The chest's hinges were rusty and clotted with sand. They creaked as Dale tried to raise the lid. He held the penlight in his mouth and used both hands. The hinges creaked again and the lid stuttered up.

Even the wood felt old and spongy, and he had time to wonder how Dagget's people got that aged, distressed effect – did they soak the wood in brine, maybe? – before the penlight's ray fell upon the sparkling contents.

*   *   *

Chapter 57

Kelly jerked awake with a gasp, and sat bolt upright in the crowded clothiers' shop. Not even Steve's sleepy interrogative mumble, and the warmth of his hand enfolding hers, helped quell the sudden surge of adrenaline thrumming through her bloodstream.

Around her, indistinct shapes in the gloom, a few of the others twitched or muttered or turned over. But no one else got up.

She didn't know what had slapped her so abruptly awake. If she'd been having a nightmare — which would have been more than understandable, given what the past few days had been like — she didn't remember any of it.

Had she heard something?

All she heard now was the ordinary night-noises of the island. Monkey-hoots and birdcalls, the rustle of wind in the palm fronds, the rhythmic surf, distant thunder over the sea.

Kelly fished out a tiny keychain squeeze-light and shined its dim blue glow around.

Sarah's cot was empty.

That must have been what woke Kelly . . . Sarah, getting up in the night for a quick bathroom visit or a drink of water or something.

Nothing to worry about, then.

She settled back down beside Steve. Like all of them, he was grimy and sweaty and gross. They'd been working too hard on loading up the *Adventure* to bother much with personal hygiene, and being careful to conserve their

fresh water.

Which was how it had been for sailors in the olden days, ironically enough. Kelly hadn't delved into the lore of 17th-century seafarers as wholeheartedly as her father had, but she'd picked up enough here and there. They would have to get used to being grubby for a while. The contestants had a head start on that, since they'd been stuck on the island for several days already without much in the way of laundry facilities and showers.

Still in his sleep, Steve tucked his good arm around her. He mumbled something else she couldn't make out.

"Mmm," Kelly said by way of reply.

Content, she snuggled close, thinking that it was a little weird to be finding any sort of comfort and happiness in the midst of everything else that had gone so apocalyptically wrong. Or maybe it was the only thing that made sense. Grab it while she could. Life was too damn short and uncertain.

Tired as she was, she discovered that her eyes didn't want to close. She realized she was waiting to hear Sarah come back. It was sort of how she'd felt as a kid, when her parents had gone out and the babysitter put her to bed. She'd lie there in the dark, wide awake, unable to shut her eyes until she at least heard their car pull into the driveway. Until then, the house didn't feel complete . . . or safe . . . or right.

Kelly sat up again.

No Sarah.

Even with the worst of it over, why would anybody want to wander off by themselves in the middle of the night? If, that was, Sarah *was* by herself. Maybe she and Dale . . . no, not likely . . . Kelly knew all about Dale and Sidney. Besides, there was a big motionless lump in Dale's spot.

More deliberately, Kelly shined the blue beam from one sleeper to the next, doing a headcount.

Jimmy's face screwed up in a grimace when the light hit him. He thrashed over onto his other side, and as he did, his arm snagged on Dale's blanket, sliding it partway off. Revealing not Dale all curled up, but a couple of bolts of calico cloth from the shop's shelves.

Closer investigation showed Kelly that Connie's bed was empty, too.

Her stomach had a deep, nagging unease growing in it. She got to her feet as quietly as she could, stepping over snoring bodies to poke her head outside.

Rum Town, the damage it had taken softened by the shadows, was silent and still except for a few scurrying rats. The *Adventure* bobbed in its moorings, ready to take them away from here to try their luck in the wider world

the next day. It was a prospect that simultaneously filled Kelly with anticipation and dread. She'd be glad to see the last of Veradoga, which was nothing but bad memories of blood and loss and terror now. But she was almost as afraid of what they'd find when they left the island.

She didn't see any sign of Sarah, or Dale, or Connie.

Dale and Sarah, okay. Ann's daughter had latched onto Dale, and hadn't wanted to let him out of her sight.

Dale and Connie, maybe. The two of them had been hanging around together earlier in the afternoon, up on Lookout Point. Kelly had even thought that it was nice to see someone tolerating Connie . . . especially if it was someone besides Kelly herself. And at least with Dale, Connie didn't have to wonder if he was only interested in one thing.

All three of them buddying up, though? That didn't make sense. Busy as the day had been, they'd still all seen Sarah's hurt jealousy when she'd noticed Dale and Connie on the Lookout.

Unless Dale had gone the diplomatic route and convinced both women to step aside with him and get their issues out in the open?

Maybe. If this had still been the show, Kelly wouldn't have doubted it. But given what they'd all been through, a little catfight over a guy — a gay guy, even! — was hardly worth stirring things up over. It could wait until they were off Veradoga, couldn't it?

Kelly eyed the low, turbulent masses of black clouds and decided that it wasn't going to dump acid rain on her in the next few minutes. She slipped out of the shop for a better look around.

Unease was giving way to irritation. None of them should be splitting off and doing their own thing. This was still a dangerous place, even if they were no longer being stalked by a deranged murderer.

Her father. Her dead father. The one she'd shot.

She flinched.

No one else was moving around out here. Kelly really didn't want to go searching from building to building. Didn't want to have to look at the bodies again, people she knew, people she'd cared about, piled in Doc Brookstone's office and probably already gone moistly, greenly soft with decay from the heat and the tropical humidity.

But, damn it, how irresponsible could those three be? Going off without a word to anyone? Didn't it occur to them that someone else might wake up, find them missing, and worry?

Kelly turned at the corner by the tavern. Impact and pain crunched her toes, slammed up her leg. She flailed for balance, missed it, and took a tum-

bling header over something solid and hard and all sharp edges and angles.

The breath was knocked out of her in a grunt when she landed. She felt bone-jarred, rattled, scraped and embarrassed.

A wheelbarrow. She had stubbed her toes and cracked her shins on a wheelbarrow, tripped over it, and gone sprawling.

"Who left that fucking thing there?" she said to nobody, folding her leg to cradle her bruised, indignant toes. Thank God she'd put on her hiking boots. Still hurt like a bastard, but she didn't think she'd broken any.

They'd been using the wheelbarrows to trundle supplies up the gang-plank and onto the *Adventure*. Anything and everything that they might be able to use or barter. She'd thought that they had all gotten put back in the equipment shed, but here was one left out.

And it was a disgusting mess, too. Caked with clots of dark mud, streaked with sludge, vines and leaves tangled around the front wheel. Looked like someone had pushed it halfway across Veradoga and back.

She rubbed her shin, her elbows, the heels of her hands, and all her other assorted hurting places. A few were oozing blood, and it felt like she'd lost about a yard of skin. It smarted. Her toes were throbbing inside her boot, in time with her heartbeat. In a cartoon, she thought, they would have been flashing red and swelling up and down like balloons.

Resisting the urge to give the wheelbarrow a kick – she'd probably stub the other set of toes – Kelly picked herself up and brushed the seat of her shorts.

Hadn't she just been thinking, not two minutes ago, how stupid and irresponsible it was for people to wander off by themselves? Might get hurt. And here she was, doing that very exact thing.

"Idiot." Kelly shook her head and turned around.

If Sarah, Dale and Connie wanted to pull this kind of dumb stunt, fine. No need for her to break her neck trying to track them down in the middle of the night. When they got back, she'd be ready to give them hell.

She started toward the shop, then paused as she saw someone limp-staggering down the cobblestoned street. He was stooped over, awkwardly holding his back like an arthritic old man. His shirt was off, and he had something that looked like black strips wrapped around his chest.

"Dale?" Kelly said, aiming the light at him.

He jumped, yelping in surprise and pain. "Who – ?"

It was Dale, all right. He looked awful. Filthy, mud-splashed, his hair a corkscrew tangle with leaves and bugs caught in it. He was even more banged up and scraped up than Kelly. His eyes were sunken and staring, from a face

that would have been right at home in a pictorial shot in a war-zone.

"It's Kelly Dagget," she said. "God, Dale, what happened to you? Where have you been? Are you okay?"

"Kelly." He sagged against a wall, shoulders heaving. "Oh, jeez. I didn't think I'd make it."

"You're hurt," she said, seeing that the black strips were long pieces of tape holding a pad of folded, blood-soaked cloth against his back.

"Stabbed," Dale said.

"Stabbed?" Her voice rose. Inside the clothiers' shop, she could hear movement and other voices, querying, alarmed.

"We have to get out of here!" Dale's hand shot out and seized Kelly's wrist. "I mean, now! Right away!"

"Stabbed by who?"

His mouth worked. His throat bulged as he swallowed. "Connie."

"What?"

The others crowded out into the street, jostling, babbling. It was confusion and chaos. Letitia shoved through to examine Dale's back. Everyone was talking at once. Kelly shouted for quiet, didn't get it.

"Shut up!" Mike's bellow was loud enough to even stun the birds and monkeys into silence.

"Tell us what happened," Kelly said to Dale.

He gasped as Letitia peeled the tape away. "It was Connie. She . . . she told me . . . she said she knew where the treasure was. The gold. The half million."

"Fuck, man!" Jimmy said. "You went after the stupid *gold?* You greedy dumbass!"

"I know," Dale said, hanging his head. "I know, greedy dumbass, I know! She was just trying to get me alone, so they could pick us off one by one."

"They?" Karl asked. His brows came down, his expression dark.

"Her and B.J.," Dale said bitterly. "She lied to us about everything. He wasn't dead. It was them all along."

Amid the outbursts of profanity, Kelly reeled back against Steve. "She said my dad . . . my dad was the killer."

"She told me they'd found the gold, and she'd share it with me if I helped her," Dale said. "I didn't even see him until all at once there he was, and he stabbed me in the back with a pocket knife or something. He could have killed me!"

"I knew we couldn't trust her," Tala said, over more scattered curses and growls.

Letitia dabbed peroxide on the bleeding wound. It foamed, and Dale hissed through his teeth. "I got away," he said, voice tight. "But they're still out there. We have to get out of here before they come back to finish us off. They're crazy! B.J., he was like a . . . mad dog or a wild animal or something. Connie, too."

"I can't believe you went for the gold," Jimmy said again. "What were you thinking?"

"Leave him be," Letitia said.

"If it wasn't my father . . ." Kelly said slowly. She felt herself start to shake.

"Easy, love," Steve said. "Right now I think none of us really know what's going on here."

"I just told you," Dale said. "It's Connie and B.J., and they're going to kill all of us!"

"He's right," Ambrose said. "I don't want to die. Let's just go, okay? Can't we just go?"

"What about Sarah?" Kelly asked.

She got a sea of blank faces in response. A few of them glanced around, only then realizing that Sarah wasn't there.

"Sarah?" Dale echoed.

"Didn't she go with you and Connie?"

He floundered, mouth opening and shutting, confusion in his eyes. "Sarah? No . . . I . . . she isn't here?"

"I woke up and she was gone," Kelly said. "All three of you were gone. So I figured . . ."

"No," Dale said. He looked numb. "I never . . . I didn't . . . I thought she was here."

"Oh, no," Tala said, biting her lower lip. "What if she followed him, and . . ."

"We'd best go look for her," Steve said.

Karl nodded. "I'll get some lights and weapons together."

"No!" Dale said. "Are you insane? You can't go out there!"

"This is your fault, asshole," Jimmy said. "If she followed you and they got her —"

"Hold on," Kelly said. "Everybody, settle down. We can't charge off into the jungle in the middle of the night."

"But we have to find Sarah," Ambrose said.

Everyone started talking at once again, arguing, waving their arms, shouting at each other.

They'd wait until morning. By morning, it might be too late. Forget that,

it might be too late already! Board the ship and set sail. Take the cars and organize a search. Stick together. Split up into pairs. Barricade themselves in town, just in case B.J. and Connie showed up. Maybe Sarah had been in on it. Bullshit, she was in on it. Or maybe *all* of them had been in on it together! Sarah and Dagget as well as B.J. and Connie! Bullshit squared! What if the killers came after them in town? Everyone should have a gun. Nobody should have a gun, in case one of them was in on it too.

And so on, around and around, until Kelly thought her head was going to explode.

*   *   *

Chapter 58

Sarah Parkins opened her eyes to daylight . . . sort of. The sunrise was as awful in its seething orange brilliance as the sunset had been. Fumingly hot, hellish, and unreal. The patches of sky visible between the smoggy-brown clouds looked blistered. Like her mother's skin.

She was wet with dew, or whatever passed for dew in the jungle. It took her a few groggy seconds to figure out where she was, and how she'd ended up there.

Dale, Connie, the cave, the map. Memories came back to her in bits and pieces.

She looked at the cave, but there were no signs of life. The wheelbarrow was gone. In its place, a wild sow nosed around in the soft, dark soil, grunting and snuffling.

Dale and Connie.

Not sex.

A treasure hunt.

They wanted the gold. The prize money.

Which didn't seem exactly fair.

If they did all get off the island, and gold was still worth something in whatever kind of world awaited them out there, it should be divided among everyone. Players and production team both.

She'd watched as Dale pulled down a screening shield of bushes. Connie had shone the flashlight in, and that was when Sarah decided she'd wait for

them, confront them when they came out.

But then Connie had started to scream. And there'd been other sounds. Horrible sounds.

Then . . . nothing.

Had she fainted? Had she fallen asleep? Dreamed the whole thing? Imagined it?

But she could see how the bushes at the mouth of the opening were pulled down. And she could see the tracks the wheelbarrow had left.

"Dale? Connie? Are you there? Hello?"

The pig snorted and lumbered away, making low indignant sounds in its throat as if Sarah had first startled and then offended it.

Sarah got up and approached the cave entrance. Her nose wrinkled at the foul air that came wafting out of the shadows.

"Dale?" Her voice shook a little. "Connie?"

It smelled like the apothecary, where the bodies of her mother and Doctor Brookstone and the others were still waiting on the pyre she'd meant to give them.

This was a death-place too.

Don't go in there! her mind warned. *You don't want to go in there.*

True. She didn't want to. But she had to see.

With the bushes torn down, the blistered orange daylight permeated far enough for her to see a little way in. She moved cautiously down the passageway.

Connie Berkwelter's gutted corpse was the first thing she found. Sarah's eyes bulged and a scream welled in her throat. It came out as a thin squeak, and died away altogether when her gaze traveled past Connie to the facedown man in the sand.

Something was wrong with his leg and something even worse was wrong with his crushed head, but . . .

"Trip?"

The bag he always carried confirmed it. The satchel lay several feet from his body, the flap open and some of the contents spilled out. Its long strap was partially buried under a heap of loose, fresh-dug sand. She could make out places in the pile that still held the shape of the shovel-scoops. The hole was irregular and sunken, making her think of a gaping, toothless mouth.

She wanted to cry, but she was still too stunned, too numb, too disbelieving. She couldn't really be seeing all this. A dream, it had to be a dream. She was still sleeping. That was the only possible explanation.

Or she had gone crazy.

Around the hole, the rough cave walls curved. They were ridged with ledges that looked like natural formations in the stone . . . perfect shelves to hold rows of bare, grinning skulls.

There were more bones at the rear of the cave, bones scattered like driftwood and tangled in the threadbare scraps of ancient clothing. Some were snapped or crushed, surrounded by a trampled pattern of footprints in the sand. It reminded her of those dance diagrams she'd sometimes seen in old cartoons. But these tracks went all around the hole, and she supposed they must belong to whoever had been digging.

Her gaze came to rest on the one intact skeleton, and she shivered. Sarah tried desperately to cling to the dream idea, but this was too vivid, too real. Her mind couldn't make up something in this much detail and clarity.

Insanity, then.

Okay. Insanity. Going crazy was better than having to deal with what she'd seen and experienced.

Crazy was good. Crazy was all right. Crazy, she could live with.

Sarah moved closer, smiling in admiration.

The authenticity of the clothing was fabulous.

She had been Edith Creighton's assistant, and the two of them had spent countless hours poring over illustrations and descriptions. They'd used all sorts of tricks and techniques to give the rags on the skeletons at Dead Man's Cove and Bloody Bay the proper aged-and-weathered look. And they'd done a very good job.

This, though, was way better than anything she or Edith had ever been able to pull off. These clothes really did look like they'd been here for three hundred years.

Squatting beside the jointed bones held together by skin that resembled cured leather, Sarah fingered the cuff of the frock coat. The spiderweb-fine embroidery and gold brocade would have been museum-worthy if it hadn't been so faded, so brittle . . .

The arm moved.

She recoiled, sucking in a breath, then laughed at her silliness. She'd dislodged it, that was all. The arm was balanced just so –

The bony fingers, dry but fearfully strong, clamped around her wrist.

*   *   *

Chapter 59

The sun was lost behind a bed of red-black clouds. The daylight filtering through made everything look thinly painted in old blood.

There was no wind, not so much as a breath of it. Had the *Adventure* been a strictly traditional sailing ship, they wouldn't have been going anywhere that day, no matter how much they wanted to.

Everything was in readiness, or in as much readiness as they could get it. Kelly paced the deck. She could feel their gazes on her. Following her.

All she had to do was say the word, and they could get underway. Goodbye, Veradoga. Goodbye and good riddance.

They were all as eager to leave as she was. Some of them even more eager. Ambrose shifted from foot to foot like he had to pee. Dale would have been checking his watch every few seconds, if he'd been wearing one.

None of them would question her decision, or second-guess her if she said to start the *Adventure's* engines and untie the mooring lines, haul anchor, and get the fuck out of here. They'd do it without hesitation. With sighs and cheers of relief, most likely.

Now, more than ever, she probably should have been wearing that damned Captain Kelly outfit.

She was the captain, all right. Like it or not.

But if she gave those orders . . .

Karl had led a small search party at first light, he and Mike and Jimmy looking for Sarah or any sign of where she might have gone. While they'd done that, Letitia and had gotten the injured Steve and Dale settled on board, and Ambrose and Tala helped Kelly make sure they had their salvaged cargo and belongings stowed.

"One hour," Kelly had told Karl. "If you haven't found anything by then, come back and we'll discuss it some more."

She'd watched them go, dolefully sure that they wouldn't return either … that they'd die just like everyone else had died. Shot, like Pete had been. Tortured and executed in some hideous fiendish way, like what had happened to Joe Baxter and Bev Phillips and the group of men who'd gone with Robbie Willets.

It didn't seem possible that B.J. and Connie had been able to do all that. Not when they'd been accompanied by camera crews almost constantly.

An hour later, Karl and Mike and Jimmy had emerged from the jungle. Unscathed, but also unsuccessful. No Sarah. No B.J., no Connie.

And now Kelly had a crucial decision to make.

Stay, or go?

Escape while they could and leave Sarah to her fate?

Or keep looking for her, and risk all of their lives?

Not that leaving was a guarantee of safety. Their lives could be at just as much risk at sea. They didn't know where they could go, whether they could get there, what they might find.

Kelly looked from one pair of eyes to the next, to the next. Some met hers steadily. Some looked away. Some pleaded wordlessly for salvation, and an end to this nightmare.

Whatever she said, she didn't know if she'd be able to live with it.

Sarah was her responsibility.

So were these others.

Sarah might be dead already, and by staying, the rest of them would only endanger their own lives.

If Sarah *was* still alive, and they abandoned her, they might as well have killed her themselves.

They might all die out there in the open ocean anyway.

Here, on the island, they'd have shelter and firewood and water and food. And murderers. And memories.

"It's a damn coin flip," she said, whispering it so that no one else overheard.

A coin flip of life or death.

*　　*　　*

Chapter 60

The girl took one long look into the empty black fire of Smythe's eye sockets, uttered a shrill cry, and swooned into a limp and senseless heap.

He stood, tendons creaking as he moved. His hollow gaze traveled slowly over what had been done to his dear Luisa, and their child.

A vast, blinding rage swelled up and swallowed him, and he gave himself to it gladly.

Their precious bones! Kicked about, trodden on, crushed! The fragile little skull . . . in fragments. His family, defiled without so much as a murmur of respect. Desecrated!

The man who'd been left on watch was dead, and there would not even be any disciplining of him, any punishing of him. His head was so shattered that his spirit was forever beyond reach of summoning.

That only angered Smythe further. His cave invaded, his treasure stolen, his wife's and son's bones scattered like jackstraws . . . and he could not even wreak righteous revenge on the lazy buggering imbecile who'd let it happen!

Smythe circled the hole where the chest had been and stood over the freshly dead man. There was another corpse as well, a woman, slouched with her guts laid open in her lap to provide a feast for the first exploratory, buzzing flies.

And here . . . a shovel, an iron bar . . . tossed aside when the digging was done. A swath in the sand showed where the chest had been dragged out.

Had it been the work of this girl? She seemed barely more than a child,

not strong enough for such a feat on her own. There must have been others, others who escaped with his gold.

He lifted her slack weight. She was heavy and warm in his arms, the beating of her heart a tangible thudding drumbeat through her flesh.

This wretched creature had the pulse and breath of life. When Smythe himself did not. When Luisa and their child had been robbed of it.

He could kill her now. Kill her with his bare hands. Or with his teeth. Tear into the softness of her neck and let her hot blood pour into the sand.

What stopped him was the knowledge that she could not have done this alone. Perhaps she had not even done it at all. Perhaps she had come later, come after the true thieves.

It was someone else who had done this.

Smythe went around the cave, touching the bare skulls on their ledges one after another. Power surged in his bony hands as he once again summoned forth his crew.

They appeared before him, smoky forms growing substantial with fury as they realized what had been taken from them.

The gold and silver and jewels . . . their treasure, for which they had fought and suffered and died . . . stolen.

And the girl?

She would tell him who had done this.

He would find those responsible.

He would make them pay.

Dearly.

*　　*　　*

Chapter 61

The engines, hidden in the *Adventure's* hold, rumbled as the ship cut smoothly across the dark, glassy waters of Veradoga Harbor.

Kelly looked back at the debris-strewn, shrapnel-peppered ruins of Rum Town, and thought that it looked more authentic than ever. As if it really had been bombarded by cannonfire, sacked and burned.

Their wake frothed and churned in a swirling, rising bulge.

That wasn't right. Kelly had never seen the water look like that before. A bulge? As if something large were coming up, surfacing, breaching like a whale . . . a submarine . . . a sea monster . . .

"What *is* that?" she asked.

A black, rotted, jagged spire emerged from the center of the churning froth. It resembled a tree trunk or telephone pole, sheared off into an uneven point. As it continued to rise, Kelly recognized it.

She didn't *believe* it, but she recognized it.

The top of a mast. Broken yardarms, dripping brine and seaweed, leaned from it at drunken angles. Sodden, rotted flaps of sail still hung from them. A crow's nest, black with slime and studded with barnacles, came next.

"It's a ship," Kelly heard herself say.

The sea continued to swell and roil, heaving up more of the derelict bulk. She saw more waterlogged strips of sailcloth, and tattered rigging.

The other survivors, the rest of her crew, stared with identical expressions of gape-mouthed astonishment.

Now Kelly could see the dark shipwreck's forecastle, and the aft deck. Seawater poured over the sides, making waterfalls cascade through the railings. The hull and deck planking was bloated, distorted, eaten away into monstrous cavities and cancerous-looking holes. Rows of blunt cannon snouts were lined along the gunwales, their brass greened with verdigris.

"Captain Smythe's ship," Kelly said.

Gilded lettering on the hull, nearly worn away but still legible, told her she was right. *Good Lady Jane,* the scrolled letters read.

Water ran in freshets and froth down the wreck's corroded sides. The ship's undulations slowed as the sea around it gradually calmed.

"Our anchor must have snagged her and dislodged her from the bottom."

Steve Quinlan was at her side. Kelly didn't know when that had happened, when he had emerged from Letitia's makeshift infirmary.

"Look!" Mike called, pointing.

A smaller craft, a longboat, was crossing the cove. Its oars dipped and lifted and dipped again, propelling it along at a steady pace. A figure stood at the prow, a thin man in what looked like a long coat and a plumed hat. Someone sat beside him . . . a woman . . .

"It's Sarah," Steve said.

"But who . . ." Kelly's voice faltered as she got a better look at the men rowing the longboat.

They weren't men at all.

Not anymore, at least.

She was aware of commotion all around her. Panic and fear. Denial. Horror. Someone was shouting Sarah's name. Others were screaming, or praying, or both at the same time.

A hand closed on Kelly's. She looked around, expecting Steve, and found herself facing the stormcloud-colored eyes of Tala Greywolf.

"We *have* to leave here," Tala said. "Now."

"But Sarah —"

"Too late. Forget her. She's among the dead. Lost to us. If we delay, we'll join them."

A decaying old rope ladder had unrolled down the side of the *Good Lady Jane* as the longboat came alongside, and though it didn't seem capable of holding the weight of a seagull, let alone a person, Sarah was climbing it. The tall man-shape that had been in the longboat's prow was already aboard. His head turned toward the *Adventure.* For a heart-stopping moment, Kelly felt their eyes meet.

"There he is," she said. "Captain Smythe himself."

"It's a ghost ship," Jimmy said.

Smythe's crew, grey and foggy, insubstantial apparitions that might have stepped out of a black-and-white movie, swarmed up the ladder and fanned out over the *Good Lady Jane's* deck. They moved with the quickness and precision of long-practiced sailors.

"Tala's right," Steve said from Kelly's other side. "Get us out of here, love."

"This isn't real," Karl said. "This isn't happening. We're hallucinating."

"Ghost ship," Jimmy repeated. "Ghost pirates. Holy shit. Ghost pirates. They're coming after us. They're hoisting their colors. Look."

Kelly's blood ran cold.

Give me enough to sound convincing, like I know what I'm talking about, she'd told Dad's experts on pirate lore.

As a result, she knew exactly what those flags meant. One was wilted and darkish grey, once black. The yellowed design on it wasn't the familiar skull-and-crossbones that would have been used in the *Pirate Adventure* show's opening credits, but displayed a Grim Reaper with white outlines of wings, a scythe in one skeletal hand and an hourglass in the other. Elliot Smythe's own flag.

The other scrap of faded, dripping cloth was a dusty rose hue. Plain and unadorned. Once, it would have been a solid flag of blood-red. The symbol for attacking without mercy. No quarter given. No surrender. Death to all.

"No," Dale said. They were all clustered around Kelly now, shoulder to shoulder, staring at the pirate ship. "No, game over, this isn't happening, this can't be real."

"It's not real," Karl said. "Hallucination."

"That we're all having?" Ambrose sounded like he would love to believe them, but couldn't quite manage it.

Sarah stood beside Smythe, alive but expressionless, blank, and dead-eyed. Catatonic. She didn't seem aware of where she was or what was happening, let alone capable of showing any response to the people who'd been calling and waving to her.

Smythe, now at the helm, extended an arm and leveled a thin, pale finger at the *Adventure*.

"Oh, dear Lord." Steve had gone ashen, and was trembling. "The helicopter crash. I remember now. It was one of them. Just . . . appeared out of nowhere. Right there in the cabin. I saw it attack Leslie. That's why we went down."

"All those stories about the island," Kelly said. "And the curse. It's true, the whole thing's true. All these years, bound here to protect their treasure. They must have wanted to get rid of us. That whole run of bad luck, Steve! The

279

accidents. And then, when it wasn't working, when we kept bringing more people to the island, that's when the murders started. It wasn't Dad. It's been them, all along. Smythe and his crew."

"You people are out of your minds," Karl said. "There's no such things as ghosts!"

"Get your head out of your ass, man!" Jimmy smacked Karl on the upper arm. "Look at that thing! That's a ghost-ship! They're coming to kill us!"

"But why?" asked Letitia, who looked like she was about to faint. "If they wanted us to leave, that's what we're doing!"

"Yeah, so let's do it, let's oblige already!" Dale reached past Kelly for the *Adventure's* wheel. "Crank the engine, floor it, whatever the heck you do, and let's get out of here before they catch up!"

"But Sarah's on that ship," Kelly said. "They've got her. We have to do something. Help her. Rescue her."

Jimmy laughed wildly. "From *that?* You want to fight a bunch of pirate ghosts? With what? These fake cannons we got?"

"They happen to be real cannons," Steve said. "They actually do fire."

"So what?' Jimmy rounded on Steve. "They're fucking *dead* already!"

The yelling and arguing, the panic, flared up again. Kelly barely paid attention. She couldn't look away from the figure of Captain Smythe, who still seemed to be staring right back at her. Evaluating her. His adversary. He would fire on the *Adventure*, riddling it with holes, sending a deadly storm of wood-splinters. Crippling the ship. Then they'd board. And then . . .

Then what?

If they were ghosts, what could they do?

She thought of everyone who'd already died, and what had happened to them. Obviously, ghosts or not, these things *could* affect the real world in a very serious way. They could torture, mutilate, rape and kill.

God, how in the world had it come to this? An actual ship-to-ship battle? Broadsides and boarding parties and the whole nine yards? There was no way they could win. Smythe's crew had them outnumbered five to one . . . Smythe's crew was made up of supernatural undead monsters!

If the *Adventure* could outrun the *Good Lady Jane,* they might have a chance. The *Adventure* had engines, while the *Good Lady Jane* only had sails. Sails that were ragged shrouds made up of more holes than canvas. There wasn't even any wind . . .

Which meant, really, that the *Good Lady Jane* shouldn't be moving at all. Yet here she came, gliding across the harbor toward them, cresting the swells made by the *Adventure's* wake.

Letitia was at the rail, screaming to the pirates. "We're going! We're leaving! We're sorry! The island's all yours! Just let us alone!"

"They're still chasing us," Jimmy said. "I think they're about to shoot those what-do-you-call-thems."

"Long nines," Steve said.

"We're going to die if they catch us." Tala spoke serenely, but her complexion had gone grayish. "They'll kill us all."

The shot from one of the long nines was a muffled cough. It whizzed through the air and splashed into the sea only a dozen yards aft of their stern.

"Warning shot," Steve said.

"Why?" Ambrose tried to pull Letitia down, out of the line of fire. "They got what they wanted. We're leaving."

Even Karl had given up his protests and denial and was arming himself. Although the *Adventure* was chugging toward the open sea at a good clip, the pirates were gaining. All of them could see the phantoms swarming up the rigging, busying themselves with the cannons, readying muskets and cutlasses and worn ropes on rusty grappling hooks.

"Because they're pirates," Kelly said, speeding up until the engines roared. The ship leaped ahead in a powerful surge. "It's what they do. Dead or alive, it's what they do. They'll take what plunder they want, slaughter us, and either seize the ship or scuttle and burn it."

"Plunder? We don't have any plunder, for Christ's sake!" Karl said.

"We have provisions," Steve said. "Goods. Most pirate booty wasn't actually all doubloons and pieces-of-eight."

"Enough with the fucking history lectures!" Dale yelled. "Professor Charles got voted out, remember? Jeez, you people make me crazy! So what if they want the gold? It doesn't matter! They can't have it! It's mine, damn it, *mine!* Fair and square! I found it, I got it, I'm going to keep it, and no dead-fucking-pirates are going to take it away from me!"

They all looked at him.

Dale went scarlet. Guilt and sheepishness might as well have been tattooed in big letters across his face, but they were quickly suffused by a defiant, indignant anger.

"What are you talking about, mate?" Steve asked.

"Nothing. What? Nothing!" Dale jabbed a finger toward the other ship, beginning to fall behind. "In case you didn't notice, we're about to get attacked here!"

"Hey, Karl." Jimmy's gaze didn't shift from Dale as he spoke. "What ever happened to that map you found?"

"How the hell do I know, and who the hell cares, anyway?"

"What map?" Kelly asked.

"You took the map, didn't you?" Jimmy ignored her, and took a step toward Dale. "You snuck out and dug up the gold, and hid it on board, and that's why they're after us. They want the damn treasure!"

"Too bad for them! I told you, it's mine!" Dale's lip curled in a belligerent sneer. "Finders keepers. I would have won this stupid game anyway."

"What map?" Kelly demanded, louder.

"We found it when we were searching through the rubble of the fortress," Karl said. "A fancy treasure map with a big red X on it. We figured it was for the final challenge. The half million in gold. You know, the grand prize."

"You numbnuts!" This from mild-mannered Ambrose, of all people. He shoved past Jimmy to confront Dale. "You brought all that on the ship? That's what they want!"

"Then give it to them!" Letitia cried. "Maybe they'll take it and go away and not hurt us!"

"No way!" Dale threw appealing looks around the circle. "Look, we can split it, okay? I don't mind sharing. I wouldn't have kept it all for myself."

"Lying, greedy, son of a bitch," marveled Jimmy. "Had to get the money, huh? Had to get the gold."

"Hey, it seemed stupid to go through everything we've been through and leave it on the island," Dale said. "I mean, what a waste!"

"When did you – ?" Karl began.

"Last night," Kelly said, thinking about the wheelbarrow she'd tripped over. The one that had been covered with mud and foliage, as if it had been trundled through the dense jungle growth. "You stashed it on the *Adventure,* just before I saw you in town."

"I was going to tell everyone," Dale said, all sulky now like a spoiled kid. "I was going to share."

"What about Connie?" Ambrose asked. "You said she told you about it."

"Jeez, I lied, okay? So sue me! We were going to dig it up and go fifty-fifty on it, me and Connie, that was her idea. But . . . uh . . . look, it doesn't matter right now."

"I think it does," Kelly said. "You told us that Connie and B.J. attacked you, and that's how you got stabbed."

"Guys, come on!" Dale gestured at the *Good Lady Jane,* which had dwindled to half its former looming size behind them but was still in pursuit. "Can't we do this later? If there *is* a later."

"Nuh-uh," Letitia said, planting herself in Dale's personal space. "I think

we better know what really went on last night. With B.J. and Connie and Sarah, all of it."

He flung exasperated hands in the air. "Connie's dead, okay? B.J. too, as far as I know . . . just like Connie told us. I didn't even see Sarah last night. She must have followed me, and that's how she wound up with Captain Cryptkeeper over there. You can't blame me for that. You guys on the show were the ones who thought it'd be such a neato idea to bury the swag in his fucking cave in the first place!"

"Cave?" Kelly exchanged a glance with Mike and Steve. "What cave? We didn't bury anything in any cave."

"Oh, bullshit," Dale said. "I saw the whole setup. The skulls, all the bones, the works. I thought it was more special effects, like Old Bony back at our beach. How was I supposed to know it was for real? No wonder he's been so pissed at you people and put this whole curse thing on the show. *You* disturbed his resting place, not me. Well, not me first."

"Dale . . ." Kelly said carefully, "what, exactly, did you find? What kind of treasure?"

"You know!" He rolled his eyes. "Gold and silver coins, ropes of pearls, jewel-studded cups, medallions, all that stuff."

"No," Mike said.

"Yeah-huh," Dale insisted.

"There wasn't silver, pearls, cups or anything like that in the chest we buried," Kelly said. "And we didn't bury it in any cave."

Jimmy slapped himself in the forehead. "How much is buried on this island anyway? So now Dale *didn't* find the half-mil grand prize? What, did he find the real thing?"

"I do believe he did," Steve said. "Captain Smythe's own swag."

A gust blew a lock of Kelly's hair into her face. She swiped it absently aside, trying to coax more speed out of the *Adventure* and hoping that she didn't run them right over one of the reefs that she knew ringed Veradoga's rocky coast. "This is . . ."

"Are you telling me I dug up the wrong fucking treasure chest?" Dale hit the railing with his fist. "I don't believe it! Jeez!"

"Nice one, Dale," Karl said, his tone like acid. "Very slick. Congratulations. You grave-robbing asshole."

"I just did what any one of you would have done if you had any brains in your head!"

Dale might have gone on blustering, but Jimmy chose that moment to drive a fist into his nose.

"Shut up, man!" Jimmy shouted as Dale reeled back. "I had enough of your crap! You just shut up! You got us killed, you —" He launched into a torrent of Spanish, most of which Kelly figured was obscene.

Dale put his hands to his face, then stared at the blood on them. His nose was crunched, and gushing. "Brick!" he yelled at Jimmy. "You fuggig brick!"

"Break it up and that's an order!" Steve was using his sharpest Mr. Quinlan voice, for all the good it did.

Mike and Karl interposed themselves as Dale and Jimmy lunged at each other. The four of them made a scuffling, struggling knot of bodies on the deck. Letitia jumped into the thick of it as well, either trying to pull them apart or trying to land a few kicks and punches of her own on Dale. Tala had her hands over her eyes, like a little girl during the scary part of a movie. Ambrose danced around the melee, obviously wanting to help but just as obviously not knowing what to do.

Kelly swiped again at her hair, wind-tossed into her face.

She froze. Wind-tossed?

Above her, the edges of the *Adventure's* furled sails fluttered. The flag, which had been slack, was lifting in the freshening breeze. She could see the show's logo, bright colors and bold graphics, snapping back and forth.

"Steve! The wind's picking up!"

He was at her side in an instant. "Don't worry, love. We've outdistanced them. Even if they could get that tub under full sail, they couldn't catch us now."

Kelly looked over her shoulder. The *Good Lady Jane's* faded flags, the Grim Reaper and the solid *jolie rouge*, were flapping. The ragged sails, which should have let the wind pass through their gaping rents, were belled out full.

"They're gaining speed, though," she said. "It's impossible, but they are."

"Just get us around the point," he said, indicating the sweeping promontory that curved out like a rocky claw from the island's coast. "It won't be at their backs then, and we'll leave them far behind."

"Okay," Kelly said.

A series of rattling bangs came from somewhere in the belly of the ship. They sounded like a string of firecrackers going off. The ship shuddered. The engines made a rough, blatting, choppy sound.

Gouts of dark, oily smoke billowed up through the hatches. There was an explosion below, thunderous, making the deck jump beneath Kelly's feet.

Then, with a final grinding cough, the *Adventure's* engines died.

*   *   *

Chapter 62

The rise and fall of the waves, the strengthening wind, the creak of mast and flap of sail, the salt spray leaping as the prow forged ahead . . . bliss.

And to be closing on an enemy ship again? Purest ecstasy.

The *Adventure,* for so was the name was emblazoned on its hull in letters two foot high and painted in sparkling gold, had been heading away from Smythe's ship at a daunting clip.

Yet now, it faltered and slowed. Smoke arose from the hold. A careless flame? The powder magazine?

Smythe saw them on the deck, dashing this way and that, waving their arms like panicked birds unable to take to the air. His dry lips split in a smile.

His eager crew had lost none of their shipboard skills in the intervening centuries. They performed their duties as expertly as any captain could have wished.

He brought the *Good Lady Jane* about on a course that would position them broadsides to the *Adventure.* He could see the enemy crew scrambling about. They yanked at lines, they shouted madly at one another. Trying, he surmised, to set their own sails.

It would not matter. He had them now.

At the bosun's signal, fiery brands were touched to fuses. Six starboard cannons boomed. Six coils of white smoke, spinning like whirlpools before being torn apart by the breeze, belched from the barrels.

The cannonballs arched high and splashed down, missing the *Adventure*

by mere yards.

Smythe laughed his cold, dusty-dry laugh as the attack spurred renewed terror and panic among his prey. His men laughed as well. Only the girl, whose light had been snuffed like a candle flame, was oblivious. She stood at his side, slack-featured and glazed of eye.

To be at sea again! To be aboard his own ship again, after so long! It revitalized him. He almost felt alive. His crew seemed more substantial now, their voices audible instead of mutters and whispers heard only in Smythe's mind. They were no longer as misty and grey as they'd been. Color was returning to them

Even the *Good Lady Jane* herself was being invigorated by the chase, and the thrill of battle. The sails were re-knitting even as he watched, the melding together as if stitched by some invisible hand. The gouges in the mast and the holes in the hull were diminishing, drawing in on themselves.

The cannons fired another volley. Five shots found their mark. The aftcastle of the *Adventure* opened with four holes like startled eyes. The fifth shot went high and glanced off the mast. The sixth missed and sent up a white plume as it plowed into the sea.

He'd cripple their ship and bring the *Good Lady Jane* alongside for boarding, and the matter would be settled by blade and pistol. No quarter. No mercy. When all hands of the *Adventure* were dead, their bodies cast to the sharks, the plunder of the ship would be his.

Other cannons roared. They were attempting to return fire, fools that they were. Their shots fell far short, coming nowhere close to striking the *Good Lady Jane.*

They had left the calmer waters of the harbor for the rougher open seas. Ahead was a curving jut of rock, beyond which Smythe knew the winds would be crosswise, and less favorable. But he would be upon them long before they reached it. The *Good Lady Jane* knifed easily through the waves, almost seemed to leap like a frolicsome young horse.

Again Smythe's cannons thundered. They had come even with the *Adventure* and the cannonballs shredded planking and masts and rails into a lethal hail of splinters. Bodies were thrown end over end, arms and legs flailing wildly. A tangle of torn sails and rigging came down in a heap onto the damaged deck.

Smythe gave the order to board.

*　　*　　*

Chapter 63

The deck of the *Adventure* was in chaos, people running and screaming all over the place. Dale could hear Kelly Dagget and Steve Quinlan barking orders that could barely be understood above the booming cannons.

What a farce! One day of pirate camp couldn't get them ready for this!

Dale sprang down through the hatch. The air was dense with smoke and diesel stink, gaggingly foul.

He fought through it and came to the cramped room with its hard benches and low ceiling, the room in the hold where the twelve of them had made the crossing from Jamaica to Rum Town. Hadn't been that long ago . . . seemed like a lifetime. Seemed like forever.

The *Adventure* rocked from another cannonball onslaught. Dale almost went head over heels, but kept his balance. He clambered over piles of junk, kicked and pushed more junk out of his way.

He hurt all over, muscles aching from the previous night's grueling labor, the stitches popped open so that his stab-wound was bleeding again, the broken nose courtesy of that prick Jimmy Hernandez feeling like it was full of needling wasps. Every breath was a snuffling gargle of his own blood and snot.

But Dale wasn't going to let any of that stop him, He didn't care if he had to spend the next year in a hospital bed while plastic surgeons put his face back together. He could afford it. He could afford the finest medical care money could buy.

The chest was hidden under a bunch of spare blankets and hammocks and clothes. He'd planned on finding a better place for it, down in the bilge maybe, once they'd gotten away from this miserable fucking excuse for an island.

He had about killed himself getting it in here without anyone else noticing. He'd been sure that they'd see him, or hear him, struggling to maneuver the wheelbarrow up the gangplank and then lower the chest on ropes and winches. He still wasn't entirely sure how he'd done it by himself. That part was kind of in a haze.

Actually, everything after leaving the cave was kind of in a haze.

Dale crawled to the chest, took the tarnished old key from where he'd tucked it down his pants, and opened the lid. He had the penlight he'd gotten from the guy who'd stabbed him, clenching it in his teeth again. Its beam struck sparkles from the riches, gleamed on precious metal, glowed in the jewels.

When he'd first seen the treasure, Dale hadn't been able to resist an urge to plunge his hands in, scoop up piles of it, and let it trickle down through his fingers. He did it again now, chortling to himself like a greedy miser in some old melodrama.

His. All his. Not the prize money at all. Real, actual, genuine, authentic pirate loot. Not Dagget's. None of the others had any sort of claim on it. *He* had found it, *he* had dug it up and brought it here. That meant it belonged to Dale Allen Sheffield, and no one else.

Well, except for the real, actual, genuine, authentic pirates. They sure seemed to want it back. They were fully prepared to hack and slash and burn and kill to get it.

If he honestly believed that surrendering and turning the treasure over to them would save the *Adventure* and their lives, Dale would have done it. Absolutely. Right away. Without question.

But the pirates would kill them anyway. Just for the fun of it. They might be quick in dealing with the others, but somehow Dale had a feeling that they'd reserve a special fate for him. He'd heard what had been done to the other people. Mousy little Heather getting her head cracked like a walnut shell . . . that guy who'd had his intestines nailed to a post . . . the woman who'd been buried to the chin below the high-tide line . . . the guy that had been found char-broiled in a barrel full of burnt gunpowder . . .

Probably, whatever Smythe would do to Dale would make all those tortures look like kiddie rides. Even if Dale returned the treasure.

Of course, doing the noble thing might spare the others . . .

Screw the others!

He burrowed his hands into the coins and jewels, loving the music they made as they clinked together. Pearls slid in cool, smooth succession between his fingers.

And screw giving it back! If Smythe wanted it, he'd have to take it over Dale's dead body. What did a ghost need with treasure anyway?

He pawed through the glittering mounds of silver and gold, sifting through the larger items that had ended up toward the bottom. He'd seen one thing in here . . . where was it . . . aha!

Dale held up a knife, which for all he knew might have belonged to an Incan prince or a Spanish conquistador. It had a jeweled hilt that felt as if it had been crafted for Dale's very own hand, and a shining blade unblemished after all this time. Like it hadn't ever been used.

The *Adventure* quaked from a monstrous grinding crash. Not cannonfire this time, but a colossal slam of wood on wood. He heard cries of pain and fear, and furious howls that sounded simultaneously bloodcurdling and hollow. He heard the ringing clash of swords, the crack of pistols.

A boarding party. A by-God son of a bitch boarding party!

He couldn't stand waiting down here to defend his treasure, but he couldn't stand to just leave it, either. As a compromise, Dale scooped handfuls of loot into cotton pouches, and crammed them into his baggy pirate clothes. They made heavy, uncomfortable bulges and he jingled when he walked, and he was sure he looked absurd, but he didn't care.

Up on deck, everything was smoke and shouting and gunfire. The two ships were locked together by lines and grappling hooks. The *Adventure* looked like a tornado had whirled across it, splintered wood and debris strewn from one end to the other. Barrels rolled. Winch-hooks on ropes swung in crazy pendulum arcs.

The sky was the color of burning blood, shedding a gruesome red light over the scene. The spectral pirates poured over the side of the *Good Lady Jane,* whooping and shrieking.

Though Dale could mostly see through them, they were solid enough . . . solid and real enough to kill.

He saw Ambrose face-down on the deck, a crimson pool spreading around him. He saw Letitia huddled against the mast, hands pressed to her side, blood dribbling through her fingers.

Steve Quinlan was down, with so many long jagged wood-splinters sticking out of him that he looked like a porcupine. Kelly Dagget stood over him, wild, a gun in each hand.

Karl had splinters sticking in him, too, but was toe-to-toe with a pirate,

wielding his cutlass in savage swipes. He wasn't arguing anymore that this was all a big hallucination. His face was set, and grim.

Dale hesitated. His eyes darted frantically from side to side.

He saw Jimmy, limping, gasping, trying to hide behind a cannon. He saw Tala, maybe unconscious, maybe dead, her long black hair gripped in a pirate's bony fist the way cavemen dragged their women in cartoons. He saw Mike backed against the rail by a grinning horde of phantoms.

Screw the others, he'd thought earlier.

Yeah.

As Dale spun, with a half-formed notion of diving overboard and swimming for it, he was brought up short by the sight of Sarah Parkins.

"Suh . . . Sarah," Dale said, and swallowed. "Hi."

"You killed Trip," she said.

"What? Huh? Look, I . . ."

The skeletal captain from the cave, in his frock coat and plumed hat, stepped up beside Sarah. He looked quite a bit less skeletal now, Dale noted in the part of his brain still capable of reason.

"It was you," the apparition said, his voice a harsh rasp, his hollow gaze fixed on the jeweled knife in Dale's hand.

Sarah's face was pale and doughy. In the depths of her empty eyes, something flickered. "You left Connie," she said. "You left her to die. You left me. You killed Trip."

"No," Dale said. "It wasn't like that."

Smythe leveled an antique-looking pistol at Dale.

A cannon went off with an enormous explosion. The *Adventure* bucked. Dale slipped, his feet shooting out from under him. The pistol-ball meant for his heart skimmed harmlessly by.

He landed on his hip and side, the bags of coins and jewels like rocks digging into him. But he ignored the pain, wanting to stab at Smythe before the captain could recover and shoot him again.

Dale thrust with the knife —

No, he thrust with an empty hand because the knife had been jarred from his grasp and gone spinning away when he fell.

Smythe's pistol swung. The barrel, hard as an iron bar and hot as a brand, shattered Dale's wrist. He shrieked.

"Now," Smythe said, drawing a nicked, battered old cutlass. "Now you will pay."

*   *   *

Chapter 64

Kelly knew she was going to die.

They were all going to die.

Steve might be dead already. The rest of them might be dead already. As far as she knew, she was the only one left. She couldn't see past the crowd of pirates closing in on her.

She had shot them again and again, using Steve's gun as well as her own. But she'd lost count of her bullets and doubted that they'd give her a chance to reload.

It didn't matter, anyway. They kept coming. Dead, they couldn't be killed. The bullets went into them but drew no blood. They wouldn't stop, wouldn't fall, wouldn't die.

Then, through the wind-torn smoke, she saw Captain Smythe approaching. His cutlass dripped dark red, spattering drops of blood on the deck. His men parted to let him through.

Kelly Dagget drew herself up, taking a deep breath. How many shots left? Any at all?

She didn't wait for the formalities. The gun in her right hand came up . . .

. . . and clicked on empty.

"No!"

Smythe's cracked lips peeled back in a grin. He swung the cutlass at her.

Kelly jumped back. She flung the empty gun at Smythe and knocked off his hat. His bare scalp, with its long straggles of hair, stretched taut over his skull.

Could he be hurt? He seemed more real, more *there* than the others.

"Eeeh-yah!"

The cry startled her, surprised the pirates.

Jimmy Hernandez came swinging down on a rope in the best swash-buckler tradition. His heels hit Smythe in the chest, and sent the captain sprawling hard to the deck.

Kelly ducked. Jimmy careened around in a wild figure-eight, smacked into the mainmast, lost his hold on the rope, and dropped into a dazed heap.

Smythe was trying to get up, moving in awkward jerks like a half-swatted bug. Kelly shifted Steve's gun into her right hand and fired. She hit him in the elbow, snapping off his withered arm like a dry twig, and he went down again. No blood, but he was hurt, yes, he was hurt all right.

She aimed at the patchy, bald crown of his head.

Pulled the trigger.

Got another useless click.

"No! Damn it, no!"

"Kelly . . . love."

She looked down, and Steve's eyes were open. Clouded with pain, but open. His hand twitched fitfully toward a small barrel that lay nearby.

Gunpowder? She looked at him, dumbfounded. What was she supposed to do with this? Blow herself and the ship to bits before the pirates could finish the job?

The pirates had drawn away from her to cluster uncertainly around Smythe, as if waiting to see whether or not their captain could recover. Smythe did seem to be regaining his coordination, even . . . healing? Regenerating? Mending?

Kelly didn't know. She scanned the smoldering, ruined deck and saw that she wasn't the only one left alive. She saw Mike, Letitia, Karl. All wounded, but upright. Saw Jimmy struggling to push himself up.

The same expression was on each of their faces. Kelly wondered if it was on her own.

She yanked the stopper out of the little keg of gunpowder. A drizzle of black grit spilled out. Someone's crew kerchief — red, *Tortuga* — was crumpled nearby and she stuffed one end in through the hole, then held the other into a burning pile of ropes until it ignited.

"Throw it!" Karl called, pointing at the crowd of phantoms around Smythe.

"Kill her," Smythe's hoarse voice replied.

With a helpless, squawking cry, Kelly chucked the keg of gunpowder. It flew, trailing its blazing fuse —

Then tumbled past the pirates and rolled toward an open hatch.

Kelly swore, stumbling back as the pirates advanced. She saw Karl running on the littered, smoking deck. He weaved between obstacles like a football player through the defensive line. He dove and reached and rolled, snagged the gunpowder keg just before it fell through the hatch, and came up with it cradled in the crook of his elbow.

She thought he was going to chuck a Hail Mary right into the middle of Smythe's crew.

He ran with it instead.

"Karl, don't!" she screamed, realizing what he was about to do.

Karl didn't stop. He charged into the midst of the pirates, elbowing and shouldering his way until he was practically on top of Smythe.

The explosion was tremendous. A deafening thunderclap that turned the world inside-out.

Kelly was thrown backward, airborne, feeling as though she'd been struck head-on by a runaway truck. She heard nothing but the ringing blast, saw nothing but a fireball brighter and hotter than the strange, fuming orange sun.

*　*　*

Chapter 65

The fire burned brilliant magnesium white, snapping with hot yellow sparks. It fanned out over the deck, raced along ropes and rails, scurried like a horde of rats. A tongue of flame reached the *Adventure's* row of cannons and found another barrel of gunpowder.

Dale barely noticed. He crept along on his knees, dragging himself, groaning. His right hand clamped over the stump of his other arm, squeezing. He could feel blood spurting against his fingers, spurting in time with the pounding of his heart.

Smythe hadn't killed him. Smythe had turned and walked away, leaving Dale there to gibber in horror at the sight of his own severed hand still convulsing from the final scrambled nerve impulses.

Left him . . . for Sarah.

She had picked up the jeweled knife, running her thumb along the blade in slow, dreamy, hypnotic strokes. Dale had closed his eyes, so wrapped around the terrible agony of his arm that he'd almost been looking forward to the *coup de grace*.

But it hadn't come.

When he finally looked up, Sarah had been gone.

He'd seen swirling masses of smoke, heard the sounds of fighting. Then had come an eardrum-bursting explosion that shook the ship.

Tucking his stump against his belly, hating the hot, soaking feel of blood through his shirt, Dale crawled. His fingernails carved scratches in the wood.

Splinters ran up under them. His index finger caught on something and tore the fingernail off.

Dale saw some of the others, still alive. They were cutting at the ropes that bound the ships together. The *Good Lady Jane* was sinking, and losing cohesion, rotting away before their very eyes. But the grappling hooks and lines would make sure that the dying ship pulled them down with her.

No one was looking his way. He croaked a smoky, desperate plea for help that went unheard.

The *Adventure* tilted, and Dale felt himself slide along the sloped deck planking. He tried again to scream for help, tried to grab for purchase. His bleeding stump banged the wood, and pain seared like a lightning bolt all the way through his body.

His legs slid out through the gap where the gangplank went. He caught at one of the posts. His entire body was hanging over the side, swinging above the churning water where the *Good Lady Jane* was being sucked down.

The last line snapped, its ends flying. The *Adventure* rocked back, slammed down with a jolt. Dale lost his grip and dropped feet-first.

The salt water raged like battery acid on the raw meat of his arm. His head went under. He choked on the brine, vomited, choked again on that. He beat frenziedly at the sea, scissoring his legs.

He couldn't surface. Couldn't swim with one hand . . . couldn't swim with the extra weight of the pouches. Dale clawed into his clothes, trying to rid himself of the treasure. Coins turned over and over, glinting, winking gold as they spun away into the darkness of the sea.

Crimson clouds surrounded him, pumping from the end of his arm. Scarlet billows, like in that old song that Sidney had sometimes liked to sing when he was in the shower, or puttering around in the kitchen.

Dale's abused lungs rebelled. His throat stung from the brine and puke he'd inhaled. A bubble of air, the last of his breath, popped out of his mouth and rose with mocking ease, shimmering toward the surface.

The waver of light beckoned him, taunted him. His limbs felt encased in lead, and no matter how he fought to swim, he couldn't make any progress.

Something long and thin, snakelike, wrapped around him. A rope line, trailing from the *Good Lady Jane,* snared him, entangled him, tightened around his body and dragged him toward the depths.

Into the darkness. Into the black. He quit struggling and let himself fall, spinning in the sucking whirlpool of the pirate ship's descent.

* * *

Chapter 66

Mike doused the *Adventure's* entire engine room in an inch-deep layer of fire-retardant foam, then wiped the worst of it away so he could get a look at the engines.

He soberly shook his head. "Nope."

Kelly took this to mean that they were a total loss. But she had to ask. "How bad?"

She spoke loudly, probably louder than she needed to. Not her fault. Her hearing hadn't come all the way back yet, and there was a drilling high-pitched whine that seemed to resonate in her skull like a vibration.

"It's toast," Jimmy said, also loud. "Look at this. Someone fucked with the engines but good." He tapped at a few places in the wiring and machinery. "Rigged them to blow when they heated up."

The ship heaved and wallowed as it rode out a violent swell. Conversation went on standby as they found handholds. The dizzying rise and stomach-lifting drop made Kelly utter an involuntary groan.

Not, Kelly supposed, that they needed to talk about it. She knew as well as Mike did who'd sabotaged the ship. This was one that they couldn't blame on Smythe and his curse.

Smythe, after all, had wanted them to leave.

Her dad, on the other hand, had said he'd see to it that they weren't going anywhere.

She bumped her fist against the wall, not hard enough to hurt. "So we're adrift and damaged, with a bad storm coming."

The sky had gotten uglier, the wind rising into a gale and stirring the sea with whitecaps. Ominous thunder chuckled like Satan Himself. The jet-black clouds blotted out any hint of daylight, and what spearing forks of lightning they saw were immense even from miles away.

She found the last few members of her crew in the largest cabin. Letitia had been forced to pluck a pistol-ball from her own side with tweezers, and stitch herself up. Kelly wasn't sure where she'd found the grit to do that and then still be able to take care of the rest of them. Cuts, burns, bruises, a few broken bones, dozens of splinters . . . no one had gotten away unhurt.

Except for Sarah . . . physically, at least. She had come out of nowhere when Kelly realized that the sinking *Good Lady Jane* was going to tow the *Adventure* into the depths, and used a jewel-handled knife to help them slash at the lines. Since then, she'd gone where she was led, and when left to her own devices, just sat hugging herself and rocking back and forth, staring vacantly into space.

She gave them the bad news about the engines, and didn't have to tell them what it meant. No Jamaica. No hospital in Kingston. They had what was left of the sails, and not enough able-bodied crew to handle them.

And the weather was getting steadily worse.

Kelly felt Steve's hand cover hers and give a weak squeeze. "Do . . . what you have to . . . love," he said.

She could barely hear him at all, the words low and muffled and thick from the drugs. He was drifting in and out of consciousness, so she wasn't sure that she heard her, either, when she leaned over and told him to get some rest.

"We'll look after him," Letitia promised, patting Sarah on the shoulder. "Won't we, honey?"

Mike was waiting for her at the helm, even his massive chest and arms having to fight to keep the wheel from spinning crazily as the *Adventure* was tossed around at the whim of sea and storm.

"Hard to port, Mr. Glass," she shouted, and wondered if this was what it felt like to lose your mind.

Thunder crashed directly overhead. Wave crests, curling under and foaming eerie white against the black water, swept them along.

Silhouetted by flash after flash of lightning, a dark mass loomed ahead.

The ship scraped over a reef with a series of shudders and jolts. The prow tipped, ran aground a sand bar. Waves piled up beneath aft section, raising it, turning the ship, heeling it over.

Kelly shouted unheard in the wind for everyone to hold on, to brace themselves.

The ship was coming apart, the squeal and crack of torn wood drowning out everything else. Decking planks popped up in rapid succession.

A violent, jarring impact tore Kelly loose. She had the sensation of flying, of cartwheeling through the air.

Then she landed and slid, her body gouging a trench in wet sand. She fetched up flat on her back, breathing hard, looking up at the angry sky, amazed to be alive.

She tested herself to see if everything was working, found to her surprise that it all still was, and sat up.

The *Adventure* was on its side like a beached whale, half in and half out of the surf. The hull was in pieces, waves surging in and out, churning with flotsam and an oily sheen.

One by one, the survivors painfully pulled themselves free of the shipwreck. Staggering, supporting each other, they stumbled up the beach toward the dubious shelter of jungle.

"Where are we?" Letitia asked, her arm around Sarah.

Mike grinned and pointed. His grin, though, was humorless and strange.

Not thirty feet from where they stood, was a post with a skeleton sprawled at the bottom and a sign nailed to the top.

Kelly sank down on her knees in the sand, leaned her forehead against Steve's, and shook with mingled laughter, sobs and relief.

"Buccaneer Bay," Jimmy said. "How do you like that, Tish? Right back where we started from."

*　*　*

The End

About the Author

Christine Morgan lives in the Pacific Northwest with her husband, daughter, and trio of cats. She is a graduate of California's Humboldt State University, with a B. A. in Psychology. Her overnight-shift job as a residential counselor in a psychiatric facility allows her ample time to write as well as the occasional flash of inspiration.

She divides her writing time among a variety of genres – horror, fantasy, childrens' fiction, and erotica among them. Her previous books include the *MageLore* and *ElfLore* fantasy trilogies, the Silver Doorway series of children's books, and the other Trinity Bay horror novels, *Black Roses, Gifted Children* and *Changeling Moon*. She was nominated for an Origins Award for her zombie short story "Dawn of the Living-Impaired," and various others of her works have appeared in anthologies, magazines, and several online forums.

A longtime gamer, Christine can often be found at regional conventions, running games as well as promoting books. She has a fond relationship with the folks at Steve Jackson Games and other names in the gaming industry, all of whom have been incredibly supportive and helpful. In 2003, Christine and Tim released their first role-playing game supplement, the controversial *Naughty and Dice: An Adult Gamer's Guide to Sexual Situations*.

Christine's other interests span a wide gamut – robotic combat, British comedy, documentaries, and reality game shows make up the majority of her television viewing habits; horror, mysteries, and thrillers dominate her bookshelves; and she enjoys cooking and crafts.

Christine welcomes and appreciates feedback from readers. She can be reached by e-mail at christine@sabledrake.com and invites visitors to her websites, www.sabledrake.com and www.christine-morgan.com.